D1095681

SUNRISE

By Mike Mullin

Tanglewood • Terre Haute, IN

Published by Tanglewood Publishing, Inc., 2014

Text © Mike Mullin 2014

Cover photograph by Ana Correal
Design by Amy Alick Perich

Tanglewood Publishing, Inc.
4400 Hulman Street
Terre Haute, IN 47803
www.tanglewoodbooks.com

Printed by Maple-Vail Press, York, PA, USA
10 9 8 7 6 5 4 3 2 1

ISBN-13: 978-1-939100-01-6

Library of Congress Cataloging-in-Publication Data

Mullin, Mike.
  Sunrise / Mike Mullin.
  pages cm. -- (Ashfall trilogy)
  Summary: Nearly a year after the eruption of the Yellowstone supervolcano, survival has become harder than ever and Alex and Darla must risk everything to try to create a community that can withstand the ongoing disaster.
  ISBN 978-1-939100-01-6 (hardback)
  [1. Volcanoes--Fiction. 2. Survival--Fiction. 3. Science fiction.] I. Title.
  PZ7.M9196Sun 2014
  [Fic]--dc23
  2013050876

To Peggy Tierney
for believing

Chapter 1

I left the farmhouse in the darkest hour of the night to make a weapon. The light from my oil lamp drew a pitiful circle of gray against the snow around my feet. Other lamps and torches shone here and there amid the ramshackle refugee encampment surrounding Uncle Paul's farm, fading pockets of humanity in the chaotic dark. People huddled within the lights, cleaning guns and sharpening knives.

By sunrise I'd reached the dead forest behind the farm and cut a *jahng bong*. A staff was a ridiculous weapon for the coming fight, but it was the best I could do.

1

The eruption of the Yellowstone supervolcano had plunged Iowa and Illinois into chaos. Communications went down. Air travel ended. Roads became impassable due to the ashfall and brutal winter it triggered. Towns were on their own. And now, eleven months after the eruption, the towns of northwest Illinois had begun waging war on each other.

Almost two weeks before, a few hundred men from Stockton had attacked Warren. A short, sad battle ensued. The Warrenites lost their stored food and their homes. Many lost their lives. The survivors fled to my Uncle Paul's farm. Mom, Darla, Alyssa, Ben, and I had arrived yesterday, finding the farm transformed into a rough refugee camp.

Today Warren's mayor, Bob Petty, planned to lead a counterattack. The adult refugees would attempt to retake Warren and reclaim their food. Everyone was hungry. Replacing the stockpile of frozen pork stolen by the Stocktonites would be impossible. All the slaughterhouses and nearly all the farms had been shut down for months. If the counterattack failed, most of us would starve to death.

Apparently the term *adults* didn't include me, despite the fact that I was sixteen. Our family had three decent weapons: the two AR-15 rifles I'd brought back from Iowa and a bolt-action hunting rifle. Mom, Aunt Caroline, and Uncle Paul would carry those. I was under strict orders to stay behind with Darla; Ben; Alyssa; my sister, Rebecca; and my cousins, Max and Anna. Orders I planned to ignore.

My wild trip through Iowa had taught me one thing at least—if I wanted something, I'd better be willing to fight for it. By myself, when necessary. If I hadn't gone after my parents, they'd still be stuck in the FEMA camp in Maquoketa. If I hadn't gone after Darla, she'd be dead or a slave in a flenser gang. But my dad might still be alive. Instead, he had died helping the rest of us escape. I jammed my new staff into the snow beside me, ramming it against the frozen ground hard enough to jar my elbow.

I tried to blend into the throng of refugees preparing to march to Warren, but Aunt Caroline noticed me. Her mom-vision would put an eagle's eyesight to shame. "Alex, you can't go with—"

"Where's Mom?" I said.

"We were wondering the same thing," Uncle Paul said. "We're supposed to move out any minute."

"I thought you were heading out at dawn," I said. "I figured I'd have to run to catch up."

"We were supposed to." Uncle Paul frowned.

"I'm going to find Mom." I turned away.

"We'll help," Uncle Paul said, and the three of us jogged to the farmhouse.

As I stepped into the tiny foyer adjoining the living room, I noticed the smell. Sweat and a fecal stink blended with the stomach-turning stench of rotting wounds. The living room had been converted into a pitiful makeshift hospital. In the primitive conditions, Dr. McCarthy and his assistant, Belinda, were losing the battle to keep their patients clean and healthy.

They were an amazing team, working tirelessly in horrible conditions to try to save lives. They constantly came up with creative solutions to the lack of technology: scavenging Froot Loops to treat scurvy, creating a gravity-flow transfusion system, scrounging antibiotics, and more. They shared a mutual admiration that had clearly grown into a romance, even though they had yet to admit it publicly.

I glanced over the injured, unwilling to let my eyes linger lest I get sucked into the horror of missing limbs and oozing wounds. Alyssa and Max were helping Dr. McCarthy. Well, Alyssa was helping. Max was following her like a puppy and generally getting in the way. It was no different from high school—the new girl always attracts all the attention. I didn't see any sign of Mom. I turned back to the foyer and ran up the stairs, taking them two at a time.

"Mom?" I yelled in the hallway at the top of the stairs. No answer. Uncle Paul and Aunt Caroline joined me in the hall. Aunt Caroline had hung dozens of family photos in the stairway and hall. About a third of them were missing, which seemed odd—I could have sworn they had all been there the day before. The blank spaces in the walls seemed like empty eye sockets, staring at nothing.

I knocked once and opened the door to the first bedroom. Darla, Rebecca, and Anna were huddled together, wrapped in a faded bedspread. Since the hospital had displaced us from the living room and the comfort of its fireplace, we'd been forced into the icy cold upstairs. All the girls shared Anna's room, and all the guys were in Max's. It beat sleeping in the refugee encampment outside. "You guys seen Mom?" I asked.

They all shook their heads. Darla had been shot, and during her ordeal as a prisoner of a cannibal gang, the Dirty White Boys, her wound had become infected. Otherwise, she probably would have insisted on going with me to Warren. She was healing well and didn't need a bed downstairs, but she was still weak.

Anna slid out from under the bedspread and ran to us, wrapping her arms around Aunt Caroline's stomach in an awkward, sideways hug.

"Mom—" Anna said before a choked sob cut her off.

Aunt Caroline stroked Anna's hair. "Shh. It's all right. I'll be back tonight."

Uncle Paul laid a hand on Anna's shoulder, leaned in close to his wife, and whispered, "We really shouldn't both—"

Aunt Caroline pressed her hands over Anna's ears. "We already talked about this. I'm going. Those starving people camped outside are my neighbors too, not just yours. And besides, I'm better with a rifle than you are, and you know it."

"Yes, but—"

"If anyone should stay, it's you."

"But what if . . . who'll take care of the kids?"

"We're going to be fine," Aunt Caroline said, lifting her hands from Anna's ears to end the conversation.

Anna choked out a series of words too garbled for me to understand, and Aunt Caroline bent over, talking to her in a low voice.

I stepped up to the bed and leaned over, putting my face close to Darla's. "You okay?"

"I'm fine," she whispered. "I should go with you."

"I'll be careful."

Darla snorted. "Not sure you'd know careful if you tripped over it."

"Tripping over careful? That's ironic."

"If anyone could do it, it'd be you. You'd probably break your nose in the process."

I smiled. Somehow it didn't bother me when Darla teased me—girlfriends get special privileges like that. Although "girlfriend" didn't even begin to describe what Darla meant to me. "I'll be back tonight. I promise."

"I'll still worry." Darla reached one hand out from under the covers, wrapped it around the back of my neck, and pulled me closer for a kiss.

When the kiss broke, I pressed my lips together, savoring the warmth she'd left, trying to hold on to it. "I love you."

"Love you too."

"Do I need to leave?" Rebecca asked. "I do *not* want to be here while my sappy brother makes out with his girl-friend."

"No. I have to go." I kissed Darla's forehead and left the room, stepping around Anna, Aunt Caroline, and Uncle Paul to continue searching for my mother.

I found Ben, Alyssa's older brother, in the second upstairs bedroom. He sat under the window, wrapped in a blanket, reading a book. "You seen my mom?"

Ben didn't reply. When he was interested in something, he had an amazing ability to block out all distractions—

including me. It had something to do with his autism. I couldn't imagine what book had drawn him in that deeply—he was gaga over all things military, and as far as I knew, there were no books on that subject in the farmhouse. I drew the door closed and moved on to the master bedroom. Yesterday Anna had asked Mom to share the girls' room, but she'd refused, and Aunt Caroline had invited her to sleep in the master bedroom instead.

At first the master bedroom looked empty, but a noise from behind the bed prompted me to investigate further. Mom sat on the floor with her back wedged into the corner of the room. Empty picture frames were scattered to her left. She was sorting pictures of me, Rebecca, herself, and Dad, creating some kind of impromptu collage. As I watched, she swept all the photos up off the floor and started dealing them into a new pattern, as if they were cards in a bizarre game of solitaire.

Mom wore only jeans and a light sweater despite the subzero temperature in the house. Her face was flushed, and she trembled as though her muscles were composed of seething colonies of ants rather than flesh. She was sweating so profusely that droplets fell from her nose and chin, splatting onto the photographs. A rifle lay on the floor near the foot of the bed.

"Mom. You okay?" A stupid question. She most certainly was not okay. She looked terrible.

"Mom," I said a little more urgently. She still didn't answer. Her eyes were bloodshot. I waved my hand in front of her face, and she kept sorting photos. But when I went to put my hand on her shoulder, she grabbed my hand, clutching it with surprising strength.

"Mom," I shouted, "what's wrong?"

"We'll stay here," she hissed through her clenched jaw. "You'll be safe here." She tried to pull me down beside her.

I resisted. "We've got to go, Mom," I said as gently as I could.

"What's wrong? I heard a shout." Darla was standing in the doorway, leaning against the jamb.

Mom raised a hand, her tense and crooked finger pointing at Darla. "Get away," she hissed.

"What's wrong, Mom?" It made no sense—she'd been fine yesterday. "Leave!" Mom screeched.

I twisted my arm free, turned, and ran from the room. My aunt and uncle were moving down the hall toward the commotion. I ran past them and leaped down the stairs three at a time. I stepped into the living room, where Dr. McCarthy was chatting with a patient.

"Dr. McCarthy," I said, "something's wrong with Mom."

"I'll be right back," he said to his patient before he stood and followed me back up the stairs.

I hung back at the doorway with Darla when we reached the master bedroom. Dr. McCarthy knelt beside Mom, talking too quietly for me to hear. He placed his hand against her forehead.

Darla had slumped down, sitting on the floor with her back against the jamb. "What's wrong with your mom?" she asked.

I knelt next to her. "You should get back to bed."

"Whatever. You didn't answer the question."

"I don't know." I draped her arm over my shoulder and helped her up. As soon as we stood, Mom started screaming—high-pitched, unintelligible squawks like a parakeet on meth. I wavered, unsure what to do. Uncle Paul and Aunt Caroline crossed the room toward Mom and Dr. McCarthy. As they reached my mother, a trumpet sounded outside—the call to move out.

"We have to go," Aunt Caroline said.

"Take Darla back to bed, Alex," Dr. McCarthy said. "Send your sister in, would you?"

"Is Mom okay?" I asked.

"I think so. Give us some space."

I hefted the rifle Mom had left on the floor in my free hand and left the room behind Uncle Paul and Aunt Caroline. As I helped Darla get settled back into bed in the girls' room, I told Rebecca, "Dr. McCarthy needs help. Something's wrong with Mom. They're in the master bedroom."

Rebecca shot a worried look at me as she disentangled herself from the blankets. "Is she okay?" Rebecca was only fourteen, but with everything that had happened in the last eleven months, she'd gotten a lot less childish.

"I don't know. I'm sorry. I've got to go."

Rebecca nodded and rushed past me. I kissed Darla goodbye again and turned the other way, following Uncle Paul and Aunt Caroline down the stairs and out of the house.

When I caught up with them, Aunt Caroline turned toward me. "Alex, you can't come."

I clenched the rifle more tightly. "I'm going."

"Just because your mother can't come doesn't mean—"

"I'm going." If Aunt Caroline thought I was going to give up the rifle, she was as crazy as my mother.

Uncle Paul stared at me for a moment, his face stony. "You know how to use that gun?"

"Sort of."

"Let me give you a refresher."

Aunt Caroline sighed and turned away.

As we marched away from the farm, Uncle Paul coached me on the crucial parts of the AR-15: the charging handle, selector lever, magazine release button, rear sight, and front sight. I focused on each rifle part, blocking everything else out of my mind, walking mechanically, and listening with single-minded intensity. I had to learn everything Uncle Paul was teaching me. In a few hours, my life would depend on it.

Chapter 2

The night before, Ben had told me there were two good ways to attack Warren: an overwhelming show of force or a sneak attack. So, of course, Mayor Petty chose a third.

We were strung out in a bedraggled line, trudging along Stagecoach Trail toward Warren. Almost three hundred refugees had volunteered, hoping to retake their homes and reclaim the stockpiled pork, corn, and kale that were all that stood between us and starvation. Most of the ragtag army had guns, but a few had come along with nothing more than knives or sharpened poles.

"I'll be right back," I said to Uncle Paul and broke into a trot, headed for the front of the column. Stagecoach Trail was a paved, two-lane highway, not a trail, although it was now covered in packed snow and ice. FEMA had plowed it not long after the blizzards that had followed Yellowstone's eruption, leaving ten-foot snow berms lining both sides of the road. We were slogging down an ice-walled half-pipe: a perfect kill zone. Anyone firing from the tops of the berms could slaughter us.

I caught up to Mayor Petty at the front of the column. He wore a ski mask, but despite the frigid air, sweat was beading at the corners of his eyes. "We need to get off the road," I told him.

He shot me an annoyed glare. "We will, we will." Gasping breaths interspersed his words. "No sense wearing ourselves out in the deep snow before we're close."

"What if they're ready for us? They could have scouts out. We'd be sitting—"

"We'll move off the road after we pass the cemetery."

"What if—"

"That's enough," Mayor Petty shouted.

"At least put some scouts out." I waved at the towering snow berms blocking the flanks of our column.

"Be my guest." The mayor turned away.

I stopped in the road, and people flowed around me as I thought about the problem. I could scout one of our flanks, sure, but without skis or snowshoes, I'd quickly fall behind. What we really needed was a small group on each flank on skis. Or better yet, a plan that didn't involve approaching Warren by the most obvious route.

Someone shouted behind me, and I spun just in time to see a man in a thin brown overcoat fall headlong onto the icy road. The guy beside him—who wore a much warmer looking down coat—retracted his leg, making it look like he'd intentionally tripped the first man. I glared at him: Did he think we were marching down a kindergarten hall rather than headed to war?

I stepped back to offer the fallen guy a hand. The whole situation made a lot more sense when I saw his face: Ed Bauman, the former flenser and member of the Peckerwoods gang whose life I'd saved a few weeks before. He'd reformed—he abhorred his cannibalistic past—but he still wasn't trusted or even liked.

"What're you doing here?" I said.

"Headed for Warren, same as you." Ed was carrying an old broom handle, sharpened at one end. A Bowie knife was tucked into his belt.

"I'm surprised the mayor let you come along."

"Might be he hasn't noticed yet."

I shrugged. Anyone who wanted to come along on this mission had to be crazy—Ed probably wasn't much crazier than the rest of us. But I didn't particularly want him at my back. I pushed past him and went to rejoin Uncle Paul and Aunt Caroline.

The light was dim and yellow—normal, since the volcano. The sky reminded me of the skin surrounding a scab. As I dragged my feet down the road, the sky seemed to darken further. I glanced from one side of the road to the other, but the horizon was sliced short by the snow berms.

My dread increased as we approached Elmwood Cemetery outside of Warren. It occupied a low hill on our left, so we could see the tops of a few grave markers and tree stumps above the berm.

As Mayor Petty led our column past the entrance to the cemetery, I caught a flash of motion from the corner of my eye. A dark figure rose from behind a monument, and suddenly there were dozens of people popping up from every hollow, tree stump, and stone marker on the hill above us. I screamed a warning, but my voice was drowned out by the roar of incoming gunfire.

Chapter 3

A woman a few steps ahead of me was hit. Cyndi Reitmeyer, I remembered, even though I'd only spoken to her twice. Everything slowed, and I watched in horror as the top of her skull pirouetted lazily away, trailing torn bits of her knit hat and bloody strands of molasses-colored hair.

Before I could bring my rifle to bear, someone slammed into my right shoulder, hurling me to the edge of the road. I yelled a protest but shut up when I realized I'd been pushed into the only safe space— so tight against the snow berm that the attackers couldn't get an angle down to shoot me.

Aunt Caroline and Uncle Paul were crouched nearby. Ed was at my shoulder—he'd thrown me against the berm, maybe saved my life. Mayor Petty was screaming, "Up and over!" and gesturing at the top of the berm.

"Idiot," I yelled. "We need to flank them. Come on!"

Uncle Paul nodded, and I started elbow-crawling back the way we'd come. Uncle Paul, Aunt Caroline, and Ed followed me. The chatter of gunfire was continuous; chips of ice showered us as bullets struck the ice above our heads.

The road had filled with the newly dead and dying. Blood coated the ice, seeping toward both sides of the road. The air itself seemed alive with screams of pain, the acrid stink of gunpowder, and the sickly stench of blood.

I glanced over my shoulder. We'd split into four groups: One tried to climb directly toward the attackers. Mayor Petty was urging them on at pistol-point. Another crawled along the base of the snow berm, following me and Uncle Paul. A third group was running in panic, their numbers thinned steadily by gunfire from above. The fourth group lay bleeding in the road.

As we crawled out of the immediate area of the ambush, I caught Uncle Paul's ankle and yelled, "Up and flank them?"

Instead of replying, he turned and started clawing his way up the snow bank.

"Up!" I bellowed, following him. Ed, Aunt Caroline, and dozens of others started up alongside us.

At the top I flopped into the snow alongside Uncle Paul and tried to click off my rifle's safety. My thumb slid over the lever twice. My fingers were shaking, and my vision had narrowed as if I were looking out from the end of a dark tunnel. I dragged my thumb along the smooth metal of the rifle, concentrating, and managed to bump the lever to single shot. I only had one magazine, and it wasn't full. Twenty-three shots in all.

The next two minutes were a cacophony of noise, terror, and adrenaline. From the direction of the road, the ambushers were behind good cover—gravestones, tree stumps, the brick gateposts, and the two gatehouses, but that did nothing to protect them from us on their flank. They were totally focused on killing people in Mayor Petty's group as fast as they could reach the top of the snow berm.

I aimed at a guy peeking up over the top of a gravestone and pulled the trigger. A moment later he disappeared—but I had no idea whether I'd hit him or someone else had.

Some of the ambushers turned toward us. I threw myself forward and to one side, rolling behind a tree stump. I heard a resonant thunk, and the stump vibrated against my head. The world lurched around me in a herky-jerky syncopation, counterpoint to the screams, the pop of gunfire, and the reek of powder.

I peeked around the side of my stump and shot again. More and more of us were reaching the top of the snow berm behind me, flanking and overwhelming the ambushers. I scrambled away from my stump, taking cover behind a stone monument and firing. Soon the ambushers began to flee, and we advanced, pushing them back. A few of the people in Mayor Petty's group made it to the edge of the cemetery, sheltering behind the gatehouses. It looked like we would rout the rest of the ambushers.

"I'm going to see if I can do anything for the wounded," Aunt Caroline yelled. She slid down the snow berm and ran toward the nearest of the dozens of people who lay bleeding in the road. I moved forward, ducking behind a stump, scanning for targets.

Under the constant chatter of gunfire, I heard the low growl of an engine. I looked for the source of the sound. Two pickups drove side by side, coming down the hill at the outskirts of occupied Warren. A column of men with rifles jogged behind the trucks. Each truck had a belt-fed machine gun mounted to the roof of the cab. Aunt Caroline, Mayor Petty, and at least a hundred others were still on the road.

As I watched in horror, both machine guns opened fire.

Chapter 4

I shot at the closest truck, firing as fast as I could pull the trigger. The two guys manning the machine gun jerked spastically and fell. My ammo ran dry. I dropped the now-useless rifle from my shaking hands.

The second truck moved in front of the first, hugging the right side of the road, tight against the snow berm. I scrambled to the top of the berm as it approached, keeping on my belly. Ed slid up beside me—I had no idea where he'd come from. Rivulets of blood dripped down the shaft of his broomstick, staining the snow with a trail of livid droplets.

The gunners on the second truck were spraying bullets across the middle of the road. Mayor Petty went down screaming. Aunt Caroline was trying to drag an injured man up the berm. No way would she get over the top in time.

I froze. My vision narrowed to a black-rimmed tunnel, centered on Aunt Caroline. She jerked spastically, thrown backward by the slugs tearing through her midsection. Her scream was audible even over the chaotic shouts and gunfire, as loud in my ears as if it were the only noise in a quiet cemetery, rather than merely one more wail among the chorus. I felt it as much as heard it—piercing me, opening my field of vision, and unfreezing my legs.

The truck was almost past my position on the berm. I threw myself off it, jumping toward the gunners.

I stretched out, elbow up as if I were doing a taekwondo high block, aiming for the side of the closest guy's head. I hit him perfectly, my elbow connecting with his temple with a crack that was audible even over the gunfire. We went down in the bed of the pickup, our limbs thrashing and tangling.

I rolled, looking up just in time to see the other gunner draw a pistol and aim it at my head.

Chapter 5

A shadow passed over me as the gunner's hand tensed on his pistol. Ed soared over us in a flying leap, his broom handle held below him like a hawk's talons. More than a foot of bloody broom handle sprouted from between the gunner's ribs, driven through by Ed's falling weight. The gunner dropped. Hot blood spattered my face, and the sharp end of the stake thunked into the truck bed beside my neck. I roared wordlessly, more from surprise than terror.

I threw the twitching weight of the man off me, rolling onto my knees. Ed was lifting the machine gun from its mounting on the cab of the pickup.

Bullets whanged around us as the column of men behind the trucks fired. The driver of the pickup thrust his arm out the window, trying to bring a pistol to bear on Ed. I lurched forward and grabbed the driver's wrist in both hands, hauling it backward against the window frame. His elbow broke with a crunch, and the pistol slipped from his hand into the road.

Ed had freed the machine gun from its mounting. He turned it around, braced it against the back of the cab, and opened up on the men behind the truck.

The rear window of the truck shattered from the gun's recoil. Thousands of pebbles of tempered glass rained down in a tinkling sheet. Ed adjusted the machine gun, bracing it against the strip of metal above the window, and opened fire again.

Men died. Some fell quietly, becoming inert piles of bloodied flesh and clothing. Others screamed, falling into writhing heaps of agony. Those who didn't fall under the Ed's scything gun scattered, running back the way they had come.

Ed's ammo ran dry, but by then our side had taken full control of the other truck and machine gun. The fight was over. I slid out of the bed of the truck, collapsed to my knees, and vomited onto the frozen road.

Chapter

6

I hadn't seen Uncle Paul since the beginning of the fight. Not far from me, someone was frantically working on Mayor Petty's right leg, cinching a belt around his thigh—an improvised tourniquet. Blood pulsed from half a dozen wounds spread across both of his legs.

I pushed myself upright, catching sight of Uncle Paul as I rose. He was about fifty feet off, kneeling by Aunt Caroline. Uncle Paul was cradling her head in one hand with his other pressed to her stomach. Her face was nestled against his coat.

"Alex," Aunt Caroline said as I approached,

"you're okay." She forced a wan, bloodless smile.

"How are . . ." I noticed the tears streaming down Uncle Paul's face and the blood welling between his fingers.

"Can't feel my legs," Aunt Caroline replied. "Paul says they're fine. His ears turn red when he lies."

Uncle Paul fixed his stare on me. "We need to get her to Dr. McCarthy. Now." His voice was ragged.

"I'll get a truck." I ran back to the pickup Ed and I had liberated. The cab was empty, but the truck was still running. Ed was helping two other guys lift Mayor Petty's considerable bulk. I grabbed Petty's shoulder, and we slid him into the bed of the truck.

"Drive," I told Ed. "I'll help load. We need to pick up Aunt Caroline and get back to Dr. McCarthy. Fast."

Ed nodded and vaulted out of the bed.

I ran ahead of the truck with three others. We loaded the injured into the bed and dragged the dead to the sides of the road while Ed inched the truck forward. By the time we got to Aunt Caroline, the bed was full. People lay practically atop each other, and the floor was awash in blood. We laid Aunt Caroline on the open tailgate, and Uncle Paul crouched next to her, holding on to her with one hand and the side rail of the truck with the other. I helped a woman who'd been shot in the foot hobble into the cab and squeezed in beside her. Ed goosed the gas, and we raced back toward the farm.

I was out of the cab, sprinting to get Dr. McCarthy, even before the truck rolled to a stop. I found him on the leeward side of the partial stockade wall. A large fire had been built there, and five pots of water were suspended above it on a wire. The tables from Uncle Paul's kitchen and dining room were beside the fire, one clear, the other stacked high with blankets, bandages, towels, and medical instruments.

"How many injured?" Dr. McCarthy barked.

"Sixteen on this truck," I gasped. "More coming on the other truck and on foot."

"Truck? Never mind. Run to the house. Get Belinda. And round up anyone who's steady enough to help."

I turned toward the house. Dr. McCarthy was already gone, running the other way, toward the truck.

Belinda, Alyssa, and Max were in the living room, caring for convalescents from the last disastrous fight between Stockton and Warren.

Alyssa gasped as she caught sight of me. "What happened?"

I glanced down—my clothing was caked with blood. Some of the blood had already dried and started to flake off; some of the blood was still fresh, glistening in the firelight. "It's not my blood. Dr. McCarthy needs help. Sixteen injured. Badly. More coming."

They dropped what they were doing. Belinda ran past me with Alyssa at her heels. I grabbed Max's arm as he tried to pass by. "Max—"

"Let go! I can help too."

"Your mother is out there. She's hurt."

Max hesitated, looking at me over his shoulder. "Is it—how bad?"

"It's not good. She's been shot."

"I've gotta go." He tugged on my arm, but I tightened my grip.

"You've got to hold it together. Help Dr. McCarthy and Belinda. Can you—"

"I've got it." He turned, fixing a determined gaze on me.

I let him go, and he left at a run. I dashed up the stairs to the girls' room, entering without knocking.

Darla wobbled to her feet. "Alex, Christ—"

"It's okay, it's okay," I said. "The blood's not mine. Rebecca, Dr. McCarthy needs help outside. Anna, you and Darla stay here and take care of the people downstairs." I leaned in as if to kiss Darla's ear and whispered, "Keep Anna here. Aunt Caroline's hurt. Bad." Darla nodded. Everyone leapt into motion, and I went to look for Ben.

I found him in the exact same place he'd been that morning, reading the exact same book. "Ben!" I yelled. He didn't even look up. "Ben!" I finally had to walk into the room and grab the book. My glove left a bloody smear on the page.

"You are covered in blood, Lieutenant," Ben finally said.

"It's not mine," I said for at least the third time. And what was up with calling me Lieutenant? I didn't have time to ask. "Can you—"

"I presume the attempt to retake Warren failed?"

"Miserably," I said, but Ben just kept talking.

"You should have used misdirection or surprise. An attack on Stockton or from an unexpected—"

"I know, I know!" I shouted, but Ben kept right on talking. "Shut up for a second, would you?"

Ben started moaning and rocking back and forth in his chair. I cursed myself for an idiot—yelling at Ben was never helpful. "Can you help Dr. McCarthy?" I asked.

"Ben is not qualified as a field medic," he replied, still rocking.

"Right. Sorry I yelled." I turned to go.

"Lieutenant!"

I turned back. Ben was still now.

"Stockton's leader will expect you to spend time regrouping. If you attack their base in Stockton now, you might take them by surprise."

"I've got to go help Dr. McCarthy," I said as I left.

The field hospital outside was a hive of frenzied activity. Dozens of those too old or young to fight had descended on the hospital, helping to unload the truck, bandage wounds, and comfort the injured. Belinda had triaged the injured into three groups: those who needed medical care immediately, those who might be able to wait, and the two unfortunates who'd died on the way back to the farm.

Aunt Caroline was in the second group. Belinda said that since she hadn't bled out already, she probably wouldn't in the next few minutes. Uncle Paul stayed with Caroline, his hand pressed to her belly as if he could hold her together by pure force of will.

We had three trucks now: the two we had just captured and one I had brought back from Iowa. All three raced back and forth to the battlefield, picking up survivors. Ed drove one of them. A few hours before, I wouldn't have trusted him with a captured truck. I would have assumed he'd take off, maybe return to the flenser gang. Now, I didn't give it a second thought.

Max rushed to do whatever Dr. McCarthy asked, stopping only during the rare lulls to gaze longingly at the blanket where his mom lay. We ran to fetch more thread for stitching wounds. We refilled the pots hanging over the fire and kept the fire stoked. We washed patients' wounds. We held their hands. We unloaded the trucks when they pulled up with more wounded. Three more people died, and Max and I moved their corpses off the table to clear the way for those who might yet be saved.

More injured came, at first on the three trucks, but after about two hours, the walking wounded started to show up. Dr. McCarthy moved in a mechanical blur, plunging his bloody hands into nearly scalding water between each patient, racing to stabilize them so they could be passed off to Belinda to be stitched up, or passed off to Max and me to be laid out with the rest of the corpses. I didn't think nurses had usually stitched wounds in the old world, the pre-volcano world, but Belinda was good at it, her hands fast and sure.

Almost three hours passed before Dr. McCarthy had time to examine Aunt Caroline. Her skin was yellow and bloodless. Max, Uncle Paul, Alyssa, and I lifted her as gently as we could. Max whispered over and over again, "You're going to be okay, Mom. You're going to be okay."

It sounded like he was trying to convince himself. Aunt Caroline gasped loudly as we set her down.

Dr. McCarthy used a pair of shears to cut her clothing away from her stomach. Two crusty, puckered wounds marred the bone-white skin just above her waist. Blood had pooled in her belly button, so that the wounds looked something like a screaming face. Dr. McCarthy had me help roll her onto her side. Her back was unmarked, other than a huge, ugly bruise spreading along her spine.

Dr. McCarthy tapped on her knees—hard—with his fingers. I had no idea why. He turned to Uncle Paul, gesturing toward the fence with his head. "We need to talk—over there, maybe."

Aunt Caroline hadn't moved or done anything but moan since we'd moved her to the table. But when Dr. McCarthy started to move away, her hand shot out, clasping his arm. "No. Tell him here. I need to know too."

Dr. McCarthy said, "Should Max—"

"He can stay too."

Dr. McCarthy sighed and gathered himself. "It's not good. Two bullets. No exit wound. A huge contusion along the spine. They missed your abdominal aorta somehow, or you'd have bled out already. But the bad news is that both bullets are still in there. Since you have no autonomic response, one or both of them must be lodged in your spine."

"I'm paralyzed."

Dr. McCarthy nodded once.

"I can move my arms. It could be worse."

A strangled cry escaped Dr. McCarthy's mouth, quickly choked off.

"It is worse, isn't it."

"Yes. If I had a modern operating room—if I were a trauma surgeon, if I had a full support team, maybe. But . . ."

"I'm going to die." Aunt Caroline said it flatly, with quiet assurance, like she'd known it all along. Max made a choking sound and turned away. Uncle Paul clenched his wife's shoulder, his knuckles white.

"Alex," Aunt Caroline said, "go get Anna."

I stood there dumbly too overwhelmed to move.

"Now, please. I don't have forever."

I ran for the living room.

Darla insisted on coming with Anna. I put an arm around Darla's waist to support her. She held Anna's hand. When we stepped into the foyer, I saw Mom standing at the top of the stairs.

"Alex, you're—"

"It's not my blood, Mom. Aunt Caroline's hurt. We've got to go."

"I'll come with you. Maybe I can help."

When we got outside, another patient was on the table where Aunt Caroline had lain. I looked around in panic—could she have died in the moment or two I was gone? Then I saw her not far from the fire, wrapped in a blanket. Max and Uncle Paul knelt by her side. Anna wrenched free of Darla's hand and ran to her mother. Mom went to stand behind Uncle Paul, extending her hand halfway as if she wasn't sure whether she should touch her brother-in-law or not.

How would Mom even survive this? Losing my dad, her husband, only two days ago and now her sister-in law? Then I thought of Uncle Paul. He'd lost his brother and now his wife was dying. Would he go crazy like Mom had? I swallowed hard, as if to eat my fear.

Anna threw herself into Aunt Caroline's arms before any of us could stop her. A shadow passed over Aunt Caroline's face, and she cried out in pain, but she held on when Anna tried to pull away, clutching her daughter even more tightly. "Oh, Anna," Aunt Caroline breathed.

I clung to Darla. I wasn't sure if I should stay or go. I wanted to be anywhere else—another place, another world, one where mothers didn't die. But I knew I couldn't run fast enough to escape the weight in my chest.

"He . . ." Anna said to her mother, her voice tremulous, "Alex said you were hurt."

Aunt Caroline smoothed her hand slowly along Anna's back. "Dr. McCarthy says I'm dying."

Anna yelped, holding her mother tighter, and Aunt Caroline moaned, her eyes squeezing shut.

"Anna . . ." Uncle Paul laid a hand on Anna's shoulder, and she relaxed her desperate grasp.

Anna was sobbing now. Max was biting his lower lip, trembling like a flag caught in an uncertain wind. Tears flowed freely from Uncle Paul's eyes. Aunt Caroline was the only one who wasn't crying.

Anna choked out a few words, "You can't . . . I need . . ."

"Anna," Aunt Caroline whispered. "When I'm dead, will you still love me?"

"Y-yes."

"Then I'll still be with you. And love you." Aunt Caroline lifted a hand toward Max. Her hand wavered, and Max caught it.

"I'm proud of you, Max. You're becoming a good man."

Max crumpled over her hand, bawling.

"Don't go," Uncle Paul pleaded. "I love you."

"I'll never leave you," Aunt Caroline said. "I love you too."

Three hours later, she was dead.

Chapter 7

My dreams that night were bizarrely vivid: staccato flashes of perfect memory, like images captured in the hyper-saturated flash and pop of a dying light bulb. Cyndi's skull flying apart—pop. The gunners on the pickup, crumpling as I shot them—pop. The sharp end of Ed's broomstick, protruding from a man's chest—pop. The ragged wounds on Aunt Caroline's stomach—pop.

I woke screaming.

Ben moaned and Max sobbed. The darkness hid our faces but not our pain. A few moments later, the covers lifted, and Darla slid in beside me. Even though we were both fully clothed against the cold, I felt the edge of her ribcage digging into my side. "Shh," she whispered, "go back to sleep." Tangled in her arms and legs, I found I could.

Later that night I dreamed of the uncertain rhythm of gunfire. It emanated from the darkness all around me. Some gunners played frenzied sixty-fourth notes on their automatic weapons. Others, a steady four-four time of careful pistol shots. Sometimes multiple guns fired together in a thunderous roar; other times they all lapsed into brief, fearful silences during which the only sounds were the bleating complaints of the goats stabled in the downstairs guest room.

Darla shook me awake. "Someone's shooting."

My violent dreams and the evidently real gunfire were too much. I felt as if I'd been sucked into the airless darkness under a huge wave, crushed by the weight, my life ripped by the shifting currents. I pulled the covers over my head, smothering the noise.

Darla ripped the covers off both of us so forcefully that the blanket tore. The freezing air was like a slap to the face. "Get up. Now," she said, her words as much a slap as the air.

"I froze yesterday. When they shot at Aunt Caroline. I could have—"

"There's no time. We'll talk about it later. If whoever's shooting out there makes it to the house, everyone will be in danger. Rebecca, Anna, Max . . ."

She was right. I took a deep, shuddering breath and hurled myself out of the bed.

"I'm going back to the other room for my boots," she said.

"Just wait here," I said as I jammed my feet into my boots and pulled a knit cap on my head. She was still debilitated from her ordeal with the Dirty White Boys and in no condition to be running around outside. I started to tell her so, but she was already gone.

When I got out to the hall, she was sitting on the top stair, wrenching on her boots.

By the time we got outside, the shooting had trailed off. A few distant pops echoed in the darkness enveloping the farm. One of the ramshackle lean-tos at the edge of the encampment was ablaze. Flames leapt from its canvas-and-stick roof, threatening to ignite neighboring shelters. People were running everywhere, frantic shadows silhouetted by the fire. But nobody seemed to be fighting the fire.

I ducked back into the house and grabbed a stack of water pails from the kitchen. Darla and I ran—not toward the fire but to the farm's hand-pumped well.

"Fill buckets as fast as you can, okay?" I said to Darla. "I'll organize a fire brigade." I didn't think she should be out there at all. Filling buckets would at least keep her away from the fire.

To my relief, Darla nodded and started working the pump handle. I put myself squarely in the path of the first person I saw—Lynn Manck—a guy I barely knew.

"You!" I yelled. "Grab buckets from Darla! We're forming a line, got it?"

I was a bit shocked by his reply: "Got it!" he shouted and took his place next to Darla. I ran from person to person, chivvying them into a line. I ordered another guy to join the brigade, shouting at his back. I didn't notice

until he turned that I was shouting at Uncle Paul. I started
to stammer an apology to him, but he was already halfway
to the spot where he was needed.

Later I wondered why it had been so easy. Why did
everyone leap to do what I told them to? Why hadn't they
organized a fire brigade before I got outside? I was sixteen—
a kid in their eyes—and I certainly wasn't used to anyone
listening to me, let alone obeying my instructions.
Everyone seemed to know that we *needed* a fire brigade,
but they couldn't start *being* a fire brigade until someone
organized it. It reminded me of an experiment I did in
fourth grade, dissolving massive amounts of sugar in boiling water to make crystals. Nothing happens until you
dangle a string into the jar. I guess it was the same with
the fire brigade—someone had to be the string.

The fire was fierce. The last person in the brigade had
to rush in, hurl their water, and duck back from the billow-
ing smoke and sizzling heat. Once the line was established,
I started to help throw water. I concentrated on wetting
down the neighboring shelters and putting out stray
embers, stopping the fire from spreading.

Eventually the fire burned itself out, and we began the
laborious process of dousing the coals.

The distant gunfire had ended completely. I wasn't sure
when it happened—I'd been wholly absorbed in fighting
the fire. Now that the fire was out, it was too dark to see
well. I sent a couple of people to get torches.

As we finished stirring the ashes of the lean-to, making
sure all the embers were out, Ed loped out of the dark-

ness. His face was sweaty despite the frozen night air, and he held a semi-automatic rifle.

"Thought we were out of ammo for those," I said.

"We are. Still, it looks scary—and it makes a darn good club." Ed slung the rifle across his back.

"You know what happened?"

"Just three or four attackers. Probably from the Stocktonites occupying Warren. Totally disorganized. Threw some torches and took some pot shots."

"Anyone hurt you know of?"

"No." Ed sidled closer, his voice dropping to a whisper. "It'll get worse. If they come back in force, or better organized . . . we're defenseless."

The tired reek of wet ash filled my nose, making every breath feel like an effort. "Ben thinks we should attack Stockton. Go after their heart to force them to pull out of Warren."

One of the guys who'd been helping put out the fire, Steve McCormick, interrupted us. "We're done here. Fire's out cold. What'd you want us to do now?"

Why was he asking me? I guess once you've volunteered to be the string in the sugar solution, to start creating crystals, you can't stop. "You know who lived in the lean-to that burnt?" I asked.

"Yeah, Linda Greenburg and her twin boys, Roan and Mateo. They got out okay."

"Check on them. Find someplace for them to stay and get them settled, would you?"

"Roger. I'll squeeze them into our shack, at least for

tonight." Steve jogged away with his torch, carrying away half our light.

Ed said, "Ben's right. All of Stockton's troops must be in Warren. We should go now, take them by surprise."

I groaned. "I don't know if I can walk to bed, let alone all the way to Stockton."

Ed seized my arm, whispering urgently into my ear. "Look, Alex, if you're going to lead, you've got to put that away. The weakness, I mean. It's okay to feel it, but you can't show it. Not to anyone except maybe me or Darla. People want strong leaders."

My head spun. I was getting leadership advice from an ex-cannibal? My world made less sense every day. "What if I don't want to lead?"

"Too late for that, you already started."

"I'm only sixteen."

"It's a different world, Alex. A lot of great leaders started as teenagers. Alexander the Great, Joan of Arc—"

"Didn't she get burned at the stake?"

"Yeah, and Alexander died young, thousands of miles from his home."

"You're not helping here."

"I watched what happened in the Peckerwoods gang. The leaders who showed fear, who showed weakness— they moved from the top to the bottom of the food chain, if you get what I'm saying."

"You're *really* not helping now. Look, Ed, you saved my life in that fight. Twice, maybe. We're even. You don't—"

"You're wrong. We're not even. We'll never be even.

No matter what I do now, I'll never atone for what I did. What I was. But I swore to try."

"If you want to round up people to attack Stockton, go ahead. I'll wish you luck. But I can't, Ed, I just—"

"You're the only one who can. Mayor Petty might not live, your Uncle Paul is in no condition to do anything, and Doc McCarthy's way too busy. People follow you."

"That's not my problem." I violently wrenched my arm out of his grasp and turned away, looking for Darla.

She was standing right behind me.

"Alex," she said softly. "He's right."

Great. Now my girlfriend and the ex-cannibal were in cahoots. Leave it to the apocalypse to turn my world completely upside-down. I started to turn away, but she wrapped her arms around me and tucked her head below my chin. She smelled of smoke and sweat. "I can't, Darla. . . . I just can't."

"Christ, Alex. You're one of the smartest people I've ever met, but you're wrong more often than a roomful of stopped clocks."

"It's just—"

"No. Listen. You've been leading since the day I met you. Who took me to Worthington when I was too wrecked by Mom's death to even function? Who got us to his uncle's farm through the middle of what was basically a war zone?" She lifted her head to look at me, the fierce light of the torch flickering in her eyes. "Who moved hell and earth, convinced his family, friends, and even a unit of freaking Black Lake to help find me? Those Black Lake mercenaries are out for no one but themselves, but you wrangled their help anyway. This is what you were born to do, Alex."

"I'm sixteen!"

"So. Freaking. What."

A hundred emotions waged war within me. Pride at the way Darla was looking at me, at her faith. Love for her, for her unwavering support. But mostly fear. I knew what I needed to say—but I didn't want to say it. Didn't want to admit my weakness, even to her.

"I . . . I froze out there. When they were shooting at Aunt Caroline. If I'd moved faster, maybe I could have saved her."

"Alex, it's—"

"What if it happens again?" People around us turned to look. I'd raised my voice far louder than I'd intended.

Darla held me tighter, waiting until everyone turned away. "Every time I made a mistake, my dad used to trot out this lame saying he had. He'd say, 'I'm glad you're not perfect, bunnykins. You see, the aliens carry off all the perfect people for study. And I'd like you to stick around.'"

"Bunnykins?"

Darla's face flared so red, I could see the color in her cheeks even by torchlight. "I swear to God, Alex, if you tell anyone that nickname, I'll twist your balls so hard that your new locker-room nickname will be Slinky."

My knees came together instinctively. "Maybe I'll call you Bunnykins in private?"

"No. You won't."

I gave her my best evil grin but felt it fade from my face as I remembered the point of the conversation.

"It's not your fault, Alex. Aunt Caroline is dead because Stockton decided to steal our food. Not because you hesitated for a split second in the middle of a battle that would have made most guys shit their pants and hide. You can do this. We can do it."

"You're not coming. You need to rest. It's seven miles. At night."

"Can we take the trucks?"

"I need to check whether they have enough gas." Somehow, I'd decided to go without even realizing it. Darla was tricky like that.

"Well, if they do, I'm going too."

I didn't respond right away. I was thinking—hoping to hit upon something, anything that would convince Darla to stay behind. It wasn't that I didn't want her around; I was terrified she'd get hurt. Normally, she was at least as capable as I was—stronger, in fact. But not now. "I need someone to organize a defense here. Someone I can trust."

"Ask Uncle Paul."

"His wife just died. I'm not asking him to do anything but mourn. Which is all I want to do."

"I'll ask him. I'm going with you. I'll drive and guard the trucks."

I didn't like it. But arguing with Darla was usually pointless. "Round up some people to come with us. I'll do the same. We'll meet at the trucks in half an hour."

"Got it."

One of the beauties of Darla was that when it was a
serious matter, she didn't rub it in—winning, that is. I
reached out and gently turned her face back toward me.
She launched herself at me, wrapping her arms around me
and kissing me like she meant to imprint her taste on my
lips forever. When the kiss broke, neither of us said anything. We turned to walk our separate paths out into the
uncaring night.

Chapter 8

I checked the trucks first—all three of them had between a quarter and a half tank of gas. Plenty to get to Stockton. Then I started running around trying to convince people to join us.

The first guy I talked to, Lynn Manck, agreed right away. I'd barely gotten the words "attack Stockton" out of my mouth when he said, "I'm in." While we were talking, Nylce Myers stopped to listen and volunteered without being asked.

They couldn't have been more different. Lynn was a huge bear of a man, a farmer in his fifties who sported a beard so long, he must have been growing it out for years. Most guys had beards now—razors were hard to come by—but Lynn's was magnificent. By contrast, all I could grow were stupid-looking wisps of facial hair. He'd lived on a small farm on the outskirts of Warren all his life. His kids were grown and gone—he hadn't heard from any of them since the volcano had erupted. But he and his wife still lived on their farm—or had, until the invaders from Stockton had driven them out.

Nylce probably massed less than half of what Lynn did. She was short and slight, in her early twenties. I'd heard from Uncle Paul that her fiancé was a salesman for Kussmaul Seeds—he'd been on his route in Nebraska when the volcano blew. Which meant he was almost certainly dead. I had no idea how she'd be in a fight, but she seemed determined enough.

The next guy I collared, Kyle Henthorn, was more skeptical.

"Shouldn't the mayor have a say-so?" he asked.

"He's unconscious. Dr. McCarthy had to amputate both his legs. Might not survive."

"Hmm, and what'd you say the plan was again?"

That stumped me. Ben hadn't mentioned a specific plan. Just the general idea of attacking Stockton, now, while they were still recovering from yesterday's fight. "I need to talk to Ben. If you decide to help, meet us at the trucks."

"You're going to get military advice from a teenager?"

"Yep. Look, I realize you don't know him, so you're just going to have to take my word for it. Ben's probably the smartest person I've ever met, and he's spent basically his whole life studying all things military."

Kyle shrugged skeptically, and I turned away to look for Ben.

I found him in the upstairs bedroom of Uncle Paul's house, asleep. I reached out to shake him awake, stopping when I remembered how much he hated to be touched. Instead, I said his name—over and over, until I was yelling it.

He finally woke, flailing his arms. "Who is yelling Ben's name?" he mumbled.

"It's me. I need your help."

"Ben's sleep should not be interrupted." He rolled over so his back was toward me.

"Your plan for attacking Stockton. I want to try it. But I'm having trouble convincing enough people to join. And we only have three pickups. Is there any way to make it work with only a couple dozen folks?"

"What time is it?" Ben asked, back still turned.

"What's that got to do with anything?"

"If the lieutenant wants to know whether he should carry through with his planned attack, he must tell his strategist what the current time is."

Oh-kay . . . "I don't know exactly. Sometime between one and two in the morning, I think."

Ben was quiet for a moment. "You should proceed with the attack. With two dozen men—"

I started to say, "They won't all be men," but Ben talked over me.

"An effective attack can be executed. But it must be done quickly, and the attackers must take the defenders by total surprise. Here is a plan with a good probability of success. . . ."

As soon as Ben finished explaining his plan, I ran. We had no time to waste. I grabbed a small backpack, a water bottle, and an empty semi-automatic rifle. As I reached the front door, Dr. McCarthy stopped me, laying a hand on my shoulder.

"I'm in a hurry, Doc," I said. His eyes were nearly solid red, and his face was slack with exhaustion. "We're headed to Stockton."

"I heard," he said.

I tried to turn away.

Dr. McCarthy held onto my shoulder. "Alex. Haven't enough people died? Where will it all end?"

"With us starving to death, if we don't get our food back."

"I just spent sixteen hours trying to save the people who got shot in the last fight. Most of them died. My overalls were so caked in blood that when I took them off, they stood up on their own. As if I were still in them! How many more people have to die?"

"What do you suggest? What're we going to eat? We could eat our dead, I suppose. Do you want to be the one to suggest that to Uncle Paul? To Max and Anna? That they eat their mother?"

Dr. McCarthy recoiled, drawing his arm back from my shoulder. I bolted out the door.

I stopped by the barn, picking up a coil of rope. Only twenty people, including me, Darla, and Ed, were waiting by the trucks. Twenty to attack a town that had held almost two thousand before the eruption. It seemed the height of foolishness to even try. But I believed in Ben's plan. In Ben himself. We loaded up the trucks and headed out.

We drove south on Canyon Park Road to avoid Warren. The roads deserted, the only noises were the rumble of our engines and the crunch of our tires on the thin layer of frozen snow. We turned on several minor roads, working our way over to Highway 78, the main route between Warren and Stockton. Neither Ed nor I knew the roads well since we weren't from Warren, so Lynn gave Darla directions.

When we reached the intersection of Highway 78 and Highway 20, which led directly to Stockton, we pulled the trucks against the snow berm on 78, where they'd be hidden.

I called everyone together and explained the plan, splitting us into two squads of six and one of seven. Darla would stay behind with the trucks. I wasn't sure how to choose people to lead the other two squads. Ed could have done it, but no one would trust him—a former flenser—as a leader. Someone had to be in charge, though, so I called for volunteers. Nylce and Lynn spoke up, which made sense, I guessed. They were the first ones to volunteer for this whole crazy plan. I wished Uncle Paul were with us. He was always steady in a crisis, and I knew I could have trusted him to lead a squad.

Ben had told me to circle around Stockton at this point and approach from the south. What he hadn't explained was how I'd even *find* Stockton after we left the road. It was dead black. And any light would have made us painfully obvious.

I led the column over the snow berm on the south side of Highway 20. We trudged through the thick snow, hoping we were moving in the general direction of Stockton. The walk seemed interminable.

I'd been counting in my head, trying to estimate how long we'd been out there. I reached four thousand—more than half an hour. Surely we should have reached Stockton by then? I started curving to the right, straining to catch sight of Stockton's barricade of upturned cars.

My count passed six thousand. Still no Stockton. A wall loomed suddenly in front of me: not Stockton's car wall, but the backside of a snow berm. We must have walked in a huge arc, winding up back at Highway 20. I took a left, following the berm. No doubt Ben was correct, that it would be better to approach from the south, from a place where there was no road. But we couldn't attack Stockton if we never found it.

Not five minutes later, we finally reached the wall of cars. A sedan was propped on its front bumper, trunk thrust in the air. On either side of it, more cars were wedged together tightly, forming a solid barrier.

On the other side of the berm, I remembered, there was a log gate blocking the road. That would surely be guarded. I led our troop south along the car wall in near silence. No one talked, but in the frozen night, every crunch of our boots in the snow tightened the cold knot of fear growing at the base of my spine.

I glanced overhead constantly, fearing the moment when someone would appear atop the wall. The scene played over and over in my mind—the figure barely visible in the darkness, swinging a gun toward us, opening fire.

I also looked for a particular kind of car in the wall. I needed an older truck with hefty side mirrors mounted on steel brackets, not the modern, plastic, breakaway type. When I found one, I signaled a halt with an upraised palm.

I stopped—waiting, watching, and listening for any sign of opposition above where we stood. I started counting silently: one Mississippi, two Mississippi. About the time I hit four hundred, I heard a low mumble behind me, and turned to glare, raising my hand in a stop gesture. The grumbling silenced. I forced myself to wait a full ten minutes, as Ben had recommended, counting all the way to six hundred Mississippi. I neither saw nor heard any sign of guards on the wall.

The mirror bracket was just above my head. I grabbed the metal bar and tugged hard, putting my whole weight on it. The bracket and truck were rock-solid. I pulled myself upward. It was no different than doing a chin-up in gym class. I hooked an elbow over the mirror and reached higher. I could barely grab the back of the cab. I pulled myself up until I was standing on the mirror bracket. From there, it was fairly easy to scramble up into the bed of the truck and climb the rest of the way by shimmying up the side rail.

I waited another full two minutes up there, flattened against the tailgate atop the truck. I saw a couple of flickering lights off in the distance, but they didn't move. Apparently, no one was patrolling this section of the wall. The truck I was on was held upright by a log wedged under its rear axle. The log sloped down to the ground, forming the hypotenuse of a right triangle.

When I felt certain it was safe, I got the rope out of my backpack, tied one end to the tailpipe, and tossed the other end down to Ed. Then I climbed down the inside of the wall. That was much easier than the climb up had been—I just lowered myself down the exhaust pipe until I reached the log that supported the truck. Wrapping my legs around the log made it easy to slide the rest of the way to the ground.

Eighteen people followed the path I'd blazed over the truck. Every grunt and clunk jangled my already-rattled nerves. I moved away from the wall. I'd come down beside a cemetery, so I took a position along its fence, scanning back and forth for any sign of opposition. I couldn't help but remember Elmwood Cemetery outside of Warren, the carnage there yesterday. I hoped Stockton's cemetery wouldn't see similar bloodshed—if this went off perfectly, no one had to die.

The last person over the wall untied the rope and returned it to me. We broke into our pre-arranged squads, and Lynn and Nylce led their groups along the wall in opposite directions. I sent a silent prayer out with them, that they'd both be up to the task they'd volunteered for. Then I took my squad straight for the center of Stockton.

My squad left the graveyard, jogging through what looked like a residential neighborhood. It was tough to tell—buildings, except for those right on the street, were hidden by the darkness. The streets were dark and silent—deserted.

We'd been running for only three or four minutes when I caught sight of a small fire up ahead, flickering in the surrounding darkness. I raised a hand, signaling stop. Working in whispers and gestures, I split my squad into two groups, sending Ed and two others to swing wide and sneak up to the fire from the other side, and leaving three guys with me to approach directly.

I gave Ed's group time to work their way around the fire while I waited, counting off two minutes in my head. Then I bent low and stalked along the road, directly toward the fire.

As I got closer, I saw two figures beside the fire—one silhouetted, with his back to us, and another facing us on the far side. The plowed track in the road split where they were camped, one branch continuing straight and the other veering to pass under a huge overhead door, directly into a warehouse. The warehouse looked massive, extending far beyond what the circle of firelight could illuminate. The sign over the closed overhead door read FURST ELECTRICAL AND CHEMICAL DISTRIBUTORS, EST. 1951.

I dropped to a crawl, moving in the darkness along the edge of the road. When we got so close that I was sure the guys by the fire *had* to hear us, I held up my hand, all five fingers splayed. My fingers didn't shake, which surprised me. On the inside, I was trembling like an autumn leaf. I lowered my fingers one at a time: five . . . four . . . three . . . two . . . one.

All of us jumped to our feet, sprinting toward the fire. The two guards lurched up, spinning and peering into the blackness toward us. One of them bent, reaching for a long gun propped against his chair. Ed materialized from the darkness behind him, pressing his gun to the guy's neck. I reached the fire, training my rifle at the other guy. The rifle was empty, but he didn't know that.

He said, "What the—?"

"Any more guards here?" I asked, gesturing with my rifle.

"Who in the seven hells of Sheba are you?"

"I'm holding the gun, so I'll ask the questions. Got it?" Without waiting for an answer, I ordered Ed, "Search them."

Ed slung his rifle across his back and frisked both of them, coming up with a bowie knife and a machete. They both had shotguns too, which Ed promptly confiscated. He passed the machete and one of the shotguns to other members of our squad.

"Are there more guards here?" I repeated.

"Cliff's in charge. Ask him."

I aimed my rifle at the other guy—Cliff. "Talk."

"Cain't. *Doctore* wouldn't like it if ah did."

"Doctor? What doctor?" I asked.

"Cain't tell you."

Ed turned back to Cliff, bowie knife clenched in his fist at about chest level. The blade shone orange in the fire-light. He wrapped a hank of Cliff's long, greasy hair around his left hand, forcing his head back.

"Ed. What're you doing?" I asked.

Ed slipped the edge of his knife along Cliff's throat.

"This guy's in charge. Kill him, and the other one'll talk."

The other guy backed away, running right into the barrel of a shotgun held by Steve McCormick. That stopped him in his tracks.

We didn't have time to waste. One of the other squads could run into trouble sweeping the walls. I stared at Cliff. He was sweating despite the cold. Could I do it? Order Ed to kill this man while I watched just to get the other guy to talk? If we didn't gain control of Stockton through surprise—before any gunfire broke out—some of us would die. Maybe all of us. Was that worth taking Cliff's life? I thought of my dad, how vicious he'd been with captured slavers in the Maquoketa FEMA camp. I understood him better now.

Would Ed even do it? I lifted my gaze to Ed's face. The flat look in his eyes told me yes, he would. He shrugged as if to say get on with it.

I nodded. "Do it," I said. "Cut his throat."

Ed's grip tightened on the knife handle.

"W-wait," Cliff stammered. Ed checked his cut. A thin line of blood, dark and viscous, appeared along Cliff's neck. Two black runnels parted from the line, trickling toward Cliff's collarbone.

"J-just hold on, hold on," Cliff said. "There's no other guards nearby. Just us."

"What're you guarding?"

"Warehouse."

I scowled at him. "Duh, what's in it?"

"All our supplies. Spare guns, ammo, gas."

"How many guards are on duty in town right now?"

Cliff hesitated. I took a step toward him.

"Six, just six. Us, two on the west gate, two on the east gate."

"No patrols?"

"Not tonight. Everybody's up in Warren."

"You're bullshitting me," I said flatly, glancing at Ed, who still held the knife close to Cliff's throat.

"N-no. Everyone's in Warren, I swear. *Doctore* cleaned us out, sent everyone with the *primus* to fight in Warren."

"But they left you behind."

"*Doctore* wanted a few men held back. Just the most trustworthy. To guard the town."

"Who's this doctor guy?"

"Red. He runs things here now. Calls himself a *doctore*, trainer of gladiators. Calls us a *familia*. Thinks he's some kind of reborn Roman, even studies Latin. Whatever—I just do what I'm told."

"So why're you in front of this warehouse?"

"Little food's left. It's in there too. Been broken into twice. Gotta guard it."

"From your own people," I said. Cliff nodded. They must be starving to try to steal from their town's own food stores. The thought made me a little sick. "Six on duty tonight, how many in the daytime shifts?"

"J-just twelve more. They're in the sack right now."

"Who's in charge?"

"*Doctore*'s here. He sent *Primus* Alton to Warren."

"Where?"

"He's got a house up by City Hall."

"And where're the guards sleeping?"

"Y-you're just going to kill me, ain't you? After I tell you everything?"

"Ed's going to kill you right now if you don't tell me everything."

Cliff's Adam's apple bobbed, triggering a new trickle of blood down his neck. "Barracks are near City Hall too. In the Stockton Bowling Lanes."

"Ed," I said, "detail two men to guard this warehouse and hold him." I gestured at the second guard. "Cliff is going to take the rest of us to visit this *doctore* of his."

I got the rope out of my backpack, cut a hank, and bound Cliff's hands behind his back.

"You're going to lead us directly to *Doctore's* house. And you'll be quiet about it. Or Ed will finish the cut he started in your neck."

Cliff led us down the street until we reached an old, two-story brick building labeled CITY HALL AND POLICE DEPARTMENT. A few businesses were scattered on the other side of the street, including a bowling alley with its front window covered in black paper.

"That the barracks?" I asked Cliff in a whisper.

"Yes," he replied.

As we crept past the bowling alley, the stillness of the night was shattered by gunfire.

Chapter 9

The gunfire was coming from somewhere to the west, near the car wall. "Shit," I muttered. "Run! To *Doctore's* house!" I prodded Cliff with my gun, and we all broke into a sprint.

I glanced over my shoulder. Cracks of light shone around the edges of the bowling alley-cum-barracks' windows. A new fusillade of noise broke out somewhere northeast of us—there were two separate firefights going on. Everyone in Stockton must have been awakened.

Just past the tiny downtown area, the character of the street changed; it was lined with Victorian mansions set so close to the street that they loomed out of the darkness, turrets and gables hanging threateningly over our heads. As we ran, lights appeared in several of the windows. "Which house is it?" I yelled at Cliff, prodding him again with the barrel of my gun.

"First one," Cliff gasped, pointing at a particularly ornate house.

I glanced over my shoulder again. A man with an oil lamp and rifle was emerging from the side door to the bowling alley. I cursed myself silently—I should have set up an ambush at the door of the barracks. That's what Ben would have told me to do. But by then it was too late.

I swerved into the side street between the last commercial building and *Doctore*'s house. A light was moving around on the second floor. Cliff lagged behind, and I let him, racing ahead. Ed was alongside me, the three remaining members of my squad trailing behind.

I ran to the back of the house and flung open the storm door. There was a small window set into the top of the back door. Inside it was dark. I raised my foot, launching a front kick at the lock. All my desperation and fear flowed into that kick. The lock was solid, but the jamb wasn't. It splintered with an obscenely loud crack, and the door banged open.

In the dark, we raced through the main floor of the house, crashing blindly into unseen furniture, looking for a staircase. Finally I spotted a dim ray of light. I ran toward it, my empty gun held at shoulder level in front of me, commando style—at least I thought it was from what I'd seen in video games.

I pulled up at the base of a grand Victorian staircase. Polished wood and elaborately turned balusters gleamed in the light of an oil lamp. The lamp sat on the floor next to a whip-thin guy, so short that even I could have looked down on him if he hadn't been at the top of the staircase. His brown hair was chopped into a cruel buzz cut, his upper lip adorned with a wispy Hitler mustache. He had a large straight knife, almost a sword, in his right hand and a short blade with a wicked serrated spine in his left. He played with the shorter blade, rolling it across the back of his hand over and over, as if it were a habit ingrained through hundreds of hours of practice. Other than the motion of that hand and blade, he was preternaturally still.

Ed was on my right, another squaddie on my left. All three of us aimed our guns up the stairs. Ed had the shotgun he'd taken from one of the warehouse guards—the only gun that was loaded. "You brought knives to a gunfight," I called up the stairs.

I fought to keep my hands steady, to keep the tremors rattling my innards from leaking out. If my gun shook, surely he'd notice, realize I was bluffing. Then what?

The guy at the top stared at us over the tip of the larger knife. The smaller knife flashed in the lamplight, its motion unceasing. "Knives to a gunfight?" he said. "Really? That hoary old saw? It's not such a bad strategy as you might think, bringing a knife to a gunfight. Within twenty-one feet, the guy with the knife can win every time."

I didn't believe him, but it didn't seem like the time or place to argue the point. "Put your knives down. On the floor. Now!"

He continued in a conversational tone. "If there were only two of you, you'd be dead already. Julia, my throwing knife, would enter your body just above the suprasternal notch. It would puncture both the trachea and the jugular vein. You'd asphyxiate, drowning in your own blood. In the meantime, I'd charge the other guy. His hands would shake—like yours are. He might not even get a shot off, and if he did, it would miss. The first blow with Claudia, my *gladius*, would sever his arm at the elbow. It's tough to pull a trigger when your hand isn't connected to your arm. The second blow, the killing blow, would be an uppercut through the stomach, the liver, and into the descending thoracic aorta. He'd go into hypovolemic shock in seconds and be dead of blood loss within two minutes."

The other two guys in my squad, Cliff in tow, clattered into the foyer.

"Shoot this guy, Ed," I said. "I'm tired of listening to him."

Ed raised the shotgun to his shoulder.

The guy dropped both his knives. They stuck, quivering in the hardwood floor, handles up, ready for fast retrieval.

I charged up the stairs, Ed and the rest behind me. The guy didn't move, not even when I reached the top and grabbed his knives. When I stood, I was just inches from him, so close I could smell him—an alcohol scent like cheap cologne.

"Where's *Doctore*?" I asked.

He smiled and said nothing.

"Ed, watch him. The rest of you, search this floor. Find *Doctore*. Make sure there's nobody behind us."

Ed took the lamp from the floor. I stepped around him to let the other guys past and tucked the *gladius* into my belt.

I was stowing Julia, the smaller knife, just as the front door near the base of the stairs burst open. A stream of guys dressed in black rushed in, guns raised. I stepped behind our captive and raised his own knife under his chin. He barely flinched.

A forest of rifles aimed up the stairs toward us. "Tell them to put their guns down," I said, pressing the point of the knife into his chin.

The guy in the lead yelled up at us. "Orders, *Doctore*?"

He very nearly growled his response. "Standish, you idiot. To start with, don't give the enemy intel—the fact that I'm in charge, for example."

"Tell them to put down their weapons," I said.

"S-s-sorry, Red," Standish said.

"You know why they call me Red?" the guy asked. As he talked, the knife I held nicked his throat, a thick line of blood dripping downward.

"I don't know, and I don't care," I said. "Tell them to put their guns down!"

"Red is the color of the knife, the color of blood, the way of iron, the way of the new world, the world of men. Our laws are the ancient laws, the Laws of Steel," Red said. His voice crescendoed to a shout, "We are!"

"The Reds!" the men below us screamed in unison.

"Johnson!" Red called.

"Sir!" a guy in the middle of the pack yelled back.

"Standish failed me. You are hereby promoted."

"Yes, sir!" he called back.

"Shoot Standish." Everyone was still for a second. "Now!" Red hollered.

One of the guys in the front started to swivel, but Johnson was faster. He lowered his gun and shot, hitting Standish in the back with a three-round burst. Standish flew forward, crumpled.

"Jesus," I yelled, "I almost stabbed you! If a firefight starts here you're—"

"Cliff led them here," he said. "Shoot him next."

Cliff tried to move around behind me, but Johnson raised his gun and shot. Cliff was standing so close to me that I could hear the meaty thunks of the bullets hitting his torso.

"Tell them to put down their guns! Now!" I rammed the knife up into the soft underside of his throat, drawing more blood. "I'm *this* close to stabbing you."

Red's voice came out as a croak. "Do as he says."

The men in the foyer below us—eleven of them now—laid down their guns. Drawn by the gunfire, the rest of my squad had returned. "Floor's clear," one of them said. "Just him up here."

"Yeah, he's *Doctore*," I replied. "Tie 'em all up. We need to check on the other teams."

Lynn's patrol at the west gate had been spotted before they could take out the guards. Lynn was dead. The rest of the squad had overpowered and killed the two Stockton guards.

That firefight had put the guards at the east gate on alert. They pinned down Nylce's patrol, and things were stalemated until Darla, hearing the gunfire, rammed the gate with her pickup truck, killing the guards who'd been using it for cover. Everyone on Nylce's squad was okay, but we were down a pickup. Darla seemed to be fine.

"I thought you were going to guard the trucks?" I said when I finally caught up to her.

"I never left the truck," she replied, giving me a shit-eating grin.

It took what little remained of the night to get organized. I sent Darla and Nylce back to the farm with our two remaining trucks to try to recruit reinforcements. Ed consolidated all our captives—including the guy I'd left at the warehouse—on the main floor of *Doctore's* mansion, tied and under guard. I split everyone else up into groups: three to guard the east gate, a pair to guard the west gate, a pair to guard the prisoners, two pairs to patrol the walls, and two pairs to patrol the streets of the town. I told the street patrols to enforce a curfew—keep everyone at home, indoors.

We were woefully undermanned. I hoped Darla and Nylce would return quickly and bring a couple of pickups full of help. The one bit of good news was that with all the rifles we'd taken from Red's soldiers, all our people were armed now. Ammo, however, seemed to be in very short supply—nobody had more than thirty rounds. When I finished setting up all that, Ed and I grabbed a lantern and headed to the warehouse.

It was locked up tight. "Guess we'll have to bust open the door." I started hunting for a log to use as a battering ram—both the overhead door and pedestrian door were metal, and kicking them would only bruise my foot.

"Uh, boss?" Ed said. I paused to look his way. He held a ring of keys, jingling them so they glinted in the light of my lantern.

"Where'd you get those?"

"Took 'em off Cliff's corpse."

The third key opened the pedestrian door. Inside, we saw a huge stack of electric water heaters, their boxes forming a wall that blocked our view of the rest of the interior. We crept farther into the warehouse. Most of the racks were loaded with oddments—plumbing fixtures, pipes, electrical boxes, and the like. Along one wall, huge spools of wire rested on their sides.

Finally we found the food: a wall of nearly empty shelves with a few forlorn boxes scattered here and there. A case of sugar-free grape Kool-Aid. A dozen tiny glass bottles of saffron. Two cases of Sriracha hot sauce. A few hundred small paper packets of Sweet 'N Low, Equal, and Splenda in a moldering cardboard box. I'd like to see the Iron Chefs do anything useful with *those* ingredients.

Farther along, we found the weapons—hundreds of them laid out in neat rows on floor-to-ceiling shelving. Old black powder rifles. Bolt-action rifles. Pump shotguns. Skeet shotguns. A huge selection of revolvers. I didn't see any semi-automatic rifles, and the few semi-auto handguns looked old and poorly maintained. I also didn't see any ammo. A huge section of shelving near the guns might once have held bricks of ammo, but the shelves were empty except for a bottom shelf that held three large wooden crates. I pulled the first crate out onto the concrete floor.

It had no top. I lifted my lantern, letting light spill into the box. Inside were hundreds of cartridges—for rifles, handguns, and shotguns—in a bewildering assortment of calibers. Some of the cartridges were shiny yellow brass, others gray—steel, I figured, although I wasn't sure. The other two crates held the same chaotic mix of loose ammo.

"We can work with this," Ed said.

"It's going to take too long. It's almost dawn. Let's carry a box to the east gate and sort it while we wait for Darla and Nylce to get back."

"Yessir," Ed replied.

"Don't 'yessir' me," I said.

"Nosir." Ed grinned, a rare crack in his normally grim visage.

I laid six of the best-looking rifles on top of the wooden ammo crate. Ed grabbed one of its rope handles, and I grabbed the other. It was heavy—barely manageable between us. We trudged to the gate, reaching it just as the black sky began to fade to the yellow-gray of morning.

Steve McCormick was there with another guy. They were working on the gate, trying to complete a jury-rigged repair of the hinges Darla had shattered when she rammed it. "All quiet?" I asked.

"So far," Steve replied.

Ed and I knelt in the packed snow behind the wall and started sorting ammo. I found five cartridges for one of the bolt-action rifles we'd brought with us. It looked like a twin of Uncle Paul's hunting rifle, and I'd learned to fire that over the last year, although Darla was a much better shot than I was. "I'm going to go check on the patrols and the west gate. Get as many rifles ready as you can—we'll need them when Darla gets back. If you see anyone coming, fire two quick shots. That'll be the signal that you need reinforcements. I'll tell everyone."

"Got it," Ed replied.

"If it's Darla and the truck, fire once."

"Yessir."

I rolled my eyes at his yessir—a useless gesture, given how dim the early morning light was—and took off jogging alongside the car wall, looking for our patrols.

It took me almost two hours to find everyone. We were spread ridiculously thin—seventeen people to patrol a town that still held hundreds of terrified residents. I ended up back at *Doctore*'s mansion. Our captives were sprawled across the living room, their arms and legs bound. The two guards I'd left there were sitting on folding chairs near the door, overseeing. The prisoners had been complaining about the lack of breakfast. I told our guards to gag anyone who got too annoying; I didn't plan to hold anyone long enough for them to starve to death.

Just as I finished that unpleasant conversation, I heard a gunshot—not from the east gate, but closer. Did it mean Darla was back? If so, why wasn't she at the east gate? I left the mansion, running down the street in the direction I thought the shot had come from.

I caught up with one of our patrols about two blocks off. "You guys fire?"

Kyle Henthorn, a burly, red-faced guy in his early thirties, replied, "Had to fire a warning shot. Guy came out of that house." Kyle gestured with his rifle at a house across the street. "Didn't want to go back in. Had to put a little scare—"

A rifle shot echoed across Stockton, and Kyle fell suddenly quiet. There was a short pause, and then two more shots rang out, coming from the direction of the east gate.

"The attack signal. Come on!" I dashed pell-mell toward a side street that would carry me in the direction of the east gate, with Kyle and the other patroller close behind me. We had to get there fast—if we were being attacked, there was no way Steve, Ed, and one other guard would be able to hold them off.

It seemed like it took forever to get back to the gate, even though it couldn't have taken even five minutes. Stockton's not that big of a town. I didn't hear any more shots, which I took as a good sign.

As I approached the gate, I saw the pickups pulled up just inside the wall. Darla was back! I slowed to a trot—I was exhausted and starving. I'd had next to no sleep the night before and no food for nearly two days.

The people on the wall were silhouettes in the dim, morning light. I tried to pick out Darla; I hoped she was still in the truck, but I couldn't see through its windows.

Knowing Darla, she'd be on the wall, even though she had
to be at least as tired and hungry as I was. And I knew she
was still weak from her injuries at the hands of the Dirty
White Boys.

As I scrutinized the figures on the wall, one of them
turned toward me. She—I thought, although I couldn't
tell who it was—raised her arms over her head, waving
them back and forth frantically. What was wrong? I broke
into a sprint.

Chapter 10

The woman abruptly quit waving. Everyone on the wall fell flat all at once. I ran even faster.

Darla had obviously brought two full truckloads of reinforcements; there were about twenty people crouched behind the wall or the low log gate. Every one of them had a long gun—Ed must have gone back to the warehouse for more—and were aiming at the road beyond the gate.

Several hundred yards past the gate, I saw a panel van slewed diagonally across the road. Behind it, the top of a semi was visible. Dozens of figures were clustered around the van and spread out to either side, aiming rifles back down the road toward us.

"Get your idiot ass out of the middle of the road," Darla shouted.

"Take cover, sir," Ed yelled at the same time.

I veered—putting the edge of the car wall between me and the guns—and sprinted the rest of the way to the gate.

"What's going on?" I gasped.

"Right after I turned onto Highway 78 about halfway between here and Warren, a line of trucks came over the hill north of me," Darla said. "They chased us all the way back here."

"How many?"

"Two panel vans and nine semi tractor-trailers."

"Same ones that were loading the pork from the warehouse in Warren?" Ed asked.

"Must be," Darla said.

"This doesn't need to turn into a fight." I pulled my coat, sweater, and shirt up from my belly. My undershirt rode up too, exposing my skin to the frigid air. I yanked the undershirt down and started trying to tear off a hunk of it.

"What're you doing?" Darla asked.

"I need a white flag," I said.

"Are you crazy?" Darla exclaimed. "You're not going out there."

"We've got their leader, they've got our food." I struggled with the shirt. It wouldn't tear. "Someone's got to go explain things—work out a trade."

"Someone," Ed said. "Not you."

"I'm not asking anyone else to take a risk like that! What if they start shooting?" The shirt was incredibly frustrating. No matter how hard I tugged, it wouldn't rip. I took the knife off my belt.

"I'll go," Darla said.

"No!" I jerked the knife so hard that I nicked my belly.

"That's no good either," Ed said. "Say they take you hostage. He'll do anything to get you back."

Darla scowled and stepped away, moving along the inside of the car wall.

"He's right," I said as I finished cutting off a chunk of my T-shirt.

Darla had reached an old Chevy Silverado. She grabbed a piece of conduit, ripping it free of the brackets that held it to the underside of the car. The wires inside the conduit didn't break, though. "They made these old trucks too dang well," she muttered as she yanked on the conduit, trying unsuccessfully to break the wires.

I stepped over to her. "He's right, you know. I'd do anything to get you back. Anything."

"Let me see your knife."

I handed it to her, hilt first. She took it and started sawing away at the wire. I stood and watched quietly.

The chunk of conduit came free, and Darla handed back the knife. Our gloved fingers touched as I took its hilt. "I know," she whispered.

"I'll go," Ed said. I hadn't even noticed him following us. He grabbed one end of the hunk of cloth I was holding, but I didn't let go. "If they take me hostage, nobody'll care."

"No," I said, "I'd care."

"He's right." Darla handed the conduit to Ed. It drooped from his hand, a bit too floppy to make a really good flagpole.

"I can do it," I said, pulling on the rag.

Ed held the rag tight. "But you shouldn't."

"Alex," Darla said softly, "let go."

I dropped the rag, and Ed tied it to the top of the conduit. He handed me his rifle and held the improvised flag high over his head. He walked slowly toward the gate, waving it over his head. Darla and I followed as far as the gate so we could peek above it.

Ed's march from the gate to the panel van seemed interminable. He held both hands above his head, one waving the white flag, the other open and turned out toward the enemy. When he was about twenty yards from the panel van, two guys ran up and patted him down. Then all three of them walked slowly around the panel van, disappearing from view.

That made me uncomfortable. What would I do if Ed never came back? Send someone else? Go myself? It wasn't that I distrusted Ed; the last couple of days had changed my view of him forever. The problem with the past is that you can never truly escape from it. Ed would always be a former member of a flenser gang. But despite his cannibalistic past, he'd saved my life—probably twice— and been there for me in every way that mattered yesterday during the fight and its aftermath.

Darla was leaning against the car wall beside me. I turned and muttered to her.

"What if he doesn't come back?"

"He'll come back."

"They might not let him."

"If you don't quit obsessing about it, I'm going to slap you."

"But—"

Darla flattened her hand and wound up in an exaggerated gesture. I put an arm up to block. She changed direction and swatted me on the butt, far harder than necessary to make her point.

"What's with the extra English?" I said.

"That? That was a love pat. Wait until I'm feeling better." Her grin was wide and wicked. It faded suddenly, and she leaned in to kiss me. "Alex, you're doing great. Ed's going to come back. Try not to worry so much."

I smiled despite my churning thoughts. The arguments we'd had with Uncle Paul about my age when we first reached the farm seemed like scenes from a previous lifetime now. Whether Darla and I could share a bed seemed utterly trivial in comparison to the life-and-death decisions we were making now.

When I turned back to the wall, nothing was moving. A few dozen guys pointed their rifles down the road at us. We pointed our rifles back. No one shot. The wait stretched out forever.

Darla leaned close. "I brought our food stash with me. The stuff we brought back from Iowa. It's in the truck."

Good thinking," I said.

We passed the time by sharing the food with all our

fighters. Those trucks contained Warren's whole supply
of frozen pork—I'd be willing to bet anything on it. Soon
we'd either have plenty of food or we'd be dead—it didn't
make sense to save anything.

Finally Ed emerged from behind the panel van, walking slowly, flanked by two guys. They dropped back, and
he hoisted the white flag over his head again, trudging
across the no-man's land between us.

"What's the word?" I asked Ed a few minutes later as
he clambered over the log gate.

"They want proof. That we're holding Red."

"Guess we can go get him."

"Alex," Ed caught my arm, leaning close and speaking
softly, "they're terrified of him. Even though we've got
him and he's tied up. I don't know what kind of hold he's
got over them, but—"

"He's certainly vicious enough," I said.

"Maybe that's it," Ed said.

"It doesn't matter right now. Take the truck. Get Red
and his lieutenant."

"Yessir."

"Don't yes—"

"Nosir."

I started to protest again, but Ed and Darla were
already on their way to the truck. Instead, I went to
explain what was going on to Nylce and the rest of our
people manning the wall and gate.

Half an hour later, Ed and Darla were back. Red and
Johnson were in the bed of the pickup, huddled under a

blanket. I lowered the tailgate, climbed up beside Johnson, and drew my knife. Johnson flinched. Red smiled, looking at the knife the way I might look at Darla after we'd been apart for a few hours.

"Here's what's going to happen," I said. "I'm going to cut you free, and you're going to march out to those trucks and tell your buddies that I've got Red, alive and unhurt. He'll stay that way if you play along. Got it?"

"Yeah," Johnson said, eyeing me warily.

"Then you and whoever's in charge over there are going to walk halfway back to us—unarmed. Darla, Ed, Red, and I will come out to meet you. Three of us, three of you. No weapons. Anything goes wrong, either side can kill everyone out there. Got it?"

Johnson turned to look at Red, waiting.

"Do it, Johnson. Like he says."

"Yes, sir," he replied.

I sawed the rope off his ankles and wrists, handed him the white flag, and helped him out of the pickup and over the log gate. He moved stiffly, his feet dragging in the thin layer of snow that had blown over the icy road.

About fifteen minutes after Johnson disappeared around the van, he came back, walking alongside another guy. Neither of them was carrying any obvious weapon, but they could have hidden an arsenal under their coats.

I cut free Red's ankles, leaving his hands bound, and Red, Ed, Darla, and I headed for no-man's land. Ed and I had to lift Red over the gate, but it was easy—he didn't weigh much.

When we'd finally gathered in the approximate center of the kill zone, I gestured at Johnson and the new guy, telling Ed, "Check those two for weapons."

"Yessir." Ed stepped toward them, but they each took a step back.

"Why don't we check you?" the new guy growled.

"Go right ahead," I replied. I still had two knives on my belt—I hadn't thought to leave them with my rifle—but I didn't mind giving them up. I'd taken them from Red, after all. I put my hand on the *gladius*'s hilt.

The two guys took another step back, fumbling under their jackets for something. Ed and Darla moved toward them. Johnson pulled a pistol from under his coat, but Ed was on him before he could bring it to bear, twisting his arm so hard that the elbow audibly popped.

I was three steps away, Darla two. The other guy got his pistol from his back. I slipped behind Red, wrapping one arm around him in a confining embrace and raising my knife so the tip rested just under his chin. My hands shook with adrenaline, and the knife made a tiny cut in his skin, adding fresh blood to the scabs I'd left there earlier.

The new guy leveled his pistol at me. "Drop the knife. Now," he said. "Or I'll shoot."

"Go ahead and shoot," I replied, glad that the quaver in my hands wasn't evident in my voice. "Maybe I'll have enough strength left to jam this knife into his throat, maybe not. Either way, both sides will open fire, and we'll all die. That what you want?" I was surprised nobody had started shooting yet. Looking past the handgun leveled at me, I saw the stopped trucks—men peered past their edges, gripping their rifles, wide-eyed and tense.

Red tried to say something, but when his throat tensed, my knife pushed deeper into his skin, and he abruptly shut up.

"Put your gun down!" I yelled. "Now, goddamn it!"

The new guy just stared at me. Then I realized: he was staring at Red.

Red's head twitched—a barely perceptible shake.

"Can't do that," the new guy said.

There was no reasoning with them. Whatever hold Red had on them was insanely scary. I had to negotiate directly with Red. "Lower the gun to your side. I'll ease off on the knife enough so he can talk." I slid the knife downward about half an inch. My fist was against his chest, the knife thrust upward, its point toward his throat.

"Let me go now," Red said, "and you can all leave here alive."

"We're not going anywhere without our food," I replied.

"My food," Red said emphatically. "Possession's nine-tenths of the law, as they say, and I *am* the law. So I own ten-tenths of that food."

"If that's the case, then I own you. And your town." I briefly pushed the knife tighter against his throat to emphasize the point.

"Temporarily, maybe."

I could hardly believe his sangfroid. My hands were shaking—the adrenaline was starting to wear off, and I was fighting an internal battle with my stomach. "You need a solution worse than I do. This goes south, my people at the gate will start shooting. We'll all die out here. And my people will still have your town. They'll—"

"*My* people will have the food," Red said.

"Their families are in Stockton. They'll be more willing to work out a deal than you seem to be."

"You haven't proposed anything."

"Your people at the trucks lay down their weapons and move a few hundred yards off. We'll leave Stockton, take the trucks, and go home."

"And we'll starve for certain. I'd rather take my chances on a firefight."

"Without *our* food, *we'll* starve."

"Not my concern," Red said. "But I'll allow you to take one truck. My choice of which one you keep."

"I've got the upper hand here," I said. "I'll allow you to keep one truckload of *our* food. And I'll choose which truck you get."

"We split them, six and five. I choose which five you get."

We haggled for half an hour more. Finally we settled on an eight/three split. Red would choose which three of the semis or panel vans he'd keep. Neither side would disarm, but we'd keep Red captive until the last minute, as insurance for his side's good behavior. In addition, we'd keep both the remaining pickups. Red also insisted that I return his knives, Julia and Claudia.

It took most of the day to make the trade. Red's people sorted the trucks out, getting eight of them in a line facing back toward Warren, and the other three facing

Stockton. I thought Red would choose three semis to maximize the amount of food he could keep, but he picked two semis and a panel van. Later I found out that the van held all the weapons, ammo, alcohol, and seeds his people had looted from Warren.

It was a miracle nobody got shot. Ed collected all our people from Stockton, and we moved past Red's men—both groups eyeing each other warily across the sights of their rifles. Finally by late afternoon, we were all loaded in our idling trucks.

I turned Red loose and gave him his knives. "Be seeing you," he said with a smile that held more threat than mirth.

"Jesus, I hope not." I slammed the pickup's door, and we pulled out—a motley column of seven semis and one panel van led by our captured pickup truck.

As we turned from Highway 20 onto Highway 78, toward home, the tension and stress finally overwhelmed me. I'd been awake for nearly two days. My whole body shook. I rolled down the passenger window of the pickup and barely got my head out in time to spew stomach acid all over the side of the truck.

Chapter 11

I returned to my uncle's farm a hero. Not that there was a ticker-tape parade or anything. Nobody knew when we'd be back or whether we'd even make it back at all. But they knew what the line of trucks trailing behind us meant.

Folks dashed out to meet us even as I climbed out wearily from the pickup. My door was still smeared with streaks of vomit. I trudged to the rear door of the panel van now parked in the road. By the time I reached it, I was surrounded by a crowd. I twisted the handle and opened the door.

The crowd gasped as the contents came into

view: a precarious jumble of frozen hog carcasses filled the truck from floor to ceiling.

Alyssa laughed and flung her arms around me. "That's bringing home the bacon," she said as she kissed my cheek.

Darla cleared her throat, glaring at me. What was up with that? *I* hadn't done anything.

"We need to debrief, Lieutenant," Ben said.

"Not now," I said. "I'm dead on my feet."

"Your recall will be clearer while the events are still—"

Ben kept talking, but I quit listening. "Tomorrow," I said firmly.

Uncle Paul clasped my arm. The skin around his eyes was nearly black: Emperor Palpatine in a younger body. "Alex . . . you did good. I'm sorry. I should have been there—"

"You were right where you needed to be. With Max and Anna. If things had gone bad in Stockton—"

"We should have a feast," Uncle Paul said, "to mourn and celebrate. Roast some of this pork."

"I'm dead on my feet. Would you take care of it?"

"Sure thing." He started talking about the details, and my attention wandered.

I looked around for Mom but didn't see her anywhere. Maybe she was still in the bedroom, sorting pictures. Instead, I saw Lynn's wife at the edge of the crowd. She craned her neck, looking back and forth, bewilderment and fear writ plainly on her face.

"I've got to go."

I pushed through the crowd until I reached her, Darla

on my heels. "Mrs. Manck?" I started, dreading what I had to say.

"Where's Lynn?" she asked, her face twitching, lips curling down as if she already suspected the answer. "Is he okay?"

"He didn't make it. I'm sorry."

Her face was porcelain white. She stood rigid except for the tremors chasing across her cheeks. "No. No. You could be wrong. Maybe he's only hurt."

"We brought his body back."

"He's not . . . it could be someone else's body."

"I wish. I wish it were anyone else. Me. Or nobody."

Mrs. Manck sagged. She looked as if she might faint. I stepped toward her, opening my arms to catch her, give her a hug, offer whatever insufficient comfort I could. Instead of embracing me, she lashed out.

I was totally unprepared for the violence of her blow. Her fist caught my jaw, rocking my head sideways with a snap I felt all the way down to the base of my spine. I raised my arms to block—too late, of course—and stepped back.

She didn't move forward. Her hands fell to her sides, and her trembling grew more violent as if her fury had migrated inward from her fists.

Darla hadn't moved. Now she opened her arms, just standing there. Tears streamed down Mrs. Manck's face, and she fell forward into Darla's arms.

I lowered my fists and stepped around their hug so I could see Darla's face. She mouthed, "Go on, I've got this. I'll find you later."

I was relieved, but I also felt a little guilty. I'd led the attack on Stockton; its consequences, including Lynn's death, were my responsibility. I should be the one dealing with the aftermath, not Darla. I walked on toward the house anyway.

Dr. McCarthy was working in the living room/make-shift hospital. Mom and Belinda were in there, helping him. All three of them looked utterly exhausted. I managed a tired wave in their direction and turned toward the stairs.

"Alex, wait," Dr. McCarthy called.

I took a couple more steps and sagged onto the stair-case to wait.

It took Dr. McCarthy a moment to get to the foyer; the living room was packed so tightly with makeshift pallets that it was difficult to move around without kicking a patient. "Good. You heard me."

"Yeah. I'm so tired I may fall asleep right here. What did you need?"

"I . . . I wanted to apologize. For what I said before you left. You were right. We needed that food. And you got it."

I turned my head away. "Tell that to Mrs. Manck."

"Lynn didn't make it?"

I shook my head.

I felt Dr. McCarthy's hand on my upper arm. "Maybe it's kind of like medicine," he said. "You fight to save everyone, do everything you can, but people die anyway." I didn't respond, and after a short silence, Dr. McCarthy went on. "I became a family practitioner in part so I could avoid that—the constant death—I never understood how

ER docs or thoracic surgeons handled it. How they could live with all that death. But it found me anyway. And now I think I know. How surgeons deal with it. It becomes motivation. To keep struggling, to keep learning, to save whoever you can."

"Maybe I'll feel more like struggling after I've slept." I stood, but Dr. McCarthy didn't let go of my arm.

"You did the right thing. Even though I told you not to. I'm proud of you, Alex. I got to know your dad a bit after the eruption, before he went looking for you. I think he'd be proud too." Dr. McCarthy dropped my arm and turned back toward the living room.

I trudged up the stairs, the tears I hadn't been able to cry before flowing freely down my face. It was all I could do not to sob out loud.

I reached the empty bedroom still crying, pulled my frozen boots off my nearly frostbitten feet, and crawled into bed without even taking off my coat.

Eventually the tears subsided, but I couldn't sleep. My mind ground over the events in Stockton: the guns aimed at me, Standish and Cliff as they died in *Doctore*'s mansion, Lynn's corpse laid out in dirty snow. My whole body was sore, and my eyes were swollen from crying. I was desperately tired, but my mind wouldn't allow me to sleep. I laid there for an hour or more before Darla came into the room and slid into the bed alongside me. Then finally, nestled in her arms, I slept.

Chapter 12

The pork in the trucks was originally from Warren, but Mayor Petty was still mostly unconscious and in no shape to divide it up. I talked to Uncle Paul and Dr. McCarthy about it, and we agreed to send the seven semis of pork back to Warren with the refugees but to keep the panel van. It contained enough meat to feed Uncle Paul's family—my family now—for years. I sent one of our remaining pickups to Warren and kept one—it'd be useful around the farm, at least until we ran out of gas.

It took three days to get people moved from the farm back to Warren. Most of them volunteered to stay behind and help dismantle the ramshackle structures they'd been living in, but I could tell they were anxious to get home, so I told them not to bother.

We scavenged the useful bits of the lean-tos but broke most of them up for firewood. For a while that saved us from the increasingly long trek to find uncut timber. We needed a lot of it—Darla said more than a cord per week—to keep the fires burning in the living room and in the hypocausts, the system of small underground tunnels that kept our greenhouses warm.

Fortunately the greenhouses were in decent shape. Since people had been sleeping in them and all the kale had been harvested and eaten, we had to turn the dirt and replant. I hoped our new crop of kale would come in soon enough to stave off scurvy. I didn't particularly look forward to pulling a bloody toothbrush out of my mouth every morning. All our ducks were gone, slaughtered over the past few weeks to feed the horde from Warren, but we still had a breeding pair of goats.

Dr. McCarthy didn't move back to Warren right away. Several of his patients, Mayor Petty included, were too sick to move. So Belinda returned to Warren to staff the clinic, and our living room continued to serve as a rude hospital.

Uncle Paul moved into Max's room with the rest of the guys, because he said he couldn't sleep in the master bedroom. So Mom theoretically had the master bedroom to herself. She hardly ever slept there, though—or slept at all. She spent most of her time in the living room, helping

Dr. McCarthy care for the last of the patients, particularly Mayor Petty.

Ed hadn't left either, even after almost everyone else had moved back to Warren. Finally I asked him about it while we were chopping wood. "You headed to Warren soon?"

Ed lowered his axe, leaning on the handle. "Well, uh . . ."

"Well, what?" I held the hatchet I was using mid-swing, waiting for him to answer.

"Been meaning to ask you. Couldn't find the right time. Or words. You know."

"No." I set my hatchet down. "I have no clue what you're talking about, Ed."

"Thought I'd stay here. If you don't mind, that is." Ed leaned over farther, putting more weight on the axe handle. "I mean, you know, figure I owe you—"

"You don't owe me anything, Ed."

"That's not true. But even if it was, I'd want to hang around and help. Seems like, well, stuff happens around you."

"That's a great reason to leave—not stay," I said.

"But still . . ."

I thought about it a moment. "That'd be fine," I said finally.

Ed straightened up and hefted his axe. "That's set, then."

I picked my hatchet back up. "Hey, why're you asking me? It's Uncle Paul's farm."

Ed checked the swing of his axe. "You want me to ask him?"

"No, I will."

"Thanks."

And with that, we both returned to work.

I caught Uncle Paul later that day as he carried water into the kitchen. We stood at the sink, slopping water on our hands, trying to scrub off the grime of a day's hard work.

"Ed wants to stay here," I said.

Uncle Paul grunted.

"On the farm. With us."

"Didn't he used to be a flenser?"

"Yeah. And I used to be a high school student."

Uncle Paul turned toward me, a sad smile creasing his cheeks. "Same thing, but with less cannibalism?"

I snorted. "Yeah, pretty much."

"So what'd you tell Ed?"

"I told him he could stay, but I thought it should be your decision. It's your place and all."

Uncle Paul rubbed his hands on a dishrag in silence for a moment. Then he turned toward me, looking me dead in the eyes. "Max and Anna ate today because of decisions you made, Alex. You think Ed should stay, that's good enough for me."

Uncle Paul turned away, walking toward the kitchen table. I dried my hands in a surreal silence, not really feeling them. What exactly did this new responsibility mean?

Chapter 13

Ed and I trekked to Apple River Canyon State Park about every other day to cut wood. We couldn't afford to let our woodpile get low in case something went wrong—say, some of us got sick—and we had to have enough wood on hand to keep all the fires burning until we could cut more.

We filled the toboggan we used for hauling wood faster than usual one morning and wound up back at the farm about an hour before lunchtime. As we were stacking wood near one of the greenhouses, I had the nagging feeling that something was missing.

"There's no smoke," I said.

"Whatcha mean?" Ed asked.

"The hypocaust vent. There's usually smoke coming from it."

"Huh. I'll check on the fire." Ed slid down into the hole that allowed access to the fire shelf, which was a small, stone-lined space where we kept a fire burning continuously. Smoke and heat from the fire rose along the sloping shelf and was funneled into tunnels under the greenhouses to warm the soil. I could see the door to the shelf from my vantage point above him—it was partly open to allow fresh air to enter, which was as it should be. Ed slid the door fully open and peered inside. "Fire's burned out."

"Nobody fed it this morning?"

"Guess not. I'll get it going."

I left Ed and jogged to the house. The cooking fire outside the kitchen was lit. Uncle Paul was there, roasting a large pork shoulder on a spit—our lunch.

"Where is everyone?" I asked.

"Out in the greenhouses," Uncle Paul said.

"No, I was just there."

Uncle Paul shrugged, and I entered the house through the kitchen door. Darla was in there, cutting up the rest of the hog carcass that had supplied the shoulder. She didn't know where everyone else was either. Avoiding her bloody hands, I leaned in for a kiss and then moved on to the living room.

Mayor Petty was asleep, and Dr. McCarthy sat nearby, reading what looked like a twenty-pound medical book.

"Where is everyone?" I asked.

He barely glanced up. "I think your mom went out to the barn."

A strange sight awaited me at the barn. The doors were thrown wide, letting the weak, yellowish daylight inside. The straw had been brushed away and the dirt floor smoothed. Anna, Max, Rebecca, and Ben sat on the floor, scratching numbers in the dirt. It looked like they were doing some kind of . . . math lesson? My mom and Alyssa stood farther inside, nearly shrouded in darkness. I could hear them fine.

"Remember," Mom was saying, "an average attention span is about seven minutes. Plan two activities in each fifteen-minute block. Seven minutes of direct instruction, eight of individual practice, workstations, or buddy practice. The point is to break it up. Match your instruction to your students' attention spans."

Alyssa was listening and nodding, soaking it all in. Nobody had noticed me.

"Do you realize," I said loud enough to carry over my mother's words, "that it's almost lunchtime?"

Max jumped to his feet. "Oh, crap. I haven't fed the goats yet."

"You're supposed to do that first thing," I said.

"I know. Mom used to . . . never mind. That's no excuse." Max took a step toward the door of the barn and then stopped, looking back at Alyssa. "Um, Alyssa, um, I mean teacher, Mrs., I mean Miss Fredericks. May I be excused?"

Max's face was flushed, and Alyssa was failing to suppress a laugh. Alyssa said, "Yes, you may go." At nearly the same time, my mom said, "School isn't over until lunchtime."

Max didn't wait for them to sort it out. He was off like a shot, heading for the house, where we kept the goats stabled in the guest room so they didn't freeze to death at night.

Rebecca and Anna were standing now. "We're supposed to be watering the kale in Greenhouse Two," Rebecca said.

"Go," I said. "We'll hold off on lunch until all the morning chores are done." Rebecca and Anna each grabbed two empty five-gallon pails, carrying them out of the barn.

Ben was still sitting in the dirt, working math problems. Mom was glaring at me, her arms folded over her chest, and now Alyssa was frowning.

"What were you supposed to be doing this morning, Ben?" I asked.

"Ben's assignment was changed by the Sister Unit," Ben said.

"Is the Sister Unit in charge of the chore roster?" I asked.

"Ben always does what the Sister Unit asks of him," Ben said.

"Almost always," Alyssa said. "We were on fire duty."

"The fires under the greenhouses are out!" I said.

"I'm sorry," Alyssa said. "Will the kale be—"

"It'll be fine," I said, although I wasn't totally sure about that. "Ed's getting the fires relit, and the ground holds heat a long time. But what were you doing? Playing school?"

"We weren't playing, Alex," Mom said. "These kids need to be in school."

"We need to eat," I said. "School is a luxury we can't afford right now."

"Education is no kind of *luxury*," Mom said. "Without it we're only one generation removed from barbarism."

"Without food there won't *be* another generation."

"Why do you have to fight me all the time?"

"That's not the—"

"I'll go help Ed with the fires," Alyssa said, stepping toward the barn door.

"Wait," I said.

"Well," Mom said, "you seem to have ended all hope for any more learning taking place this morning." She pivoted abruptly and marched off toward the house.

I stared, not sure whether to chase after her or not.

"I'm sorry," Alyssa said. "I just . . . Dr. McCarthy asked me this morning what I was planning to do before the volcano erupted. I always wanted to get a teaching degree, work with kids like Ben, maybe."

"You'd be great at that."

"Your mom was there, and she started telling me how she got her start teaching special ed."

My mother was a special ed teacher? She'd never told me about that. She'd been a principal for as long as I could remember.

"And anyway," Alyssa continued, "things kind of snowballed from there, and everyone was really enthusiastic about the idea, especially your mom. I figured we could teach practical classes too. I was going to ask you to run a taekwondo class, maybe have your uncle teach gun safety and marksmanship, stuff like that."

"It's a good idea, but—"

"I know. We should have waited until all the work was done. It doesn't seem like there'll ever be enough time to do everything we need and want to do."

"Could you design lessons that could be taught while you do chores? It doesn't take much brainpower to water the kale or wash clothing. I could change the duty rotations to give you time with each of your students and with Mom if you want."

"That could work." Alyssa turned toward Ben, who was still sitting on the floor, scratching columns of figures into the dirt. "Come on, let's get our chores done." He stood and brushed off his pants.

I started to leave, but Alyssa caught my arm, leaned in, and kissed my cheek.

"What was that for?" I asked.

"You're sweet." She left the barn, Ben trailing behind her, heading for the greenhouses.

I rubbed the spot she'd kissed, wondering what I'd done to make Alyssa think I was sweet. And why did my mother seem to disagree so adamantly?

Chapter 14

Dr. McCarthy and Mayor Petty were with us for almost a month. Petty clung to life stubbornly despite his amputated legs, despite the infections that raced through his body leaving him feverish and incoherent. When his condition improved enough, Belinda drove out in Dr. McCarthy's old Studebaker, a folded wheelchair jammed into its backseat. A few days later, Petty, McCarthy, and Belinda moved back to town, and the farm settled into a routine of sorts.

We tore up all the carpet in the living room. It was too badly stained with blood, urine, and other unidentifiable fluids to be salvaged. The rough wood floor underneath wasn't as comfortable, but it smelled a lot better.

Our kale crop came in blessedly fast, as if the soil in the greenhouses had stored up all that energy from going unplanted and now was pumping it into our crop. As soon as the first shoots were a few inches long, we started harvesting them, eating only one shoot per person per day to prevent scurvy.

Alyssa took all the most boring, repetitive jobs so she could practice teaching while she worked. She hung around Mom a lot, talking about her students: Anna, Rebecca, Max, and Ben. Ben was older than she, and the rest weren't much younger, but they seemed to enjoy the classes. Darla never participated, and I was usually far too busy. Occasionally Alyssa organized evening classes that we all attended. The subjects ranged from taekwondo to fire safety, marksmanship, or greenhouse farming. Uncle Paul taught most of the evening seminars, although I led the taekwondo classes, of course.

Darla got steadily stronger, working longer and longer days beside me. There was—as always—no end to the work. Clothes had to be washed by hand, wood had to be cut, kale watered. Darla kept sleeping beside me too, abandoning the girls' room where Alyssa, Rebecca, and Anna slept. Ben, Uncle Paul, Max, and Ed all slept in Max's bedroom too, so it wasn't like we could make out or anything. The greenhouses were better for that. They were warm—particularly in the middle of the day—heated by the hypocaust and what wan light filtered through the ash and sulfur dioxide still polluting the stratosphere.

Darla had started challenging me to arm wrestle every night after dinner. Before her enslavement to the Dirty White Boys, I would never have agreed to arm wrestle with Darla—getting my wrist slammed to the table did nothing good for my ego. But I found that I could beat her easily now. Still, she kept challenging me, night after night, and losing.

Finally, after almost two months on the farm, she beat me. The next night I won—barely—but then she beat me three nights running, winning easily the third time.

The night after that, she waited until everyone else had left the dinner table before she banged her elbow down, holding her hand up, ready to clinch mine. "Ready?"

"Not tonight."

"Really? You beat me, what, fifty or sixty nights running, and after three losses, you're calling it quits?"

"Four losses. And yes."

"Weak."

"My ego may be weak, not my arms. You're just freakishly strong."

"You're calling me a freak? Now you've got to wrestle."

I reached out and grabbed her wrist, twisting her arm and pulling her out of her seat toward me. I caught her by surprise, wrenching her arm around and pulling her into my lap. "I guess I like wrestling after all," I said, laughing.

I released her arm and craned my neck over her shoulder. She turned her head, and we kissed. She wrapped her newly freed arm around my shoulder, pulling me closer.

"I've been meaning to talk to you," she said when the kiss ended.

"Yeah?"

"We're running out of wood."

"Yeah," I said, sighing heavily. I'd noticed the same thing—Apple River Canyon State Park was mostly stumps now.

"I want to try to get one of those wind turbines running," Darla said.

"Wind turbines?"

"The big windmill things, east of Warren. There're sixty or seventy of them. I've been talking to your uncle, and I think we might be able to do it—rig them to run under local control and use them to heat greenhouses. We'd need a lot of components—mostly parts from electric water heaters, some big metal tanks, insulation—oh, and tools. Some heavy gauge—"

"Okay, I get the picture."

"I want to build another Bikezilla too."

"So we need a couple of bicycles and a snowmobile. We've got enough kale to trade now. You ask Uncle Paul if we could take some to Warren to trade?"

"Yeah. He said to check with you."

"What? Why?"

"I dunno. But we should go soon. The right time to deal with this is *before* we run out of wood completely."

"We'll pick kale to trade in the morning. Head to Warren first thing."

"Okay, good." Darla kissed me again and slid off my lap. I didn't mind. Somehow the talk of windmills, kale, and running out of wood had dampened my ardor. Why was Uncle Paul letting all of the farm's problems fall into my lap? I wasn't sure I wanted the responsibility: if I failed, we would all die.

Chapter 15

The next morning Ben found me in one of the greenhouses. Darla and I were picking kale, bagging it for trade.

"Lieutenant," Ben said, "are you mounting an expedition to Warren today?"

"Yeah," I replied. "We're going to try to trade some kale for electrical parts Darla needs."

"I request permission to accompany your expedition."

"Sure, you can come along." Then I hastily added, "If you bring Alyssa."

Darla shot a sharp look my way, but I ignored

her. I didn't think Ben would have any problem on a day trip to Warren, but if he did, I wanted Alyssa there too. She was the only one who could calm him on the rare occasions he melted down.

"When do we leave, sir?"

I'd told Ben to quit calling me "lieutenant" and "sir" about a million times. It didn't help. "Meet us in the kitchen in about a half hour."

Ben saluted and left the greenhouse.

The four of us piled into the captured pickup truck. Usually we walked the five miles to Warren—gas was nearly impossible to come by—but Darla had a huge shopping list of electrical components, tools, and parts. If the trip was successful, we'd need the carrying capacity of the truck.

As we approached Warren, Ben spoke up. "Where is the wall?"

"What wall?" Alyssa asked.

"The wall that Warren needs to build. Since no one has air power, tanks, or heavy ordinance, a wall is an effective means of defending the town. They should have built one by now. In fact, we need to move to town—"

"Move to town? Why?" I asked.

Ben had kept talking. "—because the farm cannot be defended effectively."

"But the greenhouses—"

"The postapocalyptic society will inevitably devolve into a feudal system. We will live in town in times of danger and travel to the greenhouses outside to farm, or move all food production inside the walls, or perhaps inside a larger fixed defense system of some sort."

"If I can get the windmills running," Darla said, "it might be easier to move the town to the windmills."

"Why not run power lines to the town?" I asked.

Ben answered, "Your solution would leave the power source vulnerable. The windmills could be attacked—or the power lines cut—leaving the town completely at the mercy of a besieging army."

As Darla turned the truck into the parking lot at Dr. McCarthy's clinic, Ben added, "Whether we move to the windmills or not, the town must adopt a better defensive posture. We should not have been able to come this far unchallenged."

"I'll talk to them about it," I said.

Dr. McCarthy and Belinda were at the counter in the clinic, reading by the light of an oil lamp. "Slow day?" I asked.

"Yes, thank God," Dr. McCarthy replied. "Only three rooms occupied. Two cases of pneumonia and a reinfected wound. Hope you aren't bringing me any business."

"Nope. Everything's okay out at the farm. Well, except for Mom."

"What are her symptoms?"

"She's not sick, really. Just hardly ever sleeps. Spends a lot of time compulsively sorting old pictures."

"I'd prescribe an SSRI if I had any or refer her to a specialist in cognitive behavioral therapy, if there were any in Warren."

"What's she got?"

"Maybe post-traumatic stress disorder? I'm not an expert. Maybe she'll get better with time."

"There's nothing we can do?"

"Wait. Reassure her if you can. She was a big help with the hospital and Mayor Petty. I think she'll pull through."

I slung my backpack off my shoulder and pulled out a large bag of kale. "For your patients. Anyone showing signs of scurvy?"

"Not yet, but they'll be starting to present symptoms soon."

"Don't tell anyone he gave you that for free," Darla said. "We've got a bunch more we're going to try to trade."

Dr. McCarthy nodded.

"Who's in charge now?" I asked.

"Bob Petty. Same as always."

"What? Really? After the forked-up mess he made of retaking Warren?"

"Yes. Really. Soon as he was getting around okay in that wheelchair, he picked up where he left off. Seems more determined than ever to run things. Couple of people suggested holding elections, but nothing came of it."

The mayor's office was a three-room brick building across the railroad tracks from Warren's tiny downtown. The front office was deserted, but I saw a bustle of activity in the conference room. Eight women sat around the table, laboriously copying a notice about food distribution. The mayor chatted with the women from his wheelchair at the head of the table.

The mayor looked up as I stepped into the room. "Alex, pleasant surprise. What brings you to Warren?"

"Glad to see you're on your . . . feeling better, I mean." I felt my face flush at my near-gaffe.

"Doc's a miracle worker."

"Yeah, he is. I've got a list of stuff we'd like to trade for. Our kale came in—we brought some to trade."

"Already? Our kale's barely sprouting."

"How long did it take them to plant?" Darla whispered scornfully.

Evidently Mayor Petty overheard her. "The town's greenhouses were badly damaged during the occupation. Folks had to clean up their own homes too. And not everyone has as fine a green thumb as the Halprins. Your aunt could grow turnips in the tailings from a coal mine if she put her mind to it."

"Not anymore," I said quietly.

"Yes," Mayor Petty replied in a similar tone. "Sorry. What were you looking to trade for, anyway? Got plenty of pork."

"Darla's got a list."

Darla pushed past me and handed the list to Mayor Petty. He slid a pair of reading glasses over his nose and peered down at the paper. "Believe Abe Miller, outside town, might still have a snowmobile. Don't know if he'll give it up or not, though. Should be plenty of bicycles around—city doesn't own any, of course. I've got no idea where you'd find all this electrical stuff."

"You should check your inventory," Ben said.

"What inventory?"

"You must have taken an inventory of all supplies available in the town. It would be a basic survival preparation."

"Now, son, we don't go messing with making lists of people's private property. I don't know what kind of big city you come from, but around here folks' stuff is their own, and we don't go making lists of it. Don't tell them they can't have Big Gulp sodas either. You want that stuff on your list, you'll have to ask around, see if they want to trade."

I groaned inwardly. Warren's population had shrunk by almost eighty percent since the eruption, but that still left several hundred people. And what did soda have to do with anything, anyway?

"You are not sufficiently prepared for another attack," Ben said. "You need to inventory all town supplies—private property or not. And you must begin building a wall immediately."

"You want to build a wall, be my guest," Mayor Petty said. "People around here are just struggling to survive. They don't have the time or energy for a project like—"

"If Stockton attacks again," I said, "you'll—"

"We beat them so bad they won't be back for more."

Wait, what? *I'd* beaten the Reds and gotten Warren's food back. Mayor Petty had gotten his ass kicked, his legs shot off, and my Aunt Caroline killed. While I was trying to think of an appropriate response, Darla spoke up. "What're you going to do for heat when all the timber's cut? We could use your help rounding up these supplies— we get them all, we might be able to rig a wind-powered heating system."

"Got that covered. Going to eminent domain abandoned houses and grant salvage rights. Plenty of burnable wood in those."

Darla said, "Even that—"

"Look," Mayor Petty said, "I'd love to chew the fat all day, but we got ourselves a project here, getting ready to publicize the new food distribution rules. You're welcome to trade with anyone who wants to or build yourself a wall if that's what you feel like doing, but I've got real work to do."

We wound up going house to house, knocking on doors and trying to trade our kale. We bought two bicycles fairly easily and then trekked a half mile out of town to buy what appeared to be the only remaining snowmobile in Warren. Lots of folks were willing to trade electric water heaters—they were useless without power, after all—but we could only fit two of them in the bed of the truck alongside the snowmobile.

I complained about Mayor Petty to Mom and Uncle Paul over the dinner table. "He's doing the best he can," Mom told me. "We're all overwhelmed, and most of us still have two good legs."

"I think Ben's right," Uncle Paul said. "He should be building a wall. And we should be living inside it and commuting to the farm. We can't defend ourselves effectively here."

"Maybe we could build an ice wall around the farm, like they had in Worthington," Darla said.

"We do not have an adequate population on the farm to patrol or defend our own wall," Ben said.

"If Warren gets attacked, everyone's going to wind up right back here again," I said.

Uncle Paul speared a slice of ham. "Nothing we can do about it."

"What if he had an accident?" Max said.

"What?" I asked.

"Yeah, like the brakes on his wheelchair could sort of accidently fail, and then he could roll off a cliff."

"So you're going to sabotage his brakes, drive him somewhere there's a cliff, and then push him off?" Anna asked.

"Maaaaaybe," Max replied.

"Maybe you're an idiot," Anna said.

"No, the mayor's an idiot," Max said.

"He's a very nice man," Mom said.

"Maybe the mayor is both nice *and* an idiot," I said. "Either way, we're not going to hurt him."

"I was just joking," Max said.

"Fine," I said, even though I didn't completely believe Max. I turned my attention to Uncle Paul. "There must be a way to get rid of him."

"Don't look at me," Uncle Paul said.

"You could try protesting or something," Anna said, "like those people who were always holding protest marches in Chicago."

"Maybe," Darla said. "But Warren's a small town like Worthington. Nobody's going to listen to outsiders."

"I've lived near here almost all my life," Uncle Paul said.

"What we need to do," I said, "is convince enough residents to complain, to make Mayor Petty change his mind and either build a wall or leave office."

"Something must be done," Ben said. "Warren's strategic posture is completely unsustainable."

"I'll try," I told Ben.

Darla released a sigh. "I'm going to get roped into helping you, aren't I?"

"It's up to you," I said, "but I'd love your company."

"Are you sure this isn't another case of Alex grabbing a lance and charging a windmill?" Darla asked.

It might be exactly that, I thought. "No. I'm not sure. But I think it's worth trying."

"I'd better come along, then. You might need some help if the windmill decides to fight back."

Everyone was quiet for a while, wrapped up in our own thoughts. I thought about trying to convince enough people to protest to force Mayor Petty to take action or step down. I had plenty of work to do without getting involved in Warren's byzantine politics.

But then I remembered the bloody road in front of Elmwood Cemetery, Aunt Caroline falling as the bullets tore into her stomach, Anna's face when she was forced to say goodbye to her mother forever. Anything I could do, any amount of work, was worth it if it could prevent something like that from happening again. We had to find a way to defend ourselves adequately, and I had to make it happen.

Chapter 16

We did farm work in the morning and early afternoon—watering, planting, harvesting, cutting wood. Darla invited the other girls—Rebecca, Anna, and Alyssa—to help her build Bikezilla II in the late afternoons. Rebecca and Anna were enthusiastic; Alyssa flatly refused. She had no interest whatsoever in anything mechanical or anything that might get her hands greasy. Or maybe she just didn't want to spend more time around Darla than she had to.

Max, Ed, and I finished a woodcutting expedition to Apple River Canyon State Park early one afternoon, so I went out to the barn to say hi to

Darla. She was holding a lit welding torch and gesturing at the flame with a metal rod, while Rebecca and Anna looked on.

"The oxygen and acetylene combine in the inner cone of flame. Right at the tip of that inner cone is the hottest part of the torch—that's the part you want to use for welding." Darla noticed me and released the lever on the welding torch. The flame went out with a pop, and the room darkened considerably.

"Need any help?" I asked.

"You're not allowed," Rebecca said.

"I'm not—"

"This is the Girls' Excellence in Engineering Klub. We're the GEEKs! No boys allowed."

"Um—"

"Particularly not older brothers of club members," Rebecca said.

"What about boyfriends of club members?" I asked Darla.

"Sorry," she said. "I'll make it up to you later."

I shrugged and headed out of the barn. On the way out the door, I thought of something and turned back. "Maybe you should call it 'Girls' Excellence in Engineering and Science Education,' so it would be the GEESE club."

Without a moment's hesitation, Anna responded, "Maybe we'll call it 'Guys are Notably Dumb and Especially Ridiculous'—the GANDER club."

I knew when I was beaten. I left the barn without another word.

I peeked in on the GEEKs now and then over the following days. They took two bicycles and the snowmobile completely apart. The idea was to weld the two bicycles together side by side, with the snowmobile track between them where their back wheels had been. The front wheels of each bike would be replaced with skis. I didn't quite understand how it was going to work—the whole process seemed to involve a lot of welding and cursing. But I knew Darla would figure it out—there was no apparent limit to her genius with all things mechanical.

One day Darla surprised me by visiting me in the woodlot—the area outside the greenhouses where we sawed and split the logs we had hauled back to the farm, turning them into firewood. "Time to call it a day," she said.

"Why are we stopping?" I asked—it was only midafternoon. "We can get in a couple more hours."

"You don't know?" Darla said. "Seriously? October 2nd?"

Oh. I'd totally forgotten my own birthday—for the second year in a row. We had a subdued party, all ten of us. There was no birthday cake, only kale and pork like always. We lit a candle, and I blew it out almost immediately; we couldn't afford to waste the wick. We did manage a pretty good rendition of "Happy Birthday to You." All in all, the best part of my seventeenth birthday was the kiss Darla gave me when it was over.

• • •

It took more than two weeks for the GEEKs to finish Bikezilla II. Then Darla and I started ducking out of afternoon chores completely to bike to Warren and knock on doors, asking folks to visit Mayor Petty and talk to him about building a wall.

I was worried when we started. I figured we'd get doors slammed in our faces, people yelling at us, maybe even running us off. And a lot of people did answer their doors with guns in their hands. Darla and I approached each house slowly, our hands in plain view, loudly calling out "hello" as we came. Most of the houses we checked were vacant.

But the people we did meet were universally friendly after they figured out who we were. Almost everyone invited us in, and some of them even offered us a snack: sometimes a bit of ham, sometimes dried kale chips. Their generosity was overwhelming. Only two months ago, we'd all been starving; now folks were sharing their food willingly—eagerly, even.

That wasn't to say that they all agreed with us. Plenty of them liked Mayor Petty. They'd known him forever; he'd kissed their babies and shaken their grandparents' hands.

On the third day of our campaign, we met a middle-aged woman living with her two teenage sons. Before I could even say hello, she spoke up, "Hell, yes, I'll talk to Petty about a wall!"

Darla laughed. "Best sales job you've done yet."

"I haven't said anything yet!" I said.

"Exactly."

The woman invited us in, and we spent a few minutes talking to her sons about the protest campaign. Word had gotten around about what we were doing. As we got up to leave, the woman said, "You hear Mayor Petty's looking for you?"

"No, I haven't," I said.

"If he had built a wall and gate, he'd have found us the moment we came to town," Darla said.

"He's put out the word," she said. "Wants to talk with you, I guess."

"We'll head down to his office now."

Mayor Petty smiled just as brightly and shook our hands just as vigorously as he had the last time we'd met him. "Why're you two stirring up trouble in my town?"

"We need to prepare to defend *our* town. Prepare for the future," I said. "I'd prefer it if you'd work with us."

"This is about that wall nonsense again? Nobody here wants to be drafted into some kind of work party to build a wall."

"I bet you could convince them."

"What I want is to convince you to drop this whole rigmarole. Dividing people against each other isn't doing the town any favors."

"I'm not dropping it," I said.

"Nobody's going to be forced to waste time building a wall while I'm mayor."

"Then you should resign."

"Not going to happen."

"I'm not dropping it."

"I'll ban you from the city."

I thought a moment before answering. "Good. Do that. The only way you'll be able to keep me out is by building a wall."

"Or by ordering you shot on sight."

Darla and I spoke at once:

"You wouldn't," I said.

"If you shoot him, I will end you," Darla said.

Mayor Petty glowered at us. "Don't push me."

"So Yellowstone is claiming another victim," I said, "democracy in Warren."

"We'll hold proper elections when my term is up," Mayor Petty said, "in two and a half years."

The mention of elections sparked an idea. "So let the people—your constituents—decide. Hold a special vote on whether or not to build a wall."

"And if I do?"

"We'll go away. Win or lose, we'll quit bothering you, quit trying to stir up public opinion."

Mayor Petty was silent for a moment. A crafty look shadowed his eyes. "I'll hold an election, all right. For mayor. You against me. You win, you run the show, build the wall, do whatever you damn well please. I win, you stay out on your uncle's farm and out of my town."

"I don't want to be mayor," I said. "I want a safe place we can move to, a walled town capable of defending itself."

"You're not so excited about wall building when you're

on the hot seat, huh? When you're the one who'd have to implement your crack-brained plan."

I thought for a moment. I didn't want to be mayor, didn't want to run Warren, didn't want to do anything but create a safe space for Darla, me, and my family. I certainly wasn't qualified to be mayor, but could I be any worse than Petty? I would at least consult Ben on military matters, Uncle Paul and Darla on engineering questions, and Dr. McCarthy on medical issues. "Okay," I said, "I'll do it."

Mayor Petty smiled in a way that was more cruel than mirthful. "First Tuesday in January. Ten weeks from now. That suit?"

"Why not next Tuesday?" I said.

"'Cause that's the way I want it. And I'm the mayor. Everyone who wants to vote'll meet at St. Ann's Church. Voting machines won't work without electric, so we'll use paper, pens, and an old-fashioned ballot box."

"We'll count the votes publicly," Darla said, "immediately after voting closes. While everyone's there watching. Won't even need to lock the ballot box, that way."

"Agreed." Mayor Petty rubbed his hands together gleefully. "I'll beat the pants off you. Wait. Don't quote me on that. Don't want anyone to get the idea I'm one of them pedophiles, do I?"

I couldn't summon nearly as much enthusiasm as Mayor Petty. I shook his hand and left his office in a state of stunned disbelief.

• • •

After Mayor Petty agreed to the election, our daily routine didn't change much. Darla and I worked on the farm every morning and biked to Warren every afternoon, to campaign instead of trying to convince people to protest. When they could spare the time—which was rarely—Uncle Paul, Alyssa, Max, Rebecca, and even Anna walked to Warren to help with the campaign. Mom came along occasionally, but she never campaigned. When I asked her what she did in town, she said she was "visiting" and evaded my questions about who she was visiting with. Ed worried that his past would be a liability and stayed behind on the farm. Ben had neither the skills nor inclination for politics.

Campaigning meant going door to door and talking with people, often while we helped them with their chores. There was no radio, no television, no flyers, and nobody had time to attend rallies, so the campaign had a decidedly low-tech feel. Darla kept meticulous notes on everyone we talked to. She said it wasn't much different than keeping track of cows. She thought we'd win, but it would be close—within twenty votes.

After about five weeks of this, something changed. People stopped answering their doors when we approached. Several said they were too busy to talk. One guy, a Petty supporter, pointed a shotgun at us. I could understand being tired of talking to us—heck, I was tired of talking, myself—but the change came about almost overnight. Nobody would tell us why.

I sought out Nylce Myers, who'd led a squad during the attack on Stockton. She was a huge supporter and one of the toughest women I had ever met other than Darla. Surely she would tell me what was going on.

"It's nothing, Alex. The mayor's people are spreading ugly rumors, that's all. I'm sure it's not true."

"What're they saying?" I asked.

"They claim Stockton attacked us because of you. They say you told them we had stockpiles of pork."

"That's . . ." my voice trailed off as I thought about it. What had I said on that icy road in front of Stockton last year? Before Darla and I started off to find my folks? I strained to remember. "Oh, f—"

"What is it?" Darla asked.

"I *did* tell them. When we were trying to buy medical care for Ed. The guy said he'd heard Warren had plenty of hogs, and I said yeah, thousands."

"So you didn't really tell them."

"But I confirmed it."

"What're you going to do?"

"I don't know. I need to think about it."

"You mind keeping this under wraps until he decides?" Darla asked Nylce.

"Sure, whatever you need."

"Thanks," I said and gave her a hug before leaving.

• • •

After dinner that night, I trudged out to the greenhouses to sit on the warm soil and think. It came down to this: what did I value more, my integrity or the town's survival? Framed that way, it was easy. I'd choose lives over morals any day. But I couldn't quit thinking about it—couldn't come to terms with my decision to lie about what I'd said in Stockton.

I'd been out there a good long while when Mom entered the greenhouse. "You don't look so good."

"I'm okay."

"You're working too hard. You look like you've been beaten more than a threadbare rug."

"Really, I'm okay. I'm thinking."

"It's Darla. She's pushing you too hard."

"She's the one who keeps me sane, Mom."

"Stay home tomorrow. Spend some time with Alyssa. Relax for once. We've hardly seen you all month."

"I can't. Maybe after the election."

"Mayor Petty says Darla's putting all this election nonsense in your head. You don't have to do everything she tells you to, you know."

"What's with you and Darla anyway? Why don't you ever talk to her? You talk *about* her enough."

"I don't—"

"You do! You complain about her to Uncle Paul, to Alyssa—even to Max! What'd she ever do to you?"

"Alex, I love you, and I only want what's best for you."

"Darla is what's best for me."

"You haven't been the same since you met her."

"I haven't been the same since Yellowstone erupted."

"That's true. None of us have. But can't you see? She's just not right for you."

"No. I can't see that." I noticed I had been scooping up handfuls of earth and clenching them in my fists. I forced myself to relax, the dirt flowing through my fingers.

"Does this have anything to do with Dad?"

"What? No. How could you even say that?" Mom's fists were clinched too.

"We all went to Iowa City. Darla came back. Dad didn't."

"It's got nothing to do with that. She's too controlling. Always bossing you around—never giving you any space to relax."

"She's a lot like you, Mom."

"I'm nothing like—"

"You are. Or were. Organized, tough, driven. She's as passionate about farming as you were about being a principal. Or about protecting the girls in the Maquoketa FEMA camp. Maybe that's one reason I love you both."

"I . . . I don't feel very tough. Not anymore. Not since . . ."

"You're still grieving for Dad. We all are. If Darla died, I'd never be the same. Take it easy on yourself."

"That's my point. She pushes you too hard. You need—"

Darla pulled back the flap of plastic that served as the inner door to the greenhouse. "Who pushes him too hard?"

Mom yelped, "My God, you just about scared me out of my skin."

"Sorry." Darla sounded anything but sorry. She stepped toward me, but Mom was between us. There wasn't room to pass easily in the tiny aisle between the closely spaced rows of kale. "What were you talking about, anyway?"

Mom looked over her shoulder at Darla. "Oh, nothing. I was chatting with my son." They stared at each other for a moment. Then Mom pushed past Darla, their shoulders brushing.

"What was that about?" Darla asked when Mom was gone.

"Mom's losing it." I tried to keep my tone light, but I could tell I wasn't fooling Darla. "She thinks you're putting too much pressure on me."

"As if," Darla said.

"Yeah, well. Her solution is to add some pressure of her own."

"You okay?"

"I'm being squished between the two women I love most."

"Eww," Darla said.

"That didn't come out right, sorry."

"What's it really about?" Darla asked.

"Dad. I think she can't, or won't, blame me for his death, so she blames you."

Darla nodded slowly.

"It's not fair. I decided to go to Iowa City—"

"I'm glad," Darla said softly.

"And Dad decided on his own to come along. I'm to blame, or Dad, or better yet, the Dirty White Boys."

"Yeah," Darla said softly, "I blamed you for my mom's death for a while. But you weren't responsible for Target escaping from prison. You didn't pull the trigger—he did. He was to blame. And you killed him."

Darla choked back a sob, and I stood, wrapping her in my arms. Pretty soon I was crying too, crying for my dead father, for my estranged mother, for the whole disaster the world had become. Somehow it felt right to let it out there, in that greenhouse, our tears watering the kale that kept us alive. Only survivors are allowed the luxury of sadness.

Chapter 17

It was bitterly cold on the day of the election. By the time we reached Warren, the strip of exposed skin around my eyes was red and windburned. Darla chained Bikezilla to a streetlight in front of St. Ann's Church. Uncle Paul rode along on Bikezilla's load bed. Nobody else on the farm was registered to vote in Warren. I briefly contemplated getting back on the bike, pedaling back to the farm and forgetting about this whole exercise in tilting at windmills. My hands were shaking, so I jammed one into a pocket and took Darla's hand with the other, hoping her touch would still the tremors.

The sanctuary was lit by a dozen torches set into sconces in stone walls. Even though I was a half hour early, dozens of people were already there. Most of them clustered around Mayor Petty's wheelchair at the back of the sanctuary. He wore a suit, tie, and elegant dark-gray coat. His coattails flopped straight down past the stumps of his legs, almost brushing the floor.

I hadn't given any thought about what to wear. I was in my normal, everyday clothes, the same clothes I'd been working and campaigning in: long johns and jeans on the bottom; a T-shirt, over shirt, and sweater on top. Over that, I wore insulated overalls and a coat. I peeled my scarves and hat off my head, and Darla fussed with my hair.

Steve McCormick approached us, asking a question about where the wall would run in relation to his house, and quickly Darla and I were engulfed. Two competing knots of people formed at the back of the sanctuary: one swirling around Mayor Petty, one around me, like eyes in the gaping face of the church. The face was lopsided, though; there were always more people around Mayor Petty than me.

As the sanctuary filled, it warmed up. The torches and the body heat of hundreds of people were more than enough to overcome the draft from the constantly opening doors. I took off my coat and slung it over a pew.

Mayor Petty's voice rose over the hubbub. "Shall we start?" People parted in front of him, and he rolled himself down the aisle toward the front of the sanctuary. I followed him, mentally cursing myself—I should have suggested starting, taken the lead. There was a folding table holding a couple dozen pencils, a stack of tiny slips of paper, and the ballot box—a crude plywood cube with a padlock on its front.

Mayor Petty turned to face the crowd. Every seat in the church was filled, and the side aisles and back were full of those standing. It was the kind of crowd that would give a pastor ecstasy and a fire marshal apoplexy. "Here's how this will work," Mayor Petty said in his booming baritone. "We'll have two short speeches, say, ten minutes each." He looked at me, and I nodded. My hands were still trembling, so I jammed them into the pockets of my coveralls. "Then you'll all form a single-file line, approach the ballot box one at a time, and vote. Write either Bob or Alex on your ballot. The votes will be counted immediately after they're all cast, right here in public. Questions?"

There were none. Petty went on, "We'll flip for who speaks first. Dr. McCarthy, if you'll do the honors?" I called heads, won, and elected to speak second.

"You all know me," Mayor Petty started. "I was born at Katherine Shaw Bethea Hospital just down the road in Dixon. I've lived in Warren all my life."

I wasn't sure what to do as I listened to him. I felt awkward standing in front of that huge crowd, so I backed up to the communion rail and sat on the kneeling bench.

"I've been to your weddings, your babies' baptisms, your parents' funerals. I've seen Warren grow from a sleepy village of fifteen hundred to a thriving town of fourteen hundred." A few chuckles rippled through the audience. Thanks to our campaigning, I knew the current population of Warren exactly: 381, of whom 264 were registered voters. Most of the nonregistered citizens were under eighteen. In fact, the vast majority of the survivors were between ages six and thirty-five. The death toll among those older or younger was horrendous. I glared at the audience—didn't they realize how wrong Mayor Petty was?

"But on a more serious note, I know this town. I know you. My opponent moved here less than a year ago. And while I applaud his taste in choosing to relocate to our fine city, he hasn't got any roots here."

That was not exactly true either. Didn't my uncle count?

"This is a time of trials. We need stability, experience, and leadership. I've led this town as your mayor for nearly ten years now. I've gotten us through some tough jams before, and I'll get us through this one."

Tough jams? What, did the only railroad crossing gate in Warren quit working?

"My opponent knows nothing about the adult world. The toughest problem he's had to face is a pop quiz in arithmetic class."

A few people laughed. Would punching a guy in a wheelchair hurt my chances of winning the election? I glanced at Darla; she was standing in the front row at one edge of the sanctuary. She had a huge smile plastered on her face and was pointing at it with both index fingers. Her eyes weren't smiling—they were glaring at me. I got it and did my best to plaster a neutral smile on my face without looking like a zombie.

"And while it's widely known that my opponent helped in resolving our conflict with the Reds, what's not so well known is how he caused that conflict. How he—through his inexperience and youth, if not outright malice—betrayed our fine community.

"A few of you know I've had a houseguest for the last two weeks. Now I'd like to introduce him to all of you: Mr. James Sawyer." Mayor Petty turned to look at the door to the vestry. A man nudged it open and stepped out. With a shock, I recognized the man I had met with outside of Stockton, the one whom I had bargained with, trying to buy medical care for Ed. He had a long, red, knurled cut along his right check, held closed by dozens of neat black stitches. Sawyer strode forward confidently, but he missed the step down from the chancel, nearly flying head over heels. He stood next to Mayor Petty's wheelchair, hands on his hips, beaming as he turned his head back and forth to take in everyone. His smile was broad, but his eyes were cold and wary.

"When I heard rumors of what he'd done," Mayor Petty pointed at me, "I knew I needed to learn the truth. I knew you needed to learn the truth. And so I sent a team to Stockton. They brought back Mr. Sawyer here, and he tells me he's so thrilled by our community that he wants to stay! Isn't that right, sir?"

"Yessir!" Sawyer practically shouted.

I was instantly suspicious. I could understand wanting

to leave Stockton and Red behind, but why move here? He could be spying, planning another attack. In fact I was willing to bet he had family in Stockton under Red's thumb. I made a mental note to talk to Darla, Ben, and Uncle Paul about it later.

"Tell the good folks of Warren what you told me," Mayor Petty said.

"I was on guard duty when this fellow," Sawyer gestured at me, "came to trade. Wanted to buy medical care for a flenser." A scattering of weak boos emerged from the crowd. "While we were talking, the subject of hogs came up. Fellow said he didn't have any hogs to trade, but he knew where we could get them. 'Thousands of hog carcasses,' he said." The boos were louder this time. "We'd heard rumors that you all were eating well, but we didn't know how *much* pork you had 'til he came along. When I reported on that conversation, Red was mighty interested. He started planning the attack that same day." The boos were overwhelming now, and Sawyer had to stop.

When the ruckus died down, Mayor Petty said, "Thank you, Mr. Sawyer. Now some of you might be thinking, 'What if the Reds attack again?' I want to assure you, that fight is settled. We licked 'em, and we still gave them three trucks full of our own supplies. We've got food. They've got food. There's no reason for them to come back.

"I know how much effort it takes just to stay warm, clean, and healthy in these terrible times. The last thing we need is some whack-a-doodle government project to build a wall. Nobody's got the time or energy for it. Those of you with property around the town don't want the government taking your land for some wall."

"I'm okay with it," someone called from the crowd.

Someone else replied, "Give 'em your own land, then. Don't take mine."

"Quiet down," Mayor Petty said. "This here's a speech, not a town hall meeting . . . thank you. Now if some of you want, as private citizens, to build walls on your own land, well that's your right, and I won't stand in your way.

"But imagine how foolish you'll feel on that fine spring day that's coming soon—I know it is, I can feel it in my bones—when the army will roll up here out of the East in their tanks and Humvees and put this part of Illinois to rights. That wall you spent thousands of hours building is going to look pretty silly then." More people in the crowd nodded.

"I've appealed to the commander of the FEMA camp in Galena for help—several times now. And while he says it's not part of his mission to intervene in local disputes, he's radioed our plight to Washington. The government out East is still a going concern. The American spirit can conquer anything, even a supervolcano. And one fine day—very soon—we're going to look to the east and see an honest-to-God sunrise." The mayor's tones were hushed, reverent. He had every ear in the room straining to listen. "And out of that sunrise the cavalry will ride— not on horses but in Humvees. And they'll carry food: fresh fruit, chocolate, and coffee." An orgiastic sigh floated from the audience. "Soon," Mayor Petty promised again.

"Now some believe," Petty glanced at me, and every eye in the room followed, "that we should further strain our limited resources and aching backs building a wall. We could do that. The people of Warren are equal to any task set before them by man or God. But how many will die— yes, die—in that endeavor? We have neither the equipment nor the trained personnel to build a wall.

"This foolish proposal illustrates why you should vote for experience over youth. Why you should return to office a trusted leader with almost a decade of experience leading this town. You can choose a man you know and trust or a boy who can't even grow a proper beard yet."

That was not exactly true. I couldn't grow any kind of beard, let alone a proper one.

"A boy who betrayed us. Vote for experience, steady leadership, and trust. Vote for the man who will hold us together until those Humvees ride out of the east. Write Bob on your ballot. Thank you."

The applause was long and thunderous. When it died down, I stood slowly. I ignored my still-shaking hands. I had prepared a speech in which I denied Mayor Petty's charges and rehearsed it a dozen times in front of Darla. It left my mind completely. I could not even remember the first word. The silence in the room started to grow uncomfortable, maybe even a little malevolent. I coughed, and it echoed.

"I did not betray this town. At least not knowingly. But what Mayor Petty and Mr. Sawyer said is true." Darla winced and hid her head behind her hands. "I told the Reds there was pork in Warren." A few people booed, but their neighbors quickly shushed them. "Or at least I confirmed it. I made a terrible mistake, and I'm deeply sorry.

"It's a cliché, that everyone makes mistakes, but it's also true. A teacher told me once that responsibility has nothing to do with making mistakes. Responsible people own their mistakes. They do everything possible to fix them. And I've done that.

"When Mayor Petty led that disastrous march on Warren, I asked him to put out scouts to flank our advance." Mayor Petty was shaking his head in denial. "My friend Ben Fredericks told you—told all of us in a public meeting—that the attack was doomed, that we should attack at a time and in a direction the Reds didn't expect. I realize that since Ben and his sister, Alyssa, are even newer to Warren than I am, it may be hard to listen to them. But these are hard times, times that call for a leader willing to hear good advice even from unusual sources." Many people were nodding now. "But Mayor Petty ignored Ben's advice.

"I listened. I organized and led the attack that invaded Stockton and gave us the bargaining power to reclaim our food. Everyone in this room has a full stomach because of that attack. Because of me."

Someone in the audience yelled, "We wouldn't have lost the food in the first place except for you!"

"Probably true," I replied. "But anyone you elect—me, Mayor Petty, or the second coming of Abraham Lincoln— would make mistakes. The difference is this: I acknowledge and fix mine.

"Let me remind you: Ben predicted that our attack on Warren would fail. He also planned the attack that reclaimed our food. And now he says we need a wall. Without air power, artillery, or tanks, walled cities will rule the land. We can either build our own or be overrun.

"We'd all freeze to death if not for the wood we burn for heat. And that wood is not an inexhaustible resource. We're going to run out. Darla and my uncle have a plan for using the wind farm to our east to provide a sustainable power source. We need resources to test and implement that plan. Resources Mayor Petty has refused to provide.

"I don't want to be your mayor." Darla winced again. "But I want to *live!*" I practically shouted the word. "I want a place where Darla and I can get married, have kids, grow old together, and die together. I'm *going* to create that place. Small groups won't be viable in the future. A decent way of life demands manpower and womanpower and division of labor. It demands a group large enough to defend itself. If the only way I can create that is to lead it, then that's what I'll do. That's why I'm running for mayor.

"I liked that story Mayor Petty told about the sunrise and the Humvees and the coffee, the chocolate, and the fresh fruit. But it's just that. A story. There's no help coming. Ever. We must, we *must* survive on our own resources with what we can make and raise with our own hands.

"So I ask you for your vote. If you vote for me, we'll start preparing for the long term. We'll build a wall. We'll develop a sustainable way to stay warm. If I'm wrong, we will have wasted some time and effort, sure. But if I'm right about the future, then a vote for me is a vote for survival itself. Thank you."

As I sat down, a scattering of polite applause echoed hollowly in the church. It was quickly extinguished, as if the clappers were embarrassed or maybe afraid to be seen supporting me.

I lost the election. It wasn't even close. So much for my political career—doomed from the start.

Chapter 18

"Did you even use three words of the speech you practiced?" Darla asked as we pedaled back to Uncle Paul's farm.

"Nope. Just two," I replied. "'Thank' and 'you.'"

"Christ on a broomstick," Darla muttered.

I bore down on the pedals in silence for a while. We were moving so fast that the wind fell like a lash across my eyes. Uncle Paul was curled in a blanket on the load bed. He either ignored the conversation or couldn't hear it. "I just . . . when he brought out Sawyer, it threw me off my stride. Everything I planned to say flew out of my head. I guess I had nothing left in me but the truth. . . . I'm sorry."

Darla swiveled in her seat to look at me. "I'm glad you're not some kind of goddamn politician, Alex. If—no, *since*—they won't listen to the truth, those fools in Warren deserve what they get."

"No, they don't. Nobody deserves what's coming. Nobody deserved any of this."

"Maybe the few who actually paid attention to you don't deserve this. But the rest? Pfft." She waved one gloved hand in the cold air.

"They all listened. Most of them just didn't like what I was saying."

We had to slow to make the turn onto Canyon Park Road. When we were back up to speed, Darla said, "We'll figure it out. Some other way of defending ourselves."

"Like what?"

"Let me talk to Ben about my ideas. Work out a solid plan."

"Okay." I wasn't ready to think about other options anyway. We had spent months of effort on the election. I needed to mope some more before I could move on to plan B—whatever it was.

"What you said in that church, in front of all those people, about us, about wanting a place we could raise a family and grow old together. It . . . I don't know how to say it . . . I was mad at you for screwing up the speech, and suddenly all that anger turned to fire."

"Fire? Like you were even madder?"

"I'm not saying this right. I *want* that future. I will kill for it. I will drag all those people in Warren kicking and screaming into something resembling sense if I have to, even though I don't care about most of them."

"I know," I said. "I feel the same way."

We pulled to a stop beside the house and dismounted Bikezilla. I took Darla in my arms, and she crushed me against her body. The world around us was frozen, quiet, and still, as if the last point of warmth in the universe burned between her chest and mine.

Chapter 19

Little changed except that Darla and I didn't have to ride to Warren every afternoon to campaign. Instead, Uncle Paul and Darla often took Bikezilla out to the wind farm east of Warren. They broke into three of the windmills, climbing inside the turbine towers to study their workings and refine the plan for converting one to produce heat.

I spent part of my time with Ben working on a plan to survive if the farm were attacked again. We built a platform atop the roof of the farmhouse, accessible from a hatch we cut in the attic. I created a watch schedule—there were ten of us, so to cover the entire day and night, each watch had to be two hours and twenty-four minutes long. With one of us constantly on watch, the workload for everyone else increased. We were always tired; tempers grew shorter as the workdays grew even longer.

Darla helped me rig a rope from the platform to a bell hung in the second floor hallway so that whoever was on watch could wake us without leaving their post. We practiced endlessly; if more than six hostiles showed up, we'd run rather than trying to fight. Everyone had a go-bag of food and crucial supplies. After weeks of practice and drills, we got to the point where we could be out the back door and away from the farmhouse less than two minutes after the bell rang, even starting from a deep sleep. Actually it took longer during the day, because we were spread out all over the farm doing chores.

Ben studied the approaches to the farm, and we did our best to block the problematic ones. For example, behind the barn there was a huge blind spot, a wedge of land that wasn't visible from the observation platform. So we spent almost a week moving snow into that area, creating a huge pile of loose snow and ice that made it difficult to walk in the places invisible to our lookout. In other places—atop the low hills around the farm, for example—we packed down the snow, creating areas that were easy to traverse and visible from the observation post.

One afternoon, Anna was on watch on the platform. I joined her, checking the sightlines, making sure that a new pile of snow Ben and I had moved that morning would funnel attackers into a spot where we could see—or shoot—them easily.

Alyssa came, opening the hatch from the attic to the platform and clomping up the stairs. The platform was not really big enough for three—we were packed on it shoulder to shoulder.

Alyssa flung her arms around me and gave me a huge, smacking kiss on the cheek.

"What . . . what's that about?" I spluttered, trying to remove her arms without knocking either of us off the platform.

"I love them!" Alyssa was practically gushing enthusiasm. Anna had turned beet red.

"Love what?" I asked.

"The earrings you left under my pillow." She tossed her head so her earrings bobbed. I hadn't noticed them before, but they were lovely—gold filigree hummingbirds with tiny ruby eyes.

"They're beautiful," I said. "But I didn't have anything to do with it."

"They're even better than the square of chocolate you left for me last week. It was a little stale."

"I didn't have anything to do with that either."

"You don't need to be coy," she said. She pressed herself up against me, and I turned my head, dodging another kiss.

Alyssa left, and I turned back to Anna. "Not a word to Darla," I warned.

She nodded, her lips pressed together, her face still flaming red.

• • •

When Darla and Uncle Paul returned to the farm after a day of studying wind turbines east of Warren, I met them outside. "I need to talk to you," I told Darla as she dismounted Bikezilla II.

"I'm freaking freezing," Darla said.

"It'll just take a second." I waited for Uncle Paul to get inside and then turned back to Darla. "Alyssa thinks I've been leaving her gifts."

"Oh?"

"I haven't."

"Figured," Darla said. "So who has?"

"I don't know. But Alyssa was all huggy when she was trying to thank me. She didn't believe it wasn't me."

Darla didn't reply.

"You okay?"

"If I turn flenser, I'm eating Alyssa first," Darla said.

"She *would* be delicious," I said.

"Hey! Don't be coveting the meat of another woman."

"Yeah, but I don't think you'd taste nearly as nice. Too tough and stringy."

Darla glared at me. "Stringy?"

"It's okay. I like my women tough."

"Your women?" Darla's glare had turned positively murderous.

"Woman, I mean, woman."

Darla smiled and gave me a quick kiss.

"Seriously," I said. "Are we okay?"

"Yes. I trust you, Alex. You've never given me any reason not to."

I held the door for Darla, and we went inside.

• • •

After more than a month spent studying the wind turbines, Darla had a new list of electrical supplies she needed: eight-gauge wire, electric stoves, electric water heaters, and more. They were mostly things that could be scavenged from homes. We biked to Warren with two sacks of kale to try to trade.

Nobody would talk to us. Doors were slammed in our faces. Shotguns poked out windows as we approached. Oh, a few were friendly enough, like Nylce, but we already had taken everything we could use from her house. We asked Mayor Petty for permission to scavenge from abandoned houses in town, and he smiled sadistically as he said no.

We raided abandoned farmhouses instead. I spent the afternoons on my back in crawlspaces or craning my neck upward in basements to pull staples and liberate lengths of the heavy wire Darla needed for her project. We raided the ranger station in Apple River Canyon State Park, cutting the water heater free with a hacksaw and dragging it out to Bikezilla's load bed.

The barn began to look like an appliance repair shop, with dozens of water heaters and stoves arranged in neat rows, some in pieces, some intact. A corner held an enormous stack of heavy-gauge wire in various lengths, each piece coiled neatly and labeled.

We used the truck to drag a huge metal tank originally used for storing pesticides from a nearby farm. We left it hitched to the back of the truck sitting outside the workshop Darla and Uncle Paul had built in the barn. Darla cut a hatch in the tank, and she and Uncle Paul started assembling a contraption inside. Darla swore it was a simple water-heating system, but the tangled mess of tubes and wire I saw in there looked as complicated to me as the guts of the space shuttle.

The GEEKs couldn't help Darla much with the project. There was only room for one person inside the tank, and Uncle Paul hovered at the hatch, talking to her in a strange language full of volts, amps, ohms, and resistances. I worried about exposure to the pesticide residue in the tank, but when I raised the issue, Darla scoffed at me. "We'll freeze to death a heck of a lot faster than those pesticides will kill me." I figured she was right and dropped the issue, although I couldn't get it out of my mind completely. I lay awake that night in bed for more than an hour. Darla claimed modern pesticides were remarkably safe. I was sure she was right, but what if that tank had stored something else? Something older?

When I finally did sleep, I dreamed that Darla had grown huge and stretched out like a cross between the *Na'vi* from *Avatar* and Mr. Bendy. She tried to kiss me, but her body bent double, folding over mine so that instead of kissing my lips, she was smooching my Achilles tendon, my head pressed to her stomach, which had somehow molded to fit my face so precisely that it was suffocating me.

I woke with a start. The bell—the one that signaled an attack—was ringing wildly.

Chapter 20

I pulled on my coat and boots, grabbed my go-bag—actually a full-size backpack with frame. I slung the pack over my shoulders and hit the door of the bedroom less than thirty seconds after I'd woken up. Darla was on my heels.

Who was on watch? I wondered as I ran into the hall. Max, I thought. The pull-down staircase to the attic was open, and Max was nowhere in sight. If we were supposed to run, then he should have been in the hall ready to go with us. I charged up the staircase, anxious to find out what was going on.

Max was on the lookout platform, but I didn't

need to ask him why he'd rung the bell. Flames were licking up the outside of the barn, illuminating everything
with a flickering red glow. The greenhouses were burning
too—wispy blue flames flitted across their skins, turning
the irreplaceable plastic into pools of slag.

I started to ask what had happened, changed my mind,
and asked a more important question. "Anyone out there?"

"I'm only half finished with my scan," Max said in a
soft voice. "But I haven't seen anyone. Could the fire have
started itself somehow?"

"I don't see how. Keep looking."

Darla crowded her way onto the platform. The fire on
the barn leapt further up its walls, and a gust of wind carried a blast of heat and choking smoke across us. "My
welder!" Darla vaulted off the platform, sliding down the
steep, icy roof.

I grabbed for her but missed. "Are you crazy?" Darla
was sliding toward the front of the house where the peak
of a small porch roof came within five or six feet of the
main roof's gutter. If she missed the porch roof, she
would fall more than twenty feet.

Uncle Paul poked his head out from the hatch.

"Get a fire brigade organized," I told him, then turned
to Max. "Stay here. Keep scanning."

Darla flew off the edge of the roof. If I tried to go
through the hatch and down the stairs, it'd take forever—
I'd have to push past Uncle Paul and whoever else was
coming up.

I hurled myself off the platform, following Darla.

Chapter 21

I flew down the roof headlong, my outstretched gloves throwing stinging particles of snow and ice into my face. I dug my hands in, trying to slow my descent, but all too soon I had reached the edge of the roof. I tried to grab the gutter as I went over, but I was going too fast and couldn't hold on. Someone was screaming—me, I realized, as my side slammed into the top of the porch roof. A sharp pain spiked through my hip and shoulder, but I didn't hear anything snapping or crunching, which meant—I hoped—I hadn't broken any bones.

I rolled sideways, sliding off the ridge of the

porch roof in an uncontrolled tumble. Suddenly I was in the air again, still turning as I plummeted into a snowbank beside the concrete steps.

I slowly pushed myself free of the snow, spitting bits of ice and blinking to clear my eyes. Darla was already up, about twenty feet ahead of me, running pell-mell toward the burning barn. My leg and hip hurt as I put weight on them, forcing myself to a run, trying to catch up with Darla, my pack bouncing against my back.

"Wait!" I yelled. "We've got to get the panel van out. Our pork!" We hadn't bothered to move the pork out of the panel van—it made a handy freezer, parked in the barn next to Uncle Paul's old tractor. If it burned up, we would starve.

Darla didn't even slow down. "My welder first! Before it explodes!"

I redoubled my efforts to catch up with her. Running into a burning barn to grab tanks of explosive welding gasses did not seem like the best idea Darla had ever had. So of course, that was exactly what she did.

She hurled open the side door of the barn and ducked inside, into the workshop area. The barn was choked with thick smoke. My eyes stung as I followed her inside. The heat was oppressive, overwhelming, and suddenly I remembered charging back into Darla's barn after Target had set it afire, trying to save our backpacks almost a year and a half ago.

Darla disconnected a hose from a tank. A split second later, there was a pop and flash above us, as whatever gas escaped from the tank ignited near the exposed wooden ceiling. In seconds the entire ceiling was ablaze. Darla passed the first tank to me—it was so hot that it singed my hand, even through my gloves. I ran for the door, carrying the tank, Darla close behind me with the second tank.

The doorframe was afire now too. I plunged through the curtain of fire, running another dozen steps or so on pure momentum before I dropped the tank into the snow at my feet. The snow sizzled and melted around the tank. Only then did I notice that my coveralls were on fire. I dropped into the snow next to the tank and did the stop, drop, and roll I had learned in elementary school.

Darla was already running back toward the burning barn. "Stop!" I yelled.

"I've gotta get the welder. Go for the truck!"

I forced myself upright and sprinted to the vehicle door. The top part of the wooden sliding door was alight. I grabbed it near the base and started trying to wrench it open. I slid it back three or four feet—enough to see the nose of the panel van inside. I thought I saw a flicker of movement behind the front windshield but dismissed it as a quirk of the dancing flame and shadow.

But then the van's headlights popped on, and its engine roared to life. I was still crouched at the base of the door, straining to open it.

The van accelerated. It was aimed directly at my head.

Chapter 22

I lunged backward, trying to get out of the path of the van. There was a mighty crack as the van hit the inside of the rolling barn doors, sending bits of flaming wood flying everywhere. Half the barn door spun free. It struck the side of my head. Everything went black.

• • •

"Alex! Alex! Alex!" Darla was standing over me.

"Quit yelling, would you?" I mumbled.

"Are you okay?" She pulled off my ski mask,

looking for blood. My head felt like it was burning up from the inside. "We've got to get farther away from the barn. Can you walk?"

I reached up took her hand, and levered myself upright with her help. The barn was fully engulfed in roaring flames. Uncle Paul and Ed were kneeling in the snow with rifles butted against their shoulders, firing at the panel van. It slid through the curve from our driveway onto Canyon Park Road and raced north. If Uncle Paul or Ed had hit the van at all, they hadn't done any damage to it.

"We need to follow them," I said. "Get our pork back."

"Sure you're up to it?"

I stumbled toward the pickup truck instead of answering. It was parked beside the burning barn, close enough that I couldn't even approach the passenger door. I slid across from the driver's side instead, letting Darla take the wheel. Uncle Paul and Ed climbed into the bed behind the driver's side.

As soon as she put it in gear, there were two loud pops from the passenger side. The right side of the truck suddenly dropped a few inches. I ducked—the noises sounded vaguely like gunfire. My head swam.

"Christ and the Michelin man!" Darla yelled. "The fire melted our tires."

The wheels spun, hampered by the weight of the still-attached metal pesticide tank and the popped tires, and slowly the truck inched forward. Darla got it going pretty fast down the driveway, fighting to hold the wheel steady. When she tried to make the turn onto Canyon Park Road, the truck slid sideways instead of turning, burying itself in the snow berm. The tank we were towing slammed into the bank of snow just after we did, throwing up a huge spray of ice.

Darla jiggered the truck back and forth, trying to get going again. The panel van was almost out of sight. She leapt out the door, disconnected the chains attaching the tank to the truck, and tried again. We were completely stuck. We climbed out of the truck and ran for Bikezilla, which we'd left parked by the side door of the farmhouse, but by the time we were mounted up, the panel van was long gone.

I tried to dismount the bike seat, caught my foot on the bar, and fell into the snow beside us.

Uncle Paul knelt to help me up. "You okay?"

"No," I replied. "I mean, short term, I'm okay. But long term, we're all screwed. Get everyone together in the living room, would you?"

"I'll be right there," Darla said. "I've got to move the welder and gas tanks farther from the barn. It's going to collapse."

"I'll help," Ed said and left with Darla.

Uncle Paul helped me into the living room and then went upstairs to find everyone else.

Max was one of the first ones downstairs. "What happened?" I asked him.

"Nobody woke me. For some reason I woke on my own and went to check if it was time for my shift or not. Nobody was on the platform, and the barn was already burning."

"Who was supposed to be on watch?"

"Your mom," Max said in a low voice.

Anna had come into the room while we were talking. "Your mom's been missing a lot of watches. Max and I didn't want to tell you—give you something else to worry about. I guess we should have said something."

"You think?" My fists were balled—all that bullshit about Darla and now this? "I'm moving to Delaware," I muttered.

"Delaware?" Anna asked.

"Only state where you're allowed to divorce your parents," Max said.

"And you know this how?" Anna asked.

"It doesn't matter," I said. "We're damn lucky they didn't torch the house. Then we'd all be eating smoke right now. Go back up on watch," I told Max. "I don't think they'll come back, but why take chances? I'll fill you in later."

Max got up but stopped beside me on his way out. "I'm sorry."

I grabbed his arm and clasped it, bringing my face close to his. "It's not your fault—"

"I wish I'd woken up earlier."

"I trusted Mom. You should have told me she was missing her shifts."

"I know," Max said quietly. "But you two'd been fighting anyway. Anna and I talked about it—we didn't want to make things worse."

"Next time someone isn't pulling their weight, tell me.

Our lives could depend on it."

"I will," Max said. He left to return to the watch platform atop the house.

Everyone except Max gathered in the living room, their go-bags still on their backs. I threw three logs on the fire and blew on it until flames licked up, bathing the room in dancing firelight. When I turned away from the fire, my eyes caught Mom's. She didn't look away. Her face was calm, placid even, motionless except for the shifty, red shadows cast by the fire.

I was so angry I wondered if I would spontaneously combust. "How could you?" I yelled.

"How could I what?" Mom replied calmly.

"The watch! I trusted you!"

"What are you talking about?" Rebecca said, incipient panic lifting her voice at least an octave above normal.

"The watches! The barn! The greenhouses—"

"Alex," Uncle Paul said in a low, urgent voice, "take a deep breath. You're scaring your sister."

"You're even freaking me out a little," Ed said.

Darla took hold of my hand, her concern plain in her eyes. "What happened exactly?"

I swallowed back another yell, closed my eyes, and sucked in a lungful of cold air that tasted vaguely of smoke. I held the breath for maybe ten seconds and then let it whoosh out. I found I was calm enough to explain our situation. I finished my recap of the disastrous night with an overview of the food we had left: "The front quarter of one hog, about five pounds of kale plus any we can salvage from the greenhouses, some wheat we were saving for seed, about ten pounds of flour, and a bit of cornmeal. Maybe enough food for a week or ten days."

"We've got kale seeds," Uncle Paul said. "We can trade for more pork."

"Not many people left in Warren willing to trade with us," Darla said.

"Maybe I could talk Dr. McCarthy into being a straw man for us."

"What?" Rebecca asked.

"Being a middleman," Uncle Paul said.

"Good idea," I said. "That might work."

"We could dig more corn," Darla said.

"It's not that bad," Mom said. "All we have to do is move to town, which is what we should have done weeks ago."

"This farm is not defensible," Ben said. "We must combine forces with the town to survive over the long term."

"I don't think they want us, Ben," I said.

"I'm sure if you made a sincere apology, Mayor Petty would come around," Mom said. "He's not a bad guy, you know. He'd keep us safe."

"I did apologize, Mom," I said. "In front of everyone. And now most of Warren won't even talk to me."

Mom started to say something, but Darla spoke over her. "Moving is a good idea. But not to Warren. What about moving east of Warren where the wind turbines are?"

"You still have the defensibility problem," Ben said.

"I've been thinking about that," Darla replied. "We could build a one-room structure—a big timbered hut. Have it back right up to a wind turbine. I could cut sniper ports into the turbine's support column, build the green-houses right next door, and we can use the same heating system to keep everything warm."

"That could work," Uncle Paul said thoughtfully.

"It would be like a Viking longhouse," Ben said.

"Exactly!" Darla cried. "Make the walls thick enough to withstand most gunfire, build gun ports on each side, and connect the greenhouses with tunnels so we don't even have to go outside to work."

"What about water?" I asked.

"If we can find a drilling rig in decent shape," Uncle Paul replied, "we might be able to drill a well inside the longhouse. The water table is high around here."

"They used to dig wells by hand." Darla shrugged.

Mom stood up. "There's plenty of water in Warren! All we have to do is move there! Why isn't anyone listening to me?" she yelled.

"Mom," I replied quietly, "I'm not going to Warren."

"This is about *her*, isn't it?" Mom shot a hateful glare at Darla.

I rolled to my feet and stepped between them. "It's not about her, Mom, or at least not in the way you think."

"You . . . you'd move out to some wasteland instead of following your mother?"

I nodded slowly.

"Come with me," she whispered. "Let's go to Warren—you, me, and Rebecca. Get a fresh start. Be a family again."

"No," I replied as gently as I could. I was still angry at her, but I couldn't see the point of further aggravating things.

My mother choked back a sob, spun, and fled up the stairs. I sat in silence for a few moments. Outside, the barn collapsed with a mighty crash, shaking the foundation of my new home.

Chapter 23

Darla made me strip down beside the fire to check my wounds. I thought she should have to strip down—she'd gone sliding off the roof of the house too—but she refused. "I'm not the one who nearly got run over by a panel van," she said. I had a mess of nasty bruises all up and down my left side, and my head still hurt terribly, but otherwise I seemed to be okay. Darla helped me back into my clothes, and we trudged upstairs to bed.

The next morning Darla and I set out at first light to try to track our attackers. We took two rifles but planned to keep our distance; all we wanted to learn was where our panel van and, more importantly, our pork had gone.

It took less than half the morning to answer that question. The tracks were clear: four pairs of boots coming in, the four tires of our panel van coming out. We followed the tire tracks until Warren came into view. Darla slammed on Bikezilla's brakes, bringing us to a sliding halt on the snowy road.

"What're you doing?" I asked.

"You're just going to charge in there?"

"Yeah, get our truck back."

"What if the whole town was in on it? We go charging in there, we might never come out."

"Yeah, you're right." I started to turn Bikezilla around.

"Wait," Darla said, "let's go around Warren. Scout sites for the longhouse."

We found a perfect site later that same afternoon about five miles east of Warren atop a low rise with a stand of large, dead trees lining the creek at the bottom of the hill.

It was almost fully dark by the time we got back to the farm. Rebecca met us in the foyer before I'd even had time to take off my boots. Her eyes were red and puffy. "What's wrong?" I asked.

"Mom," Rebecca replied. "She's gone."

Chapter 24

"What happened?" I asked Rebecca.

"After lunch she asked if I wanted to go to Warren with her. I didn't know what to say. I asked if we could wait until you got home, and then I went to help Uncle Paul. She left sometime this afternoon. Her go-bag and some of her clothes are gone. . . ."

Rebecca's mouth clamped shut, trying to hold in a tremor that rolled across her lower lip. I took her in my arms, remembering that she'd only turned fifteen a few months ago. In the old world, she'd have been a sophomore at Cedar Falls High, hanging out with her friends, complaining about homework—a normal kid. She buried her face against my chest, muffling sobs. "Shh," I said, "it's okay."

"Why would she leave us?" Rebecca said through her sobs. "Why would she leave me?"

"I don't know."

"It has something to do with Dad, doesn't it?"

"Maybe so. Maybe she blames me or Darla. Tomorrow Uncle Paul, Darla, and I will go to Warren to see if we can talk to her."

"I want to go with you," Rebecca said.

"The whole city of Warren might be up in arms. No—"

"She's my mother! I'll keep quiet, keep my head down. You won't even know I'm there."

I thought about it. She was no age to be traveling with us into what might be an ambush. But I was only two years older. And we'd all spent hundreds of hours practicing with the rifles. "You can come—"

"Thank you!"

"*If* you promise to do whatever Uncle Paul or I tell you to. Instantly. No questions or backtalk."

"I will," she promised.

The next morning Darla and I pedaled Bikezilla back down the road to Warren, with Rebecca and Uncle Paul riding in the load bed. We'd gotten the pickup truck unstuck using a makeshift winch and some levers, but we only had one spare tire for it. One of the goals of this trip was to acquire at least two new tires. With new tires, we hoped we would be able to use the truck to pull the big metal tank free of the snowbank.

We stopped about a mile from Warren and hid Bikezilla by dragging it over the embankment of snow that flanked the road. We approached Warren on foot, fighting our way through the deep snow covering the fields outside of town. Even with four of us breaking trail in turns, it took over an hour to reach the town.

The streets of Warren were deserted and silent—normal since no one in their right mind wanted to be outside in the subzero temperatures. The five of us flitted from house to house, keeping abandoned houses between us and the few that were occupied. At least the weeks of campaigning were good for something—both Darla and I knew exactly where everyone lived.

We reached the back door of the clinic and eased it open, slipping inside like invading winter ghosts. Dr. McCarthy and Belinda were reading at the front desk by the light of an oil lamp—he had a paperback novel with a beach scene on the front, and she had a heavy medical textbook.

"Another slow day?" I asked.

"Yes, thank God." Dr. McCarthy smiled as he stood and shook my hand. "Was meaning to get out and check on you folks soon. Just hadn't gotten around to it."

"You hear about last night?" Uncle Paul asked.

"Last night?"

"Someone burned our barn and greenhouses," I said.

Dr. McCarthy swore. "It's not the volcano I curse most in this mess—it's the knives we keep sticking in each other's backs. The Reds are back?"

"No," I said flatly. "Whoever attacked us came from here."

"You're sure?"

I nodded.

Dr. McCarthy swore again. "There's a lot of bad feeling around. Some folks feel like you led the Reds here. Mayor hasn't been helping things any. But I didn't think it had gotten that bad."

"Is the mayor behind the attack?" Uncle Paul asked.

Dr. McCarthy paused, scowling. His nose wrinkled as if he were catching a whiff of well-rotted road kill. "If he is, I haven't heard anything about it. Doesn't seem like his style—he'd want to arrest and try you, all official-like."

"Whoever attacked our farm last night has our panel van and pork," I said. "We need it back."

"Is it safe to talk to Mayor Petty about it?" Uncle Paul asked. "You think he'll try to arrest Alex?"

"If you'd asked me an hour ago, I would have said it was perfectly safe. Now . . . I don't know."

I wasn't sure what to say to that, and the conversation lapsed into uncomfortable silence.

"Why don't I walk downtown and feel him out?" Dr. McCarthy said at last. "If things seem on the level, then we'll all go meet with him."

"Ask him to come back here," Darla said. "Whether he's behind it or not, someone in this town means us harm. I'd rather not walk around outside any more than we have to."

"I'd like to talk to my mother too," I said.

"Me too," Rebecca said.

"She's not out at the farm?" Dr. McCarthy asked.

"She left yesterday," I said. "I'm hoping she's here."

Dr. McCarthy laid one hand on my shoulder and another on Rebecca's, squeezing gently. "Things okay?"

"Not really," I said. I bit the inside of my cheek hard, suppressing a sudden urge to cry. Rebecca turned, pulling away from his hand.

"I'll do what I can." Dr. McCarthy let his arms drop and reached for his coat.

Dr. McCarthy was gone for more than an hour. I paced nervously, wondering if he would come back with a posse in tow to arrest me. I trusted Dr. McCarthy, but once he told Mayor Petty I was here, anything could happen.

But only three people were with Dr. McCarthy when he returned. First through the clinic's door was the mayor, his wheelchair pushed by Sam Moyers, his twenty-something nephew. Sam wore a sheriff's badge on his coveralls and a huge chrome revolver strapped to his hip, which was strange. When Darla and I met with him before the election, he told us he'd worked on a road crew before the volcano. He was no kind of sheriff.

Behind them, Mom walked in. Rebecca called out and ran to her, stopping a few feet away as if she were caught between the opposing forces of two magnets, suspended in the room between me and Mom.

I started to smile involuntarily and then felt my lips freeze on my face. I wasn't sure whether to laugh or cry. Why had she left us without so much as a goodbye? What did it mean that she was here?

Uncle Paul spoke up before I could, addressing Mayor

Petty. "We're looking for our pork."

"Doc told me all about it," Mayor Petty said. "Terrible, just terrible."

"You have anything to do with it?" I asked.

"Of course not! In fact, I brought our new sheriff along to take your report. We'll do everything we can to help you track down your stolen property."

"New sheriff?" I whispered to Uncle Paul.

"Vaughn Frenchman died before you got here last year," Uncle Paul replied. "Pneumonia."

"Was high time to appoint a new sheriff. And Sam will be a fine replacement," Mayor Petty said.

"Alex," Mom said, "I talked to the mayor. It's all worked out. We can all move here. You sign an apology statement, and everything's forgiven. We'll get one of the empty houses—more if we want—and a share of the town's food."

I was too whipsawed by the multiple conversations to respond at first. Instead, Rebecca said, "C-couldn't you have told us where you were going? Told *me*? I thought you'd left us!"

"Oh, honey." Mom held her arms wide for a hug. "I'm so sorry. I only wanted to take care of things. Take care of you. I should have told you where I was going. Will you forgive me?"

Rebecca sniffled loudly and then ran into Mom's arms, clinging to her.

"Mom," I said as calmly as I could, "we can't move to Warren. It's not safe here. There's no wall."

"We had an election over that issue, son," Mayor Petty said. "And we settled it."

"It's safer here than on our own," Mom said. "And there's plenty of food. We can be a family again."

"I'm sure Mayor Petty will loan us some food, given that our farm is part of Warren," Uncle Paul said. "Help us get going at our new location."

"Sorry, Paul. The new food distribution policy allows for sharing only with people inside the town limits for the duration of the emergency. Technically that means Mrs. Halprin's family doesn't qualify. But I'm willing to make an exception if he signs that apology." Mayor Petty waved a piece of paper.

"I'm not moving to Warren," I said.

"You won't sign a simple apology just to stay with your mother? You'd rather move to the frozen wasteland around those windmills?"

"I wish you hadn't told them where we're going," Darla said, her disgust plain in her voice.

"You stay out of this!" Mom said.

"Mom! It has nothing to do with the apology! I already apologized. I'll sign the stupid paper—I don't care about that." I snatched the paper out of Mayor Petty's hands and groped futilely for a pen. "What I want is a future. A safe, stable future. We can't get that in Warren."

"There's food here," Mom said. "That's a future."

"For a while," I replied. Mayor Petty extracted a pen from the pocket of his jacket and held it out to me. I scribbled my name at the bottom of the page.

"You really should read that," Darla said.

"What does it matter?" I didn't care—about Warren, about Mayor Petty, or about what any of them thought of me. I was trying to convince myself I didn't care about Mom either, but it wasn't working.

Mayor Petty took the paper and pen from me as a slick smile creased his face. "The family reunion is touching and all, but I believe you wanted to report a theft?"

"That's right," Uncle Paul said. "Panel van we got from Stockton. You know the one."

"Reds took it back?" Sheriff Moyers said.

"Tracks led here," Uncle Paul replied.

"Maybe they drove it through here to make it look like someone here took it."

"Could be," Uncle Paul admitted.

"You know, if you had a wall, people couldn't drive through town willy-nilly," I said.

Both Mom and Mayor Petty shot me nasty looks.

"I'll write up a report when I get back to the office," Sheriff Moyers said.

"Could you canvas the town?" Darla asked. "Peek in every shed and garage large enough to hide a panel van?"

"I'll keep my eyes peeled," Sheriff Moyers said.

"Need that food bad, Sam," Uncle Paul said. "Might starve otherwise."

"I heard you," Moyers replied.

"Paul," Mom said, "nobody here is starving. You and the kids are welcome here—you should move with me, maybe even talk some sense into my son if you can."

"Might come to that," Uncle Paul said. "But I figure we'll try it Alex's way first." Mom tried to interrupt, but Uncle Paul kept talking. "Don't care much what happens to me, but I'd like to see Max and Anna have a decent place to grow up. Looks to me like this winter's going to outlast our supply of wood. But the wind'll keep blowing, so rigging those turbines is worth a shot."

We talked—argued, really—for more than an hour after that. But nothing changed. The only "investigation" Moyers and Petty would make into our missing food involved filing a report. Mom was determined to move to Warren with or without me. Uncle Paul and Darla were equally determined to move to the wind farm.

At one point Rebecca and Mom stepped into the hallway that led to the exam rooms. When they reemerged after about ten minutes, Rebecca pulled me into the hallway.

"Alex," Rebecca said as soon as we were alone, "I'm staying with Mom. In Warren."

Mom was abandoning me, and now Rebecca had decided to join her? I turned away, trying to hide my reaction.

"Don't look at me like that," Rebecca said.

"I wasn't looking at you at all," I replied. "And like what, anyway?"

"Like I just strangled your new puppy on Christmas morning."

"It's just . . . what went wrong? Mom used to be . . . I didn't always like her, but I always could rely on her."

"She held us together," Rebecca said.

"Exactly. If our family was a building, she was the

steel frame that supported us all. Now she's like the wrecking ball."

"I think Dad was a bigger part of that structure than you ever gave him credit for. It's . . . she's . . . she needs us, Alex."

"We can't move here. It's not safe or—"

"I know. I feel like I've been drifting along ever since the eruption, just doing what Mom and Dad, Uncle Paul, or you tell me to do. Maybe this is what I'm meant to do. To help Mom—maybe be a bridge connecting you and her. I *need* to do this. You understand?"

I nodded slowly. I thought I did understand. My decisions were at least partly selfish: I wanted to create a decent future for myself and Darla. But Rebecca understood that Mom needed her now and was willing to sacrifice safety to support our mother. It was strange that out of the half-dozen people in the clinic, the most mature was my fifteen-year-old sister.

"What if Warren gets attacked again?" I asked.

"When you get settled, show me the route to the new homestead. I'll memorize it; practice it—both during the day and at night. I'll keep my go-bag ready and make sure Mom has one too. If another attack comes, we'll run."

I nodded again. For the second time that day, I struggled to fight back tears. Rebecca's face was tight, determined, but I saw a quiver in her lower jaw. I held out my arms for a hug. She crashed into me, and I folded my arms over her shoulders.

"It'll be okay," I said, patting her back. "We'll be close."

"I know," she said, "but I'll still miss my annoying big brother."

"And I'll miss my whiny little sister."

Bikezilla was lighter on the way back to the farm without Rebecca. It should have been easier to pedal. But it wasn't.

Chapter 25

When we got back to the farm, we realized we had completely forgotten to look for truck tires. Darla needed to sort out the wreckage of the barn, so the next day, Max and I loaded a jack and tire iron onto Bikezilla and went in search of an F-series truck with good tires. We biked from farm to farm, peeking in garages. Often we had to dig through mounds of snow to find the vehicle hiding beneath.

It took three days of searching to find a truck with tires that would work. We visited dozens of farms, and not one was occupied. All of Uncle Paul's neighbors had fled—or died. When we got new tires on our truck, we easily pulled free the pesticide tank-cum-water heater, dragging it back to the temporary outdoor workshop Darla had set up beside the ruins of the barn.

Everyone else was busy too, salvaging kale and wheat from our destroyed greenhouses, tools from the barn, and packing up everything we'd need from the house. Darla, Ben, and Uncle Paul conspired endlessly, drawing up huge lists of what to take. Strange stuff appeared on their lists—for example, I was assigned to remove the toilet seats from both toilets and pack them. Darla planned to dig a pit toilet inside our new longhouse and needed the seats for that project. We stripped wires and pipes from the walls and took the glass from the first-floor windows, which were boarded up as a security precaution anyway.

Alyssa was especially helpful to Anna, who had lost her best friend when Rebecca decided to move to Warren. Nearly all the day-to-day work of running the farm—cooking, cleaning, and chopping wood—fell to Alyssa, Anna, and Ed, while the rest of us were getting ready for the move.

Then we had to move everything to the site Darla and I had picked five miles east of Warren amid the wind farm. Low on gas, we decided to drive the truck there only once. But the truck—even packed so full that the mound of supplies overtopped the cab—couldn't hold all the stuff we needed to move. So Max and I wound up serving as movers. We pedaled back and forth from the old farm to the new site. It was about seven miles by the direct route, but we pedaled two miles out of the way to avoid passing through Warren, so each trip took more than an hour and a half one way.

It took six days to move everything. We tried to stack the supplies neatly in the snow at the new homestead, but they inevitably seemed to spread everywhere. It began to look like a cross between a flea market and an old trailer park instead of a farm. By the end of that week, Max and I were so tired that we'd quit complaining about how tired we were—we simply didn't have the strength anymore. We collapsed into our bedrolls every night, moaning as our kinked muscles screamed in protest. When the pain faded from unbearable to only debilitating, I would finally fall asleep.

Everyone else stayed at the new site, working. The first thing they built was a large, crude igloo. At first there were arguments over who got to sleep in the truck and who had to sleep in the igloo. But after two nights, the arguments ended: it was much warmer in the igloo.

On day two they started building the first greenhouse. The greenhouse was more important than the longhouse, more important than a well or an outhouse. We had less than three weeks' worth of food, and even if everything worked perfectly, it would take at least four weeks for even the tiniest, edible kale sprouts to appear.

I asked myself every day if we were doing the right thing—if the short-term risk of starvation was worth the long-term security we'd get if we could make this plan work. Everyone was hungry and short-tempered. Uncle Paul said the work we were doing required a diet of eight or nine thousand calories per day, but we were rationing our food supply, getting two or three thousand calories a day at most. Uncle Paul developed a persistent cough; he didn't have a fever, though, so we couldn't convince him to go into town to see Dr. McCarthy. Everyone lost weight, going from rail thin to skeletal.

We decided to butcher the last two goats. They were dying anyway, because we didn't have anything to feed them. Over the next week, we ate nearly every scrap of those goats: we cleaned the intestines and ate boiled tripe, fried the brains (which were delicious, like scrambled eggs but richer and fattier), and even cracked the bones and sucked out the marrow.

The greenhouse Darla designed would be about ten feet high at the north side and have a sloping, south-facing roof, so the wall on the south side would need to be only two feet high—barely tall enough to crawl into that section to tend our crops.

We built the greenhouse around the tank contraption Darla had been working on. She'd connected more than a dozen heating elements from electric water heaters inside the tank. The idea was that when the wind blew, the electricity from the wind turbine would heat the water. When it wasn't windy, the water in the tank would serve as a heat reservoir, keeping our greenhouse warm until the next windy day. I mean, it was more complicated than that— Uncle Paul and Darla argued over circuit breakers, transformers, and resistance values in ohms—but that was the basic idea.

We had lost all our plastic in the fire, so the greenhouse roof had to be glass. Even with all the panes we'd salvaged from the old farmhouse, we didn't have enough. So we started trekking to the nearest abandoned farmhouse to loot its windows. They turned out to be modern, double-paned glass—much better than the glass in Uncle Paul's house, Darla said, but the glass was coated with some kind of UV inhibitor—great if you don't want your curtains to fade, but not so good in a greenhouse that's too cold to start with. So we spent hundreds of hours laboriously scraping the glass clean with razor blades.

We tore the farmhouse's roof apart, salvaging the rafters to build the walls of our greenhouse. The amount of labor everything took was staggering. To get a nail, for example, you had to start by making a hammer. We had plenty of hammerheads, but all the shafts had burned with our barn. So you had to cut a shaft with a hatchet, clean out the remains of the old shaft from the hammerhead, fit the new one to the socket, jam it in there, then hammer wedges of wood into the socket from the other side to tighten up the fit.

Then, of course, you still had to pull the nail out of a rafter, set it on a flat rock, and beat it more or less straight so it could be reused. Now repeat that part of the process eighty-two bazillion times, and you have an idea of what many of my days were like.

By the time the greenhouse was finished, we were pretty much out of food. And we hadn't even planted anything yet. Darla and Uncle Paul started working on

connecting the heating system to the wind turbine, which
involved figuring out how to refit a complex, formerly
computer-controlled system for manual control. Even turning the turbine to shut it off in a wind too forceful for its
design was complicated. To work on the turbine, they had
to climb a ladder attached to the wall inside the tower. The
base of the tower was pretty roomy, about twelve feet wide,
but it narrowed at the top almost three hundred feet up. So
working in there made me feel both acrophobic and claus-
trophobic. Since I was no help at all working on the turbine,
I took everyone else out into the fields to dig for corn.

We started by clearing the snow from an area about
ten feet square. Sounds easy, right? Not so much. The
snow was more than four feet deep and heavy with ice. To
clear a ten-by-ten area, we had to dig up and remove more
than four hundred cubic feet of snow—that's more than
two full dump truck loads, Darla told me later.

The ash layer under the snow was surprisingly
uneven—several feet thick at one side of our excavation,
almost nonexistent at the other. Which was strange—in
most places around Warren, the ash layer was a consistent
thickness of only two or three inches.

As we dug into the ash, we figured out why. Someone
had already harvested this field. The cornstalks were there,
flattened by the weight of the ash and snow, but the ears
were all gone. We moved across the road and tried again.

This time Max and I dug a small test hole only about
two feet square. When we found ears of corn at the bottom, everyone joined in, widening the hole. By the end of

the day, I felt more hopeful about our chances. We had more than twenty grocery sacks stuffed with corn ears.

There was more good news back at the greenhouse. As we approached, we could see the huge arms of the windmill turning slowly in the breeze. That meant heat!

I was a little disappointed when I got inside the greenhouse. It didn't seem any warmer in there than it had that morning. I dropped the bags of corn I was carrying, peeled off my left glove, and held my hand against the metal wall of the tank. It was stone cold.

Darla flung her arms around me from behind. I knew it was her instantly—although I couldn't have said exactly how.

"We got it working!" her voice practically frothed with excitement.

"It's cold."

"That tank holds almost four thousand gallons of water. It's going to take days to come up to temperature."

"Oh." I'd been expecting instant heat.

"That means it will hold heat for days, so even when the wind isn't blowing, we'll stay toasty."

"Cool. Want to shuck some corn?" I asked.

"I love it when you talk dirty," Darla whispered in my ear, pulling me into an even tighter hug.

"Shucking corn? I don't get how that's dirty," I said.

"Would you rather have me explain it now or show you later?" I couldn't see Darla's face, but her evil grin was easy enough to imagine.

"This is the Show-Me State, right?"

"That's Missouri, silly."

"Let's move there."

Darla released me from the backward hug, and we sat on the cold dirt in the greenhouse. I dumped a bag of corn out between us.

The first ear I shucked looked strange. Instead of light yellow kernels, they were grayish black. I rubbed at the ear. Some of the black stuff came off, as if it were dirt or dust or something, although it was too dark for dirt—pure black without a trace of brown.

"What's this?" I asked Darla, holding the ear out between us.

She looked up from the ear she was shucking and let out a string of curses that I was fairly certain included an anatomically detailed description of what she'd called "shucking corn" a few minutes before.

"What's wrong?"

"Smell it," she said.

"Smell what?"

"The Iowa State Fair queen's powdered ass. The ear of corn, of course."

"Geez. Sorry." I raised the ear cautiously to my nose. It smelled terrible—like old, wet cardboard.

"It's some kind of mold. Normally you'd send it out and have it tested for mycotoxins. The corn was wet when the ash buried it. That's why you harvest it dry, or dry it before you store it, so it can't mold. I was hoping freezing would do the trick, and I guess it helped for a while."

"Can we still eat it?"

"If it's a type of mold that's toxic, then no. You can't even feed it to pigs or goats."

I grabbed another ear and started peeling back its wilted brown sheath. It was moldy too. We sampled ears out of every bag we'd harvested. They were all moldy, although some of them only had a light dusting of mold, while others were almost uniformly black with it.

I held out one of the least moldy ears. "You sure we can't eat this? What happens if we do?"

"I don't know," Darla said.

"I'm going to try it—"

"That's not—"

"I'll cut a handful of kernels off this ear and boil them 'til they're mush. If I don't get sick, we'll try a little more."

Darla was scowling at me. "It's not safe."

"We need the food."

I left the greenhouse to hunt up a pot and start a cooking fire.

About a half hour later, I was crouched over a pan of boiling water and corn when Ed sidled up to me.

"Let me eat that," Ed said.

"Did Darla put you up to this?" I asked.

"Yeah," he replied, "but I wouldn't have agreed to do it if she wasn't right."

"She usually is." I stuck a spoon in the pot and stirred it. "But not this time."

"You're both right," Ed said. "We need to find out if we can eat that corn. And that means someone needs to try it."

"Exactly."

"But not you. You're running things around here—"

"Uncle Paul is—"

"Be serious, Alex. He looks to you whenever a real decision needs to be made. We all do. So you can't afford to be laid up sick. I can."

I didn't like his argument at all. It seemed wrong somehow. I'd decided we needed to test the corn on a live volunteer; I should be the one to take the risk. But Ed was adamant. I took the pan off the fire, setting it on the snow behind me to cool. A couple of minutes later, I offered the pan and a spoon to Ed.

He ate all the corn I'd boiled—maybe thirty or forty kernels in total. He said it had an off taste, like wine spoiled by a bad cork. I had no idea what spoiled wine tasted like, so I had to take his word for it.

And then we waited, hoping and praying that Ed would be okay, that the only readily available food we had would prove to be edible, and that we wouldn't all starve.

We had the answer to our prayers in less than an hour. Ed started vomiting so forcefully that I was surprised not to see his internal organs on the floor.

Chapter 26

I stayed up all night trying to take care of Ed. There wasn't much I could do for him. I held an old stewpot for him to vomit in. After the first time, he brought up nothing but bile. But despite his empty stomach, he woke from his uneasy slumber about every thirty minutes, retching. I wiped the spittle off his lips and the sweat from his forehead.

A few hours before dawn, I took the stewpot outside to dump it out. There wasn't much bile in the pot, but it was making the whole igloo smell sour. I scrubbed out the pot with a little snow and stumbled back through the double flap of fabric that served as our front—and only—door.

I tripped over Anna's legs on the way back inside. She sat up and grabbed my arm.

"Sorry," I whispered, "I didn't mean to wake you up."

"It's okay," she said, "I was already awake."

I tried to move away, to get back to Ed, but Anna didn't let go of my arm.

"What are we going to do, Alex? What are we going to eat? I mean, I'm not hungry yet."

Liar, I thought. We were all hungry. Always.

"But we need to eat something," Anna said.

"Anna," I whispered, putting as much confidence into my voice as I could, "we'll figure it out. None of us is going to starve. I promise."

"Okay." Anna let her hand fall away from my arm.

"Get some sleep if you can," I said.

"You too."

I crouched by Ed's bedroll the rest of the night, wondering if I'd lied to Anna.

• • •

In the morning Ed was weak but at least not getting any worse. He had a low-grade fever, and he was still trying to turn his stomach inside out but less frequently than he had during the night.

Uncle Paul found me by Ed's bedroll. A huge coughing fit racked Uncle Paul, and he knelt beside us. "You okay?" I asked.

When it subsided he said, "Yes. What's the plan?"

I knew instantly what he was asking about: food. Hunger has a remarkable way of focusing your attention. "What do you think we should do?"

"Maybe spread out, try different fields. All the corn around the old farm was good two months ago. Maybe there's some around here that hasn't molded yet."

"Makes sense," I said. "Get it organized, would you? I need to stay with Ed."

"No, sir," Uncle Paul replied, "you're not getting off that easily. You've been running things—and doing okay at it, except maybe for letting us spend too much time building the greenhouse and not enough gathering food. I should have said something, but I got so damn caught up in the excitement of making it work, you know? I'll keep watch over Ed today. You go out there and act confident and get them organized and find us some food."

I started to protest—Ed needed care, and I was the one responsible for his sickness. Shouldn't I be staying to watch out for him? But we all needed food. I felt like taffy on one of those stretching machines at the state fair, but the machine was spinning out of control, stretching me thinner and thinner until surely I would snap.

I reached across Ed to my own bedroll and picked up the semi-automatic rifle I had been carrying. The selector lever was on "safe", but I still carefully kept the muzzle pointed straight up. I passed it to Uncle Paul. He was a maniac about gun safety. If you made a mistake—pointing the gun at something you didn't intend to kill, for example, even if the gun was unloaded, even if the safety was on, even if it was only an accidental wave of the hand holding the gun—then you would have to practice the motion you had screwed up a hundred times, passing the gun back and forth as you counted out loud.

"Fire once if you need help. If you fire more than once, everyone will come at a dead run."

Uncle Paul nodded, took the gun from me, touched the safety lever, and checked the chamber. "Got it."

I left the igloo to get a corn-digging expedition organized. Alyssa approached me as soon as I was outside. She leaned in close, whispering in my ear. "Thanks for the chunk of roasted goat. I gave half of it to Ben."

That didn't make any sense. "We're out of goat meat."

"You put the last piece under my pillow."

"It wasn't me." I called everyone together to get them organized for a day of scavenging.

I split us into three teams of two, sending each team to a different field. The plan was to dig up three ears of corn, check them for mold and then if they were moldy, move to a spot at least a hundred feet farther from the igloo and try again. Every team had a shovel, a garden hoe, and a gun. I gave the other assault rifle to Darla, our hunting rifle to Alyssa, and a revolver we'd taken from the Reds to Max. The shovels and hoes all had crude, improvised handles—the original handles had burned—but they were a lot better than digging with our hands.

We spent all day outside digging. Each of the three teams returned with the same cargo: twenty-four ears of moldy corn.

Chapter 27

The only good news? Ed had quit vomiting. I boiled a few leftover scraps of goat fat in water and held the bowl to his lips while he sipped the resulting broth. The rest of us went to bed hungry.

The next morning I called everyone together in the greenhouse. The tank in the greenhouse was warm! It had begun to thaw the frozen dirt around it, and the air in the greenhouse was noticeably warmer than in the igloo. It wasn't yet warm enough for plants—I could still see my breath in the air—but the progress was hugely encouraging.

"We can't keep putting all our eggs in one basket," I said.

"I'd kill my brother for an egg," Alyssa muttered.

"I do not have an egg," Ben said.

"We're all hungry," Darla snapped.

"Let me finish, please," I said as calmly as I could. "Maybe we'll find corn that's edible, or maybe we won't, but whatever happens, we've only got another three or four days before the lack of food starts to seriously affect our ability to work." There were nods all around. Max looked scared, but Anna was smiling, although I couldn't imagine why.

"Darla said she learned about fire building in your old Boy Scout handbook, Max. Did you pack that?"

"Yeah . . ." Max said. "I'm not sure exactly where it is, though."

"Find it. See if there's anything in there that'll help. Something we can eat."

"I'm about hungry enough to eat paper," Alyssa said.

Both Darla and I glared her to silence.

"Help Max out if you feel up to it, Ed," I said.

"I'm okay today," Ed said. "Little shaky is all."

"We'll send out two digging teams," I said. "Alyssa and Ben, and Uncle Paul and Anna. One hole per field today. We're looking for soybeans—maybe the mold won't have affected them—or maybe we'll get lucky and find some clean corn."

"Got it," Uncle Paul said, trying unsuccessfully to stifle a coughing fit.

"You sure you're okay to go dig?"

"I'm fine." He practically growled his answer.

"Darla and I are going to take half our seed stock and head into Warren to try to trade."

"You be careful," Uncle Paul said. "Whoever torched the old farm is probably still there."

"I'll be on the lookout for my fan club," I said.

"I'll bring him home safely," Darla said.

Uncle Paul nodded.

"Okay," I yelled with false enthusiasm, "let's find some food!"

Nobody cheered.

• • •

Darla and I hid Bikezilla outside Warren and sneaked in, sticking to streets where most of the houses were abandoned. It was just as easy as the last time we'd done it, three weeks before. There were no sentries, no walls, no effort whatsoever at defense. The town was smothered in a blanket of denial even deeper than the snow.

Belinda was at the front desk of the clinic. "Good to see you," she said. "We were talking about you this morning, wondering how you were getting on."

"Good to see you too," I said. "Is Doc McCarthy around?"

"He's with a patient."

"Mind if we wait in one of the exam rooms? I don't want anyone to know we're here."

"That's fine." Belinda led us to the last exam room along the hall.

Darla and I talked about food while we waited. What our favorite foods were before the eruption. A Mulligan's deep-dish pizza for me, county fair roast turkey legs for Darla. Our favorite ice cream: Ben & Jerry's Cherry Garcia ice cream for me; Häagen-Dazs pineapple coconut for her. Our favorite vegetable: tempura fried green beans for me, anything made with a potato for her. And so on. There's nothing as interesting as food when you're starving.

When Dr. McCarthy came in, the first words out of his mouth were, "You look even thinner. You getting anything to eat?"

"No," Darla replied.

I said, "We got the greenhouse—"

"Can we trust you to keep this secret?" Darla interrupted.

Dr. McCarthy nodded. "Doctor-patient confidentiality and all that."

"We got the greenhouse working. If the soil's warm enough, we'll plant tomorrow. But we're out of food, and we've been on short rations for three weeks."

"No rations at all yesterday," Darla said.

"Town's still got plenty of pork, and we wouldn't have any at all if it weren't for you. Let me try to talk some sense into Mayor Petty."

"No," I said, "it won't help. If he shares food, it's an admission that he owes me. I don't think he wants to admit that to anyone, even himself."

"What can I do?" Dr. McCarthy asked.

I passed him a bundle of seeds wrapped in part of an old T-shirt. "Take these. Tell Petty they're yours, and try to trade for at least four hog carcasses. More if you can get them. That's half our supply of wheat and kale seed."

"All right." Dr. McCarthy took the bundle and zipped it into one of the pockets of his coat.

"Do you mind going now? I want to get back to the homestead before dark."

"I'll do my best," Dr. McCarthy said before he turned and left.

A few minutes after he left, someone knocked on the door of the exam room.

"Just me," Belinda called from outside.

"Come on in."

She opened the door and stepped in, carrying two small baggies of Froot Loops. "We've got two bags of these left. We don't need them to treat scurvy anymore—everyone's eating kale from the town's greenhouses—so usually I give them to kids as a treat."

"Save them for the kids," I said.

"Thanks," Darla said, reaching out to take the two baggies.

Belinda smiled. "I'd better get back to the front desk in case someone comes in."

We ate the Froot Loops one at a time, savoring them. They practically exploded in my mouth, so sweet that they made me dizzy, a riot of brightly colored chemical flavor so radically different from our usual gray diet that they might have been food for panchromatic aliens.

We ate about a third of the Froot Loops and then put the rest away to share with the others. We didn't resume the conversation until the Froot Loops were packed away out of sight. Then, of course, we continued talking about food.

• • •

Nearly two hours passed before I heard a knock on the exam room door. I opened it and found myself face-to-face with Mom. She had a pillowcase over one shoulder, and over the other I could see Rebecca standing behind her.

Mom started forward, arrested herself mid-step when she saw Darla, and then recovered, holding her arms out toward me, asking for a hug. I stepped into her arms, patting her on her back.

Rebecca followed her through the door, and my forced smile metastasized into a real one. I disengaged from Mom and wrapped up Rebecca in an enthusiastic hug.

"There's almost nothing left of you, Bro," Rebecca said. "Going to start calling you Beanpole."

"You feel a bit pudgy, Sis. Gonna start calling you Rotunda."

"It's not funny," Mom said. "You're dangerously thin— do you even weigh ninety pounds?"

I shrugged. I had no clue what I weighed. Mom moved as if to pick me up, but I backed away. "We're doing okay. We've just got to get through this rough patch until our greenhouse starts producing."

Mom hugged me again, which only annoyed me. She hadn't even acknowledged Darla yet. "I wish you'd move back to town. I couldn't bear it if I lost you."

"If things get bad enough, we will. I'm not going to let anyone starve to death."

Dr. McCarthy entered the room, which was not designed to hold five people. Darla slid onto the counter, sitting with her legs dangling off the floor and freeing up some space for the rest of us. My heart fell when Dr. McCarthy pulled out the packet of seeds I'd given him from the pocket of his coat and handed them back to me.

"No luck," he said. "Petty won't trade. Says he doesn't want people amassing private hoards of food."

"Makes sense," Darla said. "If he controls the food, he controls the people."

"Claims the town has enough seed," Dr. McCarthy said. "I know you didn't want him to know the seeds were from you, but after he'd turned me down I told him, trying to convince him to at least loan you some food until you're on your feet."

"And he wouldn't," I said. I wasn't the least bit surprised.

"No." Dr. McCarthy was frowning. "Sorry."

"I was at the mayor's office when they talked," Mom said. "I tried to convince him to share."

"It's okay," I said. "We'll figure something else out."

Mom dropped the loaded pillowcase she'd been clutching on the exam table, making a loud thunk in the tiny room. "I gathered up all the food I had. And Dr. McCarthy and Belinda contributed some too."

"What will you eat?" I protested.

"I'll work something out with Bob."

Since when had my mom started calling the mayor by his first name?

"Maybe we'll tell him we were robbed," Dr. McCarthy said, "or I'll ask a few of my patients to help out. Or we'll go hungry for a few days until the next food distribution. It'll work out."

I said, "We can't—"

"Yes, we can," Darla said firmly. "We can pay them back when the greenhouse starts producing."

I nodded, seeing the sense of that, and looked into the bag. There was a ham, part of a pork shoulder, a cloth bag that might have held cornmeal, and a plastic bag stuffed with kale leaves. "Thanks," I said.

"I wish I had more," Mom said.

"I brought you something too," Rebecca said. She held out a paper shopping bag with handles.

I glanced into the bag. It held a five-pound bag of dried cat food—Purina Naturals—and three cans of Alpo dog food. "Huh?"

Darla hopped off the counter, peered into the bag, and then looked at Rebecca, "Smart. I'm amazed that pretty face can hold your super brain in." Darla held out her fist, and Rebecca bumped it.

"I don't get it," I said.

"I've been poking around some of the abandoned houses here," Rebecca said.

"And," Darla said, "I bet you found that all the 'real' food has been taken. But in a couple of places, they'd left the pet food behind."

"Yeah," Rebecca said.

"Perfectly good calories in this stuff," Darla said as

Rebecca passed her the bag.

"Alex," Mom said, "do you hear what she's saying? You're going to eat dog food instead of moving back here with your family? That doesn't make any sense at all. What did I do, what did I say, that you hate me so much?"

"I am living with my family, and I don't hate you, Mom."

"Come back—"

"I'm glad you're here and eating well, Mom. I'm glad Rebecca's with you. But other than the food situation, we're safer than you are. There's food here, practically undefended—"

"That's not true," Mom said. "There's at least a dozen armed men stationed around the meat locker at all times. More around the town's greenhouses."

"So they're defending the food, but not their own citizens," Darla said.

"I wasn't talking to you," Mom said through gritted teeth.

"I can't have this argument right now." I picked up the pillowcase of food Mom had brought and slung it over my shoulder.

"Alex," Mom grabbed my arm, "we need to put this family back together."

"You're welcome to join us any time you want at the new homestead—although if you don't start treating Darla better, that may change." I yanked open the exam room door and strode through. A muffled sob from Mom escaped behind me. I did not look back.

Chapter 28

"Crap!" I yelled as soon as we had left the clinic. "I need to teach Rebecca the way to the homestead in case they need to bug out."

"I'll go get her," Darla offered.

I felt like a total wimp, but I let her go back in there and face my crazy mother alone. I was hungry, sore, and tired, but mostly I was afraid that if I saw my mother again, I'd say or do something I'd regret. I waited in the icy air outside the clinic.

When Darla got back, she had Rebecca in tow. "Mom told me not to come," Rebecca said.

"But here you are," I said.

"Well, she told me not to go poking around in abandoned houses either."

"Glad you did," Darla said.

"Be careful," I said. "I'm not too popular around here. I'm afraid someone might take their frustrations with me out on you."

"I keep a low profile," Rebecca replied.

We slunk out of town, avoiding as much as possible every place we might be seen. Once we got back to Bikezilla, we traversed the route to the homestead twice, pointing out landmarks to Rebecca, who was riding in the load bed. Doing the whole route twice for Rebecca meant we had to travel back and forth a total of five times—almost twenty-five miles of biking. By the time we got back to the homestead for the third time, it was dark, and I was hungry enough to try the cat food. It wasn't bad—crunchy, like corn nuts.

Max was outside, cooking something over a stew pot. It smelled like paint thinner.

"Success?" I asked skeptically as Darla and I got off Bikezilla.

"Maybe," Max replied. "The Boy Scout Handbook said you can eat almost any kind of pine bark in an emergency. There's a stand of dead pine trees on the hill at the far side of the creek. I cut a bunch of bark and tried some—it was tough and tasted like something pooped out of a petrochemical plant."

"That's . . . encouraging," Darla said.

"Thought I'd boil some—see if that helped. Want to try it?" he asked.

"Sure," I said. Heck, I'd been eating cat food on the way here. Could pine bark be any worse?

It was. Pale, fibrous, and a little bit slimy, it tasted like turpentine. Cat food was a vastly superior gastronomic experience. I must have made a face, because Max said, "Well, the book said it didn't taste very good."

Darla grabbed the fork from me and stabbed a piece. "Beats not eating," she said. Then she put the piece of bark in her mouth. "Or not."

The corn-digging crews had come back empty-handed again—or rather, everything they brought back was moldy. Still, we ate well. Slices of ham with sides of boiled pine bark and dry cat food. Nobody had had anything to eat in two days, so we needed to start recovering our strength. I figured I'd start rationing the food again in the morning.

We slept in the greenhouse that night, nestled up against the tank. I was fully warm for the first time in weeks.

We planted the next day, filling the greenhouse with neat rows of kale and wheat, drawing warm water from a spigot Darla had installed on the side of the tank to water our plantings.

The tank had to be kept full, or the heating elements might burn out. So when we finished planting and watering, we hauled more than a hundred buckets of snow, dumping them through a hatch at the top of the tank, where the snow melted almost instantly in the warm water. Working by torchlight, we finished well after dark.

The next morning I assigned Max and Ed, who was fully recovered now, to harvest more pine bark. It tasted horrible, but none of us got sick, and everyone seemed quite a bit more cheerful now that we were getting regular meals again. I sent Ben and Alyssa out to keep looking for a soybean field or corn that had escaped the mold.

"What's next?" I asked Darla. "Build the longhouse?"

"I don't know. Maybe another greenhouse first?" she said. "I'd like to have some redundancy—if we only have one greenhouse and it fails, we're screwed."

"So start raiding more of the empty farmhouses around here for glass?"

"Yes, but there's another problem. I don't know if the wind turbine can support another greenhouse."

"I tried to figure it out," Uncle Paul said, "but there are too many variables. If I had a working computer and a copy of ETAP, it'd be a cinch. But . . ." He shrugged.

"And even if one turbine will produce enough juice to heat two or more greenhouses," Darla said, "we still have the redundancy problem. If our wind turbine goes down, everything dies, and we're trying to dog paddle up brown floater creek."

"So let's fire up another turbine," I said.

"We need a butt-load of wire for that," Darla said. "Most houses only have forty or fifty feet of eight-gauge—"

"We've got tons of the wire that we took out of the old farm."

"Most of it's not heavy enough," Uncle Paul said. "We need eight-gauge or larger."

"So where are we going to get that?" I asked.

"Remember those huge spools of wire we saw in the warehouse in Stockton?" Darla asked.

I didn't like where this conversation was going at all. "Yeah. . . ."

"That's what we need," Darla said.

"Red isn't going to just give us that wire."

"No," Darla said, "we're going to have to take it."

Chapter 29

Three nights later, Darla and I were crouched outside Stockton's wall of cars. Uncle Paul had objected strenuously, but finally I had overruled him—and been completely shocked when he accepted my decision. His chronic cough would have made it far too dangerous for him to come. We might have found an electrical supply house in Dubuque, and there were dozens of them in Chicago, but going to either of those places would be a multiday trek over unfamiliar ground.

We hid Bikezilla more than a mile from town and approached on foot. We spent more than half the night just observing the guards. There were two-man patrols outside the wall circumnavigating the city, but more than ten minutes separated each patrol. The guards stationed at regular intervals atop the wall were a bigger problem. They were more than five hundred feet apart, but we would have to be very quiet to slip between them.

A guard was stationed right on top of the place where I'd crossed the wall before. We found a spot where two subcompact cars were jammed together about halfway between the fixed sentries and waited for the next patrol to pass.

After the patrol walked by, I counted off two minutes in my head. We had five, maybe six minutes before the next patrol got close enough to catch us. Darla and I scuttled silently to the wall.

I jammed my right boot into the crack where the two cars nestled against each other and reached upward. I couldn't get a grip on anything. I took off my gloves, tucked them into a pocket, and tried again. This time I could cling to the molding around the cars' windows, digging my fingernails between the rubber gasket and the metal. It was so cold that my fingers burned, as if I had plunged them into a fire. I knew I would get frostbite if I didn't get over the wall fast.

I raised my left boot, jamming it into the crack above my right. I slid my hands upward along the windows and pulled my right boot free, slowly ascending the crack one short step at a time.

When I got close enough, I reached out for the rear

bumper of the car on my right. The rifle on my back shifted, banging into the car's hood with a resounding clang.

I froze. The night was inky black—if I didn't move, the sentries might not see me. Would they investigate the clang? Or assume the next sentry along the wall had dropped something?

I counted off the seconds. Thirty. Sixty. A bead of sweat rolled along the bridge of my nose. I was poised to jump down and run if I were spotted. Ninety. One hundred twenty. The next patrol would be along in two or three minutes. My fingers had quit burning—lost all feeling, in fact. I had to move now—get off the wall or over it. I pulled myself up, slipped over the top of the cars, and dropped into the snow on the inside. I pulled my gloves on with a quiet sigh of relief and then froze, listening. No alarm was raised.

About five minutes later—after the next patrol had passed—Darla dropped into the snow alongside me. She had left her rifle behind.

Silently we slunk through the dark streets of Stockton until we reached the warehouse. There were two guards sitting by a small fire near the front door. The two semis loaded with pork that I had allowed Stockton to keep were there, parked across from the warehouse, so their metal backs were clearly visible from the guards' fire. One of the semitrailers was standing open and empty. The other was chained and padlocked.

Was Stockton running out of food, or had they moved some of it somewhere else? And what would Red do if they did run out? I hoped I could convince my mother and sister to move out to the homestead before then.

I shook off my gloomy thoughts and led the way to the back of the building. A few bushes—what had once passed for landscaping—had died against the back of the warehouse. They were mostly buried by the snow. Darla crept up between two of the bushes, running her gloved fingers along a seam in the corrugated metal exterior of the building.

"With a crowbar and a hacksaw, I think we could break in here," she whispered.

I couldn't see the seam well at all—it was too dark. "We'll come back," I said.

We retraced our steps, brushing snow across our path, trying to disguise our tracks. Getting out was much easier—there were good holds on the undersides of the cars. We climbed together, stopping at the top to check for the patrols, and then dropped into the snow outside Stockton. Darla retrieved her rifle from the snowbank where she had hidden it, and we began the trek home.

We returned to Stockton the next night. Darla had a large wrecking bar; a small, flat pry bar; a hacksaw; and an extra hacksaw blade. She had wrapped each item in cloth secured by duct tape to keep it all from clanking. We left our rifles behind, but I brought along a revolver we had acquired during our attack on Stockton more than eight months before.

Getting across the wall was easier the second time. We already knew what to expect from the guards. Less than half an hour after we had reached Stockton, we were huddled at the metal seam in the back wall of the warehouse.

We dug a hole in the snow with our hands, trying to access the base of the wall. When we had exposed the whole seam, Darla jammed the flat pry bar between the corrugated metal panels near the base, forcing it deeper into the seam by striking the curved end of the pry bar with her palm. That made the seam open enough that I could slip the extra hacksaw blade between the metal panels and saw at the rivets holding the panels together.

Every noise we made sounded like a scream in the silent night: the thump, thump of Darla beating on the pry bar and driving it deeper, the scritch-scritch of the hacksaw blade worrying at the rivet. We stopped every now and then, listening, wondering if we'd be discovered.

When the bottom rivet gave way, the seam opened considerably. I reversed the hacksaw blade and started working my way upward, one rivet at a time.

I cut six of them before we could bend the panel enough to slip through. It was springy and wouldn't stay bent, so Darla held it open for me while I wormed through. Then I turned and forced it open with my feet, holding it for her.

There was no light whatsoever inside the warehouse. I extracted a flint and steel and tinder from my pack. I couldn't see much in the brief flashes the sparks made from the flint, but after a moment, one of the sparks caught in the shredded cottonwood bark I was using for tinder. I used the burning bark to light a candle I'd brought along. We never used candles back at the homestead—we were down to two stubs plus the one I held in my hands—but hauling an oil lamp on this commando raid had seemed impractical.

The warehouse was like a giant candy store to Darla. Actually, better. If there'd been a candy store right next door, I'm pretty sure Darla would have ignored it, preferring to ogle the racks of supplies. Nearly everything we needed was here: pumps, wire, piping, plastic sheeting, water heaters, and more.

Darla found the type of wire we needed on an industrial-size spool resting on its end on a pallet. She unwrapped two huge coils of wire, walking around and around the spool to do it and cutting the wire with a bolt cutter that was conveniently laid on a nearby shelf.

When she settled the first coil over my shoulder like a life ring, I staggered under the weight. It had to be more than a hundred pounds of wire. I thought I could get across the wall carrying it. Maybe. She put an even bigger coil across her own shoulders.

I noticed that she carefully placed the bolt cutter back in exactly the same position she had found it in. The spool of wire didn't look depleted at all, despite the burdens weighing us down.

On the way out, I passed a shelf that held boxes of nails—thousands of large framing nails, perfect for our building projects. I remembered the hours of mind-numbing work pulling and straightening nails for reuse. I grabbed two boxes.

Darla held out a hand in a "stop" gesture. She took the two boxes of nails and put them back where I had found them. Then she grabbed two boxes from the back of the shelf, where it wouldn't be as obvious they were missing, and stowed them in my backpack. She hoisted an armload of some kind of circular leather belts designed to transfer power on an old-fashioned machine. I pointed at some similar rubber belts—surely those would work better for whatever she had in mind, but she shook her head. She passed me the belts, and I stuffed them into her backpack.

To get back through the seam at the rear of the warehouse, I had to take off the roll of wire and push it through first. Once we were both outside, we worked on disguising the spot where we'd entered the warehouse. We brushed snow over our tracks, and I broke off a huge chunk of the nearest dead bush, planting it in the snow directly in front of the spot we'd broken open.

Getting over the car wall was difficult enough carrying nothing. With a backpack loaded with nails and a huge coil of wire, it was almost impossible—well, for me, anyway. I watched as Darla flowed to the top of the wall seemingly effortlessly, marveling at her strength. She stopped at the top, motionless, waiting for the sentries to pass. When she gestured for me to follow, I huffed and puffed my way up, slipping once and nearly tumbling backward off the exhaust pipe I was clinging to. Jumping down on the other side was no fun either—my collar of wire left a huge bruise across my neck and shoulder, and the nails jingled alarmingly in my backpack. But either no one heard or we were long gone by the time they got to the spot where we had crossed the wall.

The next day, Darla and Uncle Paul worked on bringing another wind turbine online. Max and Anna went to the nearby stand of pine trees to harvest more bark. It may have tasted terrible, but it was helping to keep us alive. Alyssa and Ben went to search for edible soybeans or corn, while Ed and I took the truck to drag another big metal tank to the wind farm to serve as the core of the heating system for the second greenhouse.

Nearly every abandoned farm nearby had tanks they had used for storing liquids—pesticides, fertilizer, or fuel, according to Darla. The trick was finding a farm with old tanks; the new ones were mostly made out of plastic, and we needed metal for its heat conductivity. I was still concerned about pesticide residue, but Darla insisted there was nothing to worry about.

When Ed and I finished procuring the tank, we started disassembling another farmhouse, collecting glass, pipes, wire, and lumber to build the second greenhouse.

I wanted to start our new living quarters—the longhouse, as we were calling it—but Darla had a point. With only one greenhouse, any failure could cripple our homestead. With two, we had a chance to survive a disaster.

For a few weeks, we teetered on the edge of starvation. Pine bark was filling but not very caloric. We had eaten all the food Dr. McCarthy and Rebecca had given us—even the cans of dog food. (If I ever have to eat pet food again, I hope it's dry cat food. Alpo is absolutely *disgusting.*) And I found out why Darla had taken the leather belts. Cut into small pieces and boiled, they were edible. Sort of.

Just when I thought I would have to go back to Warren to beg for more food, Alyssa and Ben got lucky. Along the top of a high ridge about a mile east of our camp, they found a field with corn that hadn't yet molded. I sent half our group to dig corn but told Alyssa and Ben to keep prospecting for soybeans. Two days later they returned to camp again triumphant, carrying a bag stuffed with fuzzy seedpods containing soybeans. I wasn't sure how to process or cook them, but Darla knew. Our food situation got better.

It was easier not to worry as we watched the plants in our greenhouses sprout. Those tiny green shoots meant life and hope. When the largest kale plants hit two inches, I plucked one leaf from each of the best-looking plants and shared them with everyone. If pine bark had vitamin C, then it'd prevent scurvy, but I had no idea what its nutritional content was. I figured we had better add kale back into our diets as soon as possible.

After dinner one night, Darla pulled me aside. She led me into the greenhouse. I hoped she wanted to make out. When we got through the double doors, I took her in my arms and gave her a kiss. She broke it off after only a few seconds. "We need to talk."

Well, crap. At least she wasn't pulling away from the hug.

"The kale at the lowest side of the greenhouse isn't sprouting," she said.

"I noticed that," I said.

"It's too cold over there, too far from the tank."

I nodded. "What do we do?" If there was one thing I

was certain of with Darla and a technical problem, it was that she wasn't bringing me just the problem. She would have a solution in mind, and it would be something that required my help, or she would have already done it.

"I want some flexible tubing and a pump. We'll bury the tubing out around the perimeter of the greenhouse and use the pump to circulate hot water through it."

"Sounds good. Let's do it."

"There was a full roll of flexible tubing in the warehouse in Stockton."

"No! Absolutely not." I let my arms drop from her sides.

Darla, however, kept her hold on me. "And there were a couple of pumps that might work."

"Can't we raid one of the abandoned farmhouses around here? They have tubes, right?"

"They're called pipes. And they're not flexible. Yes, I might make that work—the pump would be a bigger problem, but maybe we could find a sump pump that I could make work."

"Fine. Do that."

"I'll need connections and fittings. Solder and flux if I use copper pipe. The only place I've seen that stuff around here is at Furst Distributors in Stockton. So either way we need to go."

"Forget it. If we keep going back, we're going to get caught."

"How? We've been over that wall twice now. It's easy."

"How would I know? Bad luck is usually something you aren't expecting. And anyway, it's stealing." She raised her eyebrows at me. "I mean, a little wire we can't get anywhere else, I can live with. But we can't keep looting their supplies."

"Like Red cares? He steals all our food, and you're going to get squeamish over a few plumbing and electrical parts he's not even using and will probably never miss?"

"What Red does is his business. What I do is mine. Theft is theft—"

"We need—"

"Maybe it's excusable when it's done to survive and no one is hurt by the loss of the goods. But we'll survive without the flexible tubing or pump."

"Maybe," Darla said thoughtfully. "But if we're going to get the first greenhouse producing as much as it should, build the second, and a longhouse? We're going to need access to supplies. If not Stockton's, then someone else's."

"We're not. Going. Back. To Stockton." I lifted her hands from my shoulders and left the greenhouse. Darla could usually talk me into anything. But not this time.

Chapter 30

Two nights later we were back in Stockton. Darla had sworn we would play it safe, she would do everything I asked her to, we would take our time getting back in, and blah, blah, blah. So I made us wait in the snow outside the wall for two hours, making sure the guards hadn't changed their patterns. They hadn't.

We slipped over the wall fast and easily, two black-clad ghosts flitting into the city. The seam at the back of the building was exactly as we had left it. We wormed our way inside where it was dark and quiet. Nothing had changed. The shelves of hardware were the same as we'd left them, except for a thicker layer of dust.

Darla cut two massive coils of black, flexible pipe that were designed to be used with irrigation equipment. The coils were much lighter than the collars of electrical wire. We took two pumps out of their boxes and stowed one in each of our backpacks. We closed up the empty boxes and left them on the shelf so it would look like nothing had changed—at least if no one ever opened the boxes.

It was difficult to make the panel at the back of the warehouse open wide enough to push through the huge coils of tubing. I put my feet against one side of the slit and grabbed the other side with both gloved hands, pushing with my legs and straining to make it open wide enough that Darla could get the rolls of tubing through. A rivet above the ones we had cut broke with an atrociously loud ping. Darla blew out the candle, and we froze in the darkness, waiting, listening, praying that no one would come investigate. No one came.

Working by feel now that the candle was extinguished, we finally got the tubing through and slipped out ourselves. I'd bent the panel so much that I couldn't get it to reclose correctly. I worked on it for a while and then settled for camouflaging the hole with dead bushes and snow.

Once we were well away from the warehouse and its guards, I whispered to Darla, "I want to go downtown. Look for something."

"You crazy?" she whispered back. "That's where their troops are headquartered, where Red's mansion is. You didn't want to come creeping around the lion's tail, and now you're going to stick your head in his maw?"

"Yeah. You're right, I guess." I had wanted to check out the jewelry store I'd seen downtown—see if there were any engagement rings left, but no way was I going to tell her that.

We slipped back over the wall and returned to the homestead in silence, each of us lost in our own thoughts.

Chapter 31

It took more than two months to build the second greenhouse. The guts of the first one—the tank with its heating elements—were finished before we arrived at our new homestead, and we had all the glass and building materials salvaged from the old farmhouse. Now we were in the process of tearing down the three nearest abandoned farmhouses and taking the glass, lumber, pipe, and wire we needed.

The unmoldy corn and soy improved our diet immensely, and we quit eating pine bark. Two wind turbines turned out to be more than enough to heat both our greenhouses. In high wind we shut down the turbines so they wouldn't be damaged. They weren't designed to spin all that fast, Uncle Paul said. They were geared for slow and steady operation—that was more efficient and also safer for birds. Not that we'd seen any birds since the eruption. Those that weren't killed by breathing in the ash had no doubt fled south to try to survive the volcanic winter. We also had to shut down the wind turbines if the wind blew steadily for several days. The greenhouses would overheat otherwise.

Once we had two greenhouses and two turbines online—giving us some hope of surviving even if something failed—we started building the longhouse. It would be a simple, one-room structure, about forty feet long and twenty feet wide. We had saved exactly enough space for it between the two greenhouses, so it would be bordered on its two long sides by a greenhouse, and one of the short sides would butt directly against the base of the wind turbine. That way, residual heat from the greenhouses would warm our living quarters, and we could enter the turbine tower or either of the greenhouses without going outside.

We planned to build a sniper platform near the top of the turbine tower, but Darla and Ben wanted the longhouse to be a defensive structure too. So we built several test walls, varying thicknesses of wood, snow, galvanized roofing, and ice. Ben suggested building the longhouse out of reinforced concrete, but obviously that was completely impractical—we had no way to get rebar or make concrete.

Darla fired each of our guns at her test walls. None of them would stand up to short-range fire from the AR-15s. The bullets blew through ice and snow as if they weren't there and blasted splintered holes in any board in their path. A double layer of logs would usually stop them, but we didn't have the time or materials to build a wall that heavy. We settled on an A-frame log structure with board walls and corrugated metal roofing, covered with three feet of snow and ice for insulation. That would stop pistol fire just fine.

It seemed to take forever to build the longhouse. We cut huge logs for the support beams, and all eight of us working together couldn't drag them up the slope to our homestead. Darla and I returned to Stockton to steal aircraft wire and pulleys to construct a system for lifting and dragging logs.

Nothing had changed in Stockton except the semitrucks where Stocktonites stored their food. Both trucks were empty. "What is everyone here eating?" I whispered to Darla.

She shook her head and shrugged her shoulders.

We slipped around to the back of the warehouse and wormed our way inside through the metal panels we had separated. Nothing had changed inside either, except that everything was coated in a thicker layer of dust. Darla put two heavy spools of aircraft wire in my backpack and followed them with more than a dozen metal pulleys. Then she loaded her backpack with nails, silicone caulk, plumber's putty, brass plumbing joints, electrical nuts, circuit breakers, and electrical tape.

It was impossible to walk with a backpack full of metal pulleys without jingling a little. I was afraid we'd get caught. But no alarms were raised, so either no one heard us, or they attributed the noises to one of their own patrols.

The next day Darla used the material we had liberated to rig a pulley system so efficient that Anna could drag a massive tree trunk up the slope to the homestead by herself. While we worked, we worried over what we had seen in Stockton. The empty trucks terrified me. Were they out of food? If so, would Red attack Warren again? It was unlikely he would find us up on our isolated hill five miles east of Warren, but what about Rebecca and Mom?

That evening, Darla and I knocked off work early and snuck into Warren. We visited Nylce first, both to catch up and to find out where Mom and Rebecca were living. Evidently Mayor Petty had given them an empty house right next door to his and just down the street from the mayor's office.

Mom wasn't home, but we found Rebecca in the kitchen, sitting on the floor, washing clothes by the light of an oil lamp. I tapped on the back window.

She startled, groping quickly around the chair beside her and coming up with a small pistol. I waved and smiled, hoping she would recognize me before she shot me. She set the pistol back down, got up, and opened the back door.

"Just about nailed you," she said.

"Good to see you too, Sis." I walked through the doorway and stamped my feet on the rug. "Mom around?"

Rebecca gave me a quick hug. "No, she's out with a friend."

"Who?"

"You don't want to know," Rebecca said as she hugged Darla, who had come in behind me.

"If I didn't want to know, I wouldn't have asked."

Rebecca rubbed her forehead as if she were getting a headache. "Mayor Petty. Or Bob, as she calls him."

"Oh . . ." I fell into a chair.

"Told you, you didn't want to know."

"Yeah, you did."

"It's actually helping some. I don't get the evil eye from the other Warrenites as much as I used to."

"Well, that's something. Look, I came to talk to you about . . . where's your go-bag?"

"Right there." She pointed at a backpack sitting on one of the unused chairs around the kitchen table.

"And Mom keeps hers close too?"

"No. We've had that fight—I'm not going to win it. There's her bag." Rebecca grabbed the strap of a bag on another chair and then let it slip from her hands.

I groaned inwardly—the point of a go-bag was to have it at hand at all times—wherever Mom was, she should have taken it with her.

"What's with the questions?" Rebecca asked.

"Stockton's out of food again," I said.

"Do I even want to know how you know this?"

"Probably not," I said. "You've got to be ready to run."

"You'll have a good place to run to," Darla said. "Once

we build our sniper perch and finish camouflaging our site with snow and ice, it'll be about as defensible as any place with eight people can be."

"You think we'll be attacked?" Rebecca asked.

"Yes," I said flatly. "You've got food. Stockton doesn't. And if Red finds out where we are—that we've got producing greenhouses—he'll attack us too."

"Hope you're wrong."

"Yeah, me too. If there's any way you can leak the info to Mayor Petty without letting him know where you got it . . . he might trust a rumor more than something I told him."

"I'll tell Mom I heard it from Nylce or something. She'll tell *Bob.*" She said the mayor's name with disgust.

"Good. And tell Mom . . . tell her I miss her."

"Okay. I will. She misses you too, you know."

"She could move out to the homestead anytime she wants," I said.

"I know." I started to turn away, but Rebecca grabbed my arm, holding it in a surprisingly powerful grip. "It's going to be okay, Alex. I know it is."

As I pedaled away from Warren, I thought about her last words. I couldn't escape my worries, couldn't shake the inexorable feeling that we had it too good, that something horrible lurked just over the horizon.

Chapter 32

When we finished the structure of the longhouse, we piled snow around and atop it. We also covered the walls of both greenhouses with snow. From downslope the homestead looked like three unusual hillocks of snow butted up against the wind turbine. Once you got closer, the glass roofs of the greenhouses made it obvious that the snow mounds weren't natural, but there was nothing we could do about that.

When the longhouse was finished, we crushed the igloo and moved into our new digs. That night, we held a celebration. Darla had hooked up an electric range we had taken from one of the farmhouses, and she installed overhead lighting in the longhouse. If the wind was blowing, we could cook without building a fire. It seemed like the acme of luxury after almost two years squatting beside a campfire to cook anything. Darla had asked me to find some electric or hybrid cars—she and Uncle Paul thought they could convert their batteries to allow us to store electricity when the wind wasn't blowing—but I hadn't gotten around to looking for them yet.

I cooked kale greens in soybean oil. Darla made tortillas from the first wheat harvested from our greenhouse, and Anna made corn pone. There was a time when I would have turned my nose up at a meal like that, refused to eat it. But after surviving on pine bark and dog food, that meal was fabulous—a true feast.

Our next project was the sniper nest near the top of the windmill tower adjacent to the longhouse. I flatly refused to get involved. Just looking up into that tower made my knees shake. Darla planned to build a platform inside the tower near the top, cutting slits in the metal walls so the person on guard duty could look or shoot through. It would have a commanding view of the surrounding countryside since we were on a fairly high ridge to start with.

As we worked on improving the homestead, we all waited for the inevitable attack on Warren, waited for Rebecca to come up the hill toward us, maybe with a flood of refugees trailing in her wake. But no attack came. Darla finished the sniper's perch, and we started to do sentry duty up there. I *hated* being on sentry duty. Not the cold; that wasn't anything new. Or the boredom; I was used to that. It was the climb to and from the sniper's nest. Two hundred and eighty-four ladder rungs. Once I was up, it wasn't so bad. The platform Darla built filled the turbine tower—you had to enter through a hatch in the floor. There was no way to fall out—the slits in the tower wall were barely big enough for binoculars or the barrel of a rifle.

There were two panic buttons mounted on the floor: one that would ring an alarm only in the longhouse and another that would sound a Klaxon audible from miles away. They only worked when the wind was blowing, of course. Any other time, we'd use our old system of rifle shots to sound the warning.

As soon as the sniper's nest was finished, Darla and Uncle Paul built an electric grinder for our wheat. Then they started working on building a battery backup for our electrical power. They found a Chevy Volt with a good battery and hauled the battery—all 435 pounds of it—to the homestead. They started testing it out in the snow about a hundred yards downslope from the greenhouses. Uncle Paul said the battery could explode from over-charging, which sounded crazy to me, but he was the electrical engineer.

The rest of us started building a third greenhouse. Usually only two or three of us were available to work on it—we still had to cook, clean, wash clothes, dig corn and soybeans, and one person always had to be on guard duty in the sniper's nest. At the rate we progressed on the third greenhouse, I was afraid it would take six months or more to finish. Nonetheless, it was important to build another. We were eating okay, but we weren't building up a stock-pile of food. I wanted to squirrel away a few thousand pounds of flour and dried kale leaves in case something went wrong.

My eighteenth birthday came and went. I remembered it for once, but it was a day like any other—we worked on building the third greenhouse during the day and held a subdued celebration at dinnertime.

Uncle Paul and Darla did indeed blow up the battery from the Volt and then the high voltage battery pack from a Prius, but on the third try—with a battery pack from another Prius—they figured out how to add a circuit to prevent the batteries from overcharging. We had lights that we could turn on anytime we wanted! When Uncle Paul and Darla demonstrated the system, I raised my water cup in a toast, "Here's to reentering the 1890s!" Alyssa laughed. Darla glared at me.

I sidled over to Darla. "Sorry," I said in a low voice, "it's great. Brilliant. I honestly never believed I'd see a working light switch again."

"You don't have to be a suck up," Darla said.

"That's not true."

"Why do you say that?"

I leaned closer and whispered in her ear, "Because you're the only person in the world who wants to have sex with me?"

"That's not true either." Darla shot a murderous glare at Alyssa.

I intentionally misunderstood. "What? We've known each other two years, and you're already bored with this?" I swept both hands down my scrawny, half-starved body and had to stifle a laugh.

Darla just rolled her eyes.

"I mean, I was going to let myself go after we got married, but now I guess I can quit working out any—"

Darla stifled my speech with a long, intense kiss. Everyone else in the room was doing their best to ignore us. Living in a one-room longhouse takes some getting used to.

"Wow," I said, coming up for air, "that was—"

"Be serious for a moment, okay?"

I nodded, letting the grin fade from my face.

"Your uncle and I want to work on lights for the greenhouses next instead of helping to build the third greenhouse."

"Won't the light be visible for miles?"

"We'll shield all the light fixtures and only leave them on during the day. Might boost production a lot."

I nodded. It made sense—none of the greenhouses, even the ones at the old farm, had produced as well as they could. There just wasn't enough light in the dim, yellowish sky. "We've got plenty of light fixtures and bulbs—we can scavenge more from any of the farmhouses around here."

"Good. But we also need more flexible tubing and another pump. To heat the edges of the greenhouse."

"And so you want to make another trip to the warehouse."

"Yeah."

"It's not a good idea."

"We'll be fine."

I was uneasy, but she had a point. We'd raided the warehouse four times with no trouble at all. "Okay. We'll go next week. I need some caulk and nails too."

"Thanks," Darla said.

"But as soon as we finish these two projects, we're going to spend some time exploring other towns. And find a source of supplies that isn't in a town controlled by a knife-wielding psychopath."

Chapter 33

We'd climbed Stockton's wall often enough that we were getting good at it. Darla flowed up the outside of the wall like a black silk scarf caught by a fast breeze, dropping lightly to the ground on the other side. I followed—a little bit less efficiently and a lot less gracefully, but fast and silent all the same.

Nobody was around except the infrequent guard patrols, but that was no surprise. It was nighttime and so cold that nobody in their right mind would be outdoors. What was surprising was that there were no guards in front of the warehouse. The two empty semitrailers were still there, looming rectangles in the darkness, and the big overhead and pedestrian doors to the warehouse were both locked.

"What does it mean?" I whispered.

"They were mostly guarding the food in the trucks," Darla whispered back. "No need to waste manpower now that it's gone."

We slipped around to the back of the warehouse. Everything looked the same back there. I moved the piece of brush away from the seam we had opened in the wall, wiped the snow away from it, and held the panel for Darla. "Ladies first," I whispered.

She snorted softly and lay down, sliding sideways into the dark interior of the warehouse. Then she held the seam open from the inside so I could follow her.

We lit a candle and gathered our supplies in silence, stuffing our backpacks with caulk, nails, and electrical supplies, and then settling rolls of flexible tubing over our shoulders. My gaze landed on the leather belts hanging from a hook set in a pegboard wall. I remembered the hard knots of boiled leather, chewy and slightly slimy, sliding down my throat toward my sunken stomach. I shuddered and turned away.

Darla made a point of holding the metal flap out of the way for me when it was time to leave. "Ladies first," she whispered.

I scowled at her, although I realized she couldn't see me—we had already blown out the candle. I lay sideways on the floor, thrust my pack and the roll of tubing through, and then wriggled my way into the gap.

On the far side, someone seized my arms and yanked me roughly to my feet.

Chapter 34

At least three guys surrounded me—one holding each arm, and one I could sense as a dark shape looming in front of me.

Darla. I had to warn Darla without tipping off these guys that anyone was with me.

I slammed my heel into the wall, knocking the metal panels together with a clang. "Let go of me!" I screamed. I couldn't move my arms, so I lifted my foot again and brought it down full force on the instep of the guy to my right. There was a crunch of breaking bones, and he howled in pain.

I heard the scrape of metal on metal as someone

unshielded a lantern, blinding me momentarily. The guys holding my arms picked me up, lifting me off my feet, and slammed me facedown into the snow. On my way down, I saw that there were more than a dozen men out there. Behind them, watching everything and fingering a knife, stood Red.

The guys holding me had my wrists twisted and one hand on the back of each of my elbows. All they had to do was pull up on my wrists, push down on my elbows, and snap—my arms would break. I tried to fight anyway, lashing out with my legs. Someone fell on them, holding them down. Another guy approached with a rope. In less than two minutes, my arms and legs were trussed; there was nothing I could do but lay there like some useless, abandoned parcel.

"The other one is still inside," Red said. "Break into squads. One through the front, one through the back. Tie him, and bring him out here."

The men split up and disappeared from my field of vision. Nothing happened for a long while. Fifteen minutes, maybe twenty. Red took out a leather strap and stropped his knives. The two-foot *gladius* at his right hip. Then the hunting knife at his left hip, its spine rippled with wicked serrations. Two small throwing knives, one from his right boot and then one from his left. The snow burned my left cheek and forehead. I heard shouting, Darla's high voice mixed with the grunts and heavy breathing of men exerting themselves. Red impassively pulled a dagger from a sheath somehow attached to the back of his collar and started stropping both sides of its wicked-looking blade. Just as Red was reaching into his jacket—presumably for yet another knife—the men came around the corner, carrying a wriggling and struggling Darla, bound even more thoroughly than I was. They dropped her into the snow beside me.

"You okay?" I whispered.

"I'm trussed like a calf at a rodeo, lying in snow so cold it'd freeze the tits off a snowshoe hare. What do you think?"

"Shut up," one of the men near her said, kicking her leg.

I struggled with the ropes that bound me, which only made them bite deeper into my arms. I tried to shift my legs over Darla's to protect her in some meager way. I couldn't even do that.

"Load them on the sled," Red ordered. "Keep them in the barracks under guard tonight. I'll deal with the problem tomorrow."

We were tossed roughly onto a sled that resembled an oversized toboggan. I landed across Darla in an X pattern.

"Christ and Santa Claus," she whispered. "You gain weight?"

"Not really. How's your leg?" Four guys took up ropes tied to the front of the sled and pulled. It lurched into motion with a jerk that rocked me back against Darla's thighs.

"Ow! It was fine until now."

"Sorry."

"It's okay. Might bruise. Hope we're alive long enough to find out."

"Me too," I said. "How'd they know we'd be there?"

"Probably noticed something missing. Stationed their guards in back instead of the front, maybe in one of the buildings nearby, told them not to build a fire." The steady susurrus of the sled's runners against the icy road masked our conversation. "I'm more worried about what they might do with us," Darla said in an even softer voice.

I thought I knew what they were planning. If I had been talking to anyone else—Max, Uncle Paul, Alyssa, whoever—I would have lied. Told some pleasant untruth about a slap on the wrist. But I was lying atop Darla, the toughest woman I'd ever met. I told her the truth. "They're out of food. Have been for at least a month. But they haven't attacked Warren like last time they ran out. Red and these guys look pretty well fed. They've got to be eating something."

"Yeah," Darla sighed so heavily that it might easily have turned into a sob.

"I figure we'll be flensed," I said, putting words to what we were both thinking.

"That's what I figured too." A long silence followed, which Darla ultimately broke. "Well, shit." Her voice was surprisingly steady. "I was really looking forward to seeing what our children would look like. I figured my pretty genes would conquer your ugly ones, but you never know. Genetic crapshoot."

"Any child of yours would be beautiful," I said quietly. I desperately wanted to hold her hand, to kiss her, but my hands were tied, and I couldn't even shift my head enough to reach her lips.

"We aren't dead yet," Darla said.

I had an idea, but before I could say anything, the sled lurched to a stop in front of the downtown bowling alley. Two guys grabbed my shoulders and dragged me inside. An oil lamp, turned low, threw a dim and shadow-rimmed light around the room. All the racks of balls had been cleared out, leaving a large, open room. An improvised hearth had been built in the middle of the room and a small hole cut in the roof to vent smoke. But the fire was banked and the room frigid. Rows of cots and military-style footlockers filled the space. About three-fourths of them were occupied by sleeping men, maybe a hundred or so in total. A couple of the men woke, glaring blearily in our direction. I wondered why there were only men in Red's military: maybe he was an old-fashioned sort of tyrant?

My captors dropped me, my head thunking on the hard linoleum floor. Another pair of guys dumped Darla beside me. They turned to leave, and I called out, "Excuse me! I need to take a leak. You mind?" I held up my bound hands.

One of the men turned and growled. "Piss yourself, thief. We don't care."

The four guys who had brought us in dragged chairs under the oil lamp and started a card game. I guess they were guarding us. Not that we could do anything—I could barely move. I inched my head closer to Darla's so we could talk in whispers without being overheard.

We talked through the remainder of the night, falling quiet only when the dim and uncaring morning light seeped into the room through the cracks in the black paper covering the bowling alley's windows.

Chapter 35

Darla and I expected to be executed at first light. Nothing happened, though. The men who had been asleep in the barracks woke and left, and a smaller crew—maybe fifty or so—came in, stowed their guns and knives, and bedded down. We got four new guards; they built up the fire before settling down to another card game.

I didn't want to let myself hope—it would only be worse when my hopes were dashed—but if they were going to flense us, wouldn't they have done it already?

I tried to get our new guards to talk to us. I asked them question after question until one of them got up from the card game and kicked me in the ribs. I didn't think he had cracked a rib, but it hurt—badly enough that I quit asking questions.

By late afternoon my mouth tasted of dry ash, my stomach felt like it had shrunk to the size of a walnut, and by then I really did need to pee. I squeezed my legs together, desperate to avoid the ignominy of pissing myself. I knew I was going to die, but I wasn't as scared as I had expected to be. I had done okay; my family could eat because of the homestead I'd helped to establish, the greenhouses I helped to build.

All the men who had slept through the day shift were up, chatting in small knots throughout the room, cleaning their guns, or playing cards or dice. A steady stream of them came and went—using an outdoor latrine or wash area, I figured.

"Alex," Darla whispered, "I'm sorry."

"Don't be," I said, surprised that I meant it. I had argued against continuing our raids on Stockton, after all. "We did good."

"Yeah," she agreed, "we did."

Red slid into the barracks, as silent as a stalking cat. It took a few seconds for anyone else to notice he was there. Then the card players dropped their hands and rose to salute so fast that their cards scattered willy-nilly, fluttering to the floor around them.

"Bring them," Red ordered.

Our legs were cut free, and men hauled us to our feet. I sagged—hot streaks of pain ran up my legs from my

ferociously tingling feet. I wasn't sure I could walk. The
men half-dragged me out the door. I looked over my shoulder; Darla was being dragged through the doorway too.
Her foot hit the jamb, and she yelped in pain.

All the men in the barracks followed us—an escort of
over fifty. I mean, I knew how to fight, but this was ridiculous. "Where are we going?" I asked.

"Shut up, thief," the man at my right shoulder growled.

"Where are we going?" I repeated.

"I've got a gag," he said. "Open your mouth again, and
I'll use it."

They marched us down the road to Stockton's east
gate. Every resident of Stockton must have been gathered
there, more than five hundred people arrayed in a huge,
rough ellipse. People sat atop the car wall or stood in the
large, open area just inside the gate. In the middle of the
ring of people, a hot fire burned. Cut logs were scattered
around the fire as if to serve as stools. A bucket full of a
viscous black substance—tar or rubber, maybe—bubbled
over the fire. Darla gasped—somehow she knew what all
this was for, and she was terrified. We were too far apart
to whisper to each other.

Red stepped into the middle and drew his *gladius*,
holding it high over his head, where firelight flickered
along its steel like bolts of heat lightning. The crowd was
instantly silent.

"We were born," Red yelled, his voice surprisingly
loud coming from his slight body, "in a time of weakness.
Of sloth. Of indolence." He turned as he talked, taking in

everyone. They were either mesmerized or terrified. "The laws of our childhoods, the laws of forgiveness," Red sneered as he said the words, "of rehabilitation—they do not serve us now. They were laws for children, in a society filled with children.

"The volcano has burned away that old world. Those of us who survived have been reforged. We were born to a world of fat; we have been reborn in a world of steel.

"There are laws for a world of steel. Old laws, true laws. Laws of sharp vengeance, not flabby laws of mercy. Laws of the knife."

Someone in the crowd screamed, "Take their heads!"

Red whirled to glare at the spot the interruption had come from. The silence was absolute.

"The old laws are harsh laws and demand strict obedience. The penalty for theft is not a head. It is a hand."

Suddenly I understood what the bubbling tar was for. And the logs weren't stools. They were chopping blocks.

Chapter 36

I lashed out, launching a side kick at the knee of the guy on my right. His leg bent backward with an awful crunching sound, and he screamed, letting go of me and collapsing. Three guys moved in to try to take his place. I twisted powerfully, throwing the guy clinging to my left arm into them. I felt almost infinitely strong, like I could have flung him a city block. Two of the three guys advancing on me went down in a tangle of limbs. I heard a high-pitched *oof* and knew Darla was fighting too. I took a step forward and kicked the guy still advancing on me in the stomach. His body curled around my boot, and he fell.

"Stop!" Red yelled.

I whirled, keeping low, wishing my hands were free to block and punch. Red was behind Darla. His right arm reached around her, and the tip of his *gladius* was poised against the corner of her right eye. A trail of blood dribbled slowly down her face, as if she were a vampire weeping blood instead of tears.

"I'll blind her," Red said calmly.

"No," I said. It was more a prayer than a command.

"Jeff!" Red barked. "Put your knife to her eye." One of the men standing nearby drew a dagger from the sheath at his side and held it to Darla's left eye. Red lowered his *gladius* and sauntered toward me.

"Take care of them," he ordered someone else. A group of men scurried forward. The guy I had kicked in the stomach finally caught his breath and walked off under his own power. The guy whose knee I had shattered had to be carried.

"Now, if I cut your woman's eyes out," Red said, "I'd do it surgically. I'd pierce the epidermis right at the corner of the eye, pop the eyeball free, and sever the optical nerve and the central retinal artery. Oh, there would be bleeding, no doubt. You don't sever an artery without drawing blood. And I might nick the sclera, so intraocular fluid would leak along with the blood. But my knives are clean and sharp. My cuts are precise. She'd probably survive.

"If Jeff there tries it with that dagger, well, he's no artiste. He'll just plunge his blade into each socket. He'll probably hit the prefrontal cortex and cause permanent brain damage. He might chip the supraorbital foramen and maybe the zygomatic bone. The wounds will be nasty—a mix of exploded eye, bone, brain, and blood. She'll die. Slowly. Most likely of infection.

"Blinding is not part of the revenge you've earned. The Law of Steel takes the hands of thieves, not their eyes. But I've earned a little fun, don't you think? No one here would begrudge me that. After all, some of them want your head." The crowd hollered and whooped its agreement.

"I'm going to cut your arms free now. Tell me, what are you going to do? Are we going to have some fun with your woman?"

"Nothing," I said through gritted teeth. "I won't do anything."

"A pity," Red said lightly from behind me. "But at least we understand each other." His knife whispered at my back, and the ropes binding my arms fell away. He hadn't even nicked me.

"Kneel and bare one arm. Place it on the chopping block. Your choice which one."

I slowly sank to my knees in front of the log. Its surface was black and scarred. It had been used for this purpose before. I stripped off both gloves and forced my sleeves up to my elbows. I held up my hands, staring at them in horror. They had a slight blue tinge from the cold. I drew in a deep, shuddering breath, trying to decide which hand to sacrifice.

"No hurry," Red said. "We're happy to wait. We'll just amuse ourselves with your woman's lovely brown eyes in the meantime."

Without even thinking about it, I put both arms on the chopping block. Somewhere deep within me a terrified voice wailed no, no, no—a man with one hand is a cripple, a man with none, in this postvolcano world, is dead. My head floated—I was afraid I would pass out, but my voice was still strong and clear. "The thefts were my idea. Take both my hands. I'll pay your knife's price for both of us."

Red tsked. "That's not how the Law of Steel works. Choose an arm. Now."

My fingers curled around the edge of the chopping block. The bark was rough and ridged.

"Jeff," Red said casually, "cut out her left—"

"No!" I yelled. I pulled my right arm off the block.

The *gladius* flashed in a huge arc, and I watched in horror as Red severed my left hand just above the wrist.

Chapter 37

At first there was hardly any pain at all. My left hand and wrist lay on the snow before me, limp without the connection to my brain. Its fingers were already turning blue-gray. It was impossible to believe, impossible to take in. I still felt like I had both hands, like I could command both fists to clench, both thumbs to grip, both sets of fingers to caress. Blood seeped from the hand, staining the snow. Blood spurted from the end of my arm, keeping time with my heart.

Red seized my arm roughly, dragging me over to the fire. I was too dazed to resist. He plunged my stump into the pot of boiling tar. Then there was pain, indescribable in its intensity. The urine I had been holding released in a flood, and I passed out.

• • •

Darla's scream woke me. Red laid her down in the snow beside me. The stump where her right hand had been was covered in black, lumpy tar. Consciousness fled again.

• • •

I was cold, terribly cold. Snow bit into my chest, arms, and legs; a bitter wind lashed my back. I was naked, face down in the snow. One of Red's soldiers was hurrying away from me, carrying my boots and a bundle of damp rags that used to be my clothing. Darla was naked too, and unconscious again.

Red had retreated back to the circle of onlookers. "Let's show 'em off in style!" he roared.

The crowd roared back. It didn't sound like a collection of humans; it sounded like one gargantuan animal proclaiming its terror and rage to the black heavens. A snowball skimmed the ground near me. Another hit Darla's face so hard it rocked her head sideways, splattering ice into her mouth and nose. She screamed and then started coughing.

I tried to go to her, to push myself upright, but in my rush I had forgotten about my missing hand. I planted the stump in the snow. The pain was so intense, black dots danced before my eyes. I collapsed. A ball of ice slashed across my back, and I felt a warm trickle welling in its path.

Darla was crawling toward me, wobbly as a three-legged stool. I cradled my left arm against my chest, moaning with the pain of it. I staggered over to Darla as icy missiles rained around us. We clung to each other with our good arms and started shambling toward the open gate—the only break in the vicious circle of people around us. The volume of their roar swelled, and they rushed closer.

A chunk of ice hit my nose. Blood dripped from my nostrils, streaming across my lips, filling my mouth with the taste of old copper pennies. We ran.

The crowd surged, following us out the gates, pelting us with snow and ice. Their roar had died down, and now we could hear individual epithets, "Thief!" "Warren scum!" and worse. I kept my good arm around Darla's back, my hand under her shoulder, trying to hold her up. She was doing the same for me. My stump was tucked close to my chest, where the snowballs pelting my back couldn't reach it. We ran awkwardly, with our heads down.

Even our most enthusiastic pursuers dropped off after about a mile. My feet, which had burned like I was running across the blue flame of a gigantic gas burner, were numb now. Darla trembled under my arm—we were both shivering uncontrollably.

Bikezilla.

We had to make it to Bikezilla. Our go-bags were strapped to the load bed. They each contained a knife,

food, a fire-starting kit and, most importantly, extra clothing. It was only another mile to the place we had hidden
Bikezilla. We could make it. We would make it.

By the time we got to the right spot, we were both
shivering so badly we could barely walk, let alone run. We
had dragged Bikezilla across the snow berm near the ruins
of a bank. I wasn't sure how we were going to get Bikezilla
back onto the road one-handed. It had been tough enough
even when we were whole and clothed.

Just climbing the embankment naked, shivering, and
one-handed proved to be nearly impossible. I slipped
twice, once falling into Darla and knocking us both back
down to the road. When I finally did reach the summit of
the berm, I got the third worst surprise of the day:
Bikezilla was gone.

Chapter 38

I whimpered and sagged to my knees, utterly defeated. Red must have used the day we had been held captive to follow our tracks and find Bikezilla. He had chopped off our hands, dipped the stumps in tar, and created a show of "law" for his people, but his ultimate intent was for us to die. It looked like he might get his wish. Darla topped the berm behind me. Her hand and feet were a sickly shade of blue-gray. She didn't react much to the hole in the snow where Bikezilla had been, only nodded as if she had been expecting it. She hooked her hand under my shoulder and hauled me upright.

"F-f-farmhouse. On t-t-twenty," she said.

I remembered it. "How f-f-far?"

"T-t-two, three miles."

I nodded and sat down, sliding down the berm on my butt. When I looked back up the berm, I noticed that I had left pinkish streaks of blood in the snow. I tried to stand, but I was shaking so hard, it took three tries just to get up. By that time, Darla was down. Her teeth clacked like an old typewriter. I helped her to her feet, and we wrapped our arms around each other for warmth and support.

We had taken fewer than ten steps before we fell. I threw my arm out to catch myself—it's almost impossible not to, even if your arm ends in a fresh stump—and screamed with pain so fierce that I nearly passed out. Darla had done the same thing. We lay in the road, shaking spastically like fish drowning in air.

I forced myself to my feet and helped Darla up. We took a few more steps and fell again.

We had fallen four or five times before I got to where I could keep my injured arm tucked in and allow my shoulder to absorb the force of the falls. After nine or ten falls, I looked back. We had come less than four hundred feet. The dark shell of the bank was still clearly visible despite the waning light. There was no way we were going to travel three miles before dark. I wasn't sure I could walk another three miles at all. After dark the farmhouse would be invisible from the road. We could pass it and keep walking, oblivious, until our bodies gave out and only our ghosts could continue stalking the icy roads, searching for shelter in a barren world.

I turned Darla around and pointed at the bank with my stump. She nodded wearily, and we started retracing our steps.

Crossing the snow berm again to get to the bank was the worst part. I crawled up three-legged but still slipped backward over and over. I gritted my teeth against the pain, paying for every foot of height I gained with bloody knees and a bloody palm.

We found a hollow in a corner of the bank protected from the wind. The snow was shallow there. I dug downward. We needed a fire, something to help us survive the night. All I found were shards of glass from the bank's windows and a few chunks of burnt lumber.

Darla was digging a hole in the side of the snowdrift at the edge of this sheltered spot. I picked up a large piece of glass and tried to carve a charred stick of wood with it, holding the wood between my numb feet. I had a vague idea that I could make a fire bow. Instead I cut my only hand.

Darla had almost disappeared inside the snowdrift. I grabbed a brick and started beating it against the wall. There were no sparks, no matter how hard I knocked the bricks together. Still, I kept trying until Darla laid a shaking hand on my shoulder and motioned for me to follow.

We crawled into the tiny space she had excavated inside the snowdrift. She kicked at the ceiling of the tunnel until it collapsed behind us, sealing us in. Our body heat warmed the small space, but not enough. We needed clothing—some kind of insulation from the frozen ground beneath us. My shivering eased, and I felt a wonderful warmth spreading through my body. That made me feel worse, though. When you get so cold that you feel warm, it's a sign that your body is preparing to shut down. I knew—I'd been this far gone into hypothermia once before. I held Darla tightly, squeezing our bodies together, trying to conserve heat.

"We're going to die here, right?" I said.

"Probably," Darla sighed.

My mind wandered through a long silence. In the darkness and false warmth of Darla's embrace, I imagined we were drifting through a surreal landscape of blue fields and emerald sky.

Darla's soft voice called me back. "You . . . you think there's anything after this?"

"I don't know." I'd been devout once, attending Sunday school and services, well, religiously. But that had ended about the time I turned twelve. Now I wasn't sure. "If there is an omnipotent God, he's an asshole for allowing all this to happen."

"I hope there is something after this," Darla said. "Mom was sure of it. She had unshakeable faith—even the eruption didn't change her belief. . . . I'd like to see her again."

"You think you can get married in heaven? Or purgatory, or whatever?"

"I don't know. Why?"

"I wanted us to . . . I'd been, I thought that little jewelry store in downtown Stockton might have—"

"That's why you wanted to go downtown—you must have asked me four times."

"Twice. I wanted a ring. To propose the right way, you know."

Darla kissed me. I was so cold that I couldn't even feel it. Sad—that I couldn't appreciate our last kiss. "When you were passed out back there in Stockton and I had to put my hand on the block, I had this strange daydream—just a flash, a single image. We were standing in front of a huge crowd, in a wedding dress and tux—"

"You'd look great in a tux," I said.

"Shut up. Let me finish," Darla said. "We were holding hands, your right and my left, in front of all those people, and I wanted that picture to be true. So I put my right arm on the block."

"I wondered why. That's a pretty stupid reason to give up your good hand."

"Yeah."

"And you're supposed to be more practical than I am."

"Yeah."

"I wish I'd gone ahead and proposed, ring or no ring. I'd have liked to see that picture you daydreamed. I'd have liked being your husband."

"Look, Alex," Darla's voice had shifted, low and fierce now instead of wistful, "there are people who get married but live separate lives, people who marry and divorce before they've been together even as long as we have. They say marriage is a sacrament, that it's a legal contract, but here's what I think it is—a commitment. And by that standard, we're already married, more married than most of the people who have the license. I've watched

Alyssa, I know she still lusts after you, and she's far sexier than I'll ever be—"

"No, she's not."

"Oh, bullshit. I've seen your tongue hanging out when she sashays past. Max worships the snow she walks on."

"It's hard not to look," I conceded.

"That's not the point. Even when you thought I might be dead, you kept faith with me. And sometimes I catch you looking at me, and even though you look nothing like him, you remind me of how Dad used to look at Mom."

"I love you," I said.

"I'm not sure what I ever did to be worthy of it—"

"You—"

"Never mind. You said God's an asshole, but did you ever stop to think, if not for the volcano, we'd never have met?"

"And we wouldn't be dying in a snowdrift."

"It was worth it, Alex." I felt her teardrop land on my nose. "It was worth it."

I held her tightly. It got harder and harder to talk as we froze slowly to the ground, merging with it. Finally we drifted off, arms wrapped around each other, entering the longest night as one.

Chapter 39

I woke in excruciating pain. My skin was on fire with a heat that tingled and surged and spiked, as if thousands of sharp needles were being poked into me one after the other. I'd gone to Hell, and the welcoming committee was a thousand berserk acupuncturists.

I tried to open my eyes. A flickering, reddish light blinded me. Maybe I really was in Hell. My head was foggy; I couldn't focus. I shook my head, trying to clear it, but that resulted in pain so intense it nearly drowned out the needles in my body. I lay still for a moment, trying to collect my thoughts, to understand what was happening. The front side of my body was uncomfortably hot, almost burning. There was something rough against my skin. And someone was pressed against my back. Not Darla—but I couldn't have said how I could tell.

Darla. I forced my eyes back open, heedless of the glare, propped myself up on a wobbly arm, and looked around.

We were still in the corner of the ruined bank. A large fire blazed, shielded from the wind and Stockton by the bank's brick walls. Darla was nearby, facing the fire on her side like I was. A woman was pressed up against my back, another pressed against Darla's back. A thin man with a face as hard and sharp as a hatchet—maybe in his early forties—fed the fire while a seven- or eight-year-old girl dug in the snow and ash, finding charred scraps of lumber and passing them to the man. The little girl was wrapped up tight, in an oversized pink coat with a fur-trimmed hood. Only her cherubic red cheeks and face were visible.

"Shh," the woman behind me said. "Lay back down. You need to warm up, sleep, and heal."

"Darla," my voice sounded more like a frog croaking than human speech.

"She's okay. Let her sleep. You're safe. If we'd wanted to harm you, all we had to do was nothing."

That made sense. I lowered myself back down, noticing for the first time that both the woman and I were wrapped in several blankets. I put my head on her arm and slept.

• • •

I woke to the woman shaking my shoulder. "Wake up, wake up," she whispered. "We got to move on before daybreak. If we could find you, Red's men could too."

The mention of Red snapped me to full awareness. Darla was standing nearby, the firelight playing in red shadows across her skin. She was struggling to step into a pair of long johns one-handed. The woman—girl, I saw now—who had slept against her was trying to help.

I stood, shivering in the frozen air. To shiver was joyous—it meant my body had warmed up to the point where it knew the difference between hot and cold. My remaining fingers throbbed, my toes felt like someone was actively sawing at them with a knife, and the scrapes on my back hurt, but otherwise I seemed okay.

The woman dug a pair of long johns out of a pack next to her and held them open for me to step into. It suddenly occurred to me to be embarrassed—here I was letting my freak flag fly practically in her face. I hurried to put on the long johns, although my one-handed efforts were agonizingly slow.

They had two full sets of clothing, including winter coats, gloves, scarves, hats—even boots. Everything was too big for me and Darla, but we made do, rolling up cuffs and pants legs, wearing three pairs of socks, and stuffing a fourth pair into the toes of the oversized boots. Whenever I shoved my stump into a piece of clothing, just the cloth running over it was agonizing. It wasn't bleeding, though—the tar had frozen to a hard lump that sealed the end of my arm effectively. I let the shirts and coats hang long over the stump.

"Who are you?" I asked as the woman helped me dress. "Why are you doing this? Not that I'm not grateful."

"We've got to hurry," the man said. "We need to be miles away before daybreak."

"I'm Alex," I said, holding my hand out to him.

He shook it quickly. "Hurry!"

I tried to hurry, but I was clumsy, unsure of my new center of gravity, and suffering the aftereffects of nearly freezing to death.

"I'm Isaac, but most folks call me Zik," he said. "My wife, Mary." The woman helping me dress nodded. "And our girls, Charlotte and Bronwyn."

"Just Wyn," the youngest girl said. She was dumping armloads of snow on the fire. As soon as we were dressed and the fire was out, we left. Each of the four of them had a pack. I offered to carry one, but Zik refused.

They practically dragged us over the snow berm to the road. Neither Darla nor I were moving very well. I picked myself up on the far side of the berm and started staggering down the road away from Stockton.

"Can you run?" Zik asked. "We have to get away from here."

Instead of answering, I started jogging.

"Run as long as you can, and then we'll walk awhile."

I nodded. I wanted to talk to find out more about our rescuers, but I didn't have the breath for it.

As we approached the intersection where Highway 20 met 13, Mary asked, "Which way?"

Darla leaned toward me, gasping. "Do we trust them?" she whispered.

I thought about it for a moment. They had saved our lives, no doubt about it. But would showing them how to get to the homestead endanger Anna, Max, and the rest? What if that was the point of this whole forked-up situation? "Lead them to one of the houses we're scavenging." I paused to catch my breath. "Maybe the one southeast of the homestead."

Darla nodded, and instead of turning left on 13, the more direct route to the homestead, she told Mary to continue straight on 20.

We jogged in silence, listening for any hint of pursuit, constantly looking over our shoulders. Either no one was following us, or we eluded them. We jogged for about a mile, walked for about a mile, and then stopped for a short break and a little water. Repeating that about five times brought us to one of the farmhouses we had partially dismantled; a trip we could have made in less than two hours on Bikezilla took the rest of the night and all morning.

I almost expected to see Ed or Max at the farmhouse, but no one was there. Half the roof was missing, as if some gargantuan monster had taken a bite of the house, found its taste lacking, and moved on in search of juicier prey. We'd been working on dismantling its roof—the long rafters were perfect for supporting the glass roof of a greenhouse.

"You live here?" Zik said.

"No," I replied. Maybe it was rude, but I decided it was

best to be clear. "We're grateful—you saved our lives. But we're not sure we should show you our new homestead."

Mary whirled to face me. "We have nowhere else to go," she said. "Red will kill us if we go back to Stockton."

"So you're from Stockton?" I asked.

"Let's get inside," Darla suggested. "You have a fire-starting kit?"

"We've got something better," Charlotte said. She stepped around behind her dad and dug through his pack, coming up with a lighter. "It works."

Darla eyed it lustfully. "Nice. Come on inside." She held the front door open—we had broken the lock getting inside the first time. "I'll build a fire while you guys hash things out."

"I'll help you," Charlotte offered.

We trooped into the living room, and Darla set about collecting scraps of lumber and arranging them in the fireplace. I tried sitting on the moldy couch, but that aggravated the lacerations on my back and butt. I crouched near the fireplace instead.

"When Stockton ran out of food the first time," Zik said, "I was drafted to fight—I was there when we attacked Warren. It was horrible. The people I shot at . . . they were my neighbors, some of them my friends. We yelled at each other across the gymnasium during basketball season: Blackhawks versus Warriors. Hell, we were on the same side in baseball and softball; we fielded a combined team called the Warhawks. But I didn't dare say no to Red. He could've hurt Mary or the girls. So I went along and shot to miss.

"So when we started to run out of food again a couple of months ago, I was afraid I'd be forced to fight. Afraid I'd have to shoot at friends and neighbors again. We were already planning to flee. I . . . I wish we had run then."

"We were wondering how Stockton was getting food," I said.

"I was too—for a while, at least. We started getting packages of wheat, corn, and rice in Chinese packaging, black beans, even dried fruit: stuff we hadn't seen in more than a year. I had no idea where it was coming from. Red's not exactly the chatty type."

"Except about his damn knives," I said.

"I'd like to jam a knife so far up his ass, he'd taste it," Darla said.

"Yeah, he does go on about those knives," Zik said. "Anyway, we heard rumors. Girls were disappearing."

I instantly thought of the Maquoketa FEMA camp. We had stopped the Peckerwoods from raiding it for slaves—were they turning to another source?

"It was only rumors for a few weeks. People missing. Nobody we knew well. And then they took Emily."

Mary leaned close. The small fire Darla had built was magnified in her eyes. "They took her from me. Tore her right out of my arms! She's only fifteen."

"Who?" I asked.

"Red's men," Zik said. "Later, I bribed one of them to talk. Cost me a week's rations. They traded Emily for food. Red is selling the girls of our town to some prison gang . . . for food."

"To the Peckerwoods?" I asked.

"How'd you know?"

"They run in this area. Used to hang around Anamosa and Maquoketa in Iowa too, but most of that group is dead. Might be some still in Cascade."

Mary seized my left shoulder, rattling it so hard that my stump bumped against my chest. I couldn't suppress a low moan. Mary was oblivious. "You know them? You know where they took Emily? Where she is? Tell me!"

I peeled her hand off my shoulder. "I don't know where they took her. They could have traded her to the Dirty White Boys—that's what they did with Darla when they had her. Or maybe there are other gangs—there must be."

"They had her," Mary said, looking at Darla, "and you brought her back?"

I waited until Mary looked back at me and met her gaze, holding it. "I did."

"You could find Emily."

"No. I have responsibilities here. And my father got killed looking for Darla."

"I'm sorry," Zik said to me. He turned to his wife, speaking softly, "Honey, we've got to focus on keeping Wyn and Charlotte safe. We get them settled, then we'll go looking for Emily. I swear it."

Mary glared at her husband.

"I don't like it any better than you do," Zik said.

"So how'd you find us?" I asked. "And why?"

"We were there when they . . . shortened your arms," Zik said. "No choice. Everyone's got to attend those things—gets the bad lot feeling all patriotic and scares the pants off the good guys. We need a place to go—figured you might take us in, in return for our help. So we snuck over the wall after dark and started looking for you. You weren't hard to find. I figured that bank was the only shelter you'd be able to reach in your altogethers."

"You want to join our homestead."

Zik nodded.

"Everyone works—long days, some nights on guard duty too."

"We'll pull our weight and then some, if we can manage it."

Darla whispered in my ear. "What if they're spies?"

I thought about that idea—it didn't seem likely, but it was possible. "You wouldn't be allowed to leave the homestead without permission. Maybe not allowed to leave at all for a few months. I can't take the risk that you might lead others to us."

"We need to look for Emily." Mary's voice was freighted with anguish.

"That's a fair precaution," Zik said. "But as soon as you see you can trust us, I want permission to go looking for my daughter."

"You work out, and I'll do everything I can to help."

I held out my good hand, and Zik shook it. Suddenly I was responsible for twelve souls. I felt every one of them keenly, weights burdening my already sagging shoulders.

Chapter 40

When I stepped out of the abandoned house where we had been talking, I saw two figures in the distance, trudging down the road toward me. I backed up, reentering the house and closing the door. "Someone's out there. You all bring any weapons?"

"Just knives," Zik said.

I stepped over to the window. We had already taken all the glass, so the drape flapped in the wind, giving me an intermittent glimpse of the road. When the figures had halved the distance to the farmhouse, I could make out their faces: Uncle Paul and Max. I flung open the door and ran down the road toward them, with Darla hot on my heels.

"Uncle Paul! Max!" I cried.

"Alex!" he yelled and then doubled over coughing. By the time he was able to resume talking, we had reached him. "We were headed to Stockton. Figured maybe Bikezilla broke—" His breath caught in his throat, and he suddenly stopped. After a short pause, glancing back and forth between me and Darla, he said, "My God. Your hands."

"Red caught us," I said flatly.

"I'll kill that mother—"

"Get in line," Darla said.

"I should never have let you go there," Uncle Paul said.

"No." I grabbed his arm. "No regrets. We're alive because of the supplies we got in our raids. If you'd told me before all this started that I'd have to trade my hand to get the homestead up and running, I would have done it."

"Me too," Darla added.

Max was staring at my stump with grim fascination. "Did it hurt? Having your hand chopped off?"

"No, Max, it was completely painless," I said.

"Christ," Darla said to Uncle Paul, "what kind of idiots are you raising?"

"Sorry," Max said.

"I think we're both a little rattled," Uncle Paul said.

"Not as much as we were," Darla muttered.

I looked back—Zik's family huddled inside the still-open door. "I need to introduce you to Zik and his family. They saved our lives."

After the introductions, we all trudged back to the homestead together. I asked Uncle Paul to get the newcomers settled in and explain the situation to everyone else. Darla and I headed for our bedrolls. It was just after lunchtime, but we were dead on our feet.

When we next woke, Dr. McCarthy was there, holding a work light on an extension cord and examining my stump in minute detail. "Satan's teeth, Alex. Would you please quit bringing me unusual injuries to treat?"

"Last time," I said. "I promise."

He snorted in disbelief. "Your setup out here is unbelievable. Thought I'd never see working electricity again. I want to switch the light on and off a few dozen times just for the joy of it. Like kids do when they grow tall enough to reach the switches."

"You'd better not," Darla said from her bedroll beside me. "Wears out the bulbs faster."

"I won't. But I'm tempted to move out here."

"You and Belinda would be welcome anytime," I said. "But don't tell anyone where we are, okay?" I would have preferred it if no one but Rebecca knew, but I could see why Uncle Paul had felt the need to fetch the doctor.

"I won't. I'm not going to mention your electric lights either. You might wind up with tourists out here if I did."

"What about, you know, our arms?" I asked. "What do we do about them?"

"Other than calling us Mr. and Mrs. Stumpy," Darla said.

"What, are congratulations in order?" Dr. McCarthy asked. "You got married and didn't invite me to the wedding?"

"No . . ." I said.

"Yes . . ." Darla said at almost the same time.

"Sort of," I amended.

"Well when you figure it out, let me know," Dr. McCarthy said. "Anyway, your arms . . . I'm not sure."

Not exactly what you want to hear your doctor saying.

"You've got burns from the tar Red used to seal your stumps, and normally we'd want the burns to get some air, but if I go mucking around in there trying to get the tar off your skin, I'm afraid I'll reopen or infect your wounds. Might be best to do nothing."

"So a bionic hand is out of the question?" I said.

Dr. McCarthy smiled, but his eyes were sad. "Afraid so." He reached into his old-timey, black leather doctor's bag and pulled out a bottle of pills, opened it, and counted out ten. "Take one a day each for the next five days."

"What are they?" I asked as he poured them into my hand.

"Antibiotic. Levaquin."

I was so startled, I almost dropped the pills. Antibiotics were priceless—I could probably buy twenty weeks' worth of food with the ten pills in my hand. "Thank you."

"Mayor's been buying them. He's got a source, but he won't tell me who. I suspect he's trading with one of the gangs. Medical supplies are about the only thing he'll trade pork for. And I figure we owe you, even if he doesn't see it that way."

"You look at our feet yet?" I asked.

"No. Why?"

"Pretty sure they're frostbitten. Might be more along the side of my body." I started taking off my clothing, which was sort of embarrassing given the fact that we were in a one-room longhouse, and I hadn't really figured out how to undress myself one-handed. But I wanted him to check us both over thoroughly. Frostbite can be deadly.

One of my toes—the little one on my right foot, which had rested against the ground—was completely black and lifeless.

"That toe's going to have to come off, Alex."

"Don't you think I've lost enough body parts?"

"Too many. But if I leave that dead toe on there, all the antibiotics in the world won't help you. You'll lose the rest of your body parts—all at once."

I sighed heavily. "Well, get out your hedge clippers, then."

"I think I'll use a scalpel, if it's all the same to you. I'll need three pans of boiling water and a couple of helpers."

Ed and Max volunteered to help. The four of us lapsed into a tense silence while waiting for the water to boil. When the water was ready and the scalpels sterilized, Dr. McCarthy fumbled around in his medical bag, finally pulling out a leather-wrapped stick.

"I guess you still don't have any painkillers," I said.

"No. Sorry." He passed me the stick, and Ed and Max took hold of my leg. I bit down on the stick; the leather was slick and tasted slightly of soap and salt.

When Dr. McCarthy started working his scalpel around my toe, I screamed—I couldn't help myself. The sound that escaped around the stick sounded more like the trumpet of a tortured swan than anything human. Darla put her hand in mine, and I gripped it fiercely. Then, mercifully, I passed out.

When I awoke, I discovered that Darla had lost two of the toes from her left foot. Dr. McCarthy left us with a long list of things to watch out for around our wounds: redness, streaking, swelling, pus—the usual signs of infection. Darla and I had dealt with it before.

I slept through most of the next five days. Every now and then I would wake and stare at the stump on the end of my left arm. The tar had cracked, and red, burnt skin was visible in the cracks, forming a crazed red-and-black patchwork looking more like an arm that belonged on Sauron the Deceiver than on anything human.

It hurt terribly—far worse than it had at the moment it had been lopped off. Yet I could still feel my missing hand, still tell it to clench and unclench. Doing so sent waves of pain washing up my arm, but I did it anyway, holding up my arm, making my phantom hand form a phantom fist over and over again, relishing the pain in some sick way.

Darla lay next to me. She was always asleep when I woke. I didn't wake her, didn't want her to see me staring at my stump, manipulating my invisible fist until the pain made tears run down my face.

I woke one day to an argument. Uncle Paul was sitting on a nearby cot, trying to convince Darla to come help him wire the inside of a heating tank. She kept saying she couldn't, that one-handed, she'd only get in the way. He told her he didn't know how to do it, which sounded like

BS to me. Finally Darla sighed and levered herself up out of the cot. I pretended to sleep through the whole thing.

The next morning I woke to Uncle Paul shaking my shoulder. I was deep in a dream about flashing knives, and I lashed out, hitting Uncle Paul in the chest with my stump. The pain was so intense that tears involuntarily poured from my eyes. Uncle Paul either didn't notice or pretended not to.

"Darla needs you," he said.

I glanced at the cot beside mine; Darla wasn't there. "What's wrong?"

"She's just sitting in the greenhouse, staring at her stump. She doesn't say anything or do anything unless I ask her to and tell her directly and exactly what I need. She's like a robot."

"We've both had a rough week, if you hadn't noticed."

"Yeah, I noticed. And Darla's one of the toughest women I've ever met. But everyone needs some help sometimes. She needs you."

I rolled over to face away from him. "I'm tired," I said, which was true.

I heard Uncle Paul standing up behind me. "Think about it, would you?"

I grunted something noncommittal, and he left. How was I supposed to help Darla when I didn't even want to get out of bed? How was I even supposed to put on my boots one-handed? How would half a man be useful to anyone, let alone her? I rolled over, heedless of the pain it caused my stump, and tried to get back to sleep.

Chapter 41

I couldn't sleep. The image of Darla sitting in the greenhouse, flexing her phantom hand, had wormed into my mind and wouldn't leave. I tossed and turned for more than an hour and then threw the covers off, hunting around for some clothes.

Getting dressed one-handed is ridiculously challenging. Buttons, zippers, drawstrings, shoelaces—all of them are designed to be operated two-handed. I cussed at imaginary clothing designers in the most inventive terms I could think of. Velcro: Why didn't they make everything with Velcro fasteners? It worked fine for toddlers.

I didn't go straight to Darla. Instead I talked to Max, Zik, Ben, Alyssa, Anna, and Charlotte, looking for an item I wanted to give to Darla. Wyn had one, and she handed it over gravely, warning me that it didn't work—it hadn't brought her sister Emily back.

Darla was on her back on the dirt floor of the under-construction greenhouse. Her head was turned so she could stare at her stump, and I could see the muscles in her arm tensing and relaxing, over and over.

Uncle Paul was messing with some wire nearby. When he saw me, he smiled and said, "I'm going to go get lunch. Want me to bring you guys something?"

"No," I replied, "we'll be along in a bit." I flopped down alongside Darla as Uncle Paul left the greenhouse. Darla didn't even look at me.

"I got you a gift," I said.

Darla didn't respond, so I pulled out the item Wyn had given me, a lucky rabbit's foot, and held it in front of Darl's head, where she couldn't fail to see it.

"What the hell?" Darla said.

"Well, I thought, you know, the last time you were so . . . anyway, your rabbit, Jack, seemed to pop you out of it, so I thought—"

"You thought giving me a dead rabbit's foot and reminding me of my mother and my dead rabbit would cheer me up?"

"Um . . . yeah?"

"Christ, Alex. That is the most idiotic, wrongheaded . . . and sweetest thing anyone has ever done for me."

"So you don't want the rabbit's foot?"

"I didn't say that." Darla snatched the rabbit's foot from my hand and tucked it into her pocket.

"You hungry?" I asked.

"Yeah."

I stood and reached down with my good hand to help Darla up. I wrapped my good arm around her waist, and we leaned on each other, walking toward the greenhouse door. "We're going to get through this."

"I know. It's just—every morning I wake up, and I'm sure I still have a hand. Even when I stare at that damn stump, I can feel my hand moving, my fingers flexing."

"I know."

"Red's got to pay for this."

"He will. Sooner or later, he will."

Darla and I started working half days. We still needed far more sleep than normal; most of our energy was being spent on healing. Dr. McCarthy stopped by every two or three days for a while, checking our arms and feet, although it wasn't really necessary—they were doing fine. Maybe the antibiotics had worked, or maybe the boiling tar had killed all the bacteria in our stumps. After about three weeks, the tar on our forearms started to flake off as new skin grew beneath it. The new skin was pink, shiny, and hairless—it looked like it belonged on a newborn piglet, not my arm. One thing you could say for Red—he was precise. He had chopped through our forearms in the exact same place, about an inch from the wrist.

As soon as we could, we started trying to learn how to do everything one-handed. Darla had a rougher time of it than I—she was trying to train her left hand to do jobs she'd used her dominant hand for before.

Some tasks were ridiculously challenging—climbing the ladder to the sniper's nest, for example. I finally managed it by hooking my left elbow over each rung as I ascended. It was painfully slow, and by the time I reached the platform, I was shaky and sweating. I rested up there for nearly an hour before starting down the ladder—that was worse still.

It was even harder to relearn to shoot. Operating the bolt on the hunting rifle was a problem—the whole rifle would move instead of just the bolt. I had to move my left forearm to the top of the rifle, hold it down, rack the bolt, and then get back into a shooting position. Not exactly fast or efficient. And while I could line up one shot fine, I had no way to control the recoil. My rate of fire wasn't even a quarter as good as it had been before I lost my hand.

The semi-automatic rifles were easier, but reloading was still a pain. I could either roll the rifle onto its back to give me something to push against when I needed to seat a new magazine, or I could cradle the rifle against my body.

It didn't really matter—I had never been much good with any kind of firearm. And I didn't take myself or Darla off the watch rotation, despite the difficulty we had climbing the turbine tower. Hurt or not, it didn't feel right to ask everyone else to do something I wouldn't do.

Zik's family pitched in with a mad fervor. They seemed determined to outwork everyone, as if they were terrified we'd kick them out if they didn't. We finished the third greenhouse and started building a fourth.

All the tar gradually flaked off our stumps, as if it had been a scab, leaving behind a riotous mess of scar tissue, scabs, and new pink skin. Dr. McCarthy debrided the wound, cutting away some of the scabs, while Ed and Max held my arm still. It hurt so intensely that I nearly passed out. Then he stretched out the skin, stitching it up to protect the end of the bone. That hurt too, but not nearly so bad as the debriding.

Our arms healed faster after that. As soon as my arm quit hurting, it started to itch like ten thousand starving fleas were trapped under my skin. The itching was almost worse than the pain. Every now and then, I unwrapped all my coats and sleeves from the stump and plunged it into a snowbank. That stopped the itching—for a few minutes.

About a week later, the itching started to subside, and my thoughts turned to practical matters. A bionic hand was impossible, but could I fight with the stump? How could I make it more useful?

I went looking for Darla and found her standing on a stepladder, trying to string wire one-handed across the rafters in the shell of the greenhouse, cussing softly as she worked.

"You know what we need?" I said to her back.

She startled, hitting her head on a rafter. "Christ! Don't sneak up on me!"

"We need hooks."

She stepped off the ladder and turned to face me. "Do you want an eye patch too? Halloween was . . ." she stopped to think, "six weeks ago."

I put my good arm around her waist. "If we had hooks instead of stumps, we could climb the ladder in the turbine tower way easier. We could make the hooks the right size to hold a rifle barrel, so we could shoot and reload faster." What I meant, of course, was that she could build the hooks that size. I had no clue how to even start making a hook.

Darla started to get excited. "I could rig them on a leather cuff, run a strap back to our elbows to keep them on tight."

"Might even be better than a stump in a fight."

"Heck, yeah. I could even rig different attachments— how would you like a knife sprouting from the end of your stump?"

"Hmm. I'd probably be wearing the hook whenever I needed the knife. Could you sharpen the outer edge of the hook?"

"Sure. But I'm never going to make out with you again. Knowing our luck, you'd give me a mastectomy by mistake."

"I'll take it off," I said, trying to suppress a giggle.

"I'm putting a ratchet and a socket for screwdriver bits on mine. That's going to make some stuff so much easier."

Darla started spending most of her time working on the hooks. That slowed down our greenhouse building some, but it also seemed to banish the last of her lingering funk, so I didn't object. We were producing more food than we needed anyway.

It took Darla almost two months to finish the hooks. It was more of a job for a blacksmith than an amateur welder, she said. Several early prototypes broke. When she was finally done, my hook was a thing of beauty. A smoothly curved, C-shaped blade, sharpened to a razor's edge on the outside and rounded off on the inside. Darla's was ugly by comparison. She only sharpened the point of her hook because of the ungainly ratchet and driver bit attachments welded along its length.

I practiced endlessly, developing modifications of my taekwondo forms to take into account the deadly blade on the end of my left arm. I also spent hours upon hours of mind-numbingly boring practice with the guns—not firing them, just picking them up, aiming, and reloading. I had to be sure I could get the hook in exactly the right spot in the dark, when I was shivering from the cold, and when I was hopped up on adrenaline, which ruined my fine motor control. I got to the point where I could use the hook so well that it was almost as good as my lost hand, at least for shooting. It might be better than a hand in a fight, I mused. I could bring it to bear a lot faster than a belt knife or a gun. In close combat, the first unblocked strike can win the fight, so speed is critical.

Max found me during one of my practice sessions. I was on watch in the sniper's nest, so I made use of the time with a little drill. I would scan the horizon with the binoculars and pick out a landmark. Then I would close my eyes, spin two or three times, and try to pick up the unloaded rifle and get it aimed at the landmark without reopening my eyes. I was getting pretty good at it too.

I was in the middle of a drill when I heard a knock on the hatch. I stopped and snagged the eye with my hook, dragging the hatch open. Max poked his head up into the sniper's nest. "What are you doing up here? Sounds like a herd of elephants stomping on the floor."

"Just a drill," I explained while he climbed up into the sniper's nest, letting the hatch bang shut behind him.

"Cool," Max said. "You can do that? Find a target with your eyes closed?"

"Usually. I've been practicing awhile," I said. "What brings you up here, anyway? You're not on watch until tonight, right?"

"Yeah. I wanted to talk to you. We're almost ready to start the fifth greenhouse, and we have to wire up a new wind turbine."

"Yeah . . ." Darla and I had gone over this with everyone already. Why was Max rehashing it?

"We're going to need a ton of heavy-gauge wire. I'm going to go to Stockton and get it."

"Wait, what? Are you nuts?" I held my hook-topped stump up between us and shook it at him. "Nobody's going back to Stockton. Ever. Unless we come by a high-powered rifle, scope, and someone who knows how to use it, then I might mount an expedition to snipe Red—but from a hell of a long way off."

"I could do it," Max said. "I could get the wire we need."

"I'm sure you could. Darla and I raided that place four times, no problem. But the fifth was a bloody bitch. Maybe you'd be fine. Maybe you'd get caught on your first raid. No, absolutely not. Your dad would forbid it too."

"I'm fourteen and a half—almost as old as you were when the volcano erupted."

"And we treat you that way. You work as hard as any of us. You stand watch like the rest of us. But—"

"But you don't trust me to do the really important stuff." Max reached down to open the hatch.

I stepped on the hatch cover, holding it closed and preventing him from leaving. "If that's the case, I don't trust myself either, 'cause I'm not going back to Stockton."

"Yeah, whatever."

"What's going on?"

"Nothing," Max said. "Can I leave now?"

"No. You know, the only person who'll be impressed if you get a bunch of wire is Darla. You're not trying to horn in on me, are you?"

"What? No! I would never—"

"I know. Darla wouldn't be interested either. I mean, you're a good-looking guy, but—"

"Alyssa doesn't think so," Max muttered.

So that was what this mood was about. Max reached for the hatch again, but I didn't move. I thought about how to respond, until the break in the conversation got uncomfortably long. "Are you the one who's been leaving Alyssa gifts?"

"She thinks you're leaving them," Max said. "She got a gold-and-diamond bracelet last week."

"Hmm. I hadn't heard about that one. Where's all this stuff coming from?"

"There's lots of jewelry left in the farmhouses we're taking apart for supplies."

That made sense. Gold and gems were pretty much worthless. You couldn't eat them or start a fire with them, after all. Most people wouldn't bother bending over to pick up the Hope Diamond these days. "So you *are* the one leaving her gifts?"

"No," Max said emphatically. "You're not?"

"Are you nuts? Darla would skin me alive."

"I wonder who's doing it?" Max said. "I wish they'd quit. I don't stand a chance with her."

"That's not true. Who's the most important person in Alyssa's life?"

"You are," Max said instantly.

"Wrong. Guess again."

"You ever seen her looking at you? Wish she'd look at me that way."

"Be serious."

"Ben. She cares about Ben."

"Right. Maybe someday she'll tell you what she did to protect Ben when the Peckerwoods had them both—she hasn't told me much of it, but it wasn't pretty. She's as tough as any of us, as tough as Darla, but in a different way."

"So what are you saying?"

"You follow Alyssa around like a puppy looking for its mother's teats—you should be following Ben."

"All Ben cares about is military stuff—he seems all right, but it gets boring."

"What do you think we're headed for anyway?"

"What do you mean?"

"Think about it. We're doing okay because nobody thinks to look for us out here. This is supposed to be an empty field with a bunch of wind turbines. As far as I know, only Dr. McCarthy and Rebecca know where we are. Will that last?"

"Maybe."

"Be real. We're ranging all over this area scavenging stuff. And we're going to continue to expand. We need a huge food surplus, in case something goes wrong."

"Yeah. I guess someone will notice eventually." Max shifted from foot to foot uncomfortably.

"And what happens if Red or someone like him finds us?"

"Nothing good."

"That's why the walls of the longhouse are so thick—why we built the sniper's nest, and why we'll be building more of them. But still, if Red finds us, we don't stand a chance. He's got a standing army of something like 150 men."

"What're we going to do?"

"We need allies. Or a much bigger population. A military of our own. See where I'm going with this?"

"Yeah. I've got it."

I backed off the hatch to let him open it. "And Max, please don't do anything stupid. I've got enough on my plate, okay?"

"I won't."

I reached out my good hand to shake but thought better of it and pulled him into a rough hug.

• • •

The biggest problem that we hadn't solved to my satisfaction was water. We'd started out melting snow, but after a couple of months, we had used up all the nearby snow. With a dozen people and four greenhouses, we needed hundreds of gallons every day. The easiest way to get it was from the well at one of the abandoned farmhouses, but that meant someone had to haul it back. Two of us, on a rotating schedule, spent all day dragging a sled loaded with water bottles back and forth nearly a mile each way from a demolished farmhouse to our greenhouses. It was an incredible waste of manpower.

Darla had come up with two possible solutions. We could bury a pipe below the frost line and bring the water to us with a powerful pump. For that to work, we would need a lot of pipe and electrical wire that we didn't have. We also weren't sure how deep the frost line would become if this unending winter continued. The other— and better—possibility was to drill our own well. For that, we needed drilling equipment that we didn't have and neither Darla nor Uncle Paul knew how to use.

I put Max in charge of solving the water problem and asked Ed to help and keep an eye on him. Some responsibility might help settle Max down—at least I hoped so.

To prepare, I helped Max and Ed make ghillie suits using the technique Rita Mae, the librarian in Worthington, had taught me. The suits had to blend in with the snow, so we made them by sewing strips cut from an old white sheet onto coats and coverall pants.

As I worked, I thought about Rita Mae and Worthington, Darla's hometown. I hoped Rita Mae was okay. I hadn't spent much time with her, but she had always listened to me and treated me well, despite the fact that I had been a stranger to Worthington and a teenager.

When we finished, the suits made Max and Ed look like shaggy white Yetis—completely covered in strips of cloth sewn to their ski masks, coats, backpacks, and cover-all pants. When they dropped flat and lay motionless in the snow, they were very difficult to spot, even though I knew where to look. I liked the effect so much that I insisted on making two more suits—one for me and one for Darla, just in case.

When we finished the suits, Max and Ed started visiting nearby towns to the east. Mostly they were looking for old phone books. A Yellow Pages that listed all the well-drilling companies in northwest Illinois would be perfect. That'd at least give us a lead on where to find the equipment.

They visited Gratiot, Apple River, Lena, and Winslow. They were all empty, burned, and dead quiet. Every scrap of edible food had long since been looted and eaten. Almost everything flammable was gone: furniture had been broken for firewood, books torn up as kindling. If there were any Yellow Pages around in the first place, they were long gone.

One morning Max and Ed had just returned from an overnight trek to Cadiz and Browntown and were reporting on the towns' conditions—depressingly similar to the other towns they had explored—when Max stopped talking midsentence.

"You hear that?" Max said after a brief pause.

"What?" Ed said, but I had heard it too. We rushed to the door of the longhouse. Outside, the noise was clearer: the distant, echoing pop of gunfire. Were we under attack? And by whom?

Chapter 42

Our lookout was supposed to hit the panic button in the sniper nest if anyone unknown approached. Why hadn't anyone heard the alarm? Who was on duty in the sniper's nest? Charlotte, I thought—Zik's daughter. She was new, but she'd been completely reliable up until now. I scanned the horizon but couldn't see the source of the gunfire. "Get up top, Ed. Find out why Charlotte hasn't pushed the alarm. Stay up there. Have her spot while you shoot, if necessary."

"Sir!" Ed said and took off at a run.

I turned to Max. "Find everyone. Get them into the longhouse, fast."

"Got it."

I ran toward the greenhouse we had under construction, looking for Darla. As soon as I rounded the corner of the longhouse, I saw her, already on her way to me.

"What's happening?" she asked.

"Don't know. Want to go find out?"

"Not really. But I guess we'd better."

It took about five minutes to gather everyone in the longhouse. Darla and I used the time to change from our work coveralls into the ghillie suits. Then we strapped makeshift snowshoes to our boots. We had found plenty of bicycles during our scavenging, but no snowmobiles, so she still hadn't been able to replace Bikezilla. These snowshoes were a poor substitute.

"Stay inside the longhouse," I told the group once they were all assembled. "Ed and Charlotte are up top. Darla and I are going to try to find out what's going on. We'll be back as soon as we can, but before dark, no matter what. Uncle Paul's in charge."

"Okay," Uncle Paul said. He started to add something, but a coughing fit interrupted him. The cough seemed to be getting worse.

I threw on the backpack with my emergency supplies, held the door for Darla, and followed her outside. We set off, heading toward the sound of the gunfire. It seemed to be coming roughly from Warren. We moved slowly, constantly scanning the horizon ahead of us, stopping and listening. The shots tapered off and, after about ten more minutes, ceased completely.

When we got close enough to see the outskirts of Warren, we stopped. Nothing looked out of the ordinary. "It sounded like the shots were coming from here," Darla said.

"Maybe they were. Or maybe they were coming from the other side of town."

"If there was a battle in town, people might still have their fingers on their triggers."

"Let's go around."

We skirted Warren, keeping the outermost buildings barely in view. At the far side of Warren, as we came up behind Elmwood Cemetery, we started to hear low moans and the occasional scream. There were no more gunshots, though. We crept closer, using gravestones and tree stumps for cover. The moans were coming from the road—we couldn't see who was making the noises because of the high snow berms flanking the roadbed. We inched closer, slinking up the side of the snow berm, cautiously raising our heads just high enough to see over.

The road had been transformed into an abattoir. Hundreds of people lay along it as far as I could see in either direction. Many of them were dead. Blood ran at the edges of the road like rainwater, flowing toward Warren in an accusatory river.

Red. It had to be Red.

Chapter 43

Darla looked away, releasing a sigh that sounded like she was in physical pain.

I looked closer. There were knots of people who appeared to be uninjured, moving among the wounded and trying to help. All of them were dressed in ragged clothing, so filthy it was a nearly uniform shade of gray. Both the injured and the ambulatory were gaunt and starved. They could have been extras in a Holocaust movie.

At the end of the road nearest Warren, two figures worked frantically over a prone form: Dr. McCarthy and Belinda, I thought. Beyond them, I could see a line of men stretched across the road, guns held upright against their shoulders. No one else appeared to be armed. I rethought my first assumption—there was no sign of Red or any of his disciplined, black-clad troops.

"Come on." I tugged on Darla's sleeve and ducked back behind the snow berm as we worked our way toward Dr. McCarthy. Strange, I thought, that there would be another battle in almost exactly the same location where we were ambushed by the Reds holding Warren eighteen months before. The same place where my Aunt Caroline and Mayor Petty had been shot. Wind and snow had resculpted the surface of the cemetery, hiding all evidence of the earlier fight. From this side of the embankment, the cemetery seemed almost peaceful, its gravestones mostly buried, their tops dusted with snow. But I couldn't undo the carnage on the road alongside us; the moans of the dying prevented a moment's solace.

We reached the edge of the cemetery and climbed back to the top of the snow berm. Dr. McCarthy was below us and a little bit to the left. His hands flew over a young man's body, trying to affix a makeshift tourniquet to his arm. The guy's wrist had been completely smashed by a high-caliber bullet—the hand appeared to be attached by nothing more than ripped skin and gristle.

Farther to our left, there was a gap of about a hundred yards, followed by the line of men carrying rifles that I'd seen earlier, maybe thirty or forty of them in all. I recognized all of them—they were residents of Warren. Some of them shifted from foot to foot; a couple of them sat in the road or leaned against the snowbank; and others, including Sheriff Moyers, seemed to be a little green around the edges as if they were fighting the urge to vomit.

I wondered where my mom was. None of the victims looked familiar, and none of the armed Warrenites were women, so I hoped that meant she was safe inside the village.

"This wasn't a fight," Darla whispered, "it was a massacre."

"Dr. McCarthy needs help," I said.

"Alex, wait." Darla grabbed my arm. "Go slowly. You remember that you're not the most popular guy in Warren, right?"

"Yeah." I needed to get down to the road fast. To do something. To help. People were dying down there. But Darla had a point.

I raised my head a little higher, ready to quickly duck back below the lip of the snow berm if any of the men went for their rifles. "Sam!" I yelled. "Sheriff Moyers!"

He turned toward me, holding his rifle low. I raised my hand and hook to about the level of my shoulders and called out again. "You going to shoot me if I help Doc McCarthy?"

Sam shrugged and yelled back, "Suit yourself."

That wasn't really an answer, but I guessed it would have to do. I clambered over the berm and slid down to the road. Some of the riflemen eyed me uneasily, but none of them leveled their guns. "Strange outfit you're wearing," Sam said, "and what's up with the hook?" I ignored him.

The person closest to me was bleeding from wounds in his thigh and side. I needed bandages. I looked toward Belinda—she was cutting a strip from her patient's own T-shirt. Right, we had no bandages.

I unzipped the guy's coat and cut four huge strips of cloth from his shirt using the blade on my hook. I packed one strip of cloth into the wound on his thigh, then wrapped another around it, cinching it tight. That stopped the bleeding, at least. The wound on his side took longer to treat.

Darla had followed me down and started bandaging another victim. Dr. McCarthy brushed by me on his way to yet another patient.

"What happened?" I asked.

"Little busy right now," he said without stopping.

I glanced at Belinda. "Why aren't Sheriff Moyers' men helping?"

She made a face like she had just bitten into a maggoty apple, but didn't reply.

We worked for hours. My hand and hook dripped with other people's blood; it caked my arms, legs, and chest. The air reeked of slaughter and terror. Darla and I looked like extras from a gory zombie movie. Our ghillie suits were ruined—they would blend in nowhere but a slaughterhouse. Some of the ambulatory victims were helping; otherwise we would never have finished. Still, many of the injured bled out before anyone could reach them.

I recognized one of the survivors: Reverend Evans, who had been the director of the Baptist relief workers, the yellow coats at the Galena, Illinois, FEMA camp. He had been leading a mostly ineffective effort to keep the kids at the FEMA camp fed. What was he doing here?

I stumbled through the bodies, looking for anyone still alive to treat, looking for more life amid the silent dead. Dr. McCarthy grabbed my arm. "Stop. We need to get the survivors into some kind of shelter before nightfall. They're going to freeze to death."

"Start taking them to the clinic?" I asked.

Dr. McCarthy's face spasmed and turned fire-engine red. He looked like he'd swallowed a frog and was trying desperately to spit it back out. When he finally did speak, his words were clipped and angry. "That's what Sheriff Moyers is here for. So the refugees can't get into Warren. Mayor Petty won't allow them into town."

"Moyers and his men massacred these people, didn't they?"

Dr. McCarthy was so angry he couldn't speak. Instead, he gave a curt nod.

"Darla, I need you."

She looked up from the patient she was talking to. "Alex, I don't think—"

"You, you, and you." I started pointing at random ambulatory people until I had seven of them picked out. "Follow Darla back to our homestead." I turned back to Darla. "I need every blanket we've got plus two poles per blanket to make stretchers. Have everyone except Uncle Paul and the three youngest girls come back with you. Oh, and bring every oil lamp we've got. We're not going to finish this before nightfall."

"You sure that's a good idea?" Darla whispered.

I shrugged. "No."

"I could get back faster on my own. They're going to be up to their hips in snow."

"We need a trail around Warren anyway. Better to break it before we're all carrying stretchers. And you'll need the help to carry everything back here."

"Okay." She leaned in for a quick kiss. "Even though I don't understand you. We were doing fine on our own."

"It was never going to last. Get going."

"Yes, sir," she said. Instead of saluting, she slapped my butt.

I organized the grisly work of sorting the dead, the dying, and those who might survive. I talked to Dr. McCarthy, Belinda, and the few dozen people left who could walk, explaining my plan. Then I started helping to move corpses.

I approached a young woman bent over an even younger man who lay in the road, clearly dead—half of his skull was missing. "May I move him?" I asked her as gently as I could.

She turned her tear-washed face up to me. "W-w-will you bury him? Properly? B-B-Brock was a Christian. He wanted me to get baptized. He'd want a funeral."

Crap! I knew I had been forgetting something. "We'll need pickaxes to dig the graves. We can bury them in the snow for now. We'll come back when we can with the right tools and give them a proper burial, a real funeral. I promise."

I felt like an idiot. I wasn't sure how we were going to

feed the living, let alone bury the dead. The solution to that problem was obvious—I know I wouldn't mind if someone ate my corpse, but the thought of eating someone else's made me more than a little queasy. I had been fighting with flensers off and on for almost two and a half years—I couldn't stomach the thought of becoming one, even due to the direst necessity.

It was as if she could read my mind. "I don't think Brock would mind if you had to eat him. You could bury his bones still, right?"

"I don't think we'll need to go that far. If we cover him in snow, we can come back and bury him later." Or eat him, if things get bad enough, I thought but didn't say.

The woman got up and helped me drag Brock across the snow berm. On the other side, the snow was softer, making it easier to bury the body. As we covered Brock's corpse, I learned the woman's name. "Francine, not Franny," she said, which struck me as strange. Who worries about trivialities like nicknames during the aftermath of a massacre? She said it automatically, like it was a habit, a verbal tic that transcended the horror of the situation.

Without thinking about it, I asked her, "What happened?" Then I wished I could bite the words back out of the air. Surely she wouldn't want to talk about it.

But I was wrong. She seemed to need to talk, and as we moved the next corpse, burying it in the snow beside Brock, she told me the whole story.

All the people in the road—dead and living—were from the Galena FEMA camp, where Darla and I had been

held prisoner for eleven days, more than two years earlier.
Three days ago the guards, who worked for a FEMA sub-
contractor named Black Lake, had disappeared—just torn
down their tents, packed their vehicles so full they were
nearly bursting, and left. Francine had heard a rumor that
they had lost contact with the government on the East
Coast. Some refugees said the guards had left to try to
reestablish contact. Some said the guards were all moving
to a huge hoard of wheat stored on barges on the
Mississippi. I figured the second version was more likely to
be true—at least I knew the part about the wheat barges
was true. Darla and I had found the barges before we'd
been captured by Black Lake, and later we'd told the guards
about them when we were trapped in the Galena camp.

When the guards left, some of the refugees fled immediately—a group of them fastened a makeshift rope to the
chain-link fence and ripped down a whole section of it.
Other refugees stayed for a few days, but it quickly became
clear that no more food would be forthcoming, and the
guards hadn't left any behind.

Three or four hundred refugees were already clustered
on the road outside Warren when Francine had arrived.
They were arguing with a row of guards Mayor Petty had
sent to block the road. Some of the refugees only wanted
to pass through Warren. Some of them wanted to stay. All
of them needed food. A fight broke out, and then someone
fired a shot, and within seconds the massacre had begun.

The shooting only lasted about twenty minutes,
Francine thought. It ended when Dr. McCarthy and

Belinda charged through Sheriff Moyers' line of riflemen and started bandaging wounds even as bullets continued to stab bloody exclamation points and periods into the lives around them.

Sheriff Moyers had called a cease-fire. Even he could see that shooting the town's only doctor was a very bad idea.

Brock had been Francine's fiancé. They'd gotten engaged just before the volcano erupted, but they had been waiting to get married until they could find a Catholic priest to baptize Francine and officiate their wedding. Now they'd never be married.

Listening to Francine's story brought a quiet sense of despair bubbling up in my gut. I had always believed that the human race would survive the massive volcanic eruption at Yellowstone, would surmount this disaster, just as we had surmounted so many lesser disasters before. But amid the carnage in the road outside Warren, I wondered: did we deserve to survive?

Chapter 44

Darla wasn't back by nightfall with the transportation supplies. Sheriff Moyers lit two oil lamps. He and his men huddled uneasily in the light, watching us. After a few minutes, Dr. McCarthy rose from the side of the patient he was trying to treat in the dark, marched up to Sheriff Moyers, and took both the lanterns. To his credit, the sheriff didn't fight—he just sent one of his men to get two more lanterns from the town behind them.

I assigned two people to hold the lanterns for Dr. McCarthy and Belinda. I worked mostly in the dark, dragging corpses across the berm and interring them in the snow by feel.

Darla returned several hours after dark with the blankets and poles we needed to make improvised stretchers. She had more lanterns and able-bodied help too. As Max's lantern illuminated a woman who was missing most of one leg, he turned deathly pale and staggered to the edge of the road, vomiting on the blood-soaked ice.

On snowshoes we could make the trek from our homestead to Warren in about two hours. Without snowshoes, carrying a stretcher, it took more than twice that long. I felt a stab of relief when one of our patients died—one fewer person to carry—and then hated myself for feeling that way.

Darla had scrounged enough supplies for fifteen stretchers. We had more than enough able-bodied people to carry the stretchers, so I paired off some of the less seriously wounded with helpers—anyone who could walk would have to. Even so, it took three trips to move everyone back to the homestead. We weren't finished until after noon the next day.

I was dead tired. My eyes felt sandy and my head spun when I moved too fast. Still, I couldn't rest yet. I sought out Anna and Charlotte. They and Wyn hadn't made the trek to the massacre site—they were too young to see it, I thought, although I realized now that I was wasting my time trying to protect them. The longhouse was packed with wounded: we'd brought the massacre back home.

"Anna, I need to know exactly how much food we have. I haven't updated my inventory since last week. Check the greenhouse records, figure out how much food we can expect to produce, and when we'll run out, given all the new people here. Assume . . . I don't know, ask Dr. McCarthy for a guess as to how many of the wounded will survive."

"But the food records are your job."

I was only planning to ask her to gather some information while I slept, but then it hit me: with this many people around, I would need a lot of help running the show.

"Not anymore. It's your job from now on. It's really important."

"I know it is. But I can't do—"

"Alyssa says you're really good at math."

"Yeah, but—"

"And your handwriting is beautiful. But the most important thing is that I can trust you. You'll do great. The records are on the clipboard by my bedroll." I turned to Charlotte before Anna could protest further. "Charlotte, you're in charge of the census. Count everyone and get a total number to Anna as fast as you can. Then go back and interview them all. I want to know how old they are, if they have family here, what they're good at, what they did before the eruption, if they're wounded, where and how badly—everything, okay?"

Charlotte shifted nervously from foot to foot, but her voice sounded solid enough when she agreed to take on the project.

"Wake me up at dinnertime with a report," I told them.

I picked my way through the wounded to my bunk, collapsed into it, and fell asleep almost instantly.

• • •

Dinner was three small pancakes and a kale leaf. As we ate, Anna gave her report. "If we drop to survival rations— eight hundred calories a day for the women and a thousand for the men, then we'll run out of food in about fifty-seven days."

"I expected it to be worse."

"It depends on the survival rate," Anna said. "Charlotte looked into that for me."

"We've got the twelve original settlers," Charlotte said, "forty-three uninjured newcomers, twenty-nine walking wounded, and thirty-three more seriously injured. One hundred seventeen total. Dr. McCarthy expects ten percent of the walking wounded to die, along with a third of the others, mostly from infections. So we'll probably settle out at something like 103. I don't have the detailed census done yet."

"That's okay—you're doing great." I privately congratulated myself on delegating these jobs to Anna and Charlotte—I had barely been able to stumble to my bunk, let alone count and do math.

"Ed and Alyssa are on cooking duty this week,"Anna said. "I already told them to cut back on the rations."

"I noticed," I stared mournfully at my empty plate. My stomach still rumbled with hunger. Get used to it, I told my body silently.

"I can get you some more," Anna offered.

"No," I said firmly.

"How many greenhouses would it take to feed 103 people?"

"Oh, good question," Anna said. "I didn't figure that out."

"You can tell me later."

"No, no—I can get it now." She was scribbling figures furiously in the margins of the clipboard. After a long pause, she said, "Well, assuming we can find enough bulbs to light them all, between seven and eight. Without artificial lighting, maybe eleven or twelve—assuming they're equivalent to the ones we've already got in size and productivity."

The problem, of course, was where would we get the glass, wire, and electric heating elements we needed for all those extra greenhouses? The glimmerings of an idea occurred to me, and I spent the rest of the evening talking to Uncle Paul, Darla, and Ben about it. As Ben was lecturing me on the finer points of military logistics, Dr. McCarthy walked up. "Can I talk to you?" he asked.

Ben actually quit talking—he seemed to be getting better at figuring out when to stop his nearly constant barrage of words. "Would you mind if we continued the discussion tomorrow?" I asked him.

"I would like that," Ben said.

"Is there anywhere private we can talk?" Dr. McCarthy asked.

I led him into the base of the turbine tower. With the door closed, it was the most private indoor space we had. "What's up?" I asked.

"Belinda and I have talked it over—we're ready to move."

I held out my hand. "Welcome to . . . whatever here is called. We really should think of a name for it."

We shook hands. "Thanks. We'll go back to Warren tomorrow, load up the Studebaker, and drive it out here."

"You sure Petty will let you go?" I asked. I was thrilled that Doc was moving; Mayor Petty would probably be exactly as furious as I was ecstatic.

"What Petty wants doesn't figure high in my priorities right now. And he owes me—I did save his life."

I nodded. "Be careful. Oh, and would you stop in and see Mom? Try to convince her to move? I'd really like her and Rebecca to join us."

"Your mom seemed pretty set on staying."

"I don't get it. Why?"

"You know she's seeing someone, right? I mean, I think she is. We're not exactly close."

"Really? Who?"

"Mayor Petty. They're spending a lot of time together anyway."

That was just freaking perfect. Why? It was unanswerable. And I certainly didn't want to talk about it anymore. "I've gotta go." As I reached for the door handle, I remembered the original point of the whole conversation. "Tell Belinda I'm really glad you're moving here."

"I will," Dr. McCarthy replied as I left.

• • •

By the next morning, our population had fallen to 110. Seven people had died during the night. We had bandaged their wounds, carried them more than five miles to the homestead, and they had died anyway. I wanted nothing more than to get back into bed and sleep until the horror of it all passed.

I wasn't the only one. Everywhere there were people sitting and staring into space. A woman wept quietly in a corner of the longhouse, her face turned toward the walls. A boy folded and refolded the blanket he had slept on. Every time he finished, he would look at the square of fabric, shake it out, and start again. I had to get them moving, get them doing something, anything but ruminating on the massacre.

I called all the original settlers together—ten of them, not counting me or Anna, who was in the sniper's nest on watch. I assigned each of them a job and five or six newcomers to help. Four groups to scavenge lumber from nearby farmhouses. One group to assist Dr. McCarthy when he returned from Warren. A group to dig latrine pits, even though we didn't need a new latrine pit yet. And so on.

"Alex," Darla whispered to me. "You just assigned twenty-five people to scavenging lumber. We don't have anything like twenty-five hammers, or pry bars, or anything."

"We've got to get them doing something," I whispered back. "They're cracking up." Then I raised my voice to address the whole group. "We don't have enough tools for everyone. So your first job may be to make, find, or improvise what you need. A rock can serve as a hammer in a pinch, a pipe as a pry bar. The sooner we get these tasks done, the sooner we'll be safe—with enough longhouses and greenhouses to sustain everyone."

I expected to have arguments from some of the newcomers, but they went along, zombie-like, with everything
I asked them to do. I stayed behind in the longhouse, trying to work out how we would get supplies to build the
greenhouses we needed.

When Dr. McCarthy and Belinda got back with the
Studebaker a couple of hours later, I had a pleasant surprise—Nylce Myers, the tiny woman who'd done such a
capable job leading a squad during my attack on Stockton,
had come with them. My mom and sister, however, had not.

After dinner that night, I addressed everyone in the
longhouse. It was crowded in there, mostly because over
half the floor space was taken up by Dr. McCarthy's makeshift hospital. I wondered how many people could comfortably live in one longhouse this size. Maybe I'd ask
Anna to figure it out.

I started with some of the bad news, figuring it was
best to get that over with, like pulling off a bandage
really fast. "We don't have enough greenhouses to feed
everyone." A murmur of alarm raced through the room.
"Now, we'll be okay for a couple of months if we ration
food carefully, but we've got to get more greenhouses producing wheat and kale as fast as we can.

"There is good news here. We've built four greenhouses already. We know how to do it. We've got sixty-
seven wind turbines available for power. There's no reason why, with all your help, we can't construct a farm here
that will sustain us through this winter, no matter how
long it lasts.

"But there's more bad news too. We don't have enough wire, pipe, plastic, glass, heating elements, or caulk to finish the fifth greenhouse, let alone build more. We were getting supplies from Stockton, but that source is closed to us now." I glanced self-consciously at my hook but left the explanation at that. If they wanted to know more, any of the original settlers could fill them in.

"I propose to mount an expedition toward Chicago. All the way to Chicago, if need be. It will be a difficult trip— 150 miles through unexplored territory. I want to take a group large enough that isolated gangs of flensers won't dare mess with us, but small enough that we can flee if our scouts warn us of serious opposition. Maybe about thirty able-bodied people. We'll go on snowshoes and skis and try to scavenge bicycles, snowmobiles, or trucks along the way. If all goes well, we'll bring back the supplies we need to build more greenhouses.

"We've also heard rumors that the government in D.C. has collapsed. By heading east, I hope we'll be able to find out whether the rumors are true or not—whether any remnant of the old United States is left.

"The whole expedition will last about five weeks—a week to travel there, three weeks onsite scavenging, and a week for the return journey. I'm looking for volunteers—"

"I'll go!" Max yelled.

"Particularly among our new residents. I'll need most of the original settlers," I fixed Max under my stare, "to stay here and get as much of the greenhouses done as possible before we return with the wiring. Please see

Charlotte—" I pointed her out, "right after this meeting to
let her know if you're willing to volunteer for the trip."

There was a sudden murmur of conversation, and I
waited a moment for it to die down.

"One more thing. We've always called this place the
new farm or the homestead. But it's not really just a homestead anymore. With a hundred people living here, it's
more of a village. And a village needs a name. Any suggestions?"

"You should call it Maxville!" Max yelled. A few people
chuckled. I glared at him. What was with him tonight?
Had he found a stash of alcohol or happy pills?

"I've got a suggestion," Ed said, which surprised me.
Ed rarely said anything, particularly not when a group of
people was listening.

"Go on," I said.

"It's a word my Romanian grandmother taught me:
Speranta. It means hope."

Speranta. I rolled the word around my head and lips a
couple of times. I liked it. We spent about fifteen minutes
taking other suggestions, but in the end, Speranta won by
acclamation, and I called an end to the meeting.

Later that night, I lay on my bedroll thinking. We'd
become a village named Speranta, for hope. Could I deliver
on the promise of that name?

Chapter 45

We left for Chicago two days later. Almost everyone who was healthy enough to walk volunteered, though oddly, not Reverend Evans. I chose twenty-seven of them plus Darla, Ed, and me. Max desperately wanted to go, but I dodged that issue by telling him he had to have his father's permission. All the arguments Max could muster met the stone wall of Uncle Paul's refusal. I could hardly blame him—he had seen how Darla and I had returned from our last trek away from the relative safety of the homestead.

At the village meeting to see us off after breakfast, I announced that Uncle Paul would be in charge of Speranta while I was gone. I sprang it on him in public so he couldn't refuse. He knew exactly what was happening too, shooting me a look so dirty I felt a sudden need for a shower. Dr. McCarthy would have been an equally good choice for interim leader, but he had his hands full with the injured. Our population had fallen to 105, and I fully expected it to fall further while we were gone.

We moved cross-country on improvised skis and snowshoes. They were the only reason it had taken us two days to leave—it took that long to make crude snowshoes for everyone. I put four pairs of scouts out on skis—one pair to our front, one to each flank, and one covering our back trail. I told them to range three or four miles out and rejoin us if they had anything to report, or at the end of the day. I desperately wished for some handheld radios and added them to the list of things we hoped to scavenge in Chicago.

It seemed as though the sky were brighter than it had been. It was a hard thing to judge since it changed so little each day, but as we walked, I noticed that I could always tell where the sun was in the sky, despite the fact that I could never see it. The clouds of ash and sulfur dioxide that hid the sky were thinning.

We hit the town of Lena, seven or eight miles from Speranta, on the afternoon of the first day. We'd scouted it before, looking for a phonebook or well-drilling equipment. I already knew it was abandoned and thoroughly looted. We pushed on another three or four miles before spending the night in an abandoned farmhouse the forward scouts had found.

We covered about ten miles the next day, reaching the outskirts of Freeport just before dusk. I had never been there, but it looked much bigger than Warren or Stockton. The scouts hadn't seen anyone all day. The silence and stillness of the landscape seemed ominous—where had all the people gone?

We trudged up to a restaurant at the edge of town: Family Affair Café, according to the signpost out front. The restaurant itself was covered in a snowdrift so massive, it nearly engulfed the building. At the lee side of the café, a window had been smashed. I set up a guard rotation, and we built a small fire right there in the middle of the restaurant. With the snow covering most of the building and all of us packed tightly together, it was warm enough, and I slept well.

In the morning I sent out four pairs of scouts with instructions to explore for an hour and then report back. The rest of us spent the hour resting and repairing snowshoes.

The team I sent along our back trail found nothing, which was expected but still a relief. It was good to know nobody was following us. Another pair found the library in downtown Freeport, but the maps, phone books, and the useful parts of the nonfiction section—everything on agriculture and engineering—were gone.

The pair I had sent south had followed road signs to Highland Community College, but when they got there, they found it ringed by a huge wall built of frozen dirt. Sentries atop the wall had shot at them, and they had hightailed it back to our base in the café.

The final pair of scouts—Nylce and Francine—had followed West Avenue to a commercial district on the south side of town. When they returned, they were grim and ashen-faced. I could hardly believe what they told me. Instead of talking about it longer—which I couldn't bear to do—I asked them to take me there.

We went as a party of six—me, Nylce, Francine, Ed, Darla, and another survivor of the Warren massacre, Trig Boling. He was a lanky nineteen-year-old with a slightly misshapen face, like it had been frozen while he was scowling in a particularly energetic way. But despite his appearance, Trig was unfailingly friendly and cheerful—I liked having him around.

We only had three guns, but everyone was carrying at least one knife. We stalked through the city in silence, dreading our destination. After about ten minutes, we passed the Freeport City Cemetery—only a few of its tallest monuments protruded above the snow, lonely sentinels standing watch over a buried age.

Most of the buildings on West Avenue had burned. The first two shopping centers we passed had collapsed. As we approached the third, I noticed that Francine was caressing the handle of her knife, rubbing it as if it were a knotted muscle. Nylce's head flicked constantly from side to side as if she were afraid someone would sneak up on her in the few seconds since her last sidelong glance.

As we approached the Meadowlands Shopping Center, I saw a glint of firelight through the glass storefront of a J. C. Penney. We slowed our approach, using the snow-covered mounds hiding parked cars as cover. When we got close enough to see inside the Penney's, I realized that if anything, my scouts had understated the horror of the scene.

Three men dressed in ragged, bloodstained clothing crouched in front of a greasy fire. Around them were scattered thousands of burnt and cracked bones. Behind them, the grisly bone pile nearly reached the high ceiling. I could identify femurs, ribs, hip bones, and skulls—all of them fragmentary, roasted and cracked for their marrow.

All the bones were human.

Chapter 46

I dropped down behind the car/snow mound we were using as cover. What would Ben do? There were six of us and only three of them, but we had only three guns. Focus on the mission, Ben would probably say. The mission was acquiring supplies for the greenhouse.

"Move out," I whispered. "Back to base."

Darla nodded and started backtracking, but Francine grabbed my arm. "You can't just leave them here. They'll keep killing people."

"There are 105 people who'll die if we don't find supplies for building greenhouses," I whispered.

"Killing a few flensers won't help us find those supplies."

"Uh, Chief?" Ed said.

"What?" Obviously I needed to spend some more time working on turning this ragtag band of refugees into obedient soldiers.

"The flensers—they're gone."

I looked back at the J. C. Penney. The space in front of the fire was empty. Crap. Had they heard us? Better assume they had. "Where'd they go?"

"Two to our left, one to our right."

"Getting help? Or going out the side doors of that store to circle around us?"

"Or maybe to follow us back to camp."

That was a nasty thought. If they followed us, they could pick off our scouts two at a time as they came and went from the camp. I couldn't allow that to happen.

Nylce had the bolt-action rifle—much better for sniping than the semi-automatics. "Get up on that hill behind us," I told her. "Take Francine to spot for you."

"On it."

I handed the semi-automatic rifle I was carrying to Ed. "Take Trig. Set up an ambush over there at the edge of the parking lot. Darla and I will swing around and try to flush them out, push them toward you."

"Yessir," Ed replied.

Darla and I moved out to our right, hoping to intercept the singleton who had broken in that direction. We flitted from car to car, trying to stay under cover. I had no idea what kind of weapons these flensers might have.

We got around to the side door of the J. C. Penney without encountering anyone. There was no wide expanse of glass here, just a single glass door. Darla and I pressed ourselves against the brick wall to either side of the door and peered in.

The inside of the store was illuminated by the hellish flickers of the still-burning fire. I couldn't see anyone inside, although anything could have been hiding behind the bone pile or in the dark corners of the room. I pointed at myself and the bone pile and then at Darla and her rifle.

Darla nodded and readied the rifle. I pulled the door open and slipped through, running in a crouch for the cover of the bone pile's nearest edge.

It was impossible to be both fast and silent. The floor was littered with the cannibals' detritus. Fragments of bone crunched under my boots, and larger pieces skittered and clacked as I kicked them.

I stopped at the edge of the bone pile in a crouch. The stench of rotted meat was nearly overpowering—would have been unbearable except for the cold. There was a sort of low ridge of jumbled bones separating me from the hidden area behind the pile. Cautiously I raised my head up over the ridge and peered into the darkness beyond.

And found myself face-to-face with a flenser.

Chapter 47

The flenser's hand shook, making dark shadows play across the blade of the knife he held. He took an awkward, shuffling step forward. Bones skittered around his feet. He raised the knife as if to plunge it into the top of my head.

There are two basic approaches to dealing with a knife attack. If you can, you should dodge backward and try to create enough space to run away. If that's not an option, or if you have the training and practice necessary, you can block the strike and disarm the attacker with a variety of techniques: a wrist grab, an X-block, or a strike to the hand holding the knife. I chose a third option—one taught in no school any-where but an option I'd been practicing for months. I blocked the strike with my hand—or rather, my hook.

I raised my arm in a sweeping arc as if to execute a high outer forearm block, catching the blade of his knife on its way down with the inside surface of my hook, trap-ping the knife within its steel C.

His strike was slow and weak but still had enough force to carry his knife all the way down the hook until his fingers were nearly in contact with my stump. I twisted my arm, forcing the razor-sharp outer edge of my hook against the back of his fingers. The knife and four of the flenser's fingers flew out over the bone pile, trailing dark droplets of blood. The knife clattered to the floor some-where out of sight.

The flenser let out a polysyllabic moan as if he were trying to say something, but it was so slowed and slurred as to make it unintelligible. He struck at me with his left hand, fingers shaped into a claw as if he meant to rake them down my face. His nails were long, gnarled, and crusted with bits of dark filth—the better to pick out mar-row from bones, I assumed.

Darla was standing to one side. I stepped back, drag-ging my feet along the floor to push bones out of the way. Darla raised her rifle to shoot, and I held out my palm for her to stop. The flenser was moving toward me in his awk-ward, shuffling gait, both hands waving—one formed into a claw, the other spewing blood.

I raised my foot in a simple front kick, catching the

flenser right in the middle of his chest. He toppled backward with a crash, and an almost musical tinkling sound
of disturbed bones ensued. I stepped forward, planting my
boot on his wrist and pinning it to the floor.

"Move back, and I'll shoot him," Darla said.

"We can't just shoot him," I said.

"Sure I can," she replied.

"I don't want the rest to know where we are."

Darla put one of her boots on the flenser's chest, and
he clawed at her leg futilely with his mangled hand,
bloodying her boots and coverall legs.

I pushed down on his wrist with my boot—just
enough to let him know I could break his arm if I wanted
to. "Are there more of you here?"

"Ahhhh-ohhhh," was the only reply he made.

"Something's wrong with this guy," I said.

"Let's just kill him," Darla said. "I'm worried about
getting his blood on me."

"You know what he's got?"

"Shaking sickness, I think. Some kind of disease cannibals get. I saw it in a movie once."

"Is it just the three of you here?" I asked him.

"Ahhhh-ehhhh."

"We've got to move," Darla said.

"What do we do with this guy?"

"We need to kill him quietly. Preferably without
touching him." Darla pressed down with her boot until I
heard the guy's ribs cracking. It didn't seem right, killing
a man in cold blood like that. The first time I had killed

someone—a prison escapee who went by Ferret—I had vomited afterward. I dreamed about him for months: the crunch as the blade of my hand hit his neck; the limp, boneless way he fell; the unnatural angle of his body on Darla's mother's kitchen floor. He had utterly deserved death for what he'd done to Darla's mom, but it was still hard to come to terms with the fact that I'd killed him.

I thought about Ed. He had been a flenser once, but now he was a friend, comrade, almost an older brother. Could the guy under Darla's boot be redeemed?

Darla kept pressing, forcing the air from his chest. He batted at her leg with his damaged hand, but still she pressed down as his face turned red, then purple, and finally blue. He went limp, and Darla stood on him until I was sure he was dead. I wondered if I should have done something, stopped her.

A three-round burst of rifle fire snapped me from my ruminations.

We ran around the bone pile toward the front of the store. "Go slow," Darla whispered. "They could have split up, set an ambush for us."

I nodded my agreement, and we split up, pressing ourselves to the wall on either side of the big, plate glass windows and peering out. The gunfire seemed to have come from the spot where Ed had set up his ambush. I couldn't see him or Nylce, though. I gestured toward the nearest snow mound, which was easily large enough to have hidden an SUV. Darla raised her rifle to cover me, and I ran for the door, bent over as low as I could manage.

Once I was crouched behind the mound, I looked around—everything was silent and still.

I waved Darla forward, and she came at a run. We worked our way around the mound in opposite directions, rejoining each other at the far side. She gestured with her rifle, and I prepared to run to the next car/snow mound.

Some slight sound—a crunch of snow or breath of wind—made me turn and look up. A huge man was above me, stretched out in a flying leap from where he had been hiding on top of the SUV. He held a butcher knife in his outstretched hand. And it was aimed squarely at my head.

Chapter 48

I flung up my hands, barely managing to deflect the blade of the butcher knife on the outside edge of my hook. He fell on me, his rotten-meat breath full in my face, so close that the bits of unidentifiable filth clotting his wild beard rubbed my cheeks.

I rolled backward under the impact, reaching up to grab his wrist and try to control the knife. I kicked out, hoping to continue the backward roll and come out on top.

But this flenser wasn't trembling, weak, or slow. Somehow he had avoided the shaking disease that had afflicted the first guy. He threw his free arm out above my head, planting it in the snow and instantly arresting our roll. At the same time, he bore down on the butcher knife. I clutched his wrist with my right hand and put my left arm behind it for support. It felt like I was trying to hold back a hydraulic ram. The knife inched inexorably closer. He grinned, and saliva ran from his crooked, yellow teeth, a drop splattering against my cheek. Darla couldn't shoot him—her rifle was so powerful that at this range, the bullets would tear right through him and kill me too. I had to change the rules somehow, use his weight and strength against him.

I shoved his hands one direction and frantically wrenched my head in the other. The butcher knife buried itself in the snow beside my head with a soft, nearly inaudible thunk. The flenser fell forward—right into the blade of my hook.

I hadn't had room to do anything but line up a short, weak jab to his throat, but his weight took care of the rest. My hook sunk deep. Blood sprayed from the wound, coating the side of my face in a hot, wet glaze. For a moment he seemed to hover there, poised over me, caught on the edge of my hook. Then he opened his mouth and vomited blood, splashing the top of my head.

I shoved him sideways, but it was like trying to move a dump truck. Finally I managed to scramble out from under him. Two shots rang out—one from Darla, right next to me; the other from Nylce, up on the nearby hill. Both hit the flenser perfectly, center mass. He gurgled once more and died.

Ed peered out from behind a nearby snow mound. "That's two," he said in a stage whisper.

"You count the one we killed inside?" Darla asked.

"No," Ed replied, "I shot one who was trying to sneak around to the side door and come in behind you. So that makes three."

Nylce started to get up and come down the hill toward us, but I waved her off using a series of gestures to tell her and Francine to stay put and keep watch.

Darla handed her rifle to Trig and knelt beside me. "You get any of that blood in your mouth?"

"I don't think so," I said.

"We've got to get it off you." She grabbed a handful of snow and started scrubbing at my face.

"This guy wasn't sick." I gestured at the big flenser laid out in the snow nearby.

"He could still be a carrier. The disease might have taken longer to manifest in him."

That made sense. I quit protesting and submitted to a painfully vigorous and cold scrubbing.

When Darla was satisfied I was clean enough, I left Nylce, Francine, and Trig on guard, while Ed, Darla, and I went back into the Penney's. I wanted to check for any sign that more than three flensers were based here. If we hadn't gotten them all, we needed to either set an ambush for the rest or spend a lot of time obscuring our trail to and from the Family Affair.

I stepped closer to the bone pile inside the Penney's. In one corner there was a filthy profusion of discarded cloth-

ing, blankets, and saggy mattresses—more like a rat's nest
than a place for humans to sleep. After staring at it awhile,
I noticed there were three distinct rats nests—apparently,
we'd killed all the flensers who laired here.

Darla paused by the bone pile and dead flenser.
"Those . . . they were people once." Her voice was so soft
that I could barely hear her.

"What? The bones or the cannibal?" I asked.

"Both," Ed said, his voice barely audible.

"I wish," Darla said looking over the bone pile, "I wish
we could bury them."

I didn't want to bury them. I wanted to burn it all,
burn even the memory of this scene from my mind, burn
the spoiled, greasy taste from my mouth, burn time itself
if I could, burn away this world in which the best answer,
the only answer, was sometimes to kill. I wanted to sear
the last few minutes from my mind, or better yet sear away
everything since Yellowstone erupted. Everything except
Darla. "Can we burn them?"

"Need a hot fire," Ed said.

"I need a bucket," Darla said.

I gave her a blank look.

"To hold gasoline."

A Dutch oven crusted with unidentifiable charred food
had been tossed to one edge of the sleeping area. I gin-
gerly lifted it with my hook. "Will this work?"

"I'd rather have a five-gallon gas can, but sure, it'll do."

We dragged the other two flensers to the bone pile.
Maybe we could have just left them where they had died,

but someday this winter would end, and all the frozen corpses would thaw, creating a huge problem for someone. I believe in the rules I learned in kindergarten—you make a mess, you clean it up. Although I'm thankful that kindergartners don't have to deal with dead flensers.

Then we started trudging from snow hump to snow hump, unburying cars, unscrewing their gas caps, and sniffing. When we found a locked fuel hatch, Darla jammed her hook under it and pried it open by main force, snapping the lock. When she unscrewed the gas cap, I could smell gas even from where I stood, several feet back. Darla smashed the driver's side window with the handle of the screwdriver, popped the hood, and ripped some tubing out of the engine compartment.

Darla stuck one end of the tubing into the gas tank and sucked on the other, getting a siphon going. How she managed without getting a mouth full of gas was beyond me. When the Dutch oven was nearly full, I carried it into the Penney's and splashed the gas across the bone pile while Darla waited, thumb over the end of the hose to maintain the siphon.

It took thirteen trips to empty the car's tank. Without more buckets, there wasn't really anything Ed could do to help, so he stood guard. As I trudged up to him and Darla after the last trip, he said, "Kind of a waste of gas, isn't it?"

"No," Darla and I said together.

"Anyway, everything's clear," Ed said. "No sign of anyone else."

"Let's blow this joint," I said.

Ed groaned.

"I'll do it," Darla said. "You're covered in gas."

She was right—it was nearly impossible to carry the lidless Dutch oven without splashing. I had gas on my hook, its cuff, and all down my left pants leg.

Darla made one final trip into the Penney's. She grabbed the end of a stick that protruded from the flensers' still-smoldering fire, tossed it into the bone pile, and ran. Nothing happened for a moment, and then the gas caught with a whoosh. Within seconds the fire was so hot we had to move away from the building. Within minutes a substantial chunk of Meadowlands Shopping Center was ablaze.

As we walked back to the Family Affair, I asked Darla, "What do you think happened in this town?"

Darla didn't answer, but Ed did. "Folks in the college are paranoid, shooting at anyone who comes close. Must have been a big group of flensers here. They would have picked off loners, singletons, small parties, maybe even foraging parties from the college. The folks in the college built their wall and buttoned everything up tight. Once there was no other food source, well, my guess is the flensers ate each other. Those three were all that were left."

"Oh." I was sorry I had asked. It made sense, though. Cannibalism would be a terrible long-term survival strategy. I wondered if something similar was happening in other places. Millions of people were desperate for something—anything—to eat. How many of them would turn to the only readily available food source and, in so doing, seal their own eventual doom? Then I thought of something else.

"Could you have that shaking disease?" I asked Ed.

A pained look passed across Ed's face, and I felt guilty for bringing it up. "I might." He shrugged. "Would serve me right."

"You can quit with the pity party anytime, Ed," Darla said. "We know what you did, and we don't care anymore. You're a different man now."

Ed's Adam's apple bobbed as he swallowed hard. "Well . . . thanks."

As soon as we got back to the café, we packed up and moved on. We didn't go far that day, though. I called a halt on Business 20 on the east side of Freeport to search a gas station we came upon. It was a wreck, shelves thrown over, glass and plastic detritus everywhere. It took us hours to search it, and we found very little that we could use. Every scrap of food was long since gone. The wire map rack was crushed and empty. There were no phone books. I cursed the Internet in the most inventive terms I knew—by killing the telephone book and map business, it hadn't done us any favors.

Darla did find an "Emergency Auto Toolkit," which she shoved into my pack, nearly doubling its weight. By the time we finished, it was almost dark. We shoved the shelving out of the center of the gas station and set up camp right there. I reviewed the watch plan with everyone who was scheduled for sentry duty, spread my bedroll, and lay down.

When I finally slept, I dreamed of gnawing teeth and burning bones.

Chapter 49

Two days later, on the outskirts of Rockford, we reached a gas station that had partially collapsed under the weight of the snow and ash. We weren't quite halfway to Chicago yet. We spent most of the afternoon shifting beams and metal roof panels, unburying the sales counter. It had been looted before it collapsed—the broken cigarette displays were all empty. There was no food of any kind. But when we heaved aside a section of countertop, we exposed a book three years out of date: a combination Yellow and White Pages for Rockford.

Darla and I stayed up half the night studying

the book by the light of an oil lamp. It was a mother lode of information. There were maps in the front—not super-detailed, but better than what we had, which was nothing. We combed through the Rockford Yellow Pages section, noting places we needed to visit. There were several snow-mobile dealers listed. Two of them, on the north side of Rockford, were close together and looked promising: Loves Park Motorsports and Bergstrom Skegs. Almost a dozen bicycle shops were listed; we marked three near the snow-mobile dealers to check first. Darla hoped to scavenge enough parts to create a fleet of jumbo Bikezillas—we would need them to haul our gleanings back to Speranta.

Rockford was also home to four or five electrical and plumbing supply distributors. Darla yelped in delight when she saw some place called Grainger Industrial Supply listed. I had no idea what it was, but anything that made Darla as happy as Grainger had to be heaven on earth for budding engineers.

Then we turned our attention to food. Even if our trip was completely successful, we wouldn't get the new greenhouses all built and producing for months. We need-ed to bring back some kind of food to bridge the gap until then. Grocery stores and restaurants had been emptied out within days of the eruption. To find supplies in the quantities we needed, we'd have to be creative, think of things the ordinary looter wouldn't.

I thought about Rebecca finding pet food in otherwise thoroughly picked-over houses. Unfortunately there didn't appear to be a distributor or manufacturer of pet food anywhere in Rockford. I added a PetSmart and a PETCO to our list of locations to visit, though.

Next I looked up food distributors. Rockford had something called GFS Foodservice, but no grocery whole-salers I could find.

There was no Yellow Pages section for food manufac-turing. On a whim, I looked up Pepsi in the White Pages. There was a bottling plant nearby in Loves Park. Maybe they'd have bulk supplies of sugar or something? Heck, I'd even drink high-fructose corn syrup straight if it'd keep us alive for a couple of months.

That got us started on a game—naming food brands and looking them up in the White Pages. It worked too—it turned out that, along with the Pepsi bottler, the Rockford area boasted a Kraft Foods factory. I lost myself for a moment in a pleasant daydream about ripping into a pallet of macaroni and cheese.

"One of these places is going to have food left," I told Darla confidently. "We're going to find everything we need right here. We won't have to go to Chicago." I wasn't looking forward to visiting Chicago. After seeing the mess in small towns across Illinois, the thought of what almost ten million starving people might have done terrified me.

"I don't know," she replied. "There must have been lots of people working at all those plants. Wouldn't they already have snagged the food?"

My sudden burst of hope died in my chest. "Yeah. Guess you're right. But maybe we'll get lucky anyway."

• • •

In the morning our first order of business was visiting the snowmobile dealers. We were going to need some way to transport all the other supplies we hoped to find. A truck might have seemed the obvious choice, but that would come with its own problems. Gas, despite our luck in finding a half-tank's worth in Freeport, was nearly impossible to come by. And a lot of the remaining gasoline was stale—okay for starting fires, but no good for running an engine. Darla said it had something to do with evaporation and oxidization within the gasoline. Even if we could find gas, we'd run out soon enough and have no way to get more. Pedal power was an inexhaustible resource.

My heart sank when we reached our first stop, Loves Park Motorsports. The windows were smashed and the showroom empty. Not a single motorcycle or snowmobile remained. Darla checked the repair bays in back and reported another strikeout. Whoever had taken the snowmobiles had loaded up on spare parts too.

I poked around the sales counter at the front of the store. Advertising circulars were spread around the Formica counter and had cascaded onto the floor nearby. I picked one up; the back was a huge ad for their annual September "Preseason Truckload Snowmobile Sale."

"Why couldn't the volcano have erupted in September after the snowmobiles arrived?" I asked, showing the circular to Darla.

She shrugged and started to leave the showroom. Then she stopped, turned back to me, and snatched the circular out of my hand. "So if you're getting ready for a huge truckload sale, do you wait until the last minute to get your stock in?"

"How should I know?"

"Well, let's say you don't wait 'til the last minute. Where do you keep all those snowmobiles?"

"It's a *truckload* sale . . ."

We rushed around to the back of the store. There were three semitrailers parked in the back lot. All three were padlocked, which I took as a great sign. What's the point to putting a padlock on an empty truck?

Darla took the ratchet from the toolkit in my backpack and beat on the padlock for a while. She didn't even dent it. Ed had disappeared into the shop. He came back with a long tube—something you would use to build a motorcycle frame, maybe—and a coil of wire. Darla understood immediately. She wrapped the wire through the hasp of the padlock and around the tube a few dozen times. Then all three of us could pull on the tube, creating massive leverage.

The padlock didn't break, but the hasp it was connected to pulled free of the door. Darla and Ed pulled the door open. Inside, the trailer was packed with neatly palletized and shrink-wrapped, brand-spanking-new snowmobiles.

Chapter 50

I left half our force with Darla—four to stand guard and ten to help her construct her fleet of Bikezillas— and took the rest to visit the bicycle and ski shops we had found listed in the Rockford Yellow Pages. We struck out at the first three places we visited—they had been cleaned out completely. Finally we found what we needed at the Rockford Bicycle Company. The dirt bikes had all been taken, probably because their big, knobby tires would work okay in the snow and ice. But there were still dozens of high-end racing bikes and ten-speeds with frames, forks, and gears that would work fine as the core of new Bikezillas.

We cleaned out the bike shop completely, making dozens of trips to haul all the bikes back to our base at Loves Park Motorsports. We cleaned out the repair shop in the back too, taking all the spare parts and tools that were left. By the time we finished, it was dark. I set up the night sentries, and we bedded down right there in the empty showroom.

The next morning Darla handed me a huge list of supplies she wanted. The first thing on the list was skis— if we could get those, she could finish a couple of Bikezillas, which would make it much easier to haul supplies around.

As we headed to North Park Rental, the first place on our list, I wondered why we hadn't seen any people. Where were they? Huge swathes of Rockford had burned, but there were sections that looked intact, almost normal except for the deep snow and the eerie, unnatural silence. There had to have been a hundred thousand people or more in Rockford and millions more in nearby Chicago. They couldn't *all* have died.

And where was the government? Two years ago, Illinois had been part of the Yellow Zone, and FEMA and its subcontractors had been out in force here, keeping people from the Red Zone west of the Mississippi from flooding east. Now, nothing.

Someone had been here. Nearly every place we visited had been picked over—looted, I guessed, although did it really count as looting now that whoever owned all these shops was gone and probably dead?

The cross-country ski section at North Park Rentals looked like a bomb had gone off in it—bits of plastic packaging and cardboard were strewn everywhere.

The other sections hadn't been cleared out nearly as thoroughly; nobody had bothered with the snowboards or downhill skis. We hauled them back to the snowmobile shop by the armload.

We spent the afternoon hunting for other stuff on Darla's list: bolts, wire, welding rods, and lumber to build the bikes' load beds. We found a lot of the stuff at the Grainger Industrial Supply. Other materials came from a nearby Home Depot that had collapsed under the weight of the snow—which was actually fortunate. It was a ton of work to unbury anything, but the store hadn't been looted nearly as thoroughly as those that were still standing.

We even unearthed a huge bin of seeds they'd had on clearance: carrots, beets, tomatoes, lettuce, cucumbers, and more. In our early days of greenhouse farming, it was tough to get anything but kale to grow. Now that we had greenhouses that were both heated and lit, we could probably grow almost anything. Darla said that not all the seeds would germinate—some would have spoiled after two and a half years buried in the wreckage, but that was okay. Many were heirloom varieties, not hybrids. According to Darla, the heirloom plants were much more likely to produce viable seeds. That meant that even if only a few sprouted, we would have an inexhaustible source of more seeds.

Darla's group worked late into the night by lamplight,

and by morning they had the first of what she called a truck model ready. "I'm calling it a BZ-250," she said with a proud smile. "We're building a four-person drive model next, with an even bigger load bed. That'll be the BZ-450." The 250 was two bicycles side by side with their pedals and frames connected by steel rods. A large load bed covered the snowmobile track at the rear, and the front forks of both bikes ended in snowboards instead of wheels. It was ridiculously difficult to turn—you couldn't really lean into the turns much to help the snowboards bite into the snow, but it did okay going straight, and it could haul a ton of stuff. Maybe two tons.

Since we now had a good way to haul bulk supplies, I took my team in search of food. I wanted to check out the GFS warehouse we had found listed in the Yellow Pages. We found it—but it turned out to be a retail outlet store, not a true warehouse. It had been cleaned out completely.

Next we trekked to the Kraft Foods plant. It turned out to be a place where they made chewing gum, of all the useless things. Why, oh why, couldn't it have been a macaroni-and-cheese plant? I could probably live for years on a diet of macaroni and cheese, and kale.

The Pepsi bottler had been looted. There was plenty of diet soda left, but nothing else. The soda was useless, of course. We had all been on the world's most horrible diet in the two and a half years since the volcano erupted. If there was any high-fructose corn syrup left in the big stainless steel tanks at the bottling plant, I couldn't figure out how to get at it.

The PetSmart and PETCO were cleaned out too. Even the rawhide dog toys were gone—boiled down as desperation food, I figured. I thought about how hungry people must have been to eat dog toys. I could relate; I still remembered the hard knots of boiled leather belts sliding down my throat when I had been so close to starvation during our first months on the homestead.

The next day we checked retail grocery stores, even though I knew it would probably be hopeless. At the fifth one—a half-collapsed WalMart—I finally found something interesting. There was no food, of course; even the pallets in the back room had been cleared out. But amid the torn and discarded shrink-wrap, I found routing tags. All the grocery pallets had come from the same place, a distribution center in someplace called Sterling, Illinois. How much stuff would be stored in a WalMart distribution center? And how far was it from Rockford? I quizzed the guys with me until I found someone who knew—Sterling was a tiny town about an hour's drive south of Warren.

When we rejoined Darla's group that night, I talked to the rest of the team. Trig had worked in a WalMart. He had never been in one of their distribution centers, but he said they were huge—over a million square feet—and would have everything stocked in a WalMart supercenter, from food to camping supplies to pharmaceuticals to firearms and ammo. It was obvious where we had to go next.

Chapter 51

We spent another two weeks in Rockford. Darla and her team switched to building four-person bikes with even bigger load beds—they built seven to go with the first two-person bike so all thirty of us could ride back to Speranta. In the meantime my team continued scavenging to fill the huge list of supplies we needed for the new greenhouses and longhouses.

Darla came with us to Grainger Industrial Supply on the last day to help select and load supplies. When Darla asked for the grand tour of Grainger, I begged off. I had seen the whole place already.

"Where're you going?" Darla asked.

"I'll take a quick walk. My head hurts a little," I lied.

"You shouldn't be wandering around by yourself," Darla said.

"Ed," I called, "come take a walk with me, would you?"

"Yessir."

As soon as we were out of Darla's sight, I broke into a jog. "Got a ways to go," I told Ed. "Mind a run?"

As Ed ran past me, he said, "I will run you into the ground, sir."

I laughed and picked up the pace. The place I needed to visit was about two miles away. We had passed it several times during our scavenging trips, but there had always been too many people around—word might have gotten back to Darla.

Ed and I reached it in about twenty minutes, moving at a fast jog: J. Kamin Jewelers. The glass entry door and windows at the front of the building had been broken out and some of the stock looted. That probably happened in the days immediately after Yellowstone erupted. Nobody would bother looting a jewelry store now—a cup of rice was worth more than a cup of diamonds these days.

One row of display cases had been turned on their sides. Ed and I flipped them upright, and I rooted pig-like in the glass shards on the floor for a while, tossing aside bracelets, earrings, and loose diamonds. I found a couple of antique, wind-up watches and took those, though that wasn't what I was after. Finally I hit pay dirt: a velvet tray of engagement rings that had landed upside-down under the fallen display case. They were dazzling in their variety, with diamonds in more shapes and sizes than I had known existed: square, round, pear-shaped, even diamond-shaped diamonds. A couple of the rings featured emeralds or rubies along with the diamonds. I took them all; I had no idea what sort of ring Darla might prefer.

"Might need a couple of these too, Chief," Ed said. He was holding another velvet tray, this one full of plain gold wedding bands.

"You think she'll say yes?" I said.

Ed smiled. "I'd bet your life on it."

"That's about what it feels like." My palms were sweating despite the diamond-sharp air in the store.

"Scared to death, aren't you?" Ed patted my shoulder gently.

It didn't make any sense; I'd faced down prison escapees and cannibals. I *knew* Darla wanted to get married. Why should I be so afraid?

"I remember what it felt like when I popped the question to Mandy. Never so terrified in my life. Or so happy to hear the word *yes* . . . damn, I miss her." Ed bit his lip and turned away.

I wasn't sure what to do. Ed didn't seem like the kind of guy you hugged. I awkwardly patted him on the shoulder. "We'd better go before Darla starts wondering where we got to."

"You're doing the right thing, you know? I'd trade my soul in this world and the next for another day with Mandy. You got the chance for something like that, you grab it with both hands and hold on, even if the whole world is dying around you. Maybe especially then."

"I know, Ed. I love her."

Ed turned to face me. Tears streamed down his face. I pulled him into a rough hug, and we slapped each other on the back. We left the store together, my arm around his shoulders, but in some sense we were facing in totally opposite directions. Ed's tears honored his past, his lost life with Mandy. I felt fiercely alive, sad for Ed, but also full of wild joy for the future. My future with Darla.

Chapter 52

On the fleet of Bikezillas, the return trip to Speranta took only three days. We would have made it in two except that one of the bikes broke down and we had to stop for repairs.

As we pedaled up to the longhouse, my niece Anna burst from the doors, her wild, long blond hair escaping from her stocking cap and trailing in the wind as she ran toward us. I climbed down from my seat and opened my arms to give her a hug. Instead of hugging me back, she stopped, allowed me to hug her for a moment, and then pulled back.

"Dad's really sick. It's way worse than before," she said. "And Dr. McCarthy's got it too."

I followed her into the longhouse and almost got run over by Belinda, who was on her way out. "Alex," she said, "we need azithromycin, doxycycline, cefaclor, or vancomycin. I've been trying to convince Evans to send out an expedition to find them, but he won't—"

"Wait, what? I left Uncle Paul in charge. What's Evans got to do with anything?"

"He's . . . your uncle's taken a bad turn for the worse. Pneumonia with sputum-producing cough, 104 fever, chills, chest pain . . . Jim's got it too. They're both in bad shape."

The fact that she'd referred to Dr. McCarthy by his first name emphasized just how worried she was. Everyone knew she and McCarthy had a steamier relationship than they let on—it was impossible to keep a secret like that when you're living in a one-room longhouse. But Belinda stubbornly stuck to calling him "Dr. McCarthy" as if the formality would prevent us from catching on. "But why is Evans—?"

"We've lost a lot of people, Alex. Evans just kind of started organizing things."

"Lost?" A cold finger of fear wrapped itself around my heart and squeezed.

"Who?"

"Zik's wife, Mary, and eighteen of the newcomers. The bodies are outside, frozen—I've been bugging Evans to organize a burial detail, but . . ." Belinda shrugged.

"Okay. I need a list. Everything you need. Make sure to put every kind of medicine that might help on the list so that if one thing isn't available, I can look for a substitute."

Belinda pulled a folded piece of paper from her pocket and held it out toward me.

"No. Keep it until morning. Go over it. Read it to Dr. McCarthy, if he feels up to it. Make sure it's thorough, 'cause I have no clue what to look for."

"Maybe I should come with you."

"I've got a lead on a warehouse where there might be medical supplies." Nearly every WalMart had a pharmacy—the drugs had to come from somewhere. "It'll take me a minimum of four days to get there and back. You've got to stay and care for your patients."

Belinda made me put on an improvised cloth mask and led me into one of the greenhouses, where nearly three dozen people were on bedrolls—segregated from the still-healthy folks in the longhouse. A faint scent of sweat and feces grew stronger as we approached. Raspy coughs and wheezes filled the air. Dr. McCarthy lay on his side; a trickle of blood-flecked spittle flowed slowly from the corner of his mouth to the pillow.

Belinda wiped his mouth with a rag. "You up to going over the medication order, Jim?"

"Sure thing, hon." His voice was a terrible thing: low, raspy, and diseased. "Glad you're back, Alex."

I seized his hand, clutching it. "I'm going to go get the medicines you need, Doc. Just hold on until I get back, okay?"

"No problem," he wheezed. "I'll bury you all, right along with the rest of my patients. I must be the world's worst doctor."

"You're the best doctor in the town of Speranta by a long shot."

Dr. McCarthy started to laugh, but that turned into a long coughing fit. "I'm the only doctor in Speranta."

Belinda started quizzing the doctor on medicines, and I turned to Uncle Paul on the bedroll behind me. He looked terrible. His eyes were sunken and black, his skin pallid and sweaty, his voice weak.

"Alex," he whispered, "I'm sorry."

"For what?" I asked. "Impersonating a zombie when it's not Halloween?"

He choked out a laugh. "No, for—" A coughing fit overwhelmed him.

"Just rest and get better, okay? I'll go get medicine tomorrow. First thing."

I left his bedside, thinking about the trip to the distribution center in Sterling. There were several possibilities. The distribution center might already have been completely looted. That possibility didn't bear thinking on. The best but most unlikely case was that it was abandoned but still full of supplies. More likely, it might have collapsed under the weight of the ash and snow. If that was the case, I would need a lot of manpower to unbury the supplies we needed.

A fourth option occurred to me then—what if there were still people alive in Sterling, surviving on the gleanings from a million-plus square foot warehouse? If that was the case, I needed to bring something to trade. What would people who had been living on canned food for two and a half years want most? That was easy: fresh food.

I made my way across the room to our food storage area. We had put a bunch of old metal cabinets against the wall in the coldest corner of the longhouse. It was like a refrigerator, but it didn't drain any electricity. I figured I would package up almost all of our stored kale and get it ready to take on my expedition tomorrow.

One of the newcomers, a guy a year or two younger than I, was standing guard at the "refrigerators." "Hey, Deke," I said, reaching for the cabinet.

He laid his hand flat against the cabinet door, holding it closed. "Director Evans says nobody but him's to distribute food."

"It's me, Deke."

"Director Evans says especially not you."

Wait, what? I briefly contemplated kicking his legs out from under him. That would get his hand off the cabinet door. But it wasn't his fault. "You know who built the room you're standing in, right?"

"You did, sir. But Director Evans—"

"I know, I know. Where is he, anyway?"

"Out in the new greenhouse."

I found him supervising a group of people lifting one of the rafters that would support the greenhouse's glass roof. His idea of supervision was calling out directions. When I was running things, I made it a point to put my shoulder under the heaviest part of the beam.

"Welcome back," he called out when he saw me, his face lit by a smile that looked genuine enough.

"We need to talk." I pulled him aside. When we were out of earshot of the work crew, I said, "Why's Deke got orders not to let me into the food supply?"

"We've got fifty-six hungry people here. Eighty-six now that you folks are back. It only seemed sensible to post a—"

"I'm not debating the need for a guard. What I want to know is why he was given specific orders not to let me into the food stores."

"Just a misunderstanding," Evans said smoothly. "I'll get it straightened out. Your uncle got sicker right after you left. Someone had to step in. And the refugees look up to me—I fed a lot of them, or at least their children, in the camp in Galena."

I didn't buy the misunderstanding explanation. "How'd you wind up as a refugee anyway? Last time I saw you, you were in tight with Black Lake." To be fair to Evans, I supposed he had no choice but to kiss up to the FEMA subcontractors who ran Camp Galena; they wouldn't have allowed him to help feed the refugees otherwise.

"Not as tight as you thought, I guess. I used all my resources acquiring food for the refugees' children. I had hoped FEMA would see that I got home. But when Black Lake pulled up stakes and abandoned the Galena camp, they left me behind. I'm just as homeless as you are."

I was suddenly furious. "I am not homeless. This is my home." I whirled and stalked away. I was afraid I would punch him the next time he opened his mouth.

I went to find Ben. He, Max, and Alyssa were loading up a Bikezilla with empty jugs, preparing to haul water from the farmhouse well almost a mile away. I hopped on the fourth bike seat and rode there with them. We really needed to dig a well closer to the longhouse.

As we filled and loaded the jugs, I told them about my conversations with Deke and Director Evans.

"Evans has been running things since your uncle got sick," Alyssa said. "I figured it was okay, just a temporary thing until you got back, or I would have complained or something."

"Sometimes," Ben said, "a fast counterattack can accomplish more than a slower, more careful approach to the enemy."

"You can't, like, shoot Evans," Max said to Ben.

"You misunderstand me," Ben said. "I'm talking about a political counterattack. Although really, war is a continuation of politics by another means, as von Clausewitz wrote."

"That makes sense." I thought about it all the way back to Speranta. By the time we had finished emptying all the water jugs into one of the greenhouse tanks, I knew what to do. "Thanks, Ben," I said as I handed him the two empties I held.

"You are welcome," Ben called as he and the others set off to make another trip to the well. I went to the longhouse—I planned to spend the rest of the afternoon preparing my counterattack.

I dragged load after load of supplies in from the Bikezillas. After a couple of trips, Anna and Charlotte showed up. Charlotte had her eight-year-old sister, Wyn, in tow. Their eyes were dark and their cheeks tear-streaked. They'd lost their mother while I was gone. I hadn't seen their father, Zik, since I'd returned. I gave each of them a hug, telling them how sorry I was but knowing how utterly futile and inadequate my words were.

"Heard you could use some help," Anna said. She leaned in toward me and whispered, "I think they could use a distraction right now."

"Thanks." I was happy to have the help. I pointed out a row of plastic pots and sprouting trays I had brought in from the Bikezillas. "Fill all those with the best dirt you can find, would you?"

We worked all afternoon, filling pots and laying out seeds until nearly every counter and table in the longhouse was full. Director Evans stopped by and asked me what I was doing. "Getting ready to plant the seeds we found in Rockford," I told him. I didn't want to give him any hint of the counterattack before it hit him.

"A fine idea," he said. "How can I help?"

"We've got it, thanks."

At twilight Max, Ben, and Alyssa came to help. The only seeds we didn't lay out, ready to plant, were kale seeds.

When everyone filed in for dinner, they found the potting supplies. I raised my voice enough to be heard over the hubbub. "Before dinner tonight, I'd like to share part of the bounty we found in Rockford with all of you. Take a few pots or sprouting trays—however many you'd like to care for. Plant whatever seeds you wish. There are hundreds of choices laid out on the tables in front of you, almost anything you want—except kale." A few people laughed. "I kept all the kale for myself." More people laughed. If there was one thing I was sure of, it was that we were all thoroughly sick of kale.

"Keep your pots in the longhouse or one of the greenhouses and care for your seedlings. Whatever sprouts will form the core of your own garden, and every family will have their own plot of land in a greenhouse to raise their own vegetables."

Director Evans started to say something, but I spoke over him. "And now, before we begin planting, could I ask Reverend Evans to say a blessing over these plants, to give thanks for the nourishment they will provide?"

"A fine idea," Evans said and began his blessing.

We spent almost an hour planting. People chatted over the various seeds, oohing and aahing over the pictures on the seed packages, trading seeds until every pot we had was planted. Then we cleared off the tables and sat down to a meager dinner of roasted kale and tortillas made from greenhouse-grown wheat.

After dinner I rose and banged on my water glass with a spoon. Years ago I had seen someone do that in a movie about a wedding. It worked—everyone quieted down and looked my way. I was nervous—not about confronting Evans, though, but about the next topic on my agenda.

"First," I said, "I'd like to offer my thanks to Jim Evans for his service to Speranta in my absence. When my uncle got sick, Jim stepped in and ably kept things running. We owe our continued supply of kale to him." There were several groans at the mention of kale—exactly the effect I was hoping for. I led the audience in a round of polite applause. Evans rose and started to speak, but I interrupted him, smiling to soften my words. "Sit down, Jim, I'm not finished yet."

"I also want to thank the original settlers of Speranta." I named them all, starting with Darla and ending with myself. "Without your bravery and hard work, we wouldn't have this fine building sheltering us or the electricity that warms and lights our greenhouses. And we wouldn't have been able to lend a helping hand to our neighbors as they lay bleeding and dying on the highway outside Warren. Thank you."

The applause was considerably more enthusiastic that time.

"I owe thanks also to the twenty-nine brave souls who volunteered to accompany me to Rockford. Without their bravery and sacrifice, we wouldn't have all the seeds you just planted." I had to quit for a moment, the applause was so loud. "They also found the supplies that will enable us to build more greenhouses to feed ourselves no matter how long this winter lasts!" More applause.

"When there were only twelve of us, we could operate by consensus. Now with the influx of new people and new talents, we need a more formal organizational system. It has been my honor and privilege to guide this settlement, to lead Speranta through its founding and naming, but I couldn't have done it alone. I owe my success—in fact, we all owe our success—to Paul Halprin and Darla Edmunds, without whose engineering and mechanical genius, we would have no electric lights, no greenhouse, and no food."

The crowd interrupted me again for more applause. "And we owe our very survival to Ben Fredericks, whose military genius led us to this spot, and who designed the longhouse and sniper platform system that will keep us safe in the years to come." The crowd applauded again. Ben was oblivious, leaning against a wall and sketching something on a notepad that I had picked up in Rockford for him.

"But I recognize that with a new, larger population, we may need new leadership. That some of you may be uncomfortable with such a young leader, even one who has a proven track record of success. The original settlers are only a minority now, and all our new citizens should have a say in who governs them.

"Some days I wonder if America is dead. Why has there been no help for us from the East? When terrorists or hurricanes or floods threatened America, we pulled together. We helped each other. But the volcano seems to have blown us apart. If there is still a functioning government east of us, I didn't find any evidence of it during our trip to Rockford.

"But even if America is dead, I am still enough of an American to believe in the ideals she stood for, to believe we can reconstitute America in some small way, here in this longhouse, in spirit if not in fact. I believe in the right of every citizen to have a say in who governs them, and to that end, I offer you a choice tonight—should I stay on as leader of our new community of Speranta or not? A vote 'yes' will continue us on the path we've started on. A vote 'no' will trigger new elections to be held two weeks from now."

Jim Evans had risen to his feet. "We need a constitution, a primary, a campaign—you can't just spring this on us all of a sudden."

"I can and do demand that this be settled expeditiously. My uncle and our only doctor are gravely ill, along with dozens of your friends and family members. We *will* settle this question tonight, so that in the morning I can devote all of my personal resources to obtaining food and medical care for our sick."

Jim started to interrupt, "But it's not—"

"If I am retained as leader, it will be for a one-year term. During that time we'll adopt a new constitution to govern our community and future elections. All citizens will have a say in this document. If you choose not to retain me, then whoever you do elect can deal with it, and good luck to him or her."

Jim started to get up again, but one of his neighbors pulled him down, muttering, "It's fair enough, Jim, fair enough."

I hadn't really been nervous up to that point. I mean, if I lost the election, they deserved whatever kind of crappy leader they chose. I wanted to win, but I didn't *need* to win.

Now, though, approaching the next subject on my mental agenda, I was a wreck. My palms sweated, my heart raced, and I had to consciously slow my breathing to avoid hyperventilating.

"There's one more thing I'd like to do while we're all gathered here. A personal matter, if you'll indulge me, please.

"I . . . every day I curse the volcano, curse this winter—like all of us do. But then I remember that it brought me to Darla. I'm not sure we would have met otherwise. Over these two and a half years, I've come to admire her immensely: her toughness, her indomitable spirit, her courage, and her brilliance with anything mechanical."

Was it possible? Darla was blushing! Or maybe it was only a trick of the light.

"I owe her my life. Several times over. We all do. Speranta would not have been possible without her inventiveness and tireless work. But more importantly, I've come to love her."

I turned to face her. "Darla, I couldn't imagine spending my life with anyone else." I fished around in my pocket with my good hand until my fingers closed over the ring I had picked. Then I tried to kneel while simultaneously pulling the ring from my pocket. I tripped and nearly went face down, catching myself at the last second, my hook thudding into the wooden floor of the longhouse. A couple of people chuckled, but they fell silent as I lifted the ring toward Darla. It was set with a nice-size emerald surrounded by tiny diamonds.

"Darla," I said. I felt dizzy, and I paused to take a deep breath. "Will you marry me?"

Chapter 53

The silence was total. Everyone in the room had stopped breathing at the same time. Darla's face was bright red, and a tear fell from the corner of her eye. She was crying? Oh, crap!

"Say something," I whispered.

The silence persisted for a heartbeat longer, and then Darla finally broke it. "Yes," she whispered. Her voice was uncharacteristically soft, but in the quiet room everyone could hear. We all started breathing again at once. There were sighs and cheers and relieved laughter. I held out the ring, and Darla slipped her finger into it. It was too big, so I moved it onto her pointer finger. It fit fine there.

I stood, and Darla launched herself into my arms, nearly bowling me over backward. We kissed, and I forgot about everything else, forgot about the election I had just called, forgot about the audience, and lost myself in the softness of her lips, the warmth of her body pressed against mine, the faint smell of bearing grease that clung to her only slightly less persistently than I did.

When the kiss ended, I was momentarily disoriented by the percussive noise. I looked around. They were applauding us. From the corner of my eye, I saw Alyssa slip out of the longhouse. Her hands were clenched over her mouth. Max left too, following her.

When the applause died down, I stood at the front of the room, holding Darla's hand and grinning so hard that I figured my face would freeze that way, and I'd have no possible future other than as a pirate clown.

"One more thing, and then we'll hold the vote. Reverend Evans," I intentionally used his religious title, "would you do me and Darla the honor of marrying us, say a month from today?" I looked to Darla for confirmation of the date, and she nodded.

"It would be my honor," Evans murmured.

"In addition, I wonder if you would be willing to establish a place of worship here in Speranta. A community—even one as small as ours—should have spiritual leadership as well as secular, wouldn't you agree?"

"Indeed," Evans said.

I fixed him with a hard stare. "And in the finest American tradition, the secular and spiritual leadership should be separate."

Evans looked away. He knew he had been beaten; I could see it in his posture. "As you say."

Anna brought out the ballot box and paper ballots I had asked her to make earlier that day. I asked Evans and Zik to serve as election monitors. I needed to box in Evans completely, forcing him to acknowledge the legitimacy of the election, and I knew Zik would keep him honest.

Everyone able to walk filed up to the table to fill out their ballot. Then Evans and Zik donned masks and carried the box out to the greenhouse where the sick were quarantined, so they could vote without rising from their bedrolls. We counted the votes right there with everyone watching. It wasn't even close: I won with seventy-six yes votes and ten no. For at least the next year, I had my job cut out for me. The fate of almost one hundred people rested upon my already sagging shoulders.

Chapter 54

Late that night, pressed together amidst the crush of people sleeping in the longhouse, Darla and I held a whispered conversation.

"I'm sorry I proposed right in the middle of slapping down Evans," I said. "I just . . . I couldn't bear the thought of waiting. I mean, who knows—"

"What'll happen tomorrow," Darla finished for me. "I'm glad you didn't wait."

"Do you like the ring?" I asked. "I've got a bunch of others. One of them has an absolutely humongous diamond."

"I love this one," she said. "It's perfect."

"I liked the color. Green makes me think of spring. Of hope."

• • •

We got up before first light to get ready for the trip to Sterling. I decided to take the exact same crew of thirty who had gone to Rockford. For one thing, none of them were sick. I'd kept them all out of the greenhouse where the sick people were isolated. I loaded about half of our supply of kale and a wide selection of seeds in case we found someone to trade with.

At breakfast I announced that Reverend Evans would be in charge while I was gone. Darla gave me a sharp look, but I knew what I was doing. By putting him in charge and doing it publicly, I reinforced the idea that he was subordinate to me. And I managed to look magnanimous at the same time.

• • •

The trip to Sterling went smoothly. The Bikezillas were nearly empty and superfast. We made almost forty miles on the first day, passing through Pearl City, Georgetown, and Lanark. They were all half-burned and eerily silent. Not for the first time, I wondered where all the people had gone. I supposed they must mostly be dead, frozen in the tombs they used to call home.

We reached Sterling before noon the next day. From the routing slip, I knew the distribution center should be on Matthew's Road, but we couldn't find it. Street signs were hard to find anywhere—often buried in the snow berms at the sides of the roads, but usually we could locate a few of them. In Sterling they were all gone. I couldn't even find the posts that had held them up.

Finally, I reasoned that the distribution center had to be on a major highway and would probably be outside of town where the land for a giant warehouse was available. So we started following each highway out of Sterling a few miles, looking for a gigantic building. It had to be the biggest structure in the area; Sterling wasn't exactly a huge city.

Finally, on the eighth road we tried, we found it: an unmistakably massive, flat-roofed structure. Huge mounds of snow surrounded it on all sides, reaching almost to the roofline; someone had shoveled snow off the twenty-plus acre roof. Was it still occupied?

I left half my force along the highway, where they could watch the front door. The rest of us began a slow circumnavigation of the building at a distance, looking for opposition, for any sign of life.

The building was so massive, it took more than two hours to work our way around it, riding our Bikezillas out in the deep snow blanketing the fields around the warehouse. The distribution center's parking lot hosted hundreds of semitrailers. Mostly they were huge blobs of snow, but here and there the wind had blown the side of a few of them clear enough that I could tell what they were. More semitrailers were backed against docks on all sides of the distribution center, like carbuncles clinging to the body of the building. Nothing moved. It was possible that the roof had been cleared off soon after the eruption and the building abandoned later. I hoped there were some supplies left inside, that we wouldn't have to limp back to Speranta defeated and prepare for dozens of funerals instead of one wedding.

When we got back to the front of the building, I moved everyone closer to its walls, within rifle range of the glass pedestrian door. I called out, "Ed, Trig, and Francine—you're with me." I turned to Darla. "Keep everyone else out here covering the door. We'll have a quick look around and be out in fifteen minutes. If—"

"If you're not out in fifteen minutes," Darla said, "I'm going to storm in there and rescue your ass."

"I'm counting on it." I leaned in, gave her a kiss, and left. We pedaled a Bikezilla to within fifty feet of the door, laboriously turning it to be ready for a fast getaway.

The door was unlocked. I stepped inside—the daylight coming through the doorway illuminated a small outer office and reception area, as if the light were afraid to venture farther into the warehouse.

I stood there, waiting for my eyes to adjust. Then Ed stepped up beside me, carrying a lit lantern. I opened the door at the other side of the room and saw a bullpen filled with rows of desks. Papers were scattered here and there. The walls were decorated with posters listing rules: NAME BADGES MUST BE WORN AT ALL TIMES, NO UNESCORTED VENDORS IN THE BULLPEN, and the like. Ed's lantern cast crazy shadows around the room. He had brought Trig and Francine inside with him.

The back wall of the bullpen was made of painted cinderblock, not drywall like the rest. An aisle between the desks led directly to a metal door set in the back wall. I tried the handle—it was unlocked. I stepped through with Ed close on my heels.

Beyond the door was a massive, open room filled with huge metal racks. The racks were stuffed with pallet upon pallet of food, thousands of pounds of it just in the tiny bit of the warehouse I could see: canned corn, boiled potatoes, beef stock, and more. Directly in front of me, there was a row of pallets—dozens of them—that held industrial-sized cans of tomato sauce—enough tomato sauce, it seemed, to feed the country of Italy for a decade. Our food problems were solved!

A row of people rose from behind the pallets as one, as if some invisible signal had been passed. Every one of them had a pistol, and every pistol was aimed at us.

Chapter 55

"Hands up!" A woman commanded.

I raised my hand and hook. There was nothing else I could do. They were under good cover, behind the chest-high wall of tomato sauce, about twenty feet in front of me. There were at least a dozen of them, all armed. Of our group only Ed and I had guns, and they were on our backs.

"Down! On the floor! Now!" the woman yelled.

I lowered myself to the floor.

"Keep your hands up!"

I was facedown. I didn't see how it was possible to raise my hands—maybe if I were seriously double-jointed? I stretched my arms over my head, laying my one good hand against the cold concrete floor.

I heard boots against the concrete and then felt something small and metal press against the back of my neck. A gun barrel, I feared.

"This guy's got a hook," a man's voice said from directly behind me.

"We caught Captain Hook?" the woman said.

"He's not much older than Peter Pan."

"I'm Alex," I said.

"Shut up," they said together.

"What do we do with them?" the man asked.

"We've gotta kill them," the first woman said.

"I can't just shoot him!" the man behind me said.

"We can't let them go," the woman said.

"Um, why not?" I asked.

"Shut up," they repeated.

"If you do shoot us," Ed said calmly, despite the fact that his head was mashed against the concrete floor like mine, "the rest of Speranta will come looking for us. They know where we are."

"We know exactly how many of you there are," the woman said. "Twenty-six more outside. We can deal with them."

"And if you've seen everyone on our *patrol*," Ed said, "then you know they aren't carrying much in the way of supplies. Just some trade goods. If we don't come back soon, the whole town will be out poking around here."

"Spranta?" the man said. "There's no Spranta around here."

"Speranta," I said. "It's new. Look, we don't mean you any harm. We were just out looking for food—"

"Told you they were here to take our food!" the woman said. "We need to shoot 'em, Dean."

"We're not here to take anyone's food. We didn't even know you were here. You mind if I get up, so we can talk this over? Take my gun—you can always shoot me after we talk."

"All right, let's hear what he has to say, Thelma," Dean said, and I felt my rifle being lifted from my back. The strap was wrapped around my shoulder. I rolled very slowly and sat up so Dean could lift it off me. He was young, maybe mid-twenties, and black. I stayed sitting on the floor, figuring I was less threatening that way.

The woman was young too—they seemed too young to be in charge. On the other hand, I was a teenager leading a village, so who was I to say they were too young?

"I'd like to not get shot, of course," I said, "but I'd also like to trade. You've obviously got a lot of food, and while we're growing what we can—"

"What are you growing, snow carrots?" Thelma asked.

"Kale and wheat, mostly. In greenhouses."

"And you're heating these greenhouses how?"

I told her about our old greenhouses, heated by wood-burning hypocausts, and the new model, heated by electricity from the wind turbines. Thelma seemed skeptical, but Dean was clearly interested. I was very careful not to tell her how many people lived in Speranta or let on that so many of them were newcomers and wounded. I didn't want to say anything to dispel the impression of strength Ed had given them.

"So here's the deal," I said. "You're going to run out of food eventually."

Dean and Thelma spoke over each other:

"Got enough for fifty-seven months," she said.

"We've got thirty-four months of supplies," he said.

They glared at each other, and I spoke up quickly before the glaring match could turn into an argument. "This winter might last ten years. You help us get through the next six months, and we'll pay you back double by weight what you lend us now."

"Riiight," Thelma said, "we send you off with a bunch of our food, and we never see you again."

I thought about it for a moment. Something Ben had said flitted around the edges of my mind. That we would inevitably become a feudal society. Nobles had sealed bargains with an exchange of hostages, right? Royal children or whatever. "We know where you are. We'll show you where Speranta is. And then we trade hostages. We'll send five people here to live and work with you. You send five to us, and we'll teach them everything we know about growing food in a volcanic winter."

"That could work . . ." Dean rubbed his chin.

"We send you the food, you dump five slackers on us, and then you slaughter our people," Thelma said.

"You wouldn't have to send all the food we need at once," I said. "We've got enough grown and stored for fifty days or so. You could send a week's worth at a time, and if you don't like what your people are learning from us, pull out of the deal."

"How far is this Speranta place anyway?" Dean asked.

About sixty miles north of here," I said.

"Well, that bird won't fly," Dean said. "You're talking about food for hundreds and hundreds of people, right?"

I couldn't think of anything to say that wasn't risky. If I told him we had hundreds of people, I would be starting this deal off with a lie. If I told him our true numbers, we'd look weak. So I kept my mouth shut.

"We can't haul all that food sixty miles," Dean said. "Sure, we got trucks coming out our asses—"

"Must be painful," Ed said. Dean groaned, but Thelma cackled.

"But there's no stabilized, nonstale gas to be had anywhere in Sterling."

"I've got that covered," I said. "In fact, I'd like to seal this bargain with a gift. If you guys would come outside?"

• • •

"You gave away what!?" Darla yelled when I tried to explain the bargain to her about fifteen minutes later. "I've built ten Bikezillas, and you've lost three of them? Thirty percent! You'd be uninsurable if there were still insurance companies."

"Technically I don't think I was responsible—"

Ed leaned toward me and said, "You should take some advice my dad used to give me: Don't dig a hole deeper than your shovel. You might not be able to climb out."

"This is a great deal," I said. "We get the food we need

to tide us over until we can build more greenhouses, and they get the technical know-how to build their own greenhouses. They've got almost five hundred people in that warehouse, sitting on their butts, eating from a *three-year* food supply. If we get all that labor mobilized building something . . . ?"

"How're we all going to get home?"

"Four of us will need to ride in the load beds." I didn't think this was the best time to bring up the exchange of hostages. Not all of us would be going back to Speranta.

"It'll mean we can't load as much food."

"The gift was perfect—I don't think they really believed what I was telling them about wind turbines and greenhouses until I demonstrated the Bikezilla for them. Well, and the fresh kale helped. I don't think I've ever seen anyone salivate that much over kale before. And anyway, you can build more Bikezillas. They told me there's a snowmobile dealer in town."

"Yeah. They are impressive, aren't they?"

"Of course!" After her fury over losing another Bikezilla, I figured I was really in for it when I explained that we had promised to leave five people behind. But strangely, that didn't bother Darla nearly so much as my gift had.

• • •

Thelma decided to come back to Speranta with us. She still didn't trust me—I got the feeling she expected us to

butcher and eat her as soon as we got back to the homestead, but that only made her more determined to be one
of the hostages who would seal our deal. I asked Ed to
stay behind in charge of four volunteers from the newcomers. He agreed reluctantly, only after I promised we'd
bring him back to Speranta at the first possible moment.

I understood Ed's reluctance. The Wallers, as they
called themselves, lived crammed into the back of the
warehouse. They hid whenever anyone approached, dousing their fires and sitting silently in the dark warehouse.
It was a good strategy—they'd kept nearly five hundred
people alive for more than two and a half years, but it
wasn't a way I would have wanted to live.

We loaded up the Bikezillas with food from the warehouse. Dean gave us hundreds and hundreds of pounds of
it, stuff none of us had eaten in more than a year: pasta
and canned tomatoes, boxed stuffing, frozen steaks, canned
yams, frozen peas, and more. The backup power at the
warehouse had lasted until the weather had turned cold,
so very little of the warehouse's stock had spoiled.

Dean was willing enough to trade some of his medical
supplies for fresh kale. I wound up getting small stocks of
about half the drugs and supplies on Belinda's list. I also
convinced him to part with a few candles.

Those supplies didn't nearly fill our seven remaining
Bikezillas' load beds. Dean invited us to take all the clothing
we wanted—there was more of it in the warehouse than the
Wallers could wear in a decade or more. I also looked for
tuxes and wedding dresses, but of course WalMart didn't

stock those. When I asked Dean about it, he told me to
check Sterling Formal Wear downtown. He also gave me a
large supply of plastic roses and other decorations.

On our way out of Sterling, we stopped at the formal
wear shop, grabbing huge armloads of wedding dresses
and tuxes. We didn't bother to look at sizes or styles—just
grabbed everything we could in fifteen minutes or so. I
was uncomfortable delaying our return to Speranta even
that little bit more.

The fully loaded Bikezillas were slower, but we still
made it home in two days. Belinda ran out to meet us—she
had obviously been told we were coming by one of our
lookouts in the sniper's nests. "Lost three more while you
were gone," Belinda said.

"Uncle Paul? Dr. McCarthy?" I wasn't sure I wanted
to know.

"They're doing better," she said.

We reached the Bikezilla that held the medical supplies, and Belinda got too busy unloading everything to
answer more questions. I assigned four guys to help her
carry the supplies, then I gathered up Thelma and the
other four Wallers—they needed to be interviewed and
given job assignments by Charlotte.

I held the longhouse door for Thelma. She took one
step inside and stopped dead.

"Move on in," I said. "You're letting out the warm air."

She turned back toward me. "You've got generators
running?"

"No. The electric lights all run off the wind turbine."

"But the wind's not blowing."

"There's a battery bank scavenged from a Prius in a shack behind the wind turbine. We put them out there so nobody'll get hurt if they explode. The lights are running off battery power right now." I put my good hand on her shoulder and gently pushed her inside so I could shut the door behind us.

"It's warm in here," Thelma said softly, as if she were in a place of worship rather than our living quarters.

It wasn't, really. We didn't heat the longhouse directly. But residual heat from the connected greenhouses was usually enough to keep the temperature in the longhouse in the fifties, which felt amazing after the subzero weather outside. I led Thelma through two sets of plastic drapes that separated the longhouse from one of the attached greenhouses. Thelma stared, jaw unhinged, at the neat, closely spaced rows of kale and wheat. In the greenhouse near the heating tank, it was so warm that I quickly started to sweat and had to strip off my coat, hat, and scarves.

"You'll teach us . . . teach me . . . how to build all this?" Thelma asked.

"Well, I won't—I wouldn't have been able to figure out how to do all this in a thousand years with a hundred monkeys helping me. But Darla and my uncle Paul will teach you. That's part of the deal, right?"

"I want to learn everything."

We found Charlotte in the kitchen area making some kind of soup for dinner.

"Heard we're down to eighty-three," I said.

"Three more died," she said, giving me their names. They were all newcomers, nobody I knew well. "But we're up to ninety-eight total residents, not down."

"Wait, what?"

"Three families showed up together two days ago, not long after you left for Sterling. Evans gave them jobs and told me to add them to the census. Was that okay?"

"Yeah, fine. But how'd they find us?"

"I don't know."

I introduced Charlotte to Thelma and the four other Wallers. Charlotte had Thelma take over soup-making duties, so Charlotte could interview the others. They seemed to be doing fine, and I left them to check on the greenhouse we were building.

At dinner that night, I introduced myself to the newcomers and sat with them. They had heard a rumor that there was a new settlement east of Warren amid the windmills and that we had food. Then they had just wandered around the wind farm until they found us. I wondered how many more people would be showing up on our doorstep. We needed to get more greenhouses built ASAP.

For the next month, I spent my days working on the greenhouses. I couldn't do the electrical work or welding, but after building the first four greenhouses, I knew enough to manage the structural part of them. We finished the fifth greenhouse and started building three more plus another longhouse. We planned to build four greenhouses around every longhouse. Those would require two windmills and a battery bank to power. Every windmill we powered up would include a sniper platform; that way, we would have interlocking fields of fire covering our whole settlement. All the longhouses would be built as defensive structures with walls thick enough to resist most small-arms fire.

I asked Ben to lay out an optimal settlement plan assuming we continued to grow. He presented me with plans for two hundred, five hundred, one thousand, and twenty thousand inhabitants. I hadn't asked him for a plan for a city that size, and I hoped we wouldn't grow to anything like that large. Managing a city of twenty thousand sounded like a nightmare. Ben also came up with a numbering scheme for everything. Each longhouse would have a number, and the associated greenhouses and turbine towers a letter. So Turbine Tower 2-A would be the first tower at the second longhouse, and so on.

At night I worked on the wedding. Darla did most of the planning, but she parceled out little tasks to me—figuring out whether we could bake a cake (no, we didn't have baking powder or eggs), finding enough safety pins to hold preapocalyptic dresses and tuxes onto postapocalyptically thin bodies, and tracking down a wedding service to adapt. That last one was easy; nearly every abandoned farmhouse had a Bible, and one of them had a *Lutheran Book of Worship* with a wedding service too.

Belinda made great use of the medical supplies; only two more people died, and nearly everyone would be healthy enough to attend the wedding. Only one question gnawed at me: would Mom even come?

Chapter 56

I desperately wanted Mom to come to the wedding, but I was equally terrified to ask her. What if she said no? So I put off the trip to Warren. And put it off some more. I realized I was being terribly unfair to Rebecca—she loved Darla, and if she didn't get to come to the wedding, she would probably skin me and make a winter coat out of my hide.

Three nights before the big day, I was on guard in one of the sniper nests. We had four of them built by then, and we staffed all of them 24/7. Our security procedures would make attacking Speranta with anything less than a tank suicidal. I routinely gave myself the worst shifts, the ones that started at 2:00 A.M. or 4:00 A.M., both because I figured that was when we were most likely to be attacked, and because I had noticed that people seemed more enthusiastic about heinous tasks when I was also willing to do them.

I was scanning the horizon with a pair of binoculars, looking at darkness, darkness, and more darkness, when a knock sounded on the hatch under me. I just about jumped out of my skin.

Uncle Paul's muffled voice said, "You're lying on the hatch."

"Actually I'm having a coronary on the hatch," I said as I scooted aside and pulled it open.

"Sorry. Can't wait until we get a telephone system installed." Uncle Paul flopped on the floor, panting. "That's a ridiculously long climb."

"You're working on telephones?" I let the hatch clang shut and went back to scanning the horizon while we talked.

"It's on the list. After the wedding. Should be possible. We've got power, and we can scavenge the components."

"What about cell phones? Or some way to communicate with scouts? Ben wants me to set up a patrol schedule."

"Tougher. I don't know much about cellular switching systems. Maybe radios would be easier. I'll work on it," Uncle Paul said. "Anyway, I didn't come up here to talk about telephones." He paused for a long while. Just as I was getting ready to break the silence, he said, "Does my sister-in-law or Rebecca know you're getting married on Sunday?"

I cringed. I had been avoiding the topic, even with myself. I certainly didn't want to talk about it with Uncle Paul. "I don't know."

"Well, has anyone gone to Warren to tell them?"

"Not that I know of."

"They're going to be pretty upset if they don't get an invitation to your wedding."

"Mom'll be upset either way. Sometimes I think the only thing that would make her happy is an invitation to Darla's funeral."

"That's not fair, and you know it."

"Neither is the way she acts around Darla!"

"Maybe not. You know, the relationship with parents is never easy. It's so fraught with emotion that neither the parents nor their children can think about it rationally."

"I don't really think of myself as a child anymore."

"You're not. But becoming an adult doesn't make it easier. Harder, really."

I rolled to a new sniper port to continue my scan of the horizon. "I don't get where I went wrong with Mom, why it's all screwed up so badly."

"Assigning blame isn't going to help. If you can, think about it like a political problem. You're getting damn good at those."

I snorted, my eyes still glued to the horizon. "You liked the way I outmaneuvered Evans, huh?"

"He still doesn't know what hit him. If the relationship with your mother were purely political, what would you do?"

"I'd take the offensive." And that was when I knew
exactly what to do.

Chapter 57

In the morning I went to Warren. I left Uncle Paul in charge of Speranta and Darla working on a wind turbine—I thought my mother might be more open to the news if she wasn't staring at Darla as she heard it. Darla asked who was going with me, and I said I had talked to Uncle Paul, which was technically true, if a little deceptive. I had decided to go alone—on skis I would be fast and stealthy.

I breezed into Warren a little before lunch. There were still no sentries, no wall, not even so much as a barbed-wire fence. I skied right up to the back door of the house where Mom and Rebecca were living.

When I peeked in the window, I was greeted by a scream from Mom—she and Rebecca were sitting at a table right under the window, sewing by the light it let in. There was a huge pile of cloth scraps and old clothing on the table, which they were laboriously patching by hand.

I waved through the glass, and Mom sat back down heavily. Rebecca smiled and waved back before popping up to open the door. I knelt and started slowly untying the straps that held my boots to the skis—we had far more pairs of downhill skis than cross-country skis, so someone working under Darla's direction had converted a bunch of downhill skis so they could be attached to the toes of modified hiking boots. They worked fine, but they were a real pain to put on and take off.

Before I had even the first ski detached, Rebecca was outside. "Oh. My. God. That hook is wicked, bro." She reached out as if to touch it, and I moved my hook away.

"Careful. The edge is razor sharp."

She drew back her hand. "I'd heard about it from Dr. McCarthy, but whoa."

"It wasn't the most fun I've ever had on a Thursday night," I said.

"I always pictured you more as a Peter Pan type than Captain Hook."

I wondered how long the Captain Hook comments would follow me. The rest of my life, probably. "Yeah, me too."

"I kept meaning to come visit," she said, "but it got crazy busy."

"Same here." I gave her the short version of recent events while I wrestled off the skis. Then we were inside. Mom stood in front of the door, hands wrapped around herself as if she were cold. Well, she probably was—it was freezing in there. I had gotten used to the longhouse, which was usually above fifty. Mom's house was cold enough that I could see my breath in the air.

"Alex, your hand . . ." Mom said, still clutching herself.

Go on the offensive, I reminded myself. "It's fine, Mom." I held my arms wide for a hug. "Good to see you."

She opened her own arms, wrapping herself around me, and for a moment it felt like everything was all right. "How've you been?" she asked. "I mean, other than . . ."

"The hook's not bad once you get used to it," I said. "And everything else is going well. We've got enough food, finally. . . . you should come visit. Bring your mending. We've got an electric sewing machine hooked up you can use. Or we can get you new clothes pretty easily." The Wallers had more clothing than both our settlements could use in a lifetime.

"You've got electricity?"

I kicked myself mentally. We could handle a few more refugees, but not the floods that might show up if word got around about how well-off we were. But I couldn't rewind the conversation. "We only use it for sewing when the wind is blowing and the batteries are fully charged. Heating the greenhouses is the top priority. But yeah, nobody sews by hand in Speranta anymore."

"Well, I'd love to see that and to use your sewing

machine, but I've got new duties here as First Lady. And I'll be principal of the new school when it opens next month. Maybe I can come see your little settlement in a few months when the school's running well."

First Lady? What did she mean by that? And little settlement? And how was it that Warren could mow down kids in the road a few months ago and now be opening a school? Focus, Alex, that's not what you're here for. "Could you make a short trip this weekend? It's not far, only a couple hours on skis."

"I really don't have the time, honey."

"I know! We could pick you up on a Bikezilla. You could sit in it and just ride there and back—make it a one-day trip." It would be a hard day for whoever was pedaling the Bikezilla, but whatever.

Mom sat back down and picked up the jeans she was patching. "What's so important about this weekend anyway?"

I hesitated. There was no easy way to say it. "Darla and I are getting married on Sunday."

"Absolutely not!" Mom snapped.

Chapter 58

"You could consider it, at least!" I said.

"No. You are not marrying that girl." Mom held the needle as if she was going to stab it into the jeans.

"I wasn't asking for permission!"

"Good, because I forbid it."

"Mom!" Rebecca said.

"Don't 'Mom' me. That girl is bad for him."

"After all the time I spent trying to convince you to invite Alex, to let me go tell him?" Rebecca said. "You're just going to shoot him down when he reaches out to you?"

Huh? "Tell me what?"

"Alex, I swear to God," Rebecca said, "I've had bowel movements more observant than you are."

I wasn't sure whether to scream or cry—I felt like doing both. "What am I supposed to be observing?"

Mom was stitching away furiously, ignoring us both.

"Her hands," Rebecca said. "You're supposed to notice her hands."

I looked. They were the same hands Mom had always had—long fingers with angles a little too sharp to be elegant. "Her rings," I whispered. They had been gold—yellow. Now they were platinum. And the diamond on her engagement ring was, like, twenty times the size of the one Dad had given her. "Why's she got new rings?"

"She remarried, dumbass." Rebecca whirled toward Mom. "I can't believe your hypocrisy. You're going to forbid Alex from marrying Darla, you're not going to his wedding, and you didn't even invite him to your own?"

"It was only a small thing," Mom said.

"Yeah," Rebecca replied, "like fifty of the mayor's cronies and me."

"She married Mayor Petty," I said flatly, still not believing it, but at the same time understanding that it was true.

Mom kept her attention on her sewing. I spun, opened the door, and rushed outside, slamming the door with a satisfying crash.

I knelt to tie my boots back into my skis but couldn't do it; my hand was shaking too badly. This was a stupid idea. Reaching out to Mom. One thing I knew: Speranta was going to have a law allowing children to divorce their parents. I didn't know if she could forbid me to marry—in the old world, maybe, although I was eighteen now. In this new world, not a chance.

"Alex, wait."

I was so freaked out that I hadn't even noticed my sister following me outside. "Why? Nothing's going to change her mind."

"I know. But I'm coming with you. I want to see my big brother get married. It would have been *such* a delicious scandal in the old world, huh? Eighteen-year-old high school senior marries college-age girl?" Rebecca smiled sadly.

"Hurry then, okay?"

Rebecca went back inside. By the time I had calmed down enough to start strapping on my skis, I started hearing shouting from inside the house. Then crashing noises. I wondered if I should go back inside to make sure Rebecca was okay. But my presence might make it even worse.

Finally Rebecca emerged, looking flushed, wearing a heavy coat, backpack, and ski boots. She was carrying a really nice set of Saloman XADV cross-country skis in her arms. She snapped into them in less than a tenth of the time it'd taken me to get into my jury-rigged setup. "We'd better get out of here before Mom calls the sheriff—or our new stepfather."

"You think she will?" I asked.

Rebecca shrugged.

We left Warren in silence. I took a different route back to the homestead, weaving in and out of old ski and snowmobile tracks as much as possible to confuse our trail. We had traversed almost half the distance back to Speranta before either of us spoke again.

"You have extra clothing at the new farm?" Rebecca asked. We were single file with me in the lead, so she had to yell.

"Yeah. Plenty." Clothing was easy to come by now. I tried not to think too much about its provenance, though— some of it came from the closets of the dead. "Why?"

"I don't think Mom wants me to come back."

I stopped and stepped out of the ski track, letting her draw alongside me. "I'm sorry." I drew her into an awkward, one-armed, sideways hug. "How did everything get so messed up?"

She sighed heavily, leaning into me. "I thought I could convince her to, I don't know, accept you and Darla or something. But it just got worse. It was always Darla this and Darla that—if the bacon stuck to the bottom of the pan, I swear, Mom blamed Darla for it. I tried ignoring her, I tried arguing, but nothing seemed to work."

"I don't get it. Why? Mom seemed to hate Darla from the moment they met."

"Think about how they first met, in the middle of the same gun battle where Dad got shot—"

"But Darla had nothing to do with Dad's death. If anyone was to blame, it was me! I talked Dad into helping rescue Darla. I did that."

"It wasn't your fault, Alex."

"I know that. It was the goddamn Dirty White Boys'

fault. That isn't my point. So why the hell does she blame Darla?"

"Because she can't blame you."

"Why not? I'd rather have her angry at me than Darla!"

"It'd be too much like blaming herself."

I fell silent, thinking about it. When had my little sister gotten so mature, so perceptive? Or maybe she had always been that way, but I was finally open enough to notice it? But it still didn't completely make sense. "She's obviously over Dad. She married that politiciansicle, after all."

"Politiciansicle?" Rebecca asked.

"Petty. He's cold, has a stick up his butt, and you've got to lick it to get him to do anything."

Rebecca laughed. "You always did have a way with words."

I caught sight of two figures in the distance moving toward us. "Someone's coming," I whispered. I unslung the rifle from my back and dropped flat in the snow. Rebecca threw herself prone alongside me.

Chapter 59

I flicked off the safety and chambered a round, then pushed my head up just enough to see. There were definitely only two of them, headed directly toward us on skis, but I couldn't make out their faces at this distance. I held the rifle ready and watched them approach.

When they got within shouting distance, one of them spoke up, "Alex, if you shoot me, so help me, the wedding's off," Darla yelled.

I pointed the rifle away from her, safetied it, and ejected the round from the chamber. When they got closer, I could see that Darla was skiing alongside Zik.

"What were you thinking, taking off on your own?" Darla said as she reached us.

"I'm fast and stealthy on my own," I replied.

"And if you'd broken a leg or something? Who was going to go get help? Or drag your sorry ass home?"

"Oh." I hadn't really thought about that possible scenario. She sort of had a point.

"Sorry."

"Never mind. Let's get home." Darla gave Rebecca a hug, and then all four of us pointed our skis toward Speranta.

"Guess your mom's not coming?" Darla said after a bit.

"No," I said.

"What's the deal? I mean, I get that she blames me for your dad's death for some reason, but why's she taking it out on you?"

"That's the main thing, but there's more to it," Rebecca said. "You know she was feuding with Uncle Paul, right?"

"No. When? I never heard them argue," Darla said.

"It was stupid," Rebecca said. "It all started about three and a half years ago, before the eruption. Max dared me to jump off the barn into a haystack. I did it, like an idiot, and broke my arm. Mom blamed Max, since he was older and it was his farm, even though it wasn't like he pushed me or anything. And then Mom and Uncle Paul started arguing over who would take care of the medical copays. Uncle Paul sent her a check, but she wouldn't cash it. Said it had to come from Max, or he wouldn't learn. Maybe she was right, but Uncle Paul felt like she was meddling. So the point is, she was never comfortable on the farm anyway."

"But that's where she was when Yellowstone blew, right?" Darla said.

"Yeah. That's why Mom decided to go to Warren that day. To try to patch things up with Uncle Paul."

"I didn't know that," I said.

"You're a little bit oblivious sometimes, Bro," Rebecca said. "Anyway, then Mom cracked up before the battle— she would never talk about that, but I think she was embarrassed afterward. Maybe even afraid Uncle Paul would blame her for Aunt Caroline's death."

"He didn't," I said.

"Either way, caring for Mayor Petty became a way to avoid her brother-in-law. And then I guess Mom and Petty fell in love or something."

I sighed. My whole body felt heavy, like God had cranked the gravity up by twenty percent. I felt like yelling at him, Could you turn the thermostat up too, while you're at it? I didn't want to deal with it, didn't want to think about my mother anymore.

My sister skied more slowly, falling a little behind. I had to strain to make out her words. "I thought I could help, that I could be there for her, change her mind. But nothing ever really changes, does it? And now . . . and now she doesn't even want me around anymore."

I heard a choking sound—half animal snarl, half sob—and twisted to look back. Rebecca was crumpled in the snow behind me, sobbing. I performed a laborious step-turn, wishing I had skis like Rebecca's that I could snap in and out of easily. Darla and Zik skied on a bit before noticing we had dropped back. I pulled up beside Rebecca and fell into the snow beside her, wrapping my one good arm around her, supporting us both on my hook, thrust deep into the snow beside us.

"No matter what happens, *I'll* always be your family." I sat in the uncaring snow, holding my sister and sharing her tears.

Chapter 60

I woke before dawn on the morning of the wedding, dressed quietly, stepped outside, and looked to the east. Light was just beginning to emerge from the horizon, a flame-orange streak that looked more like a prairie fire than a sunrise. On the spur of the moment, I decided to climb the icy roof of the longhouse to get a better look. Getting onto the roof was easy—it stretched all the way to the ground. Still, the first time I tried to climb it, I slid back. I went inside, got a claw hammer to carry in my natural hand, and using that and my hook as improvised ice axes, I managed to scramble to the top.

I straddled the peak of the roof, getting cold while staring at the horizon. The sun still wasn't visible; it existed only as a bright smudge under a yellow-gray sky. But sometimes at dawn and dusk the sky came alight with riotous color—shows so surreal, it seemed as though we had been transported in the night to some alien planet.

That morning the sunrise was exceptional. Yellows, oranges, and reds slashed across the sky in vibrant swathes. Here and there, violets and greens emerged as if to reassure me that there was still some blue sky behind the yellow-gray murk, biding its time patiently until the thinning ash and sulfur dioxide allowed it to reemerge. The whole eastern sky flared with brilliant color, wrapping around and above me in a psychedelic embrace from the god of impressionist painters.

I waited and watched, reveling in the sunrise, until the sky faded to a uniform yellow-gray again. My legs had frozen to the roof. I pried them free and slid down to prepare for the big day.

We held the wedding in the original longhouse. We had cleared all the bedrolls and detritus of our day-to-day lives out of the middle and festooned the longhouse in plastic greenery and flowers. I stood at the front alongside the makeshift altar, trying not to shift nervously from foot to foot. Max and Ben stood beside me, Rebecca and Anna on the other side of the altar.

Darla stepped through the longhouse door on Uncle Paul's arm. She was a vision in her long white dress, its bodice made of some material that sparkled, playing flirtatiously with the electric lights overhead. With every step she took, the sparkles in her bodice picked up more of the light from the candles burning alongside the altar, making their flecks yellow instead of white, warming her as she neared me at the front of the room.

Her shoulders were bare, showing off her powerfully muscled upper arms. She wore the homemade necklace I had given her three years ago, its pendant—a 15/16 nut—nestled at the curve of her breasts. Her exposed skin was red from the cold wind outside, and I suppressed an urge to run down the aisle and lay my jacket over her shoulders. Despite its shoulderless style, the dress sported sleeves so long that they nearly hid her hand and hook. I almost laughed out loud when her skirts shifted and I caught a glimpse of her feet—she was wearing her usual black leather combat boots under all that frippery. What did brides normally wear on their feet? Glass slippers? I wasn't sure. Anyway, the combat boots were much more practical for waiting around in the snow outside while the rest of us filed in.

We had no organ or piano, of course, but we had scavenged a fiddle, and Elaine, one of the young women who had been shot outside of Warren, was a Suzuki-method violinist. She managed a pretty decent rendition of "Here Comes the Bride."

Reverend Evans started saying something, but I couldn't hear him. All the space between my ears was full—full of Darla. I had been in love with her almost since the first time I'd seen her: an overall-clad angel with a needle and thread to sew closed my wounds. But I had never felt that love as keenly as I did at that moment. I loved the small mole on her back under her left shoulder blade. I loved her earlobes and the way she giggled when I kissed them. I even loved her hook, with its ungainly wrench and screwdriver sockets.

"Ahem," Reverend Evans was clearing his throat, "would you take the family candle, please?"

Darla was holding a lit candle and glaring at me. I could read that glare as clearly as a billboard—it said, "Now, dumbass!"

I smiled an apology at her and picked up the other lit candle. Five unlit candles were arrayed on a stand between us in front of the altar: four smaller candles in a square pattern and a large one in the middle. The candles were mismatched—purple, red, and white, their sizes irregular too. Candles were exceedingly difficult to come by now and worth a fortune in trade; burning a few inches off these would easily be the most expensive part of this ceremony.

"We light the memory candles to symbolize those who have passed on and cannot be here in body, but who are surely here in spirit, blessing this union."

Darla tipped the candle she held to light one of the smaller candles. "For my father, Joseph Edmunds." Her voice was clear and brave. She lit the next one. "For my mother, Gloria Ed—" A tear raced down her cheek, and she bit her lower lip.

I lit a candle. "For my father, Douglas Halprin." I lit the fourth small candle. Did it make sense to light a candle for my mother? She wasn't here, but she wasn't dead either. Was I saying she was dead to me? She wasn't, I decided—would never be so long as we were both physically alive. I would hold onto hope even if she couldn't. "For my mother, Janice." Did I call her Janice Halprin or Janice Petty? I hadn't thought about it, so I just used her first name.

After a short pause, Reverend Evans stepped into the silence. "And now we light the unity candle to symbolize the joining of these two families." Darla and I tipped our candles toward the large one, letting our flames mingle and light it. We put our candles in the candelabrum and stepped back to listen to the remainder of the service.

The rest passed in a blur. There were readings and prayers, and Reverend Evans preached a sermon of sorts—I barely heard it. My mind burned as brightly as the candles before us, full of wonder at the beautiful woman beside me, soon to be my wife.

Then I was repeating after Reverend Evans, taking the vow that would bind us forever. I remembered what Darla had said in the snowbank outside Stockton, when we thought we were dying: that we were already married, that we had taken a vow stronger than the one that bound most married couples.

In a way, she was right. So many people mouthed these words and then ignored their meaning, ignored the hard work and sacrifice the vow required. In that sense, we were already more married than many couples and had been for more than two and a half years.

But in another way, she was wrong. There was something wonderful about saying the words here, in front of our whole community. In front of God, maybe. I had never been much of a believer, but in that moment, it wasn't difficult to feel that something holy was taking place, that we were being watched and blessed from above.

Max fumbled the ring, and it rolled around on the floor for a moment. I had visions of it falling through one of the cracks in the floorboards. We had built the longhouse fast and loose—there were plenty of ring-size cracks in the floor. But Max stopped the ring by the simple expedient of stomping on it. He plucked it off the floor and handed it to me, his face burning redder than the candles.

"With this ring, I thee wed," I said as I slipped it onto Darla's finger. She slipped my ring onto my right hand—I would wear it there forever. Darla had offered to make me a ring holder for my hook, so I could wear it on the traditional side, but I had said no. I wanted the ring against my skin, where I could feel it, reminding me of this day and of this promise.

Then Reverend Evans spoke the words I had been waiting through the whole service to hear. "You may kiss the bride."

I kissed Darla gently like the first time we'd kissed on an old couch in an abandoned house east of Worthington, Iowa, more than two and a half years ago. When our lips parted, Darla whispered, "Did I ever tell you that you're a five-star kisser?"

"No," I said. "There aren't enough stars in the sky to describe how it feels to be kissed by you."

Darla smiled and turned to the crowd, holding my hand aloft. "Let's party!" she shouted.

Everyone quickly cleared out the middle of the long-house. We didn't hold a procession—there was nowhere to proceed to anyway. I turned to snuff the candles; we might need them if our electricity failed.

The violinist was joined by a banjo player, and Max set up a scavenged drum kit. It was a strange trio, but the banjo player knew a bunch of square-dancing songs, so he led and Max and the violinist just followed along.

Flasks and bottles appeared as if by magic, people sharing their long-hoarded personal stock to celebrate. Nearly everyone offered me a drink, but I turned them all down. I didn't love the taste of alcohol, and there was no way I wanted to be drunk on my wedding night. Darla drank until her cheeks were flushed, and her smile grew a little brighter than usual.

We did as many of the usual reception rituals as we could. Darla tossed a plastic bouquet over her head, and Alyssa snagged it out of the air. She carried it back to where the band was set up and leaned over to smooch Max. He was so surprised, he dropped his drumsticks.

I went over and pounded Max on the back by way of congratulating him. He stood up and leaned close, whispering, "Someone left a necklace under Alyssa's pillow three nights ago. She thinks I did it."

"You didn't?" I said.

"No."

"I wonder who's giving her stuff? Whoever it is has been remarkably secretive—it's been going on for what, a year now?"

"A year and a half," Max said.

"You'd better tell her it's not you, before she finds out some other way."

"I guess you're right." Max shrugged, and I went to rejoin Darla.

We didn't have a traditional cake, but someone had made a dense, fudgy concoction from supplies we'd gotten from the Wallers. Darla and I cut the ersatz cake and smeared it all over each other's faces. I held her tightly and cleaned off her face with my tongue, while Rebecca looked on in disgust. I thought I was being eminently sensible, though—no sense letting all those calories go to waste, right?

Eventually the party wound down, and people started retiring to their bedrolls at the edges of the longhouse. I told the band to pack up so those who wished to could sleep. Darla and I stayed up a while longer, talking with the remaining revelers, some of whom were well and truly smashed. My feet ached and my head spun, more from exhaustion than the tiny bit of alcohol I had consumed.

"You want to go to bed?" I whispered to Darla.

"Thought you'd never ask," she replied with a wicked grin.

Usually we all slept out in the middle of the longhouse floor. There was no privacy whatsoever. A room that can sleep ninety-eight people comfortably can't really be cut up into ninety-eight bedrooms, and we didn't have the time or manpower to build partition walls anyway. Greenhouses took priority. For tonight, though, someone had erected a temporary screen made of plywood panels around one corner of the room. I lifted Darla into my arms and carried her into our makeshift bedroom to the catcalls and cheers of the partiers.

Someone had strewn plastic roses all over our bedroll. I laid Darla down atop them, and she immediately started rolling, digging around and tossing the roses aside. I brushed the faux roses off my side of the bedroll, kicked my shoes off, and lay down beside her.

Darla attacked me—that's the only way I can put it. She rolled on top of me and kissed me with a fire and passion and intensity that left me breathless and bruised. Her hand was everywhere, and she was in far too much of a hurry to bother undressing. Instead she shifted bits of clothing and undergarments, and things were going much too fast, but I wanted nothing more than to lie back and enjoy it, to let her do whatever she wanted with me.

But I couldn't. I pushed her off me, rolling her onto her back beside me.

"What the hell?" she said, loud enough that I was afraid people on the other side of the screen would hear.

"We can't," I whispered. "I mean, I want to, and we can do anything you want to except that, but . . ."

"But what?" Darla said, still talking way too loudly for my comfort.

"You already know what," I said. We had tried to buy condoms during our visit to the Wallers. There weren't any to be had at any price. They had a small stock of Triphasil—a birth control pill—but it would have cost us a small fortune in kale. We had opted to buy more antivirals and antibiotics instead.

"I don't care, Alex. I want children. Lots of them. You know that. There's no reason not to start now."

"There's every reason not to start now!" Now I was the one talking too loudly. "You could easily—"

"That tired old argument? Animals have babies without veterinarians every day. Women had babies back when medical 'science' consisted of balancing the humors in the body with leeches. I won't magically self-destruct just because I get preggers."

"Animals die in childbirth, Darla—you know that better than I do. And women used to die at a far higher rate than I—"

"At what rate?" Darla was flat-out yelling now. "One percent? Two percent? Ten percent? I don't care. I will take that risk. I want to take that risk."

"I can't," I whispered. "I can't take that risk. I can't lose you, Darla."

She was silent for a moment. When she spoke, her voice was softer. "I think we *should* take that risk. A baby would be important to our community. Important to Speranta. It would bring real meaning to the name Hope."

"You don't have a baby just to give hope to other people. And if we added another grave—your grave—to the rows outside, it would kill me. Might kill Speranta too."

Darla made a scoffing noise.

"You underestimate yourself. Without you, we'd have no Bikezillas, no greenhouses, no wind turbines—"

"I couldn't have figured out the electronics without your uncle."

"You would have, eventually. You're the heart of this community."

"No, you're the heart. I'm the brains."

"On every subject but this one, I agree with you," I said.

Darla scowled at me for a too-long moment. Then she forcefully smoothed down the skirts of her wedding dress so that they covered her long, muscular legs. She reached up to switch off the lamp. Then she rolled over, ignoring me.

And that was how I ruined our wedding night.

Chapter 61

More people filtered into Speranta over the following weeks and months. The wedding had been in April, and by mid-June, Charlotte's census had passed four hundred. People were crowded into the two long-houses we had finished.

I worried that the extra refugees would be a burden, a weight that would sink the precariously floating SS *Speranta*, but I was wrong. Charlotte had a positive genius for finding skills we needed among the newcomers. We got a guy who had paid his way through college by working in his dad's well-drilling company. With his help, we were finally able to get a well drilled inside Speranta, ending the constant, mile-long water treks to the nearest farmhouse.

Charlotte practically bounced off the walls with joy when a woman showed up who had sold irrigation equipment in her old life. I didn't see what the big deal was until we hooked her up with a plumber, and they designed and built an automatic watering system for one of the greenhouses. The new system increased production and freed up a massive amount of labor for building more irrigation systems and greenhouses.

We built greenhouses at a furious pace, managing to stay so far ahead of our population, we were able to store surplus food, begin paying down our debt to the Wallers, and buy more supplies from them. After the third such shipment, the Wallers' leader, Dean, relented on the hostage deal and allowed Ed and our other people to move back to Speranta. More than thirty Wallers accompanied Ed—they had grown tired of hiding in the warehouse and wanted to help build greenhouses. I welcomed each of them with a hug, and Charlotte welcomed them with a twenty-minute quiz.

One of the newcomers had been a hard-core organic gardener in her previous life. She convinced us to dig up our old latrine pits and compost our fecal matter instead of burying it. Dr. McCarthy argued with her about it for a while, but eventually she won him over by promising to properly monitor the temperature of our compost piles. I wasn't sure what good that would do, but it satisfied Dr. McCarthy, which was good enough for me. We also had to start peeing into a five-gallon pail fitted with a toilet seat instead of into the latrine. Evidently, human urine diluted properly is a fabulous fertilizer. Who knew? The productivity of our greenhouses climbed further.

Another newcomer, Ranaan Kendall, had served in the second Iraq war. He was young—maybe in his late twenties—but he had a ridged and grooved face, pitted from childhood acne too much sun and sand, or both. He worked with Ben to improve our military readiness. They set up flags so our snipers could account for windage, and they developed a system of arm signals so we could communicate without wasting precious ammo.

Zik left every few weeks. He was gone for days at a time, looking for his daughter, Emily. I'd quit worrying about revealing our location and had relaxed all the early rules about leaving Speranta. The secret was obviously out. I would have to rely on our numbers, defensive plans, and Ben's military genius to carry us through an attack. After each trip, Zik was surly and withdrawn for days—he hadn't been able to find any trace of his daughter. She would have been sixteen by then—if she was still alive.

I desperately wanted to know what was going on in the world. We had gotten enough refugees from neighboring states to know that Wisconsin, Indiana, and Kentucky were as bad off as Illinois. Iowa was worse, far worse. There had been some kind of collapse in the government back east almost a year ago, and FEMA and Black Lake had mostly disappeared. Food distribution had ended in the camps and cities; collapse, starvation, and cannibalism inevitably followed.

I'd been trying to get a shortwave radio. I wanted news from back east, to know if there was still a government in operation. It was best to act as if we were completely on our own, though I couldn't help but hope that some kind of functioning government was left.

One of the newcomers had been a licensed shortwave operator, but he'd left his equipment at home, halfway between Iowa City and Des Moines. I stared at the spot on a map for a while, thinking of mounting an expedition to retrieve it, but his transceiver was too far. And there was no guarantee that his shortwave set would still be there and in working condition.

We caught a break when Grant Clark trudged into Speranta. He had survived in the postapocalyptic world by traveling and trading information and supplies for food and clothing. He was the same gleaner who had sold a camp roster to Rita Mae, the librarian in Worthington, nearly two years earlier—the roster that had enabled me to find my parents. He said he had a working shortwave setup hidden in an abandoned town not far away, but he didn't want to trade it to me. He powered it on batteries scavenged from cars and sold the information gleaned from the shortwave chatter. I finally convinced him to part with it in return for a custom-made, one-man Bikezilla loaded with two hundred pounds of kale and the promise that he could make Speranta his home base and listen in on the shortwave anytime he wanted.

There was depressingly little chatter on the short-wave bands. Nothing at all from back east. All the government bands that had been full of transmissions only two years ago were dead and silent now. The religious broadcaster who I had asked for help when I was in the FEMA camp in Maquoketa was off the air. Even the strange stations that read lists of numbers were gone. We did make contact with a few isolated communities—a group in Georgia, another in Mexico, and one in the mountains of northern California. They were barely hanging on; there was nothing we could do for each other except share tips on compost piles and greenhouse construction. When conditions were good, we caught snippets of transmissions in Chinese, Spanish, or languages nobody recognized. I hoped the reason we didn't reach more communities was the difficulty in powering a radio transceiver. The possibility that everyone else was dead was too horrible to contemplate.

I asked Ben to monitor the shortwave, clicking through the bands and transmitting occasionally. He didn't want to do it at first—it wasn't a military shortwave set and therefore not interesting to Ben. We talked for nearly an hour about the importance of military intelligence, discussing all the things we might learn from monitoring the shortwave, before he finally agreed to monitor it. Once I convinced him to take the job on, he was amazing at it. He would sit at the set for hours on end, patiently listening and transmitting in impeccable shortwave code. I didn't know a CQ from a QRA from an XYZPDQ, but Ben took the time to study the manual Grant had brought with the transceiver and learn all the terms, using them perfectly.

A few days after he had started, Ben came charging up to me at the construction site where I was working. We were building . . . wait for it . . . yet another greenhouse. Our nineteenth, or Greenhouse 5-C.

"Mayor Halprin, Mayor Halprin," Ben yelled.

"Ben," I replied when he got close enough so I didn't have to yell, "you can call me Alex, you know."

"Yes sir, Mayor Alex Halprin."

I sighed. "What is it, Chief Radio Operator Fredericks?" I said it sarcastically, but it went right over Ben's head, of course.

"I have a contact. Someone who knows you and wishes to speak to you. I sent them a QRX."

"What's a QRX?"

"A request to wait."

"Who is it?" I asked.

"Station WBØSX."

"Yes, but who is that? You have a name or location?"

Ben looked at his shoes for a moment. "I forgot to ask for their QTH," he said finally. "I am sorry, Mayor Alex Halprin."

I put Ed in charge of the construction site and left with Ben, running the mile or so back to the original long-house where Darla and I lived and the radio was kept. One disadvantage of clustering our greenhouses around the wind turbines was that we were really spread out.

I picked up the mike, depressing the talk lever. "This is Alex Halprin. Over."

"You are supposed to say CQ, CQ from K9LC," Ben said.

"Alex! You survived! Guess I owe Rita Mae a pound of hamburger. Sorry about betting against you." The voice was a woman's but so crackly over the connection that I couldn't tell who was speaking.

"She is supposed to say K9LC here is WBØSX," Ben said.

"Who's speaking?" I said.

"I'm sorry," the woman's voice replied, "Kenda. Mayor Kenda from Worthington."

I heard some muttering in the background that I couldn't make out, and a new voice came on. "Alex, Rita Mae here. I knew you'd make it. Darla told me you were too stubborn and stupid to die, and I believed her."

"Thanks, I think. Glad to hear your voice."

"Well, I've been sick, but I can't kick the can yet. Afraid if I weren't here, Mayor Kenda would strap on a pair of jackboots."

"Rita Mae!" Kenda yelled, muffled in the background.

"I'm kidding. Keep your pants on back there, Madame Mayor." Sotto voce, she added, "She hates it when I call her that." For a moment the airwaves were filled by Rita Mae's cackle. "We're hard pressed here, but if you and Ben need a place to stay, you know we'll always welcome you." Rita Mae hesitated a moment. I wanted to break in but couldn't while she was transmitting. "How's . . . everyone else . . . Darla okay?"

I understood her hesitation. So many people had died, it was risky to ask about family. She'd only heard me and

Ben over the shortwave so far, so she couldn't be sure who else had survived.

"Rita Mae," Mayor Kenda said, her voice faintly audible in the background, "you've got to say 'over' and let up on the lever, or he can't respond."

"So excited I plumb forgot," Rita Mae said. "Over."

"Darla's fine," I said. "We got married, oh, four months ago. And thank you for the offer of a place to stay, but we're doing okay." I filled them in on Speranta, my election as mayor, our greenhouses, and current population of just under six hundred. So many people had died in Worthington, we had over three times their population now.

"Congratulations!" Rita Mae said when I had finished. "Alex, I hate to even bring this up, but we're sore pressed here. Flensers control all the cities near us. We've sent expeditions to Dubuque, Waterloo, and Cedar Rapids. We lost a lot of good men and women. Food's way too tight. Ammo's short. Flensers attack Worthington again, they're likely to win. There's been some talk of packing up, trying to head east—abandoning Worthington. Over."

"We're short on both ammo and weapons," I said. "We've got a good source of supplies for building greenhouses—glass, wire, pipe, and caulk—stuff like that. If you do move east, you'd be welcome here. I'm not sure how we'd cope with two hundred newcomers all at once, but if it comes to that, we'll figure it out. Over."

"Got lots of extra guns here. Be happy to share them and anything else we can spare in return for a little help on the greenhouses or our flenser infestations."

"That's not your bargain to make," Kenda protested in the background.

"Shush," Rita Mae said in her most authoritative librarian tone. "Oh, sorry, forgot again. Over."

"I'll talk to my advisers, see what I can do."

We chatted a while longer before I signed off. When I started to walk away, Ben called to me. "Mayor Halprin, may I have a small plot of land in one of the greenhouses for personal use?"

"Everyone's entitled to a personal vegetable plot if they want it. See Anna, and she'll assign you a space." I was so distracted by the conversation with Rita Mae, it didn't occur to me to ask why he wanted a plot. Ben must have been distracted too, because he turned away without a thank you or goodbye—he had gotten so much better at social niceties over the last two years that the lapse surprised me.

That night I called together my team of advisers: Darla, Ben, Uncle Paul, Ed, and Dr. McCarthy. We held informal meetings in the kitchen area of the first long-house. Anyone was welcome to listen in, and afterward I usually hung around to take suggestions and questions from our citizens. Our government was as open and transparent as I could make it.

"I want to mount an expedition. Take some supplies to the folks in Worthington. Trade for whatever they can spare. It's roughly seventy miles."

"I'm all for it," Darla said. "But you're not going to get anything like fair value in trade."

I nodded; I had figured Darla would take my side—not because she was my wife, but because Worthington had been her home.

"It would be a very risky venture for little potential gain," Ben said. "If the flenser gangs are numerous enough to threaten Worthington, we cannot mount an expedition strong enough to fight them. We have the manpower but not enough weapons."

I nodded again. Most of our citizens were former refugees from the Galena FEMA camp. Black Lake had confiscated the weapons of everyone they had interned there, so we were rich in manpower but poor in firepower. Ben had explained everything he knew about longbows to a couple of former carpenters who were trying to build a working prototype. So far, all their efforts were complete and literal busts. "What about a fast trading expedition? Thirty-two people on eight Bikezillas. Volunteers only. We'll stay off the roads, navigate by map and compass, avoid any flenser gangs too big to fight."

"That is a sound plan," Ben said.

"Uncle Paul?" I asked.

"Let's do it. I volunteer."

I nodded but made a mental note to talk to him later. He was still having horrible coughing fits. Whatever illness had lodged in his lungs had stayed there. There was no way I'd allow him to go gallivanting off to Worthington.

"Agreed," Dr. McCarthy said. "I volunteer too." Right, I was going to let our only qualified doctor risk himself? I would have to talk to Dr. McCarthy too.

"So it's settled," I said. "I'll lead the expedition. We'll leave in three days."

"Alex," Darla said, "you can't go. You can send me or Uncle Paul or someone else to lead the expedition—"

"Who'll run our engineering and construction program if you're gone?" I asked.

"Your uncle. But let me turn the question around. Who'll run *everything* if you're gone?"

I was silent for a moment thinking about that. She was right. Normally I thought of Speranta as a utopia—people worked together, lived together, and ate together, generally harmoniously. But in that moment, it felt more like a prison. I was trapped by my own success.

Chapter 62

During the question-and-answer period after the meeting, I was surprised to find that most people agreed with my decision to attempt to rescue Worthington, even though we were unlikely to get anything like fair value in trade for the supplies we sent them. Even after the apocalypse, the vast majority of people were generous and kind. The few who weren't, however—like the flensers—were exceptionally dangerous despite their relatively small numbers.

I put Ed in charge of the expedition, with Nylce second in command. Most people didn't know much about his background as a flenser. And the only people I trusted more than Ed and Nylce had duties they couldn't abandon. Max begged to be allowed to accompany the expedition. I told him he could go only with Uncle Paul's permission, which I knew he would never get.

I remembered Eli—the guy whose family Alyssa, Ben, and I had stayed with for a few days more than two years ago. Eli had helped me change a tire on the truck we had been driving when we had fled from the Peckerwoods flenser gang.

Eli's family had owned several pigs, and I wondered if they might still. Maybe they would be willing to move themselves and their pigs to Speranta. Worthington was only about thirty miles from their farm, so I asked Ed to visit Eli on the way home. We were composting a lot of material that could have been fed to hogs—kale stems and the like. And Dr. McCarthy was worried about our diet being too poor in protein. We were growing tons of black beans now, but I would feel much better if we had several potential sources of protein.

I had offered a bounty—a thousand pounds of food or ten thousand seeds for a breeding population of chickens, ducks, goats, cows, or pigs—and spread the word via the shortwave and the gleaner, Grant, but so far nobody had come forward to claim it. More than three years after the eruption, there were no live animals to be had. Silicosis from breathing the ash in the weeks immediately following the eruption had killed most of the livestock; hungry people had done in the rest.

The hardest part about sending Ed to Worthington was the waiting. I wished a thousand times a day that I had insisted on leading the expedition myself. At least then I wouldn't have been dangling on tenterhooks, wondering if I had sent Ed and the other volunteers off to their deaths. We needed a mobile shortwave set up. I knew they had existed before the volcano, but none were to be had at any price now.

Ed and I had planned for him to be gone for three weeks: a week to Worthington, a few days there, a few days looking for Eli and his family, and a week back. It should have easily been possible to make the whole trip in two weeks—a seventy-mile trek into Iowa that would have taken an hour and a half each way before the eruption—but they needed to move slowly, sending out scouts, avoiding roads and any potential opposition. The key to survival wasn't being good in a fight, it was avoiding the fight in the first place.

Ten days after he left, we heard via the shortwave that Ed had arrived in Worthington. I spoke to Ed that night. They had run into flensers, members of the Peckerwoods gang operating out of Cascade, about ten miles southeast of Worthington, and they had spent several days dodging them. Using Ben's intel, Colonel Levitov, a Black Lake commander, had cleared the Peckerwoods out of the Anamosa prison compound about two years back, but he hadn't done anything to the branch in Cascade. Ed stayed in Worthington for three days and then moved out in search of Eli's family. Ed told me that he expected to return to Speranta on his original schedule, about a week from when he left Worthington.

But two more weeks passed with no sign of Ed.

Darla noticed that I was distracted and snappish. She tried to divert my attention from worry about the expedition with sex, and yeah, that worked sometimes, but sometimes I also got the feeling she was trying to entice me into changing my mind about having kids. And we still didn't have any kind of birth control. That whole argument only added more stress I didn't need.

Then Darla tried to plan a huge party for my nineteenth birthday. I quashed that idea—no way could I celebrate while Ed was out there, lost or maybe worse. Instead, October 2nd passed like every other day—I led a greenhouse-building crew.

One day about five weeks after Ed had left Speranta, I got called to the phone. Uncle Paul and Darla had rigged a rudimentary intercom system. We had a telephone in each of our five longhouses and in every turbine tower. They hadn't been able to get any switching equipment working, so the phones were a kind of party line; if you picked up one receiver, they all rang, and the monitors assigned to every phone picked up and could hear everything that was said.

I was leading the construction of—inevitably—another greenhouse. So I had to hoof it into the adjacent longhouse to pick up the phone.

I pressed the receiver to my ear. "Mayor speaking, report please."

"Sentry, Turbine Tower 1-A reporting." I didn't recognize the voice. We had more people living in Speranta than I could keep track of now. Tower One was the first sniper's nest we had built at the original longhouse. It was still at the edge of the settlement. We were spreading out to the south and east of it. There were sixty-seven wind turbines in the area. Only about four-fifths of them still worked, though. The rest hadn't been shut down quickly enough when the ashfall hit. Still, that left enough turbines to heat about 110 greenhouses of the size we were building. "Unidentified party of nine confirmed inbound on foot, three and a half miles southeast."

Spotting an approaching group three and a half miles off was incredibly difficult in the dim yellow postvolcanic light. I made a mental note to find out who was manning Tower One and send him something. Maybe one of the boxes of brownie mix the Wallers had sent me. They wouldn't cook up right—we didn't have any eggs—but still, it was chocolate! "On-duty platoons to standby," I said. That would cause two dozen men and women at each longhouse to stop whatever they were doing and prepare to fight.

I could have called for a full mobilization, but that seemed like overkill given that we had only spotted nine people so far. "I'm on my way to Longhouse One." I handed the phone to the little girl who had been monitoring it and took off at a jog.

Could it be some sad remnant of Ed's expedition? It seemed likely. We got newcomers in all the time, but almost never in groups that large. They would usually show up as families—five or six people at most. I pulled three guys off construction duty to help me pedal a Bikezilla back to Longhouse One. Darla had continued to build four-person Bikezillas out of every snowmobile we found—the four-person models were much more practical for hauling supplies than smaller ones.

I was waiting at Longhouse One long before the group of strangers reached it. Uncle Paul stood next to me, holding a rifle. Evidently he was part of the duty platoon for the longhouse. Every now and then, he doubled over and released a series of long, dry coughs.

I stared out at the group as they came into view above the crest of the neighboring hill. One of them looked kind of like Ed. Even though I desperately wanted to see Ed again, I hoped it wasn't him. Because if it was Ed, what had happened to the other twenty-three people who'd left with him?

Chapter 63

When they got within a few hundred yards, I could see that the guy in the lead wasn't Ed. They were no threat either: bedraggled, beat down, and apparently unarmed, they were barely able to drag themselves up the rise toward the longhouse.

I asked Uncle Paul to relay the order to stand down the duty platoons. The sooner they got the order, the sooner everyone could get back to work.

There were two men and three women who looked to be in their forties, although looks were deceiving with people who had been starved as badly as this bunch. They all could easily have been in their late twenties. Nothing ages you like an apocalypse.

Two teenage guys and two young girls—eight or nine, maybe—rounded out the group.

"Hello," I called.

"H-h-hello," the guy in the lead replied.

"What brings you to Speranta?" I asked, although I was pretty sure I knew the answer.

"Heard Zik brought his family here and that they were doing all right. Heard it was safe here. That you had food."

"Nowhere's safe anymore, I guess. But we're doing okay. And we have food to share with those who're willing to work hard and contribute."

"Th-th-that'd be us."

I stretched out my good hand to him. "I'm Alex. Or Mayor Halprin. Some folks call me Captain though, 'cause of the hook, I guess."

"I'm Roy Feldman," he said as we shook.

"You look more like Peter Pan than Captain Hook," one of the teenage boys said.

I raised my eyebrows. "I've never heard that one before."

"Sorry."

I ushered them all into Longhouse One. We had walled off a chunk of it to serve as our medical clinic. I left most of the newcomers in Belinda's care, but Roy and I walked over to the kitchen area.

"How do you know Zik?" I asked once we were settled in with a bowl of dried kale chips and glasses of water.

Roy took a kale chip. He ate slowly but steadily, as if he were afraid that at any moment I would snatch back the bowl. I didn't eat any—I had eaten enough kale chips to last a lifetime. "We were neighbors in Stockton."

"Why'd you leave?" I asked, although I figured I already knew.

"People been disappearing for more 'n a year. You just wake up and they're gone. Nobody talks about it or complains. Red gets wind of a complaint, he cuts out your tongue. Heard he's got a string of 'em hanging in his bedroom. Dried up like old leaves."

Eww. His bedroom?

"We've heard reports he's trading girls to the Peckerwoods," I said.

"It's not just girls anymore," Roy said, "whole families disappear. If you're in tight with Red, you're okay, but anyone else . . . ain't that many left who aren't part of Red's circle. Figured it was time we got out before we disappeared. Went over the wall last night, me and my neighbors."

"What's he want with whole families?"

"I don't know for sure," Roy said. "But I s'pect the meat we've been eating in Stockton lately ain't pork."

Chapter 64

I convened the council that night to share Roy's news. I finished up my summary by saying, "I want Red's head on a pole. Give me some options."

Ben was shaking his head. "They have 150 men under arms behind a wall, and we have fewer than nineteen hundred rounds for our guns. Any kind of direct attack will fail."

"Alex," Darla said, "we can't right all the wrongs of this world. And when you try, that's when we get into trouble."

"But they're killing each other—"

"Let 'em!" Darla was almost yelling now. "They'll

449

get weaker and weaker. Eventually they'll be exactly like those three cannibals we killed in Freeport."

"She's right," Uncle Paul said. "We can't risk our people."

"We can welcome anyone who escapes," Dr. McCarthy said.

"If they attack us, our odds will be much better," Ben said. He and Ranaan—the Iraq War veteran—had developed an elegant plan for defending our spread-out settlement, and we had drilled on it endlessly. Whatever longhouse was attacked would hunker down to repel a siege, while all our forces from the other longhouses gathered to fall on the attackers in the flank or rear. Meanwhile our network of snipers would exact a terrible price on any attacking force. I was thankful we hadn't had to put it to the test, but I had every confidence it would work, unless we were attacked by an absolutely overwhelming force or one with artillery, an air force, or tanks.

"What would you do in Red's place, Ben?" I asked. "He's running out of food, people are fleeing, and he probably knows that we're well prepared for an attack."

Ben replied almost immediately, "I would attack Warren."

• • •

I wrote a long missive to Mayor Petty, summarizing what we knew about Stockton, and a shorter letter to my mother, begging her to reconsider and move to the safety of one of our longhouses. I even offered to put her in the newest one, Longhouse Five, where she would rarely see either me or Darla if she preferred not to.

Belinda volunteered to deliver the letters. I wanted to do it, but *everyone* on the council objected. Only Dr. McCarthy objected to Belinda going, and he was overruled.

Belinda slipped into Warren overnight, putting both letters through the mail slot at Mayor Petty's house. "It was easy," she told me the next morning. "They're sitting ducks."

The weeks crawled by without any word from Ed. Neither Mayor Petty nor my mom responded to my notes either. To be fair, we had no routine way to communicate with Warren, but it was only about five miles from there to Speranta. Someone could have come.

More escapees joined us from Stockton. Never again nine at once—they came in dribs and drabs of twos, threes, and fours.

My unease grew with every passing day. The very air around me felt charged, electric. Nothing was stable: Ed's missing expedition, Stockton's starvation and descent into cannibalism, Mayor Petty's denial about their vulnerability. I felt a little like I used to when I was sparring and my opponent launched a jump kick at me—he was committed and would have to come crashing down, and if I was in the way when it happened, I would get hurt.

Almost seven weeks after Ed's expedition left, the kick finally landed.

Chapter 65

I woke from a deep sleep to the sound of Max shouting, "Everybody up! Full mobilization!"

I was the only one who was supposed to call for a full mobilization. I sprang out of bed in my underwear. I grabbed my pants and boots and ran for the phone without taking the time to put them on. Darla was already half-dressed.

Rebecca was on the phone, monitoring reports from the other longhouses and sniper nests. "Report," I said as I stood in front of her, jamming my feet into my pants.

"Large force, two hundred plus, inbound about a

mile and a half to the northwest. They're headed right for us, right for Longhouse One. I already told everyone to mobilize."

"Good." I finished buttoning my pants—a neat trick when you have to do it one-handed—and then reached for the phone. "Longhouse One going to siege mode. Snipers stand ready. All other forces converge on Longhouse Three and await orders."

I sat on a bench to pull on my boots. "Send a runner to the door when they're at half a mile," I told Rebecca.

"Got it," she replied. Ben, over at the shortwave set, started scolding her for "incorrect military etiquette." I ran to the front door and grabbed the bullhorn we kept hanging beside the door.

They were moving very slowly. I must have waited more than half an hour before Max ran up to tell me the range had closed to a half mile. I opened our heavy, wooden front door and stared out into the black night. A few dim lights moved to the northwest in odd, bobbing paths, like ailing will-o'-the-wisps.

I raised the bullhorn to my lips and shouted, "This is Mayor Halprin. Halt, or you will be fired upon!" For a moment, nothing changed. Then the lights stopped moving. I sent Max back to Rebecca at the phone to find out if our sniper overhead could give me a more detailed report. Then someone yelled back from the group ahead; all I could make out was, "One person . . . talk."

"One unarmed person will be allowed to pass," I yelled back through the bullhorn. Then I waited. A light detached from the group ahead, growing brighter as it approached. Whoever was carrying it was moving fast, running. In less than two minutes, she was close enough that I could make out her face: Nylce Myers, who had accompanied Ed's expedition to Worthington.

Chapter 66

I ran out to meet her, giving her a hug. But we didn't have time to linger. "Who are those people?" I asked.

"Most of Warren," she said. "Everyone who's left, anyway."

"Wait, where's Ed?"

"He's . . . I don't know. The Reds got us. We were holed up in a farmhouse south of Warren last night. Only a day from home. They must have taken out our sentries. Suddenly they were among us, knives out. Ed surrendered—there was nothing else he could do. I slipped away to get help.

"I didn't have my boots on. After a few hours

hiking through the snow like that, my toes were turning black. I stopped in Warren for help—I was afraid I wouldn't make it the last five miles here. I begged Petty to send a messenger to you, and he promised he would, first thing in the morning. But the force of Reds that caught us was on its way to Warren. They slipped in and took the city at knifepoint, almost without a shot. Everyone who could, ran."

"Is Mom out there?" I asked, dreading the answer.

"She's okay. I don't know about Ed and the others, though. We found Eli. We had him and his family, his pigs, and a bunch of snowmobiles we captured from the Peckerwoods. The expedition was a huge success, but now—" Nylce's voice choked off somewhere deep in her throat. I ushered her into the longhouse and called a platoon to accompany me outside to meet Mayor Petty.

He was enthroned on his wheelchair, Mom at his right hand, Sheriff Moyers on his left. I didn't see how they had been moving him through the ice and snow—carrying the wheelchair like a palanquin, maybe?

"Mom," I said as I got close.

"Son," she said cautiously.

"I'm glad you're here," I said. "Wish you'd come earlier."

"We don't need to stay long," Mayor Petty said. "Just need to rest up, get back on our feet, and we'll go retake Warren."

"Anyone who's willing to work hard and live by our rules is welcome," I said. "And you can head back to Warren whenever you're ready." Suddenly it struck me, though: the man in front of me was responsible for the massacre outside of Warren. The man next to him, Sheriff Moyers, had carried it out. Many—maybe a third—of our settlers had been on Stagecoach Trail that night. They had lost parents, brothers, sisters, friends, and children on that road. I detested Mayor Petty, disliked him personally as well as everything he stood for. But some of the victims would hate him, and who could blame them? I still couldn't turn him away—he was, what, my stepfather now? If I sent him away, my mother would certainly follow him. And angry as I was with her, I still loved her. I needed her here in Speranta, safe. But how would I keep the other settlers from ripping Mayor Petty to shreds?

"That's fair. It's only for a few days, like I said," Bob Petty replied.

I had no illusions about his men returning to Warren. Once they got used to living in heated buildings, flipping a switch for light, and sleeping in the safety of a well-thought-out defensive system, most of them wouldn't want to return to Warren. Mayor Petty might, but I would wager nearly anything that he would be mighty lonely. "Come on, then. Let's get you checked in."

I raised my arms in a huge V at the closest sniper tower, signaling that everything was okay. If I had crossed them over my head instead, the shooting would have started.

Sheriff Moyers picked up Mayor Petty, slinging him awkwardly over his shoulders in a fireman's carry. Petty had enough of his right leg left that Moyers could hold on to it. Mom folded up his wheelchair and hung it from her back by an attached loop of cord. That answered the question of how they were transporting him—and why they were moving so slowly.

I rushed ahead to the longhouse, calling Anna, Charlotte, Uncle Paul, and Rebecca into a hurried conference. "I need you guys to clear everyone out of Longhouse Five. Move them into One through Four. I want Petty's people in Five and none of ours."

"You think Petty's group is dangerous?" Charlotte asked.

"No," I replied, "I think our people are liable to kill them."

Uncle Paul got it right away. "I'll go over there now and explain it to them."

"You go with him," I said to Anna, who was still ably managing our food stores. "Make sure there's no more than a day or two of food left in Five. It's possible that they'll disappear—I don't want to lose any critical supplies if they do."

Rebecca went back to monitoring the phone, and Charlotte prepared to do a preliminary census of the newcomers. When they finally got to the longhouse, Dr. McCarthy and I met them at the door.

Mom opened the wheelchair, and Sheriff Moyers set Mayor Petty down in it. When Petty looked up, his eyes caught Dr. McCarthy's, and they glared at each other for a moment.

"Doctor," Petty said frostily.

"Ex-Mayor," McCarthy replied.

I broke the standoff. "Dr. McCarthy will see to your wounded," I said. "The rest of you line up, please—Charlotte needs to ask you a few questions before we get you settled. Tomorrow, after you've had a chance to sleep, she'll conduct a more thorough interview and give preliminary work assignments."

"We're going to be assigned jobs by a child?" Mayor Petty asked. Charlotte was fifteen, but to be fair to Mayor Petty, she looked quite a bit younger.

"Yes," I said flatly. "If you have a problem with that, feel free to return to Warren. Now."

"It's fine, I'm sure," Mayor Petty grumbled.

Then I got the biggest shock of that evening. My mother peeled off her coat. She was pregnant.

Chapter 67

"You're, you're, you're—"

"Pregnant," Mom said. "You're going to have a little brother. Or sister."

"Half—"

"Yes. Half brother. Or half sister."

"I thought you were too old?"

"I'm only forty-one!"

"Oh." What was happening? My mother had gotten remarried, decided to have children, and told me nothing of any of it. We had grown that far apart? To be fair, I had completely forgotten how old she was, but still. "I'm glad you're here."

"Thank you," Mom said. "I—I'm sorry we've struggled with each other lately." She held her arms halfway up as if thinking about asking for a hug, but then she let them drop back to her sides.

"You don't owe me an apology." She *did* owe Darla an apology, but I didn't see anything to be gained from starting up that argument.

Mom gave me a tired half shrug instead of answering.

"I'd better go help Charlotte." I retreated to the kitchen area where Charlotte was interviewing newcomers and recording data for her census.

• • •

As the sun came up, our snipers reported seeing a huge column of smoke. I climbed Turbine Tower 1-A to get a look for myself. A hazy smudge was drifting across the sky toward us, from the northwest. I had no doubt what was causing it. Warren was ablaze.

It was almost noon by the time we got all the newcomers settled in Longhouse Five. I was dead on my feet. The only difference between me and a zombie at that point was that a zombie could easily have outthought and outrun me. But as long as Ed was out there in Red's untender care, I couldn't rest, wouldn't rest well until we had rescued him or learned his fate. I called a council meeting.

Once everyone was seated around a table, I opened the meeting. "We're going to attack Stockton and get Ed back."

Several people spoke up at once.

Darla: "You can't—"

Uncle Paul: "No, we don't—"

Ben: "There's a high probability—"

"No!" I said, banging my fist on the table. "I wasn't asking for an opinion. We *are* going to attack Stockton. Ed has put his life on the line for us over and over again. We're not leaving him or our other people with Red one minute longer than we have to. Now here's the subject of this meeting. How do we attack Stockton without getting slaughtered?"

"We use subterfuge," Ben said. "Any kind of direct attack on a walled enemy with similar numbers but superior firepower would be doomed to failure."

"What did you have in mind?" I asked.

• • •

Ben's plan involved shoveling shit. Literally. A lot of it. I, along with three other people, pedaled a Bikezilla from greenhouse to greenhouse, raiding the compost piles for our latest . . . deposits.

In the compost piles, we separated layers of feces with organic material—mostly wheat straw, sawdust, and wood chips—which helped the decomposition process somehow and kept the smell down to tolerable levels. Now we were picking the filler out with our shovels as we worked. We needed the pure . . . shit . . . for Ben's crazy project. Three other teams were doing the same thing in other greenhouses. Ben wanted a—there's really no other word for it—shitload of human feces.

By the time the bed of our Bikezilla was fully . . . loaded, you could smell us coming from a mile away. We pedaled up to the workshop we had built for Uncle Paul and Darla not far from Longhouse One.

They were outside working on an old, enclosed U-Haul trailer that was tipped on its side. Its wheels were gone, and in their place were two snowboards. Darla had a welding helmet on; she was attaching a strut to the underside of the trailer. Sparks flew from her torch.

Uncle Paul came to meet us, wrinkling his nose as he approached. "Good timing—we'll be ready to load it in a half hour or so."

"Thirty-minute break," I told the guys working with me. I rubbed my hand and hook in the snow, trying to clean up, even though I knew I would get dirty again shortly. The rest of the shit-loaded Bikezillas showed up while we waited.

When the trailer was finished, we tipped it upright so it rested on the snowboards and started filling it. Six inches of feces, then a sprinkle of warm water from one of the greenhouse heating tanks. Then another layer of feces, and so on. We had to keep the inside of the trailer wet and warm to get the effect we needed. Darla and Uncle Paul watched for a few minutes, making sure we were doing it right, and then headed inside the workshop, saying they were going to work on the fuse. I figured they were just trying to escape the stench, but whatever.

We packed the trailer so full, we could barely get the door closed. Darla drilled a small hole in the top of the door with a rechargeable drill and then sealed it with candle wax. Then my team covered the whole trailer with a massive pile of wheat straw and put a tarp over that. We needed everything to stay toasty warm overnight. Ben wanted to let it sit and ripen for a couple of days, but Uncle Paul and Darla thought it would work okay tomorrow, and I didn't want to wait any longer to leave than we had to.

I took a cold shower—we could have set up water heaters, but it would have significantly reduced the amount of energy we could devote to the greenhouses. I even splurged and used a tiny sliver of precious soap. My head spun, and I leaned against the flimsy shower wall rather than falling over. The moment my head hit my pillow, I was out.

In the morning I got a report from our scouts. Most of Warren had been burned. The area around the meatpacking plant was still intact, however. The Reds were loading pork into a pair of panel vans, trying to get it all moved to Stockton.

There was an abandoned farmhouse about a mile northeast of Warren that would work perfectly for our plan. It was close enough that the Reds' scouts would see us, but far enough that it would take them some time to mobilize a force to confront us.

I took a dozen Bikezillas—forty-eight men and women, including Darla. Three of them were hitched together in a long line to pull the U-Haul. The rest of our forces—about 250 men and women under Uncle Paul's command—

headed for Warren on foot. They would wait just outside the city for our signal. If Ben's plan worked, there would be almost no shooting. I hoped it would work—we had precious few bullets, and too many people had died already in this ridiculous war between Stockton and Warren.

We parked the U-Haul at an angle at one corner of the house and unhitched our Bikezillas from it. Then the ruse began.

We carried bags of flour, kale, and cases of pasta out the front door of the house and pretended to load them onto the U-Haul, as if we were clearing out a hidden cache of food. In reality we had brought all the food with us. One group carried it in through the back door, and another group carried it out through the front, pretending to load the food onto the U-Haul but actually passing it to the other group hidden behind the truck. They ran it around the corner of the house and returned through the back door, repeating the process.

We had hauled the same bags and boxes of food around and around in a circle for almost an hour before anything happened. A huge group of people emerged from Warren, moving toward us at a jog.

"Step it up to a run!" I called, and for a few minutes we pretended to be in a frenzy, as if we were trying to finish loading the U-Haul. When the Reds had closed about half the distance to us, I called out, "Scram!"

Everyone except me, Darla, and two others tossed the food onto the load beds of their Bikezillas, jumped on the seats, and pedaled off. Darla mounted the back bumper of the U-Haul. She had a long hank of rope in her hand. I grabbed the lit hurricane lamp that she had left hanging on the Bikezilla's handlebars. Darla picked the wax off the hole she had drilled in the trailer's door. A methane odor—like a giant fart—wafted out.

Darla jammed the end of the treated rope—a fuse— into the hole. "Time?" she asked. She meant until they reached us.

"Five minutes," I guessed. Then the Reds broke into a charge. "Three!"

"Make up your mind!" I held the lamp up, and Darla dangled the other end of the fuse into its flame. The fuse caught, burning fiercely, and the four of us ran for our Bikezilla.

As we started to pull away, I looked back at the U-Haul. The Reds were less than two hundred yards away by then. And the fuse had burned out.

Chapter 68

"Turn back!" I yelled. I tried to wrench the handlebars around, but the front forks were ganged together—I couldn't steer without Darla's help or at least acquiescence. "Trust me!"

We swung around, heading straight back toward the U-Haul trailer. Some of the charging Reds lifted their guns. I heard a bullet spanging off metal nearby and, a split second later, the pop-pop-pop of gunfire. I grabbed the hurricane lamp in my right hand, leaving my hook around the handlebars. I lifted the lamp and hurled it. It smacked into the side of the U-Haul in a tinkle of breaking glass. Oil ran down the trailer's wall, and suddenly it was afire. I had hit the side of the trailer, though, not the back. I wasn't sure if that would be enough to light it.

We swerved wildly, racing away from the oncoming Reds, who were still shooting at us. Darla veered again, putting the house between us and most of the Reds. I kept my head low, trying to merge it with the handlebars, hoping to give our pursuers a more difficult target. My butt, though, was thrust in the air so I could stand on the pedals, slamming them down in a desperate attempt to coax more speed from the bike.

As we put more distance between ourselves and the Reds, the firing started to slacken and then ceased entirely. I risked a look back over my shoulder. A bunch of the Reds were crowded around the U-Haul. A couple of them were using their coats trying to beat out the flames licking up the U-Haul's side. One of them reached for the handle that kept the rear door of the U-Haul closed. He turned the handle, pulled, and then vanished in a massive yellow-and-orange fireball. The sound and overpressure wave reached me an instant later, making the bike buck uncomfortably and my ears pop.

Three-quarters of the farmhouse had been blasted away. The roof and remaining wall toppled slowly toward the crater where the U-Haul had been, with a crackle and screech of breaking wood. The snow had melted instantly in a radius of at least fifty feet, revealing ash that looked dirty-gray by comparison to the surrounding snow. The Reds closest to the blast were gone, simply gone. Those farther away were scattered in a welter of limbs, some attached, some not.

The noise of the blast was the signal. Uncle Paul and his forces attacked.

Chapter 69

Most of the Reds ran. A few surrendered, throwing down their weapons and raising their hands. A few fought and died quickly under the combined fire of Uncle Paul's people and mine. We used the Bikezillas like cavalry, wheeling to attack the Reds in the flanks as they ran. I searched for signs of Ed or the people who had been with him. I also looked for Red—I had a score to settle. My hook clanked against the handlebars as if in agreement. But I didn't see either of them amid the chaos of fleeing Reds.

When the battle seemed well in hand, Darla and I steered our Bikezilla over to a group of prisoners who were being guarded by a detachment of Uncle Paul's troops. I swung out of the bicycle seat and approached the closest prisoner, a tall, gaunt man who vaguely reminded me of Abraham Lincoln. "You took a group of our people prisoner two days ago," I said.

He looked utterly terrified. He nodded, shaking too hard to speak. I noticed his eyes were fixed on the sharpened edge of my hook.

"Nobody's going to hurt you," I said as calmly as I could. "Where are those prisoners?"

"S-s-sent to Stockton. With a detachment. Yesterday."

"Thank you. Where's Red?"

"D-d-don't know. W-w-was with us."

"Thank you." I leapt back onto the Bikezilla, and we took off in search of Uncle Paul. When we found him, I didn't even take the time to dismount. "Have ninety-six of your men join us—eight in each bike's load bed. Ed's in Stockton, we're going after him. Keep harrying the Reds—keep them from reforming or reaching Stockton."

"Yes, sir," he replied, turning to give the orders.

Within half an hour, we were on the road to Stockton. I pushed the pace as hard as I could with Bikezillas loaded with passengers. As we flew down the road, I worried. Attacking a well-defended wall with fewer than 150 people would be suicidal. There was no chance the wall would be as lightly defended as the last time we attacked. Red was a lot of things—vicious, amoral, and scary as hell—but he wasn't stupid. But I owed it to Ed to try.

The best plan I could come up with was to attack in a

predictable place with a small force while a larger one circled around to come at them from the opposite side. If they overcommitted to defending the first attack, the strategy just might work.

A few miles outside of Stockton, I split our forces. Four Bikezillas, including mine, to make the diversionary attack; eight under Nylce's command to circle around and make the real attack from the opposite side of the city.

I waited about an hour—enough time for the larger force to get in place—and then we saddled back up and rode directly for Stockton.

When I caught sight of the gate, my heart sank. There were at least a dozen guards. More people appeared as we approached, dozens of them, maybe hundreds—a throng atop the car wall. Attacking here wouldn't be a diversion; it would be suicide. As we got close to rifle range, I raised a hand, ready to call a stop. Then I noticed something: nobody was aiming weapons at us.

They were cheering.

Chapter 70

I slowed our advance, letting our Bikezillas drift closer. The cheering swelled. When I got close enough to pick out individual faces, I saw Ed standing atop the log gate, waving. Wasn't he supposed to be a prisoner? Other familiar faces surrounded him, including Eli who had sheltered me, Alyssa, and Ben more than two years earlier while I was looking for Darla and my parents.

"Ed!" I yelled.

He jumped down on the outside of the gate and came toward us at a run. I dismounted, and we embraced, pounding each other on the back.

"Thought I was going to have to fight through half of Stockton to get to you," I said.

"How'd you know we were here?"

"Nylce. And when we took out Red's forces in Stockton, a prisoner told us you'd been moved here. What's the situation?"

"When Red caught us, I figured we were going to be turned into roasts and ribs," Ed said. "But he was in the middle of marching on Warren, so he sent a detachment to take us back to Stockton."

"I knew that much."

"Red left a big force behind in Stockton—more than fifty men. He learned his lesson the last time you caught him with his pants down. But he took all his most loyal men with him. And so I got to talking to the folks guarding us, telling them a little bit about my history, about Speranta, and well, about you. And I sort of promised them they could move to Speranta." Ed grimaced, looking at me.

"That's awesome, Ed."

"Lots of people have friends and neighbors who've disappeared. So we've had a bit of a revolution here in Stockton."

My head was spinning. I had arrived expecting to be shot at, and been welcomed with hugs instead. But first things first—the encircling force would be setting up to attack. They were supposed to wait until they heard gunfire, but if something went wrong . . . "I've got to get to the other side of town, fast."

"Open the gate!" he yelled.

Ed and the guy currently in charge of Stockton, Lawrence Mason, hopped on our Bikezilla, and we raced across town. Lawrence ordered the west gate opened, and we biked out into the snow, yelling "Nylce!" and looking for her forces. We found them about two miles out, hidden by a low rise in the road, ready to attack.

"Stockton's already free," I told Nylce as we pulled up.

"You took the city without us? Damn, Chief, I knew you were a badass, but that's just ridiculous."

"No," I said, "I didn't—Ed did. Never mind. Let's head into the city, and he can explain it on the way there."

I set my forces to guard the walls, looking out for the remnants of the Reds, and asked Lawrence to gather Stockton's population in front of city hall.

It took more than an hour to call them all together. I spent the time talking to Eli, who embraced me enthusiastically, and his wife, Mary Sue, who was as cold-hearted and suspicious as ever. His kids—Brand, Alba, and Joy—were far taller than I remembered them, but if it was possible, even skinnier. They showed me "their" pigs proudly—seven of them now, including a pregnant sow. Red had probably thought he had stumbled into the mother lode when he had captured them and the rest of Ed's expedition.

Stocktonites flowed into the intersection in front of city hall until it was packed, overflowing with what looked to be hundreds of people, though Lawrence assured me it couldn't be more than three or four hundred. They were gaunt and dirty, clothed mostly in rags, clearly fatigued and suffering. None of them were particularly old—I saw very little white hair—but they all looked years older than they probably were. There was a certain amount of hope in their stance and smiles threatening to peek from the corners of their mouths.

I climbed to the second floor balcony above one of the businesses on Main Street and raised my hand for quiet. The silence was total.

"My name is Alex Halprin," I shouted into the stillness. "I'm the duly elected mayor of Speranta. Ed Bauman has told you there is a place for you in our community, and I'm here to affirm that promise." They interrupted me with cheers. When it got quiet again, I went on.

"There is a place in Speranta for those of you who are willing to follow our laws and work hard. We have food and shelter and power—everything we need to survive this winter, however long it lasts. But we've built our settlement through hard work, and no one is exempt from that.

"If you wish to remain here in Stockton, you're welcome to do so. I want no one in Speranta who's there against his or her will. But if you remain here, you must do so under your own resources; you cannot expect us to support you with food or protect you with our troops. We will help you as we can, particularly with technical knowhow, but we have no illusions of saving everyone from this winter. We must conserve our resources to support those who support us through their blood, labor, and tears: the citizens of Speranta.

"Red's forces are broken, and if he survived the battle, he's on the run." There was another cheer. "For those of you who followed his orders, I offer forgiveness. But for Red himself, I demand justice. If he is still alive, we will find him, and he will pay for his crimes." I punched my hook into the air to emphasize the point, and the crowd grew even quieter.

"Think it over carefully. If you're ready for a new life, a new place, then start packing. Bring only what you can carry. The work will be hard, the hours long, the risks many. But if you're equal to the task, we welcome you. We leave for Speranta at first light tomorrow."

The applause was overwhelming.

Chapter 71

Nearly everyone chose to move. Speranta's population had almost doubled in the last few weeks, to over eleven hundred. We had more than two hundred people jammed into each longhouse, and they had each been designed for 150 or fewer. It took two days to get everyone settled, counted, and placed in work assignments. Every preexisting citizen with any experience at all was put in charge of a work party. We broke ground on eight greenhouses and two longhouses all at once, by far the single most ambitious expansion project we'd yet tried.

It would have been impossible to start so many buildings at once except for the supplies the

Stocktonites brought us. They freely gave us the material Darla and I had been trying to steal when we were caught and lost our hands.

Ex-Mayor Petty agreed that all the remaining frozen pork should be shared among the whole settlement of Speranta. He didn't have much choice; the Reds had thoroughly burned Warren. There was no town for the Warrenites to return to, and I wouldn't allow him to stay in Speranta without sharing the pork—we were all in this together, I figured. There wasn't as much pork left as I expected, though. The Warrenites would have been starving within a few months in any case.

Uncle Paul spent two days chasing the stragglers before he and his forces returned. He had killed or captured most of the Reds. There was no sign of Red himself, though—either he had been vaporized by our manure bomb, or he had escaped.

I had a more immediate worry than Red, though. I pulled Uncle Paul aside. "What are we going to do with all these prisoners?"

"Put 'em in a longhouse under guard?"

"Sure, but what then? We can't afford to feed people who aren't working. Heck, we can't even feed the people who are."

"I'm dead on my feet. Mind if we sit down, get something to eat?"

"Yeah. Of course not. Sorry." He lowered himself slowly onto a bench in the kitchen area, and I poured him a cup of water and grabbed a bowl of kale chips.

"God," he said wearily, "I am *so* sick of kale chips."

"You know what Darla says whenever I complain?" I said.

"Yeah. 'Beats not eating.' She says the same damn thing to me. So these prisoners. Why not put them to work? Like a chain gang or something."

"Still have to guard them. And it seems like a temporary solution."

"Hmm." Uncle Paul put a couple of kale chips in his mouth and chewed slowly. "You ever hear about that Truth and Reconciliation Commission they had in South Africa?"

"No."

"Before your time. Anyway, they interviewed victims and perpetrators of violence in the apartheid era—not necessarily to prosecute anyone, just to bring closure. We could try something like that."

"Have them talk to all the refugees and prisoners—sort out who the really bad ones were and who we might be able to integrate into Speranta?"

"Sure. A commission like that might help us get Mayor Petty's bunch integrated too."

"I know the perfect person to run it too. Thanks!"

"You bet."

Uncle Paul turned back to the kale chips as I got up to look for Zik. He was perfect to lead the commission. Anyone who had fought for Red was suspect, and who better to sort out those who might be reformed from the rest than Zik, who'd lived in Stockton and knew most of the prisoners personally? It also would give him a chance to question them about his daughter, Emily, who seemed to have disappeared off the face of the earth. I told Zik that the top priority was getting rid of the prisoners—they all needed to become members of our community or be exiled as quickly as possible.

I also set up the constitution committee I had promised over a month before when we had held the vote to confirm me as mayor. I tapped Reverend Evans to run it. If he were in charge, I figured he would have a tough time arguing that the constitution was invalid. I insisted that he put my sister, Rebecca, on the executive committee and asked her to keep an eye on Evans for me.

On the evening of the second day after battle, I summoned Anna and Charlotte into the base of the Turbine Tower 1-A, my improvised conference room. When I opened the door, though, Max and Alyssa were already in there. It looked like Max was trying to shove his tongue down Alyssa's throat. She didn't mind, though—she was pressed up against him, moaning softly. Their hands were *everywhere.*

I cleared my throat. Then cleared it again, louder. Max broke the kiss and looked over at me, startled. "I need my conference room," I said.

Alyssa tossed her hair, smiled, and marched out with her head held high.

Max's face turned tomato sauce red, and he slinked past me with a muttered, "Sorry."

I caught his arm, holding him there a minute. "Is she still getting gifts under her pillow?" I asked in a whisper.

"Sometimes," Max said.

"Did you tell her it's not you?"

"Um, not really."

I made a mental note to move Darla and my bedroll closer to where Alyssa slept. I wanted to know who was giving her gifts surreptitiously, before it exploded into some kind of drama. "You should tell her."

Max shrugged and pulled free of my grip. He nearly crashed into Anna on the way out of the turbine tower. She shoved her way past him, and Charlotte followed her into my conference room/improvised make-out spot and closed the door so we could have a private conference. "How bad is the food situation?" I asked.

Anna spoke first. "We can handle it. If we cut back to survival rations now, go on a crash building program, and borrow some food from the Wallers, we can feed everyone. But it'll be rough for about three months."

• • •

The most critical project was building greenhouses, so I threw my energy into that. I sent a team led by Nylce to trade with the Wallers for more food. Thelma, who'd started as our hostage but was now our guest, went along as an advisor—she had finally decided we weren't going to kill and eat her. Now she saved her paranoia for all the other ways she might die: a flenser raid, a rare disease, or a fall from a turbine tower were her three favorites. I normally tried to avoid her. Nylce took Ranaan Kendall—the

Iraqi war vet—along with her too. He hadn't made the trip to the WalMart warehouse yet and wanted to see it.

After dinner a few days later, Ben approached me. "Mayor Halprin, may I speak with you?"

"You can call me Alex," I said for the gazillionth time. "And sure, what's up?"

"The sniper's nest is above us," he said.

Okay. That wasn't like Ben anymore. I mean, yes, sometimes he was way too literal, but he was getting a lot better about interpreting figures of speech. He must have been incredibly nervous to misunderstand a simple expression like "what's up." "I mean, what can I help you with?"

"Could we talk in private, Mayor Halprin? I am sorry, I forgot to call you Alex, Alex."

"It's okay. Sure. Step into my office." I ushered Ben into the bottom of Turbine Tower 1-A, careful not to touch him. Normally these days a casual touch didn't seem to set him off, but he was clearly already tense. I pulled the door closed behind us and asked, "What can I do for you, Ben?"

"You can grant me permission to call on Rebecca."

"Call on?"

"May I have your permission to take your sister out on a date?"

I rocked back on my heels in both a literal and metaphorical sense. Where had *that* come from? "Rebecca doesn't need my permission to go on a date."

"It is appropriate to ask the father of the young woman for permission to court her, but if the young woman's father has passed on, one may seek permission of an older brother."

"You've been reading some really old books on dating, haven't you?"

"I have read *The Marriage Guide for Young Men, Courtship and Marriage: And the Gentle Art of Homemaking,* and *The Way to Woo and Win a Wife*—"

"No, never mind, that's okay. I don't need to know them all. Yes, you may ask Rebecca if she would like to go out on a date with you."

"Thank you, sir." Ben held out his hand to shake. I took it—every muscle in his hand was corded and straining. I could feel how much mental and physical effort the handshake cost him and cut it short after one arm pump.

I didn't catch up to Rebecca until breakfast the next morning. "Did Ben talk to you?" I asked.

She just about bubbled over right before my eyes. I could practically see the hearts rising from her head and bursting, spreading a heady scent around her. "He brought me flowers! Real flowers! What kind of guy plants real flowers in the corner of a greenhouse and tends them for three months just so he can give them to you on your first date?"

"A keeper?" I guessed.

"Hell to the yes!"

"I'm happy for you. You . . . um . . . Mom, she talked to you about, you know, all that—"

"You are truly disgusting, Alex. And yes, she did." Rebecca flounced off while I heaved a huge sigh of relief.

Chapter 72

Not long after dinner that evening, Rebecca yelled at me from the phone across the room. "Something's going on in Longhouse Five. You'd better get over here."

Normally I don't stand much on ceremony, but did she have to yell it across the entire longhouse? And Longhouse Five? That was where my mom and Mayor Petty were staying—were they in trouble or causing trouble? Everyone turned to stare at Rebecca and the phone outstretched in her hand. I ran over, taking the receiver.

The line was a confused jumble of voices. A

woman said, "Throw it up there. Over that rafter." Another voice said, "The trunk line is over there." With all the noise, I couldn't recognize either voice. Suddenly, the circuit went completely dead. Since we only had one party line, I couldn't communicate with anyone—none of the longhouses, not even the sniper post nearly three hundred feet above me.

Ed was at my elbow. I hadn't even noticed him approaching. "Full mobilization, manual protocol. Phone line's dead."

Ed ran for the door of the longhouse, unslinging the rifle from his back as he went. He yelled, "All platoons, arm and form up!" and Longhouse One instantly transformed from a relaxed, after-dinner scene to a barracks in the midst of a full mobilization. A few seconds after Ed cleared the front door, I heard three shots—the signal that we were under attack. Several more-distant three-shot bursts sounded moments later: other longhouses acknowledging the signal and passing it on.

I leaned close to Rebecca, yelling to be heard over the hubbub. "How'd you know the problem is in Five?"

"Mom was monitoring the line in Five. She started to report something, and then there was a smacking sound and a crash, and she quit responding. I asked the rest of the operators to stay off the line so we could listen in."

Some invisible cord tightened deep in my gut. I handed the phone back to Rebecca. "Line's dead. Monitor it in case it comes back." I grabbed my hat, glove, and gun and ran for the door.

Ed already had four Bikezillas formed up outside and waiting. "Leave half your force here to defend the longhouse. The other half converge on Longhouse Three."

"Yes, sir." Eight soldiers jumped onto the load bed of each Bikezilla, so we had forty-eight packed onto the four bikes. The others would have to follow on foot.

Because of the pattern we'd built them in, Longhouse Three was the closest one to Five. So Five came in view right before we reached Three. Nothing seemed out of order—nobody was outside either longhouse. I was off the Bikezilla running for the door even before we stopped.

When I pulled open the door, I was in for another shock. Longhouse Three was nearly empty. About a dozen kids and two old women were there, washing and sorting part of our black bean harvest.

"Where is everyone?" I asked.

Neither of the adults answered me. One of the kids— a girl of maybe eight or so who had survived the massacre outside Warren—said, "They went to a party."

"Shh," the older woman beside her said.

"What kind of party?" I asked.

"It was a Halloween party!" the little girl said.

"Halloween was four days ago," I said.

"But they took masks and a big rope so they wouldn't get lost on the way to the party."

"Quiet!" the old woman said.

"What are they doing!" I said to her, although I thought I knew.

"Nothing but what you should've already done," the woman said. "It should be over by now. Speranta's in no danger now."

I bolted from the room.

Chapter 73

I leapt onto one of the empty seats of a Bikezilla. Ed and the two backseat peddlers jumped on while I was straining to get the bike moving. The eight guys who had ridden in the load bed started to come aboard, and I turned and yelled at them, "Off! Now!" We would be much faster without a load.

Still, it took almost two minutes to cover the distance between the longhouses. I was running for the door before the bike had even come to a stop.

Inside, there was pandemonium. The ex-sheriff of Warren, Sam Moyers, was hanging from a rope strung on the rafters in the center of the longhouse.

His face was fading from purple to a mottled gray. His body swung slightly, wavering with the last impetus of his extinguished life. Ex-Mayor Petty was on top of a table nearby, wheelchair and all. A noose encircled his neck, the rope running up to a rafter high above our heads. Francine was behind him on the table.

My mother lay beside the table, a bruise spreading across one side of her face, her hands wrapped around her gravid belly. Another survivor of the Warren massacre—I couldn't recall his name at that moment—stood over her, training a pistol at her head. My mother wept and pled incoherently, so loudly that I could hear her over the general furor. The room was riotously full. All the Warrenites who were supposed to be in Longhouse Five were packed against the back wall. Men with semi-automatic rifles stood guard over them. Nearly the entire population of Longhouse Three, most of them survivors of the massacre outside of Warren, ringed the hanging tables in the center of the room.

Francine saw me, caught my eye. Then she raised her foot and shoved Mayor Petty's wheelchair off the table.

I charged, throwing elbows and yelling, trying to clear the crowd out of the way. The rope snapped taut, and Petty's wheelchair fell to the floor with a clatter. I couldn't get there in time—the crowd was too thick.

I slammed my right hand down on someone's shoulder, vaulting onto a nearby table. Petty's eyes were bulging, and his face was the color of a spoiled tomato. He was dangling so low that if he'd had legs, he could have just stood up. People crowded around him in the tight quarters, but they were cheering and yelling, not helping. I took two steps on the table and leapt, catching the rope above Petty's head in my right hand, sending us both swinging, crashing into the spectators.

Petty's face was purple. I reached down with my hook, sawing at the rope above Petty's head. Every evening without fail, I spent a few minutes honing the edge on my hook. So the rope parted easily, and Petty crashed to the floor. I held on, kicking out at nearby spectators' heads, trying to clear some room.

Mom crawled over to Petty, ignoring the gun trained on her and the man holding it. She clawed at the noose, and for a moment I was afraid that she wouldn't be able to loosen it, and Petty would die despite my efforts. Then she pulled it off his neck, and he gasped and coughed, flopping like an air-drowned fish.

"Silence!" I bellowed. The room fell quiet, and I dropped off the rope, bending my knees and landing neatly beside Mom and Petty.

"These are our guests! I promised they'd be safe here!"

"They're murderers!" someone yelled.

"It's on me, Captain," Francine said, looking defiantly down from her perch atop the table. "I organized it. I led it. For my dead fiancé. For Brock."

Ed and at least a dozen soldiers carrying rifles filed in. "Out!" I roared. "I've got this." The last thing I needed was any kind of shootout in the packed longhouse. Hundreds could die. Ed saluted and ordered his soldiers out. He, however, stopped in the doorway, leaving the door wide open. The icy breeze was welcome in the heat of the packed longhouse.

"How could you do it, Francine?" I asked. "How could you betray me like this?"

"It has nothing to do with you, Captain. Move on out of here, and we'll finish what we started."

"You will not!" I snatched the noose off the floor and put it around my own neck. "When you harm someone under my protection, under *our* protection, it's no different than harming me. Than harming Speranta itself. We've survived, prospered even, because we aren't a pack of animals or flensers, because we have laws and respect them, because people can work and live in safety here."

"We only want justice," Francine said.

"Justice." I practically spat the word. "Who appointed you judge? Who elected you mayor? Who asked you to join a jury? You didn't give Sam justice! This was vengeance. I should exile you all."

An alarmed mutter spread around the room. "No. It's on me," Francine said. "This was my idea. If you've got to exile anyone, it should be me."

I glared at her for a moment. "Everyone out! Back to your own longhouse," I said. "Ed, collect their weapons at the door. Put guards outside Three. Nobody leaves until we decide what to do."

Everything was still for a moment. I took the noose off my neck, letting it dangle from my hook. When they finally moved, I breathed a sigh of relief.

"Not you," I said as Francine started to join the procession. "You're coming with me." I took the pistol off her belt, checked the safety and chamber, and tucked it into the large pocket in my coveralls.

I clambered up on the next table over to check on Moyers. There was no sign of life. His face was nearly pure gray. I stretched out, reaching for the rope. A quick slice with my hook brought his corpse crashing down on the floor beside the table.

When all the interlopers from Three except Francine had left, I got down off the table. Mom was still kneeling on the floor beside Petty. He wore a necklace of bruises and rope burns, but he seemed to be recovering.

"Let's go," I said. "You'll be safer in Longhouse One."

"Alex," Mom whispered, "thank you."

Mayor Petty was perhaps my least-favorite person in Speranta. I would have been more eager to save anyone else. But I didn't see any point to telling her that. "Sure," I said, "you ready to go?"

"Our people are here," Petty said, his voice so raspy it was unrecognizable. "And we need to take care of Sam."

"At least come get your neck checked out."

Petty shook his head.

"I'll stay here," Mom said. "I need to be with my husband."

I suppressed a scowl. Hearing Mom refer to Petty as her husband made my gut churn. "I'll ask the doctor to stop by, and I'll have Darla send someone around to fix your phone line. I'll also post a team of guards outside, make sure this sort of thing doesn't happen again."

• • •

Later that night I met with my team of advisers. We talked around the issue of what to do for hours. I desperately wished that the constitution committee had finished their work faster. We needed a process for dealing with problems like this, a judicial system of some kind.

In the end we decided to choose a jury randomly and dump the problem in their laps. I closed my eyes and flipped through Anna's census book, pointing at names. Anyone from the massacre survivors or Warren was automatically disqualified—the massacre survivors might be biased toward Francine, and the Warrenites biased toward Petty—so we wound up with a jury of a dozen Stocktonites. I appointed Uncle Paul to serve as judge—he was one of the oldest people left alive in Speranta and more or less neutral.

• • •

The makeshift court convened the next morning. The trial was simple—Francine contested nothing, taking all the blame on herself. She argued that the lynch mob would never have formed except for her incitement and leadership. Her main worry seemed to be that we would exile all her compatriots. The arguments were finished before lunchtime.

The jury retired to a greenhouse to deliberate in private. Three hours later, they were back. The foreman handed a folded scrap of paper to Uncle Paul. He unfolded it and stared at it for a moment, his face grave. Then he read:

"On the count of first-degree murder, the jury finds Francine Lewis guilty. On the count of attempted first-degree murder, guilty."

"Are you ready to recommend a sentence?" Uncle Paul asked gravely.

"We are." The foreman handed another folded scrap of paper to Uncle Paul.

He unfolded it and read: "Francine Lewis shall be hung by the neck until dead."

No! She was a friend. Yes, what she had done was wrong, but who could blame her when faced with the man who had ordered the death of her fiancé? Surely she deserved no worse than exile. Surely Uncle Paul would overrule the jury.

After a short pause, Uncle Paul said, "So ordered." Speaking to Ed he added, "Take her into custody, please, Mr. Bauman. The sentence will be carried out at sunrise tomorrow."

I stormed up to the table he was presiding from. "My office. Now."

Uncle Paul followed me into the turbine tower.

When the hatch clanged shut behind us, I wheeled to face my uncle. "We are not going to kill Francine."

"Yes, we are," he said.

"She's a—"

"Alex, she killed a man. Was planning to kill two."

"Who can blame her after what Petty and Moyers did?"

"A jury of her peers can and did blame her." Uncle Paul leaned against the cold metal wall of the turbine tower.

"She deserves to be punished, no question. But killing her? No. She's not the only culpable party. Mayor Petty deserves to be on trial too."

"Maybe so. But that trial might not go the way you expect. I understand that he didn't actually order a massacre—he just told Sheriff Moyers to keep the refugees out of Warren. Somehow the shooting started. Maybe a finger slipped or one of the refugees had a gun. We'll never know."

I took a step toward him. "But the result—"

"And another thing: If we start prosecuting people for crimes they committed before they got to Speranta, we'll all wind up in jail. Mayor Petty was following the rules of Warren. Should he be liable under the rules of Speranta?"

He sort of had a point there. "But what gives us the right to take her life? Hasn't there been enough killing?"

"Alex, if you want to ban capital punishment, then argue to have that rule incorporated in our constitution. Hell, I might even join you. But the jury recommended the harshest punishment they could. And they're right. If we lose control of this—if we allow the refugees and the Warrenites to go to war with each other, we're going to lose a lot more people than just Sam and Francine."

I willed my fists to unball. "What's the saying? An eye for an eye leaves the whole world blind?"

"You can change the rules after tomorrow morning. But if you try to change this ruling, the whole system becomes suspect. You'd be saying your judgment supersedes the jury's and the judge's. That's a step down the road to dictatorship."

"We can't kill her," I said, although I was starting to resign myself to the fact that we might have to. Uncle Paul was right: We needed to put a lid on the tensions between the refugees and the Warrenites, and if I overruled the sentence, it would undermine our fledgling justice system.

"I'll do it," Uncle Paul said gently. "I affirmed the recommended sentence. I should carry it out."

I thought about the terrible burden of serving as a hangman and my history of taking all the worst jobs on myself. Part of the cohesiveness of Speranta, I was convinced, was due to the feeling that we were all in this together, that their leader was a part of the community, not above it. "No. If it has to be done, and you've convinced me it does, then I should be the one to do it."

• • •

I rousted everyone before dawn the next morning and threw them out of the longhouse. We would damn well never have any more barbaric spectacles while I led Speranta. I allowed only Uncle Paul, Ed, Darla, and, of course, Francine to stay.

"Do you want a blindfold?" I asked Francine.

"No. I'll go with my eyes open," she replied quietly. "And Captain . . . I don't blame you for this."

I turned away, biting the inside of my cheek, struggling not to cry.

When I had myself mostly under control, I helped her up onto the table. It wobbled a little as I stepped up beside her. I fitted the dangling noose around her neck, cinching it snug. "Do you have any last words?"

"I'm not as scared as I thought I'd be," Francine said. "I'm going to see my Brock."

I didn't have to push her. She stepped off the edge of the table on her own. The noose dug into her neck. Her mouth opened, as if to scream, but no sound came out. Her legs thrashed and her face turned bright red, then deep purple. A line of pale spittle ran from one corner of her mouth.

My knees shook, and I almost fell trying to climb down off the table. Darla caught me. When Francine was completely still, I fell to my knees beside her hanging body, hugging her ankles and sobbing.

Chapter 74

Nylce's expedition was back right on schedule, five days after they had left. She found me at the work-site where I was building yet another greenhouse. It didn't seem possible that she had left before the lynching debacle. "We need to talk," she said.

As soon as we were out of earshot of the rest of the work crew, I filled her in on the lynching. Then she started her report. "Our expedition was attacked by a group of Peckerwoods and Reds on the way home today. We lost one Bikezilla with a full load of supplies. Ranaan Kendall is dead. We have three injured, one seriously. Dr. McCarthy is operating now. We killed one of the attackers—the rest got away."

That hit me hard. Ranaan had survived the war in Iraq, only to die now? "I didn't know Ranaan well—he have any family here?"

"A sister, Marcella. I checked with Charlotte. Marcella's got cleaning duty in Longhouse Four today."

"We'd better go tell her before she hears about it through the grapevine." I sighed. I would rather do absolutely anything else with the next couple of hours instead of telling Marcella her brother was dead. But she deserved to hear it from me.

On our way, I asked Nylce, "How do you know it was Peckerwoods and Reds?"

"The guy we killed had Peckerwoods tattoos. And I saw Red."

Crap. I had started to believe that he was dead, vaporized by the manure bomb. But there was no way Nylce could be mistaken. How many 5'4" redheaded knife fiends could there be in northern Illinois? "I'm thinking about reorganizing our military. Putting Ed in charge, with you as his second-in-command. We need a police force too."

"I don't know anything about running an army!"

"People follow you. And I trust you. I'm going to suggest that Ed have you focus on protecting our convoys and scavenging operations—all the stuff that goes on outside of Speranta. Then Ed can focus on settlement defense. I'll take Ben off shortwave duty and make him our chief planning officer or whatever. He'll work for both of you. Have him plan convoy protection and devise some kind of an ambush to capture or kill Red." The image of Francine hanging from the rafter flashed through my mind. But it only made me more determined to catch Red. He *needed* to die.

Nylce nodded. "That'd work okay."

"I want Red's head mounted on a pole in front of Longhouse One."

"Gross," Nylce said. "Are you serious?"

"About posting his head?" I said. "No, it was just a figure of speech. About killing him? Yes, I'm deadly serious."

• • •

Ben was thrilled with his new assignment—he said he'd be an S5. I had no idea what he meant, but I didn't really care what Ben called himself so long as he figured out how to catch Red.

That night after dinner, I took Alyssa aside. "I've moved Ben off radio duty," I told her. "He's going to work for Ed and Nylce full time as a planning officer."

"He'll love that," Alyssa said.

"Yeah. But I need someone to take over communications. And I thought you'd be—"

"Um, no."

"But you'd be—"

"No."

"I really need someone I can rely—"

"Absolutely freaking not. No way. Am I not being clear here?"

I grabbed the edge of the table we were sitting at, squeezing it hard. "You're being perfectly clear, but—"

"Alex, I want to help out any way I can, but if I take on this head of communications job—"

"Chief communications officer," I said.

"Whatever. If I take it on, I won't have any time to teach my classes."

What was she talking about? "Your classes?"

"It was your idea, back on the old farm—"

"I knew you were teaching at the old farm, but I had no idea you'd kept it up after the move."

"I didn't at first. But about six months ago, I got Charlotte to assign me to a workgroup made up of all the youngest kids. We plant, harvest, weed—whatever needs doing—and I teach while we work. You really had no idea?"

"Um, no."

"You probably should get a clue about what's going on in your town, *Mayor.*"

I didn't think the sarcasm was completely fair. I spent most of my time leading the crews building new greenhouses. "Who's going to take over communications from Ben?"

"Not me," Alyssa said. "Why don't you ask your sister?"

Rebecca. Why hadn't I thought of her? She was smart, hardworking, and better with people than I was. But I always seemed to overlook her.

I left Alyssa and found my sister, who was happy to have an official role. I put her in charge of the shortwave and the phone system, and I asked her to recruit and train enough help to start monitoring the shortwave 24/7. We had more than enough manpower for it now.

We made regular trips to the Wallers' base in Sterling to trade for food and supplies for our greenhouse building spree. That left plenty of opportunity to try to sucker Red—we tried trailing a Bikezilla behind the convoy, staging a fake breakdown, and even abandoning one and observing it from a nearby ridge. None of the plans worked. Either Red was no longer scouting our convoys, or he had an uncanny ability to detect traps.

The reconciliation commission reported back, recommending that five of our prisoners be exiled and the rest allowed to join Speranta if they wished. I was reluctant to let any of them go—wouldn't they rejoin Red and help him raid us? But what would I do with them otherwise? I couldn't order them killed out of hand, even though they were all believed to have committed murders at Red's behest. Ultimately I accepted the commission's recommendations, although I had sketches made of all five of them first and warned them that if they were caught with Red or tried to return to Speranta, they would be killed. Two of the other prisoners chose to leave, but the vast majority decided to join Speranta. Charlotte interviewed them all and assigned them jobs.

The constitution committee reported back more than two months later. We needed a more sophisticated system than a typical city government since we didn't have a state or federal government over us, but a full-blown national government would be overkill. So the committee recommended that we elect a mayor, a judge, and a seven-member legislative and advisory council with a division of power similar to that in the U.S. Constitution. Each branch of government would be elected and serve for up to two six-year terms. The first term for our legislature would be two years, and the judge would serve four years, so that future terms would be staggered, with an election for one of our branches every two years.

I recruited a former state highway patrolman, Chad Brickman, to be our chief of police. He had emigrated to Speranta with the Stocktonites.

Every longhouse would have both a political and military leader. The military leaders were appointed by newly promoted General Ed Bauman. The political leaders would be elected for two-year terms. By that time, we had eight longhouses in total, so a meeting of our whole government would involve seventeen people. The serving military could have no role in politics, exactly as it had been in pre-Yellowstone America.

Our constitution also affirmed our allegiance to the United States, should it ever be reconstituted, and adopted the Bill of Rights in its entirety. Pretty much the only change we made was to lower the age of suffrage to sixteen, a nod to how young Speranta was overall. The average age of all our inhabitants, Charlotte told me, was only a little over twenty.

I tried to have a ban on capital punishment added to our constitution. Uncle Paul supported me on that, but we lost the argument. Roughly eighty percent of Speranta's population was pro-death penalty, even many who said they had been against it in the old world. I realized that I wasn't entirely consistent, either. I wouldn't hesitate to kill Red—but he had started a war with us, which made his case different to my way of thinking.

At the one-year anniversary of my election to mayor, we held another election. The new constitution was approved by over eighty percent of our electorate. A few weeks later, I stood for reelection. This time I was unopposed.

Isaac "Zik" Goldman was elected judge. Uncle Paul, Dr. McCarthy, and Nylce Myers ran for the council, mostly because I threatened them with never-ending latrine duty if they didn't. They all won. Jim Evans and Bob Petty were elected too. Despite everything, they had enough support from their constituencies among the Warrenites and ex-FEMA camp refugees to come in sixth and seventh in the council voting. The other two council members were Lawrence Mason and Margaret Feldman, both of whom were originally from Stockton. Darla had flatly refused to run for any kind of office. I retaliated by appointing her vice mayor, which meant she would have to run the show in Speranta any time I was gone. That made her exactly as mad as I thought it would; she wanted to tinker and farm, not dabble in politics. Well, what she wanted most was to start a family, but I was still holding out against that idea.

It didn't help my case when Mom had her baby. Her labor was only three hours and remarkably easy, according to Belinda. Darla redoubled her efforts to convince me to start a family. I promised her we would—I wanted the same thing—but I simply couldn't get the idea out of my head that she might die in childbirth. We faced far more likely deaths every day—a flenser raid, a fall from an under-construction longhouse roof, any number of diseases—heck, even an infected hangnail could kill in this postvolcanic world. But I could *do* something about those potential deaths. The thought that I would watch, helpless, while Darla died of a hemorrhage in childbirth had wormed its way into my brain like a parasite. I couldn't dislodge it, even after my mother's pregnancy went so smoothly.

Mom named my new half sister Sorrow, which seemed like a horrible name to saddle a child with. I hoped she would go by her middle name, Alexia. The names seemed like a rather pointed message to me, so I carefully avoided the topic on the rare occasions when Mom and I spoke. I spent almost all my free time with Darla, and Mom was still avoiding her.

When I did see Mom, it was usually because I'd gone looking for Rebecca, Alyssa, Anna, Charlotte, or Wyn. They were so taken with Alexia that they spent nearly all their free time helping Mom in Longhouse Five. When Darla was with me, I would sometimes catch her gazing longingly while Rebecca did some task that seemed utterly repulsive to me, like changing the rags that served as Alexia's diapers. But whenever Darla had offered to help, Mom would claim she had to go elsewhere, so Darla eventually quit offering.

We started gradually mixing the former FEMA camp refugees, Warrenites, and Stocktonites. One of the former Warrenites needled an ex-Stockton guard so persistently that the Warrenite took a swing at him, starting a fistfight that resulted in two broken fingers, a broken jaw, and a blackened eye. Remembering Francine's lynching, I was thankful nothing worse had happened. I was also thankful I could dump the whole mess in Zik's lap—he was our judge, after all.

Zik convened a jury to hear the men out. The jury found them both guilty, and Zik sentenced them to spend two weeks with their hands tied together. He said they'd either get over their animosity, or they would kill each other. Zik also gave them manure duty for the whole two weeks. The hearing took less than an hour. Best of all, they were mad at Zik, not me. I started to truly appreciate the genius of divided government.

More people straggled in, generally starving and filthy. We welcomed them all, and our population grew past twelve hundred. I kept our greenhouse building program going flat-out, and our food production continued to grow even faster than our population. I ordered a cutback on kale planting, shifting to more beans and wheat, which stored better than kale. We squirreled away tons and tons of food—I wouldn't relax until we had more than a year's worth stored.

I sent an expedition to raid an old highway depot, hauling off tons of rock salt to use as seasoning and for preserving meat from our rapidly expanding herd of hogs, bred from the pigs Eli had brought us. We could freeze the meat, of course, but we couldn't make bacon, ham, or even prosciutto without salt.

I woke one night to hear a whispered conversation taking place a few bedrolls over from mine. Someone had left a nightlight plugged in, and it cast just enough light that I could make out faces. Alyssa was sitting up in bed, one hand holding Anna's wrist. Something glinted from Anna's hand—a piece of gold jewelry, perhaps.

"You should have told me sooner," Alyssa whispered.

"I . . . I just couldn't," Anna said. She sounded utterly crushed.

"I like you. I like you a lot. Just not that way."

"I know . . . It was silly of me to keep hoping. I knew you liked boys." Anna's sigh was louder than her words.

"I do. Although I'm not sure why. They're all liars."

"Huh?"

"Max told me he'd been giving me gifts."

Anna's arms tensed so much, I could see her muscles swell even in the dim light.

"I swear to God I'll strangle him in his sleep."

"No. Please don't. I'll deal with him."

Anna was silent for a moment. "That might be worse for him than strangulation anyway."

"Yeah . . . I love you, Anna. Like a sister. Okay?"

Anna nodded. I could see tears shining on her cheeks in the dim illumination of the nightlight. "Like sisters." They hugged, and Anna pressed whatever was in her hand into Alyssa's hands. Then Anna stood and silently stalked back across the roomful of sleeping people.

I lay awake most of the night, thinking about what I'd overheard. I was worried about Anna—crushing on someone for two years and getting rejected, however gently, was painful. But I wasn't sure what to do.

The next morning I called Uncle Paul into my conference room and told him the whole story. I felt a little bit uneasy telling Anna's secrets, but I wanted someone to keep an eye on her, and I was afraid I wouldn't have enough time given everything else I had to do.

Later that day I heard that Alyssa had dumped Max. Max moped around for a few weeks, and then he started chasing after one of the newcomers, a stunning eighteen-year-old girl who was clearly out of his league.

The only thorn in my side was Red. He was still out there with a group of Peckerwoods. Occasionally they tried to raid one of our expeditions, which forced us to post a heavy guard on every foraging party and supply convoy, wasting a lot of manpower. But all in all, things were going well. At least until Rita Mae called on the shortwave.

• • •

A messenger ran up to me at the building site where I was working. "Rebecca says you're needed at the shortwave set, stat." I commandeered two workers, the messenger, and a Bikezilla and pedaled my way back to Longhouse One.

As I approached the table near the turbine tower door where we kept the shortwave receiver, I heard Rita Mae's rough, distinctive voice, "Is he here yet? Over."

"Running up now," Rebecca replied. "Over."

She handed the mike to me, and I mashed the talk lever. "Good to hear from you, Rita Mae. Over."

"I've got no time," she said, and I heard the pop and rattle of gunfire in the background. "The DWBs are here. Hundreds of them. They've taken half the city. Mayor Kenda's dead. We're going to have to bug out any minute now. Over."

I thought furiously. Last I'd heard, there were still flensers in Dubuque. Peckerwoods, though, not Dirty White Boys. It would take at least four days to get a force of any size all the way to Worthington. Obviously Rita Mae didn't have that kind of time. "Head for Bellevue. I'll meet you there. Over."

"We may not—" There was a pop and a hiss. The line went dead.

Chapter 75

It took all day to get ready to leave. Ed and Nylce had all kinds of questions I couldn't answer and issues I didn't know how to deal with. Charlotte and Anna were panicked about the dent that taking three hundred people out of Speranta on an expedition toward Worthington would make in the work rosters. And then, to top it all off, a council meeting was called, and I spent more than an hour twisting arms, trying to convince four of the seven of them to vote to authorize the expedition. The real sticking point was whether I would be allowed to go, but I wasn't willing to compromise on that—Rita Mae was in trouble, and I owed it to her to help. By the end of the meeting, I was cursing the stupid system of divided government we had adopted. We didn't get away from Speranta until the next morning.

Rebecca stayed up all night personally monitoring the shortwave. She heard nothing from Worthington; the frequency they normally used was dead. The delay did have one benefit: Ed and Nylce had used the time to prepare superbly—we had more than three hundred armed men and women ready, all of whom were on Bikezillas or skis. The Bikezillas carried tents, bedrolls, tools, cooking gear, medical supplies, extra weapons, ammo, and about a month's worth of food for the entire force, plus extra for the folks in Worthington we hoped to rescue. Ed would stay behind— he was responsible for the overall defense of Speranta—and Nylce would lead the military side of the expedition. We planned to be gone less than a week, but in the postvolcano world, there was no such thing as overprepared.

We made great time, reaching the Illinois side of the Mississippi, just before dark on the second day. Uncle Paul and Darla had modified one of the Bikezillas with a small battery pack and pedal-powered electrical generator that allowed us to run a shortwave transceiver and stay in touch with Speranta. The gleaner, Grant, had turned up offering to sell us another transceiver at a ridiculous price, and after hours of haggling with him, I had bought it. We could listen to transmissions any time, but to send our own farther than a couple of miles, we had to stop and string an antenna. Each night, I spoke with Rebecca and

Darla via the shortwave. Rebecca hadn't heard anything from Worthington. Darla was fuming at being left in charge of Speranta—she hadn't been able to work with Uncle Paul at all since I left, but it sounded like everything was running smoothly in my absence.

The next morning we rode across the frozen Mississippi—a five-mile trek. When we arrived in Bellevue, Iowa, midmorning, it was empty and abandoned. Rita Mae and the folks from Worthington were nowhere to be found.

• • •

Nylce sent out nearly a hundred scouts in small groups. If Rita Mae was still on her way from Worthington, it would be easy to miss her. We left a group hidden on the second floor of one of the old brick buildings in downtown Bellevue to keep watch in case Rita Mae showed up, and then we moved out, heading slowly toward Worthington.

Our scouts found no sign of Rita Mae, the DWBs, or anyone else from Worthington, and we made camp that night around an abandoned farmhouse near La Motte, Iowa, about twelve miles west of Bellevue.

The next morning we finally found Rita Mae less than fifteen miles from Worthington. A huge shotgun was slung across her tiny back, and her crazed white hair escaped from her hat in straggly wisps. She led a ragtag group of twenty-four, mostly children, six of whom were so sick that they were being dragged along on makeshift stretchers. I ran forward to give her a hug.

"Where's everyone else?" I asked. "Earl and—"

"They're dead, Alex," Rita Mae said. "They stayed behind to fight, to delay the DWBs so we could get away. I would have stayed too . . . but . . . but someone had to . . . had to . . ." she gestured at the kids arrayed around her and broke down crying. I held her head against my shoulder, amazed that she had brought anyone out. Rita Mae was beyond tough—she was easily the oldest person I had seen in more than a year, as almost all the survivors were under thirty-five—maybe she was too cantankerous to die. Still, the death toll had been horrendous. The last time I'd talked to Mayor Kenda on the shortwave, nearly two hundred people had called Worthington home.

"You're safe now," I said softly.

Rita Mae broke the embrace and looked around. Our soldiers were everywhere—some of them spread out in a defensive posture, some of them tending to Rita Mae's charges. "You've got more than a hundred soldiers here?"

"Three hundred. About a third of them are out scouting, though."

"It's enough. You could retake Worthington. Kill those sons of bitches. Kill them all."

"We could."

"But you won't, will you?"

"No." I let my breath escape my lungs. It sounded like a dying man's sigh.

Rita Mae's tiny fists were clenched. "They killed everyone, Alex. Mayor Kenda, Sheriff Earl, Mrs. Nance, Mr. Chapman—"

"I know."

"Then why? Why not restore some order to this corner of the world? The DWBs deserve to hang, every one of them, but shooting will do just fine."

"I can't restore order everywhere—"

"But—"

"And if I try, not only the DWBs will die. Some of our people will die too. Sometimes it's best to do nothing."

"All that is necessary for evil to triumph is for good men to do nothing."

"Why do you think they attacked Worthington?" I asked.

Rita Mae snorted. "We know why they attacked. They were starving. We had food and they didn't. To them, we *are* food."

"Right. And Worthington was the toughest target in the area. Now that you're gone, what will happen?"

"They'll migrate in search of food."

"Maybe. And if they come our way, we'll be able to deal with them on our own ground, using our prepared defenses. Far fewer of our people will die in that kind of battle. But what if they don't—or can't—migrate?"

"I don't know."

"They'll eat each other. I've seen it before in Freeport. Cannibalism is simply not a viable long-term survival strategy. The problem solves itself."

Rita Mae folded her arms across her chest. "That's a cold way of looking at it."

"It's a cold world."

"I want to see them hang."

"Which do you think is a more horrible way to die? The few seconds of pain during a hanging? Or having a friend knife you in the back while you sleep?"

• • •

We stopped for the day, setting up a defensive perimeter around another mostly burned farmhouse. Nylce spent the day consolidating patrols, sending scouts out toward Worthington, trying to locate the DWBs, and planning for a retreat the next day.

I circulated among Rita Mae's charges, making sure they all had food, water, and warm clothing. A few of them had minor injuries—mostly frostbite—but there was nothing that couldn't wait until we reached Dr. McCarthy and Belinda. The sick kids seemed to be improving now that they had food, warm clothing, and could ride in the Bikezillas' load beds.

We made great time the next day, collecting our people in Bellevue and reaching the west bank of the Mississippi just before dusk. We could travel faster when we were on a known route; it was easier to plan and coordinate the movement of our scouts.

We set out across the frozen expanse of the Mississippi the next morning at dawn. Less than fifteen minutes after we started out, the shortwave crackled to life. "Alex, if you can hear this, stop and set up your antenna. It's urgent." The voice was Darla's, which was strange. Normally

Rebecca operated the shortwave during daylight hours. I squeezed the brakes, and my Bikezilla skidded to a stop. I handed one end of the antenna wire to each of the guys behind me, and they ran out along the ice on either side of me, stretching the wire horizontally to its full sixty-plus-foot length. It was better to suspend the wire higher, in a building or tree, but out here on the ice, all they could do was hold it over their heads.

"Alex here. What's wrong? Over."

"It's your mother, Alex. They took her."

Chapter 76

I jammed the talk lever down so hard I briefly wondered if the mike would break. "Who took her? Where? When?" I was so rattled I held the lever, forgetting to let up and allow her to speak for a moment. "Over," I finally said, releasing the lever.

"There are five people missing—Stocktonites. Sort of a sleeper cell of Reds, we think."

"Maybe she left with them on purpose?"

"No. They left a note tacked to the door of Longhouse Five. They want five Bikezillas loaded with food. We're supposed to leave them at that wrecked bank near Stockton. And Alex, there was . . .

a pinkie finger attached to the note. It looks like your Mom's."

I ordered Nylce to detach her twelve fastest Bikezillas carrying forty-seven soldiers plus me. Nylce stayed with the remaining soldiers and the refugees from Worthington while I raced for Speranta, finishing the roughly forty-mile trek before dark. Darla met me at the door of the longhouse.

"I sent out scouts to try to track them, but we lost their trail on an icy stretch of Highway 78. I'm sorry."

My legs were rubbery from the exertion of the long ride. I held open my arms and stumbled into Darla's embrace. "It's okay. You did exactly what I would have. Get five Bikezillas loaded up with food, would you? I want to leave at first light."

"You're going to give in to them?"

"Sort of. Have someone find Ben and send him to the kitchen, please. I've got to sit down and eat something."

I went over my plan with Ben. He made a few tweaks, and then we went over it several more times, thinking through everything that could go wrong. Finally, I excused myself to go to bed. I had to be at one hundred percent the next day, which meant I needed to sleep.

As I stood up from my late, working dinner, I saw Mayor Petty wheeling himself across the floor toward me. "Who's watching Alexia?" I asked.

"Alyssa and Wyn," Petty said. "Are we leaving now?"

"Is she okay?"

"She wasn't there when they took your mother, thank God. When are we leaving?"

"Not now. First thing in the morning."

"We need to go now. God knows what's happening to her out there!"

"They want to make a trade. They won't hurt her."

"What? Chopping off a finger doesn't count?"

He had a point. "Regardless, there's nothing we can do until the morning. And Bob, I'm sorry, but you can't come."

Petty stared at me for a moment, his face turning a progressively deeper shade of purple. Then he banged his hands on the armrest of his wheelchair so hard that the whole thing rattled. "Goddamn these legs!" He drew in a heavy breath and seized my right hand. "You'll bring her home, right?"

"I will. Now let me get some sleep. We're leaving before dawn."

But I was still awake when Darla came to bed more than two hours later. "Everything's ready," she said. "We can leave at first light."

"You've got to stay and run things here."

"I already worked it out with your uncle. I appointed him vice-vice mayor. I'm going."

"There's no such thing as a vice-vice mayor!"

"There is now." Darla silenced my further objections with a kiss.

• • •

I split our forces into three groups. I'd gutted Ed's defensive force, commandeering five Bikezillas and seventy soldiers from him. Two groups left at dawn, traveling

across country. My group would take up a position on the
hilltop at the northeast corner of Highway 20 and
Highway 78. We could hide amid the stumps and deep
snow up there and observe the ruins of the bank on the
east side of Stockton. The second group with Darla would
swing wide around Stockton, hiding behind the car wall
on the south side of the city. We took the portable shortwave and the transceiver from Longhouse One so the two
groups could coordinate. The third group—five Bikezillas
loaded with food—would leave an hour after us, taking the
direct route to Stockton. They were supposed to follow
the directions on the ransom note and leave the Bikezillas
at the ruined bank. Then they would hightail it back to
Speranta on skis.

The plan went off perfectly. We all got into position,
the Bikezillas with their ransom of food parked just inside
the bank's mostly collapsed brick walls—and nothing happened. We waited, and waited, and waited. After a couple
of hours, I set up a watch schedule and went to check on
the scouts I had posted. There was nothing I could do but
try to stay calm. I wasn't, of course, but I thought I did a
pretty good job faking it.

Late that night I had fallen into an uneasy slumber,
when Trig Boling shook me awake. "Lights, Mayor," he
said, "on the road below us."

I leaped up and crawled to our forward observation
post, taking the binoculars from the soldier posted there.
Trig was right behind me. The lights were almost directly
below us, approaching the intersection. Five or six hooded

lanterns or flashlights leaked just enough illumination, I could see that a group of about twenty people was moving along the road toward the bank.

"Radio Force Two. Tell them to get ready," I murmured to Trig. He crawled away, back to the main part of our camp.

I waited another five minutes until they were well clear of the intersection below us and crawled back to camp myself. I picked up the shortwave mike, mashed the lever, and said one word: "Go."

"Roger," Darla replied.

My name is Alex, not Roger, I thought. Some people deal with tension by breaking down; others get angry. I think of stupid jokes.

We mounted our Bikezillas—six of them—and whooshed almost silently down the hillside in the darkness. It took almost a minute to drag the Bikezillas across the snow berm onto the road, and then we were flying toward the group on the road. I could see their lights now, even without the binoculars.

Each Bikezilla switched to attack mode—the back two riders kept pedaling, one of the front riders managed the steering and brakes, and the other lifted a rifle, ready to fire. Four riders on each load bed also prepared to fire. We hugged the south side of the road—Darla's group would do the same—so that we could fire at anyone in the middle of the road without hitting each other.

The men in the road didn't notice us until we were close—less than 150 feet away. Some of them turned, holding guns. "Freeze! Drop your weapons!" I bellowed. Three of them turned to aim at me, but without any light, I was only a voice in the dark. Rifles boomed from the west—Darla's group. I couldn't see them, but the muzzle flashes were clearly visible.

A short, chaotic battle ensued. Rifle shots seemed to come from everywhere and nowhere. They had lights, and we were in near-total darkness, but they returned fire at our muzzle flashes. Some of the Reds ran; we shot at them, but without lights they melted away into the darkness, and I was sure we didn't hit them all. I hoped they wouldn't show up on our flanks. I hoped my mother had the sense to throw herself flat if she was out there. People fell on both sides, and the reports of the rifles were augmented by screams and moans, a chaotic symphony of suffering.

Someone yelled, "We surrender! We surrender!"

I bellowed, "Cease fire!" A few more rifle shots sounded. Then everything fell quiet.

A new voice rang out, "Shine a lantern over here." It was Red.

When the light swung onto him, I saw that he had one arm wrapped around my mother, holding her tightly against his body. The other hand held a knife at her throat.

Chapter 77

"Mom!" I yelled.

"Alex!"

"While this reunion is no doubt touching," Red said, "I have business to attend to. You are going to allow us to walk over to that bank, pick up our food, and bike out of here. Or I will give your mother a very messy tracheotomy."

I looked around the battlefield. There were only nine or ten Reds left. I had almost fifty soldiers with rifles backing me up, and there were more in the darkness on Darla's side of the battle. A sudden stab of fear nearly paralyzed me: what if she'd been hit?

Behind me a couple of our guys—field medics—were scurrying around treating our injured.

"No," I shouted back at Red. "You're going to put your weapons down, come back to Speranta, and stand trial for your crimes."

"This knife is so sharp, it will not only part your mother's trachea and jugular, it will also sever the sternohyoid, omohyoid, and thyrohyoid muscles. It may not cut her spine, but in any case, her head will be left flopping, connected by only a few threads of cartilage."

"You do that, and we'll shoot you. So we're stalemated."

"I have nothing to lose." The knife glided sideways. My mother started to bleed.

I thought furiously for a moment. What would convince Red to let my mother go? He had an ego as large as his body was small—particularly where his knives were concerned. "Let's raise the stakes." I laid down my rifle and drew my belt knife. "You think you're the knife god? Let's find out. You and me, knives only. I win, I get my mother. You win, you get Speranta." I knew there was no way Darla would honor that promise, but I thought Red might believe it.

"I was told you *elected* your leader. Like they did in the dead age, the fat age."

Keep the pressure on his ego, I thought. "You and I both know that this is an age for the strong. You kill me, and there's nothing stopping you from claiming my place, from ruling over my greenhouses. My people." I stepped forward, letting the light from the lantern hit my knife.

"You'd stand as much chance against me in a fair fight as a strawberry in a blender," he said.

"So what are you waiting for?" I stretched my arms and neck and took another step toward him.

"You'll face me one on one? Knife to knife?"

"I give you my word."

Red threw my mother to the road and leapt, drawing his *gladius* midair and coming down on top of me in a flurry of knife blows. I tried to block his *gladius* with my hook, missed, and it bit into the back of my forearm. The scrape of the blade against my bone sent icy shivers up my spine and fiery licks of flame up my arm. His other knife slashed at my eyes, and I ducked, taking the blow on my forehead. Blood ran into my eyes, turning the world into a confused patchwork of red and black shadows.

I stabbed toward his stomach, but he was ready for me, throwing his hips backward to dodge the blow. A knife flashed from somewhere, cutting my right wrist on the inside, where the tendons and arteries run. My fingers loosened involuntarily, and my knife fell to the snow.

I was hopelessly outclassed. Darla stepped into the circle of light, raising her rifle, but he was on top of me again. If she shot him, the bullet would likely hit me too. Shadowed forms moved in the darkness. The *gladius* swept down, and I saw it barely in time to step inward, toward the strike, and throw my hook up. My hook caught his wrist, not the blade, slicing deep into the joint. The *gladius* fell, clunking harmlessly into the padded shoulder of my coat on its way down.

My head swam, and my vision constricted. All I could see out of the corners of my eyes was blackness, and the rest of my field of vision wasn't much better, rendered splotchy red by the blood pouring from my forehead. I was losing far too much blood. I had to end this fight, fast.

Red thrust with his other knife, and I dodged to the side, taking the blow on the outside of my thigh instead of in my groin. He stepped toward me, knife held low for another gutting strike. I kicked out, trying to sweep his legs from under him with a round kick. It worked, but my injured leg buckled, and we both went down. Somehow Red wound up on top of me, his knife above my throat, bearing inexorably downward.

I felt consciousness fading. I was finished. If this had been a taekwondo fight, I might have stood a chance. But during all those thousands of hours I had spent training in taekwondo, Red had been training with knives. At least my mother was okay, I thought as the knife bit effortlessly into the scarf at my neck.

The butt of a rifle slammed into the side of Red's head. Instantly the pressure on the knife eased. I threw Red off me, rolling him onto his back in the snow beside me. Darla reversed the rifle and shot him three times at a range of less than five feet, hitting him dead in the center of his chest.

The knife dropped from his limp fingers. Darla stepped over me and prodded Red's body with the toe of her black combat boot. He didn't move. "I didn't promise you a god-damn thing," she hissed. "And I *never* fight fair."

She safetied the rifle and slung it over her back. Then she was on her knees beside me, cutting strips of cloth and bandaging my wounds at a near-frenzied pace.

Mom crawled over to help. Blood ran freely from the cut on her neck, staining the snow. She glanced at Darla. "You . . . you . . ."

Darla was silent, still working on the deep cut in my left arm.

Mom hesitated a moment and then said, "You saved my son."

Darla nodded but said nothing, focused on her work.

When they had finished putting temporary patches on all my leaks, Darla pushed herself to her feet. She reached down, helping Mom up. "Can I help you with that cut on your neck?"

"I . . . yes. Thank you."

Darla turned away, presumably to get more medical supplies, but Mom didn't let go. She pulled Darla back, drawing her into a fierce embrace. Blood dripped from Mom's neck into Darla's hair. I closed my eyes for a moment—the pain had peaked and set off a wave of nausea so intense, it was all I could do not to vomit.

Our troops had taken all the weapons from the nine Reds who were left. "You have one day to leave the State of Illinois," Darla told them. "If you walk west on Highway 20 all night and all day tomorrow, you might make it. I catch you in this state again, you'll be shot."

The cut in Mom's neck was superficial. Darla used a scrap of boiled cloth and a precious strip of duct tape to hold it closed. We had three other people wounded, but miraculously no one had been killed. Darla organized a party to drag Red and his ten dead followers over the snow berm and bury them.

We camped the rest of the night in the ruins of the bank. I wanted desperately to get home—my wounds needed Dr. McCarthy's attention—but blundering around in the darkness wouldn't help.

The trip back to Speranta was slow because we didn't have enough people to fully man all the Bikezillas. I couldn't pedal at all and had to ride along like cargo. We arrived back at the longhouse well after lunchtime.

Bob Petty was waiting inside the door of Longhouse One. As I came in riding on a makeshift stretcher, he grabbed my hand, his lips worked, and he stared at me beseechingly, but no words came. I shook his hand off mine, and my stretcher bearers carried me through. Mom was right behind us. When she stepped through the door, Petty burst into tears. Mom leaned down to hug him, and they held each other for a moment.

"How's Alexia?" Mom asked.

"She's fine. Rebecca and Wyn are taking good care of her," Petty said.

Darla tried to step around the logjam at the door, but Mom reached out and grabbed her elbow. "Bob, I want to introduce my daughter-in-law, Darla Halprin."

"We've met," Petty said, shaking Darla's hand gravely.

Nylce, Rita Mae, and the kids from Worthington were back already. They had taken Stagecoach Trail, bypassing

Stockton completely. Anna, Charlotte, Uncle Paul, and Belinda were all working with the kids, trying to get them settled.

I spent the rest of the day in Dr. McCarthy's makeshift OR. He gave me a blood transfusion, reopened all my wounds, cleaned them, stitched them closed again, and rebandaged them. I was only conscious part of the time.

Early the next morning, I sent for Mom, Alyssa, and Rita Mae. They sat around my cot in what I jokingly called the sickbay. "We need to turn Speranta into a real town. We're finally producing a significant food surplus. It's time to open a real school and a library."

"I'm a little too old to be changing careers," Rita Mae said, "so I guess you'll be wanting me to open a library."

"I'd be grateful if you would. I'll see if I can get Uncle Paul and Darla to give up their stash of technical manuals so you can get those organized to start. And Ben's been collecting military books."

I turned to Mom, and she spoke up before I could. "I don't think I have time. I've got to take care of Alexia." Mom drummed her fingers on the table, forgetting her missing pinkie. When the stump hit the table's rough surface, her face scrunched up, and she moved both hands to her lap. Alyssa watched anxiously.

"I know someone who'd love to help with babysitting," I said.

Mom looked down at the table. "I'm not sure why she'd want to help me, after—"

"It's okay, Mom. We've all . . . it's been a hard couple

of years." I laid my hand palm up along the edge of the cot, asking her to take it. "I never stopped loving you. Darla doesn't know you the way I do, but if you let her, she'll love you too."

Mom wiped her eyes and took my hand. "I'd be honored to start Speranta's first school."

"I want to help," Alyssa said.

"I know," I said. "You'll both be assigned to the school full time. We'll add more teachers as soon as we can spare the manpower."

"We'll both teach," Mom said. "And I'll start training Alyssa to take over the school in case—well, when I can't do it anymore. What did you have in mind as far as students?"

"Start with the youngest kids—say, everyone ten and under," I said. "As soon as we can—as soon as I'm sure we can handle it, labor and food-wise—we'll expand the school a year at a time. Within six months or so, I hope to have everyone under sixteen in school."

"Maybe we should plan a trade school or apprentice-ship program for those older than sixteen. We need more builders, engineers, and farmers, right?" Mom said.

"Good idea. Put your heads together and figure out what you want in terms of a building to house both the library and school."

• • •

My wounds were deep; it took six weeks before I felt strong enough to resume a normal schedule. A few days of strangely warm weather greeted my return to the workforce. Late each afternoon the temperature even rose briefly above freezing; the top layer of the snow turned slushy, perfect for snowball fights. After a couple days of that, a storm blew through. We huddled in the longhouse, listening to the thunder in amazement—between the drought and winter, we hadn't had an honest-to-God thunderstorm in more than three years. When it ended a couple of hours after dark, Darla and I took a lantern and wandered around outside. The rain had frozen, leaving a crunchy layer atop the snow. The lantern's beam glittered on the ice, throwing magical yellow and orange sparkles across the snowscape.

Uncle Paul yelled to us from the longhouse door. "Turbines 8-A and 8-B didn't get shut off in time. Storm burned them out. We're going to lose four greenhouses if we don't get some power over there."

Darla sighed and dropped my hand. "I've gotta go. Don't wait up."

"Want help?"

She smiled her answer, and I wound up spending all night helping her and a crew of other volunteers string temporary lines from other turbine towers to fill the hole in our electrical grid. By the time we got back to the long-house, the sky was already hinting at grayness.

"Let me show you my favorite place to watch the sunrise," I said.

"Aren't you tired?" she asked.

"Sure. But it won't take long."

We got two claw hammers and climbed the longhouse roof together, sitting on the peak.

"I am freezing my butt off," Darla said, "literally."

"That would be a true national tragedy."

She laughed, a sound as lovely as the crystalline shards of light refracted off the new ice.

"I talked to Dr. McCarthy while I was in sickbay," I said. "There was a good obstetrics department at the hospital in Dixon. They had heart monitors, preemie incubators, all that stuff. There's no reason anyone would have looted the equipment, since nobody else has electric power—it should still be there. Doc thought maybe we could mount an expedition and move a bunch of it back here. There's some other stuff he could use too."

"Are you . . . are you saying what I think you are?"

"I am. Let's start a family."

Darla leaned over and kissed me long and softly, setting off fireworks in my brain and longing in my body that lingered well after the kiss ended.

We sat on the roof, our good arms wrapped around each other, watching the sunrise. The gray turned to a low line of deep red rising from the horizon, and then streaks of pink shot from the line, and it transformed, bursting into yellows and violets and oranges and greens and even, wonder of wonders, a patch of pure blue sky. It was the most spectacular sunrise I had ever seen.

The first sunrise of the rest of our lives.

Acknowledgments

I have a whole round table of literary knights in my corner: my wife, Margaret, slayer of unnecessary dialogue and prepositional phrases; Robert Kent, champion of the action scene; Lisa Fipps, warrior of word choice; Shannon Lee Alexander, chevalier of characterization; Jody Sparks, the emotional knight; and Josh Prokopy, the squire. Thank you all.

Thank you to the people of northwest Illinois who were so warm and generous during my research trips. Thanks in particular to the people of Stockton. I owe you at least two apologies: one for the liberties I took with the physical layout of your town and another for making my fictional Stocktonites far less friendly than the real ones.

Thank you to Krista Fry for some last-minute help on high school sports in Warren and Stockton.

Thank you to Jim Cobb, author of *Prepper's Home Defense*. The hour you spent talking to me about post-apocalyptic Chicago greatly influenced my depiction of Rockford, Illinois.

Thanks again to my brother Paul, his wife Caroline, and their children Max and Anna for lending their names to my books. Sorry the characters named in your honor didn't all survive! I also deeply appreciate the two hours Paul spent with me (during his own birthday party!) brain-storming ways to heat greenhouses with wind turbines.

Thank you to Lisa Rojany Buccieri for making me work far harder than I wanted, polishing this book. Your insightful edits dramatically improved my work, and I'm grateful. Thank you to Dorothy Chambers for uncrossing my i's and undotting my t's. Thank you to Ana Correal for another gorgeous cover image.

I cannot thank everyone at Tanglewood Press and Publishers Group West enough, particularly Peggy Tierney, whom I'm proud to claim as my editor and friend. You've all labored so hard to connect readers with my books. Truly, I owe my career to you.

About the Author

Photo by Larry Endicott

Mike Mullin's first job was scraping the gum off the undersides of desks at his high school. From there, things went steadily downhill. He almost got fired by the owner of a bookstore due to his poor taste in earrings. He worked at a place that showed slides of poopy diapers during lunch (it did cut down on the cafeteria budget). The hazing process at the next company included eating live termites raised by the resident entomologist, so that didn't last long either. For a while Mike juggled bottles at a wine shop, sometimes to disastrous effect. Oh, and then there was the job where swarms of wasps occasionally tried to chase him off ladders. So he's really glad this writing thing seems to be working out.

Mike holds a black belt in Songahm Taekwondo. He lives in Indianapolis with his wife and her three cats. *Sunrise* is his third novel. The first book in this trilogy, *Ashfall*, was named one of the top five young adult novels of 2011 by National Public Radio, a Best Teen Book of 2011 by Kirkus Reviews, and a New Voices selection by the American Booksellers Association.

Connect with Mike at www.mikemullinauthor.com.